THE THOUSAND YEAR BEACH

TOBI HIROTAKA

THE THOUSAND YEAR BEACH

TOBI HIROTAKA

TRANSLATED BY

MATT TREYVAUD

HAIKA SORU

SAN FRANCISCO

HAIKASORU
Published by VIZ Media, LLC
P.O. Box 77010
San Francisco, CA 94107

www.haikasoru.com

Library of Congress Cataloging-in-Publication Data

Names: Hirotaka, Tobi, author. | Treyvaud, Matt, translator.
Title: The thousand year beach / Tobi Hirotaka ; translated by Matt Treyvaud.
Other titles: Bit-sein beach. English
Description: San Francisco : Haikasoru, 2018.
Identifiers: LCCN 2018002552 | ISBN 9781974700097 (paperback)
Subjects: LCSH: Science fiction. | BISAC: FICTION / Science Fiction / General.
Classification: LCC PL871.I76 B5813 2018 | DDC 895.63/6--dc23
LC record available at https://lccn.loc.gov/2018002552

Printed in the U.S.A.
First printing, June 2018

CONTENTS

CHARACTERS

JULES TAPPY
A young boy

JULIE PRINTEMPS
A teenage girl

ANNE CACHEMAILLE
A fisherwoman

JOSÉ VAN DORMAEL
A fisherman; Anne's right-hand man

YVETTE "YVE" CARRIÈRE
A blind lacemaker

FELIX CARRIÈRE
A tailor and Yve's husband

ANNA
Eldest triplet

DONNA
Middle triplet

LUNA
Youngest triplet

BASTIN
Deputy mayor from Town Hall

BERNIER
A retired employee of Town Hall

DENIS PREJEAN
Manager of the Mineral Springs Hotel

PIERRE AFFRE
A local young man

RENÉ
A shipwright

GEORGES CRESPIN
A hunter

STELLA
An employee of the Mineral Springs Hotel

JOËL
The cook at the Mineral Springs Hotel

OLD JULES
A mysterious old man

LANGONI
Commander of the Spiders

CHAPTER 1:
THE VACANT SUMMER

I'm going to go to the Singing Sands and look for Glass Eyes.

This was the first thing Jules Tappy decided when he woke that morning.

As far as he could see from the window by his bed, the summer sky was an endless blue, and the wind was calm. Days like this were when wonderful things could be found washed up on the shore. Jules sprang from his bed and leaned out the window, feeling the morning air on his cheeks.

A well-trodden red dirt road ran past his house. Eventually it gave way to a narrow cobbled lane, then widened gradually into a respectable paved street that led down the hill into town.

Beyond that crowded jumble of red roofs was the fishing harbor. The sea was blue and calm, and above its vacant spread towered colossal thunderheads. Tinted pale rose by the last lingering rays of the morning glow, the clouds looked like monuments carved of marble, hard and solid and grim.

Jules knew, though, that this was not truly so. Clouds were drifting accumulations of minuscule water droplets—amorphous, ever-changing forms that could not be possessed or even fixed in place. Not objects, but phenomena.

The scent of the sea breeze at the Singing Sands rose from Jules's memory.

What sort of Eyes would he find there today?

Might there even be Driftglass?

As twelve-year-old boys often do—*almost as if* he were a real twelve-year-old boy—Jules grew excited by the promise of his own groundless hunches.

Such was the beauty of the morning.

The streetscape that sprawled below him, made in the image of a small harbor town in southern Europe and now bathed in light of a clarity permitted only to summer mornings, perfectly incarnated the concept of this Realm: a summer vacation in a small town, old-fashioned and inconvenient.

Using the cool water still in the pitcher from last night, Jules washed his face in the washbasin and went downstairs. Tiny droplets of water twinkled in his bangs, which were the same fine, soft blond as the rest of his hair.

The dining room was filled with the welcome aroma of breakfast.

In one corner stood a display cabinet containing a trophy with a chessman motif. A chess tournament was held every summer at the Mineral Springs, the finest hotel in town. The tournament had a long history, with the list of previous winners full of celebrated names and grandmasters. Jules had first entered the tournament at the age of nine, handily winning. The trophy had been placed in the display cabinet the following morning and remained there ever since, gathering dust for over a thousand years.

"Good morning, Jules," his mother called over her shoulder as she put the finishing touches on breakfast.

She plucked leaves from the herbs growing in the window planter, chopped them finely, then sprinkled them on the clam soup. Unleavened bread came out of the stone oven to be placed on the table. The tomato salad had been tossed in garlic-infused olive oil and vinegar.

Jules always liked the way his mother set the table for breakfast.

An unbleached tablecloth. Wooden bowls and china plates.

The milk jug, the pepper mill.

Knives and forks, spoons, napkin rings.

The flatbread was dense and chewy, redolent of whole grains. The tomato juice that collected at the bottom of the salad bowl was finer than any you could buy at the store. The minuscule particles of the steam that rose from the soup traced beautiful spirals in the summer light.

The light hits that chair, too, Jules thought. *The chair across from me—Papa's chair. But no one's sitting there.*

No one ever did.

Papa wasn't here.

Papa had not come to this dining room, this house, this town, this summer, for over a thousand years.

"I'm going to the Singing Sands today," said Jules. "Julie's amazing at catching crabs in the rock pools."

"Sounds good. Make sure you stay where it's safe." Jules's mother smiled the way she always did. A kind smile, but a complicated one. "How's breakfast?" she asked.

Oh, Mama, don't worry about me. I'm fine. I don't go to school, but I'm healthy and strong, and better educated than anyone in town. Or is it me being with Julie that concerns you? The way she lives her life? In all the Realm of Summer, Mama, you're the only one who worries about that.

"Delicious!" replied Jules, just as he always did. He took a bite of bread and chewed silently.

"You're going to the rocky part of the west bay, right? Would you mind stopping by Grandpa's to buy a few things?"

"Grandpa" was an old man who kept a small stall on the western rocks. Not for tourists—he sold only the freshest, finest seafood, and very cheaply at that. Jules had run errands there any number of times.

But there was something about him that Jules just didn't like.

"Just tell him I want to make fish stew. He'll put together a package for me."

Jules grunted noncommittally.

His mother added just a dash of coffee to his milk. The coffee made the sweetness of the milk stand out. What a delicate thing the human sense of taste was.

Breakfast. If the day was an engine, breakfast was its starter. Jules and his mother had been sitting down to breakfast in this dining room ever since the ChronoManager had begun keeping time one thousand and fifty years ago, and would presumably continue to do so in future. Just a boy and his mama, sitting across from each other at a table with no father, eating their breakfast together.

"Don't forget your hat. And make sure you come back for lunch."

"Yes, Mama."

Jules got himself ready and then went to the front door. He stepped outside the house, as tiny and cute as a toy, and was just adjusting the brim of his straw hat when—

"Jules!"

The spirited call came from above. He turned back toward the house and looked up. There, on the orange-shingled eaves above the front door, was Julie, standing tall.

Yes: standing tall.

Julie was a vision in white.

She wore a plain linen shift that hung from her shoulders,

her blond hair, cut short as a boy's, had faded to platinum in the summer sun,

and she wore a bracelet of white shells around her wrist, with matching anklet below.

Jules would go on to live far, far beyond his thousand-year boyhood, but the way Julie looked that morning, the whiteness of her as she stood like a sapling between the red tiles and the blue sky, he would never forget.

"All right, all right!" Julie shouted. "You should see your face!"

Her dress fluttered in the wind. She was naked underneath. For a moment, a patch slightly darker than her hair was visible between her legs.

"You'd better be careful, cousin!" Julie laughed, throwing her head back. Her teeth were her whitest part of all. "Looks like you'll trip over your jaw!"

"Julie." Jules's face was bright red. "Come on."

"Gangway!" Julie said, and then, without even a pause, leapt from the edge of the roof.

Following the gutter partway down, she swung across to a tree and slid to the ground. She carried herself as bravely as a firefighter and as lightly as flapping laundry.

She touched down right in front of Jules.

"What do you think of my dress? Mom made it for me."

She raised her arms and spun in place. In the concavities where her arms met her torso were chestnut shadows, dark smudges Jules could hardly tear his eyes away from.

"Really?" Jules said, feigning mild surprise. He knew, in fact, that Julie's mother made her clothes.

"Really."

"You look great in it."

"Really?"

The shift was simply cut and sewn, but that only emphasized the outline of her body.

"Yep."

"Really? Are you sure it's my dress you're looking at?"

Julie's lips curled into a grin. The feel of their touch came back to Jules suddenly.

"Positive."

"I wonder... Really?"

Her eyes, green-black like ripe olives, met his own gaze.

They were the only part of her that wasn't white. The restless spin of Julie's feelings always showed unguarded in her face. She loved love like a puppy, kept her distance like a mother cat, and had eyes as stubborn as a young girl's—which she was, in fact, being only sixteen.

"Well, whatever," Julie said. "I can't out-argue you." She rubbed the short hair at the nape of her neck. Her hair looked soft to the touch.

Julie didn't care whether Jules was a genius or not. Jules's unusual intelligence had attracted resentment since he was young, and it was only when he was with his "cousin" that he could forget all that.

For Julie, Jules played a similar role. Her sexual self-control was broken. She would sleep with anyone. But that didn't bother Jules a bit.

"Come on," Jules said. "Let's go"

"Now, now. No need to rush." Julie unhurriedly cleaned her ear with her little finger.

"What if someone gets to the Eyes before us?"

"No one's going to get to them. It's a secret beach. It's been a thousand years, and no one's ever found it. Why should today be the day?"

"Still, it's going to be hot later. Let's go while it's still cool."

"You sound like a mom, you know that? Yes, it'll be hot later. I understand that. But you know what? I don't care a *bit* how hot it gets. In fact, I *prefer* the heat. I'm not satisfied unless it's so hot that my hair starts to smolder."

Eventually the two of them began to walk toward the sea. They left the cobbled road to take a shortcut through the trees. They smelled the sweet fragrance of the orchard. The buzz of bees was dancing in the air somewhere.

"What're you doing tonight?" asked Julie. "Are you entering the tournament?"

"Of course I am."

The annual chess tournament was to be held at the Mineral Springs tonight.

Why would Julie ask him that?

Because she didn't want him to enter. But Jules had no intention of changing his plans. Making Julie wish he would was one of the reasons he was entering it in the first place, after all.

"Even if I string you up with Spider silk?"

This was a common figure of speech in the Realm of Summer. The "Spiders" it referred to, though, weren't the common arachnids an outsider might assume. They were something much more specific to this virtual resort—the boundless Costa del Número.

Who kept the old house that Jules and his mother called home in good repair? Spiders. Who defended this lush green orchard from pests? Spiders.

The paved road into town, the water supply that ran beneath it, the engines of the trucks going to and fro: all the maintenance the town needed—that the whole Realm of Summer needed—was carried out by robots called Spiders. You could always find one nearby if you looked carefully. They kept the Realm running smoothly, and they were everywhere.

"Hey, what's that?"

Pruned branches from the orchard were piled up a short way from the red dirt road. Gathered around them was a teeming mass of Spiders.

A gathering of Spiders wasn't strange in itself. But this one was unusually large.

"I wonder what's going on?"

The Spiders of the Realm were obviously not actual arachnids. Still, they made a very similar impression. *Spiders* really did feel like the only reasonable name for them.

No two Spiders were exactly alike. But they did share some common traits: they moved smoothly on multiple legs, and they spun "silk."

Julie stroked the soft hair at the nape of her neck again. A rattle came from her loose bracelet.

The Spiders seemed to have been drawn to a large hole, about forty centimeters across, which hung angled in midair just above the ground.

The hole was perfectly round. It looked like a large vinyl LP (still the preferred audio format in this Realm) propped up against the pile of branches. But it was not an object: it was a hole in thin air. Its crisp edges looked like the work of a sharp blade. Inside the hole there was only darkness, with nothing visible no matter how you squinted.

The Realm was a nearly perfect virtual resort space, but gaps like this did open sometimes. They were like graphical bugs. They caused no real harm, and the Spiders usually repaired them right away.

"What's wrong, guys?" Julie prodded the Spiders with the tip of her sandal. "You're sluggish today."

Spiders were highly diligent by nature.

Most holes were surrounded and blanketed with a sheet of Spider silk while still tiny. Within five minutes, the silk would morph into whatever was around the hole. The hole itself would close, the same way a wound healed. Spiders roamed the Realm constantly, assiduously repairing daily wear and tear in this way.

In response to Julie's prodding, though, these Spiders did nothing but slowly squirm. They seemed to be somehow at a loss. Julie reached down to pick up a Spider that had latched on to her ankle. About the size and shape of a round of Camembert cheese. Covered in a gray camouflage pattern. Twenty legs. Retractable eyes on both faces of its central disc, so that it could still work if flipped over. The Spider—which, naturally, had no emotions, but even so—seemed highly disturbed.

"'*What—should—I—do? This—is—a pickle,*'" said Julie, speaking for the Spider. "Don't worry, I can't just leave you like this. Let me think of something."

Julie tossed the Spider away to free her hands. Among the white shells of her bracelet was a single Glass Eye. It looked like a battered old bead of blue glass.

Putting her other hand to her bracelet, Julie stretched her arms out before her, finger pointed at the hole.

There was a small, tightening sound. The edges of the hole turned a glowing red. The hole had been caught. The dark circle began to contract, edges glowing brighter and brighter as it did, until it finally vanished, leaving a strong smell of ozone.

"Done and done."

"Right, but…there's something wrong with the Spiders," Jules said. He reached into the mass at his feet and tried to pull one free. As he lifted the Spider, ten more came with it in a dangling chain. Their legs were tangled together, but that wasn't all. Their bodies had partly melted into each other, fusing together. They let out little screams in protest at their suffering.

"That's awful," said Julie. "How could that happen?"

"Silk, maybe?"

The fused parts of the Spiders were sticky with the silk they secreted, which seemed to have dissolved their carapaces and insides, allowing them to merge. It seemed to Jules that the reparative effects of the silk had somehow gone subtly awry. The Spiders still on the ground were also melted together here and there.

"Don't worry, boys," Julie said to the Spiders, "Julie's here to help."

She took the clump of Spiders from Jules and cradled it in both arms. The light that came from within the blue Eye in her bracelet was clearly visible now. It cleanly peeled away the sticky surfaces where the Spiders had melted together, allowing them to dry healthy again.

"All done," she said, scattering the restored Spiders to the ground with a sweep of her arm. "You take it from here."

The Spiders dutifully began to repair the fused parts of other Spiders around them.

"Not bad, huh?"

"Is the Eye all right? I saw its light just now."

"Huh?"

Julie peered at her wrist. The Glass Eye had gone cloudy, like a gemstone spoiled by heat. She had overloaded it.

"Aw, and this was my favorite," Julie said, leaning her slender neck forward to hang her head. "What was I thinking, using an Eye for something like this? And you! This is all because you won't take care of yourselves!" she added, scattering the Spiders again with a kick. The little programs fled, for all the world like baby spiders skittering away.

"*Sorry, sorry—goodbye, goodbye,*" Julie said in her robot voice, giving voice to the spiders as she chased them away, right down to the last one.

Glass Eyes were essentially magical stones.

In the Realm, things affected each other just like in the real world. You could fell trees with an axe. You could get into a fistfight. If you raised crops in a field, the soil would lose nutrients. On the other hand, you couldn't wield any powers, magical or otherwise, that were unknown in the real world.

Eyes (as most people called them, for short) were the sole exception.

Eyes could affect other objects and phenomena within the Realm in ways nothing else could. With raw talent and sufficient training, those powers could be controlled. Just as Julie had done a moment ago with the Eye on her bracelet.

"I think it's almost exhausted," she said.

"Make something for me, then."

"Sure."

Julie used the Eye's last reserves to create a dragonfly.

First she turned over her hand as if looking at a watch. The Eye sat just over her slender wrist, right where the clockface would have been.

A stream of long, thin blue shadows emerged from the Eye like spun thread. They tangled and wove themselves together into a long, graceful dragonfly's body that looked like a craft project made of wire. Four transparent wings burst like knives from its thorax, and, quivering, the creation left Julie's hand and hovered in the air.

"You're free," said Julie. "Off you go."

Gathering together the Glass Eye's remaining strength, she gave the dragonfly a final kick. The details of its wireframe body were completed in an instant, and it split in two, becoming a mating pair that darted through the leaves of the orchard into the sky.

There were any number of good Glass Eyes around. But people who could use them to such vivid and pleasant effect were in short supply.

Julie smiled smugly and snorted in triumph.

"One day I'll learn to do that," said Jules.

"Ha! You need more than brains, you know."

"There's got to be a way."

"Oh, there does, does there? I see." Julie stretched extravagantly. "All right," she said. "Let's hit the beach."

She began to walk again, taking long strides. A tiny silver earring swayed in one of her ears.

An earring shaped like a fish. Only in one ear.

For a moment, Jules froze. Then he thought about the chess tournament to be held that night.

The town was bustling. The fishing boats had just come in. The central marketplace was crowded with fishmongers selling from trailers piled high with the gleaming catch. The fishmongers strove to out-shout each other, men and women alike, making customers smile with their patter. Jules and Julie cut across the paved marketplace. Slipping through the smell of cooking fish and seafood, they ducked into a dark alley with a small bicycle shop at the back.

"I've come to borrow some wheels again," said Julie. "Two bikes."

The owner nodded his assent, not bothering to leave his seat inside the store. Jules and Julie went back outside and hopped into the saddle. As they left the alley, the sunlight hurt their eyes,

"You know what that guy's into?" Julie said.

"Don't know, don't care," said Jules.

She was always like this, so he didn't bother to engage. Instead, he pedaled his bike. The strength of his tread was smoothly transformed into motive force, and the cool wind cooled his cheeks. The smell of salt grew stronger. Noting the seabirds circling overhead, he stayed on course for one more block and then turned left at the ice creamery, bringing the west bay into view. That was where the fishing boats came to port.

Two things kept the town alive: fishing and tourism. It all came down to the ocean.

The coastline was full of variety, from complex, rocky involutions to long stretches of smooth beach—everything you could want from a seaside resort. The western bay was the perfect shape and depth for fishing. The seafood that appeared on everyone's tables was taken from here.

The eastern bay was more modest in scale, but boasted stunning hills that came right up to the water's edge. Summer homes studded the hillside, overlooking the marina that catered to seasonal visitors too. There were superbly refined mineral springs bubbling in these hills, too, and of course the Mineral Springs Hotel.

Jules and Julie cycled along the road connecting the two bays, ocean to their left. The town was bifurcated by a massive, craggy mountain that extended into the sea. A narrow road snaked across the mountainside from one side to the other. Known as the Catwalk, it was just wide enough for one bicycle to pass. They traversed the Catwalk in single file, cliffs towering above them to the right, deep blue sea far below to the left. Every so often their bicycles would sway in the wind off the ocean.

Fishing off the rocks was a popular pastime with hotel guests. Trolling, too. A complex archipelago of tiny islands spread across the entire bay, and the views were superb. The pebble-like islands and their tiny beaches had been given all sorts of affectionate names.

But the Singing Sands was one name that nobody else in town knew. It was Jules and Julia's secret.

They were just about to turn at a distinctive stump onto the narrow unsurfaced road when—

"Hey, Jules!" someone called.

Jules stopped his bike and turned back to see a familiar old man sitting under a tree by the side of the road. It was Grandpa—the one Jules's mother was fond of. He wore an unpleasant leer, the precise meaning of which was unclear.

"And where are we off to today?" he asked. "With a girl, too! Can't leave you alone for a second."

The way the man was dressed had Julie agog. It was the height of summer, but he wore a long, pitch-black cloak, complete with hood. Perhaps it was a light fabric, something like linen, and cooler than it looked. He looked like a doddering old crow resting its wings.

"You're not opening the store today?" asked Jules.

"I never do when there's a big catch. Just my pigheaded way."

The old man scratched the tip of his nose with one withered finger.

The right eye that should have been beside that nose was missing.

A large scar slashed diagonally across his face. The scar was an old one, and gave the impression that his eye had been plucked out with some sharp metal implement. His cheekbones had healed crooked after the injury. The wound warped his whole face.

Narrowing his remaining eye, the old man leered at the two of them again. Did he still have more to say to them?

That, Jules decided, was the last thing they needed. "Sorry, but we're in a hurry," he said, kicking his bike back into motion. Julie followed suit, snickering. She caught up quickly and whispered into his ear as she rode alongside him.

"You ran," she said. "You ran away."

"What are you talking about?"

"He scares you that much?"

"I just don't want him to find out about the beach."

Jules refused to admit it, but Julie was right. He was afraid to look at the old man—afraid to listen to him speak. It made him think of something he would rather not.

Stopping their bicycles halfway down, Jules and Julie stepped onto a path so overgrown that it was barely even distinguishable anymore. After a short trek through the shoulder-high grass, their field of vision suddenly widened to reveal the deep blue of the sea. They were standing at the edge of a cliff that dropped thirty meters straight down. The rosy clouds Jules had seen that morning had grown even larger and now hung almost directly overhead. Struck by the harsh sunlight, they towered ferociously above, pure white and brilliant.

"Feel that wind!"

Julie shook her hair loose and let it dance in the wind that came directly off the ocean, almost knocking them off their feet. "It's so strong!" she shouted, her words carried away by the wind at once. "Yahoo!"

Jules waited until she was finished. "Let's go down already," he said.

"You really need to work on that personality of yours," Julie replied.

On top of the cliff was a stump, marking the location of a tree long since dead and fallen. A deep fissure in the surface of the rock ran from the stump, and it was possible to follow that fissure down to the bottom of the cliff. The route was almost vertical, but Julie had used a Glass Eye to create niches in the walls for their hands and feet. Jules went first, taking care not to scrape himself or tear off a fingernail against the rock. The fissure narrowed as he descended until the solid rock pressed against him from both sides.

Julie's legs brushed against the nape of his neck, his back. Her scent drew near. Jules slowed his pace. This allowed Julie to catch up naturally, so that she was gradually squeezing in between Jules's back and the rock wall. Her lithe muscles and softer parts pressed against him through her thin shift.

Jules's throat grew hot as he remembered the last time they had come here. After swimming, she had told him to lick all the salt from the sea off her body. He had complied, taking his time on the task. What sort of gasps had she let out when caressed? The smooth undulations of her stomach…

"What are you thinking about?" came Julie's voice from overhead.

"Nothing."

"Oh yeah?" she said, with what sounded like a hint of a smile.

"Nothing in particular."

"You know what's in my mouth today? A tongue piercing with an Eye in it."

Jules glanced back at her before he could stop himself.

She poked her tongue out at him cheekily. A little Eye floated against the dark backdrop like a half-melted mint drop.

"I'll give you a kiss later," she said.

Jules looked away, unable to look any longer.

"So will you do me a favor?" Julie continued.

Jules didn't immediately reply, but he did begin to move faster.

"If I say I'm going to the tournament, I'm going," he said eventually. "If I say I'm entering, I'm entering. I'm not going to bow out." His mood had turned sour. He descended with pure abandon now.

"All right, all right!" Julie said. "I won't ask you again."

Jules leapt down the final couple of yards and then helped Julie off the cliff face too. They were on a small, sandy beach where the sand had piled up against a depression in the rocky wall. This beach was not visible from the road on top of the cliff, or from the open sea.

The Singing Sands.

White sands covered the beach, fine and even.

They crunched as Jules began to walk across it.

The Sound spread beneath his feet and undulated.

The Sound.

The Sound that wasn't actually a sound.

It wasn't actually a sound, but there was nothing else to compare that certain vibration to.

The sands drank in Jules's vibrations. Those vibrations were uniquely his, as if they contained everything about him within them.

They slowly diffused from under his feet to fill the small beach entirely.

The sands, like one wild beast catching wind of another and checking the scent against memory, quietly began their own minute vibration.

When Julie stepped onto the beach too, another Sound began to spread and mingle with Jules's.

The sands, deducing from the Sounds that Jules and Julie were regular visitors, relaxed. Relief and welcome rose from the whole beach. Jules and Julie, and now the Singing Sands. The three different Sounds peacefully co-reverberated, then slowly faded away, and for a moment Jules saw, just as he always did, the echoes created by the beach of the two visitors shimmer into visibility like a mirage.

He felt both bashful and enchanted.

"That's strange," Julie said with a frown. "Jules, the Sounds are different today."

"They are?"

"Strange spikes are mixed in with them. Maybe somebody else was here. Someone we don't know. Their Sound's still here—or, no, maybe *they* are."

Jules looked up at the sky, shielded his eyes with his hands. The clouds were bathed in intense sunlight, with shadows carved dark and deep into their rough edges. Looking at one part of the cloud, where shadow and light combined in intricate patterns, he saw a momentary movement. A dull color that was neither the color of the cloud nor the shadows floated out from within the cloud's interior before being swallowed up again.

When he blinked, it was gone.

Julie stamped in place, listening to the crunch of the sand, the echo of the Sound. This time Jules listened closely too, but he couldn't tell what was different.

"That's strange," said Julie. "I've lost it."

"It was nothing, I'm sure. Let's go."

Jules stripped to his underwear and ran barefoot across the sand. Julie strolled after him, still fully dressed. The sand wasn't yet as hot as it would be later today. At the shoreline, crystal-clear waves rolled in topped with crisp foam. Jules, still running, suddenly came to a halt.

His big toe had found a stone half-buried in the sand. It peered out at him with a pale blue face.

"I knew this was my lucky day!"

One centimeter long and shaped like a teardrop, the stone was as transparent as the seawater. An immature stone rather than a young one. Probably a newborn. Julie wouldn't be able to use it in her bracelet just yet.

But even the youngest Eye had something unique to offer. Jules picked up the wet stone and held it up to the light, squinting into it with one eye.

The sea.

The clouds.

Julie.

When light shone through the stone, it revealed something like a photograph in a raree-show. The vivid outlines of the image looked very far away. Everything was still. The waves, Julie's hair in the wind: it had all stopped. The moment that Jules had seen as he peered through the Eye had been captured as if by a still camera.

Light was sealed up within the stone.

Eventually, the stilled light began to bleed and dissolve.

The bonds between the minute particles of light making up the image weakened. The particles flickered, but each retained its own purity of color, so that even as the details of the image blurred it remained as vivid as ever. Julie remained easily identifiable even after the image had almost completely dissolved. Just as she had her own unique Sound, the Julie within the Eye had a unique, unmistakable color and shine.

The Sands and the Eyes were very similar.

Just as the Sands drank in Sounds, the Eyes took in light (along with every other element) and abstracted it, each Eye extracting whatever essence had meaning to it. Just as the Sands recognized Jules and Julie from their Sounds, the Eyes saw a Light that was something quite different from what AIs usually meant by the word.

This Eye, it appeared, was in the habit of reconstructing light into something like an Impressionist painting. But there were many kinds of Eye. Some transformed light into the texture of a fabric like velvet or tapestry. Others pulled musical features like rhythm and melody from the light. One rare Eye morphed whatever it absorbed into a sepia photo of the Clément family. If you looked closely at those photos, you could see the original scenery, taken in and twisted literally beyond recognition like an optical illusion.

The Eyes were both samplers and synthesizer for the sensation of light—and not just light, but sensations from other sense organs too. Peering through a Glass Eye was a way to borrow its perspective, its worldview. Every Eye offered its own unique world to enjoy.

This was their primary value.

Without removing his eye from the stone, Jules said, "I knew today would be lucky. One's turned up already."

"Very deep, the way you don't say you found it. Good boy. Let me have a look."

"Might have been this little guy who found *me*, right?"

"An insightful and stimulating observation. Come on, just let me see for a second."

"Wow, this is amazing… Hey, cut it out, would you?"

"Cut it out, huh? Fine."

Julie suddenly began to strip off her clothes.

Her body slipped out of the white linen in a flash. She produced two pieces of fabric from somewhere inside the clothing she had just removed and wrapped them neatly around herself to cover her chest and hips as a swimsuit.

After noting Jules's thunderstruck expression with satisfaction, she reached out and plucked the stone from his hand. "I'll take that," she said. "Let's go to the other end."

The two of them walked across the beach to a small rocky area at its far edge. Although it was difficult to see from the surface, there was a deep hole carved out of the rocks below.

Within those depths lay a treasure hoard of Glass Eyes.

Jules and Julie had found any number of highly refined Eyes here, specimens of charmingly individual character. Reasoning that the conditions in the hole must favor the Eyes' development, whenever the two of them found a new Eye they brought it here as soon as they could.

They sat side by side at the edge of the rocks. Julie peered into the Eye Jules had found, then grunted in surprise. Without taking her eye from the stone, she elbowed him. "These colors are all anxious and restless," she said. "Looks like your anxiety to me. You have to treat the babies with care, or they'll catch a cold."

Jules stammered.

His contact with the stone—his fingers, his eyelids—had left his influence imprinted on it.

Just as the Singing Sands turned their footsteps into spreading waves of Sound, the Eye had acted as a mirror for what lay in Jules's heart, overlaying those hues onto the sights it had drunk in. Eyes were like that: they sampled emotion as well as sensation. The scenery inside this Eye was now rather pale.

The truth was, their encounter with the old man still nagged at Jules.

When Glass Eyes were newborn and still weak, contact with strong emotion could actually damage them in some cases.

"What should we do?" asked Jules.

Julie snorted. "Leave it to me!" she said. She held the pale blue Eye up to the sun, directly exposing it to those dazzling rays. "Feel how hot that is?" she crooned to it. "Go ahead and work up a sweat. Sweat it all out!"

At that, the stone quivered between her fingertips, forcefully expelling something.

It was the anxiety the Eye had taken in, now isolated and excreted. It amounted to about a puff of cigarette smoke, although its embodiment was more like pale blue steam, or perhaps a veil. It drifted briefly in the air before sizzling up in the sun's rays.

In this way, whatever Eyes absorbed they had the power to emit again in a different form.

These powers of transmutation could also be directed at other objects. External objects.

If the person holding an Eye could visualize and control its powers of transmutation finely enough, the world around the stone could be changed. A sufficiently skilled user could even use an Eye to create entirely new objects, like Julie's dragonfly. And even this was only the simplest manifestation of the power of the Eyes.

Jules lay back against the rocks.

Jules was unable to get a certain thought out of his mind.

Could that old man be my papa?

When exactly had this idea taken up residence in his head?

He did not know.

I'm resident of this Realm, this virtual resort space, thought Jules. *Just an NPC AI, built in from the beginning.*

My thoughts, my memories, my body—all a precisely designed set of objects running on the Realm's system.

But Papa's different.

Papa's a guest.

An unidentifiable face in the crowd of thousands who lived in the real world but held memberships in the Costa del Número. Papa used his membership to come to my house, after choosing our Realm of Summer out of countless other Realms and reserving the open role of my papa.

The Realm had many open roles like this. As long as they weren't already in use, anyone with Costa del Número membership could fill them, regardless of sex or age.

And in that way, a new Papa sat at Jules's table every day.

His family shared a range of summer pleasures with "Papa."

But not that old man. So what's this mysterious kinship, almost like a bond of blood, that I feel around him?

"Here I go!" Julie called, breaking his reverie. She leapt off the rocks and plunged into the water. Jules followed her in.

Under the surface, the rocks fell away in steps, like the inside of a funnel. Each level formed its own rocky shelf, and on each shelf was a thick bed of singing sand occupied by a host of Eyes—countless Eyes, lying quietly, passing the time.

Julie placed the Eye they had just found among their number. The newcomer was bathed in warm light from the surface. All the shelves got plenty of sun, thanks to the funnel-shaped arrangement. *It helps them get big and strong*, Julie said. Whether this was true or not, Jules wasn't sure.

Julie sank lower into the funnel, looking around at the shelves. Silently greeting all the Eyes, no doubt. Calling them by the names she had given them like pets. *Good morning, Chilled Martini! Silk Hokusai, Cracked Mirror, nice day, isn't it?* Some of the Eyes were dozing, but others were engaged in ultrafast internal calculation. *How are you feeling today, Asterism, Handbell, Ear Whorl?* As she addressed each Eye, she also checked for any there she hadn't seen before—newborns.

As she neared the bottom, Julie slowed her descent. She picked up a single Eye, then turned to Jules, smiling and giving him the thumbs-up. The Eye was a magnificent one, Jules saw as he drew closer. It was about the size of a chicken egg and looked like it would be heavy even underwater.

The milky white of the Eye was mixed with an intricate arrangement of other colors, something like an opal. When Julie raised it into the light from the surface, minuscule strands of white light rose from it like fur, making it look like a newborn mammal curled up asleep in her palm.

They returned with the Eye to the surface, where they lay on the sand gasping. The sun's rays had grown stronger, but the Singing Sands had not heated up. In fact, they were comfortably cool.

"It's really grown since the last time we saw it," Jules said, still lying on his back as he reached across to touch the Eye in Julie's hand.

Julie had lavished particular attention on Cottontail, as she called it. Its fur of white light rippled in the breeze. When Jules stroked its radiant fuzz with his finger, a pleasant Sound like shade from a tree came through his fingertip. A gentle coolness like the touch of a living thing.

"He's such a gentle, kind little guy," Julie said, smiling gently. "Let's give him a tickle." She scooped up a handful of sand and let it trickle down on the Eye. The Singing Sands were so fine that they formed a single white stream, almost like a liquid pouring from her hand. Cottontail's fuzz of light bristled as if it were a puppy startled by a splash of cold water. Then, also like a puppy, it shook itself to get the sand out of its fur. The radiance of the fur and the mineral glitter of the sands combined to create tiny rainbow rings that flew off it like bubbles in soda. Julie and Jules threw their heads back and laughed at Cottontail's surprise. Their laughter became a Sound that spread quietly across the pure, cool carpet of sand.

"You want a tickle, too, Jules?"

Julie put Cottontail on Jules's stomach and sprinkled sand on top. Jules was startled by the sensation of innumerable Sounds pinging over his skin. The thickness of the feeling of walking on the Sands was absent, and the lightness and immediacy of the sensation was heightened to a thrilling stimulation. Mixed in with this were the tiny animal-like Sounds that came from Cottontail, and the motion of its fur—and as the sand continued to pour down, the sensation was constantly renewed. Jules closed his eyes and let out a small cry.

Julie scooped up a double handful of sand and let it stream down on him from between her fingers.

The vivid stimulation arose on his stomach again, and this time he realized that what he felt was extremely close to sexual pleasure.

A shiver ran through him, head to toe.

Contained within the flow of sand was a sexual message from Julie.

A whisper, not in her voice but in the hiss of the Sands.

Jules opened his eyes. Her fingers had turned translucent as the sand flowed between them, a glowing fluorescent lattice appearing where her skin had been. The same light could be seen on Jules's stomach. The identity boundaries of the two AI programs were flickering. The boundaries of an AI's identity were defined by its skin, which was a seamless metaphor of its periphery program. That wall against the outside world had been temporarily put in a permeable state by the Sands. Their internal perception was exposed, as were the subtler sensations and feelings deeper in. These were the true "insides" of an AI. External force could not usually render them visible. Flesh and blood would appear in their place, most likely, just like normal objects. But to the AIs of the Realm, those were nothing but ornamentation. Their true selves were these intricate tapestries of light that appeared only when their boundaries were permeated. As a result, Jules was gripped by fierce embarrassment, as if someone had stripped him naked and was examining his aroused sexual organs.

Julie was showering him with feeling through the medium of the Sand…

From between her fingers, the feeling poured directly down on him…

Unnamable feeling.

An invitation that was neither word nor gesture.

In the sense that it stimulated his external periphery, it was a caress; in attempting to open him up, it was a kiss.

As the sand washed over him, Jules took a handful himself and waited for it to trickle through his fingers down onto Julie's shoulders. The same fluorescent lattice glowed on her skin as the sand flowed down from her shoulders to her breasts. The two of them embraced, kissed. The Eye on Julie's tongue stud clicked against his teeth. Their sensations, which had already begun to merge, flooded through this point of contact, mingling with each other in exchange.

But—

When Julie shook her head broadly, the silver of her earring leapt into Jules's vision.

The gleaming fish swayed.

Jules's excitement faded.

He pulled his face away from hers. Strength drained from his arms, and her breasts, pressed so tightly against him a moment ago, drew away. He heard a crackling sound, like static electricity. Julie turned her face away, as if to keep him from looking into her eyes.

Hoping to dispel the awkward mood, Jules had just opened his mouth when—

It began.

A Sound.

A terrible Sound.

A devastating Sound, roaring up at them from directly beneath like the initial shock of an earthquake.

The Sound passed through their boundaries, still in permeable mode, and went straight to their cores. Shock and pain ran through them, just as if someone had stabbed them at full strength with a blunt knife. Writhing in agony, they sealed their boundaries without consciously willing it. They could neither breathe nor speak.

But still, they understood.

This was a warning.

The Sands were bellowing as loud as they could.

Screaming and rage. Anxiety and menace. Such was the extent of the danger the Sands had sensed.

What *was* this?

Jules and Julie rose to their feet. The temperature and viscosity of the Sands changed with every step they took. Thin plumes of dry sand kicked into the air all over the beach, like the sea roiling in a storm. They felt an intoxication resembling seasickness.

Jules closed his eyes, then opened them again and looked up at the sky.

It was darkening rapidly.

As he watched, the white and solid clouds from earlier turned black as if rotting before his eyes, disintegrated like gangrenous limbs. They became a stream of bricks that filled the sky.

But could this really be the sky?

Harsh, barren mountains seemed to be growing down out of the sky. Their gray and black were those of the winter Jules and Julie had never known.

Whatever this was, thought Jules, it was not of this Realm. It had pried open the summer sky to force its way in from elsewhere.

The clouds billowed and grew as if streaming in through an unseen entrance, rippling across the sky.

Summer was under attack.

"Hey…" said Julie. All the blood had drained from her lips. "Hey, look at that."

"I see it."

"No. Over there."

Julie pointed to a corner of the clouds that was leaning at a precarious angle, like a cliff about to crumble. It was a cloud on the verge of unleashing a torrential storm—a cloud unable to bear its own weight and about to become rain. As they watched, a mass of tiny forms like a swarm of bees poured off the edge and tumbled downward.

The forms looked tiny, but each was actually quite large. Much bigger than a person. Some were as big as a house.

"They're over there, too. And there."

In Julie's hand, Cottontail's fuzz of light flattened.

"They're coming."

"Huh?"

The Singing Sands had goose bumps.

"They're coming down. That's what this little guy says."

The tiny forms began to move as one, looking like a column of mosquitos changing direction.

They were not just falling. They had their own means of propulsion; their speed and direction were under their own control. They were *descending*.

"We have to hurry."

Julie sprinted for the cliff. The Sands frothed violently under her feet, but she pushed on regardless.

A sudden clarity seized Jules's thoughts. He screamed to her at almost the same time as the Sands:

"You can't go that way!"

YOU MUST NOT COME HERE!

The frothing had been a warning. The Sands had been trying to keep her away.

But it was too late. The sensory net had already been laid across the beach, and Julie had stepped directly into it.

Then, from behind the solitary Pointed Rock—which had concealed it from them until that moment—it emerged.

A Spider.

Pointed Rock, true to its name, tapered to a point high above. It was at least five meters tall—so high that, standing at its base, you had to crane your neck to see the top. That was why Jules and Julie used it as a landmark for finding the beach.

But the Spider was taller still.

At that point, whether or not it was correct to call it a Spider was not yet clear. It wouldn't be until a short while later, after the first real battle was fought in the east bay, that everyone began to use that term.

Intuitively, though, Jules knew it was a Spider. There was something about it that conveyed its fundamental similarity to the familiar, even beloved little repairmen of their Realm.

And there was another sense in which it called for the use of the word—more than just similarity of form. Its essential nature was to ensnare everything it encountered, injecting stillness and death. "Spider" was the closest word they had, though it wasn't a true arachnid.

The Spider stood tall on ten legs. You could even say that it was *made* of legs.

Ten long, narrow legs joined together at the top, and that was all: no head, no body, no eyes, no mouth. Its legs had more than seven joints and were scabbed with a substance that defied identification, blue-green and dry but neither moss nor mineral.

It noticed Jules and took an immediate interest in him. Lacking eyes or even a head, it was not even obvious which way it was facing, but that much was clear.

With a quick motion of its legs, the Spider cleared the way between them by eliminating Pointed Rock.

Several legs seized the landmark, wrapping themselves around it like fingers. The rock did not dissolve or shatter—most of it simply vanished. The face of the part that remained was as smooth as if it had been polished.

At that moment, Jules sensed clearly the Spider's powerful appetite. Its primitive desires were communicated to him through the Singing Sands.

The spider had eaten the rock. Not with a mouth. By some other method. And the rock was now vanished from this Realm entirely.

The Spider's black legs flexed and extended as it crawled over the remains of Pointed Rock. Jules felt its drives even more strongly.

It wants to eat us. It will *eat us. But that won't satisfy it.*

What drove the Spider, Jules understood already, was not so much appetite as *hunger*—a bottomless, utterly insatiable craving. No matter how much this Spider ate, it would never be enough.

Suddenly seized by a despairing certainty, Jules looked up at the sky again. Already knowing what he would see there.

The forms in the sky had descended low enough to be made out individually.

They were coming.

An uncountable horde of Spiders.

They had different shapes, different sizes, but they shared the same essential nature, they were overflowing with exactly the same hunger, and they were on their way down.

Jules was unable to move.

I'm going to be eaten.

So was Julie. So was this beach, his house, his mama, the whole town. Nothing would be left. The Realm itself would be devoured in a moment, leaving nothing but blank memory space.

This despair spread through him like fast-acting venom. He felt paralyzed; all his perception drew sharply inward. He could no longer see any of his surroundings—not even the Spider's claw extending rapidly toward him.

There was a scream, angry and preverbal—

Someone seized his shoulders and yanked him backward. The claw grazed the tip of his nose as he fell.

"What are you *doing*?!" Julie demanded.

Jules finally snapped out of it. For a moment—and there was no other way to put it—death had bewitched him.

"Come on, this way! Hurry up!"

Still gripping Jules's shoulders, Julie dragged him with her as she turned toward the Spider and ran. They rolled under it, just barely making it through its legs. The flailing Spider lost its balance and brought its legs down heavily on the ground to keep from falling.

"Get behind me!" Julie shouted to Jules, starting to cry. Her knees were shaking so hard they almost knocked together. For all that, she remained in control of herself. "Out of the way, now! Behind me!"

They faced the Spider, the cliff at their backs. The hunger howled at them stronger than ever. The tension of a predator about to seize its prey filled the Spider's legs, right down to its claws.

As they watched, the joint at the top of the spider popped open and a white liquid sprayed out. Reacting to contact with the air, it rained down on them.

The Spider's silk looked the same as the kind that came from the familiar little Spiders. Tangled up with itself, it came down on them as a sheet of webbing.

Jules struggled desperately to free his arms, but the web was too strong to tear. It wrapped around his extremities, heavy as a wet sheet. Soon he would be unable to move at all.

Julie was unfazed. She paid no attention to the web, even as it landed directly on top of her. She simply leaned forward slightly, holding Cottontail before her chest with both hands.

"Julie, what are you doing? We have to run."

"Where to?"

She was right. There was nowhere to escape to now. Behind them was a wall of rock; before them, the Spider.

"I'm sorry about this," she murmured to the Eye.

Its fur of light rippled in response.

"It's not your fault. You grew up so big, ready to play outside, and now this happens."

She was planning to use Cottontail against the Spider.

"I'm so sorry about dragging you into this mess all of a sudden."

Her murmuring voice dropped lower and lower as she concentrated, putting everything she had into the effort. The deeper the sympathetic connection she could establish with the Eye, the more effective her attack would be. Silk continued to rain down on them, but failed to break her concentration. Talking to Cottontail was a way of both maintaining concentration and arousing its sympathy.

"Lend me your power. I won't pretend I only want a little. I want everything you have. Save us."

Her gentle, stroking voice enfolded the Eye. Its fur of light stood on end. It looked like a cornered and terrified baby animal.

"Let's drive that monster away together, you and me. Don't worry. I know you can do it."

The cloud cover was dense. It was as dark as night where they were. The only brightness lay in the palms of Julie's hands, and only her two eyes, illuminated by that light, were alive.

The Spider paused for a moment, apparently sensing something interesting about the light from Cottontail, but eventually shook itself as if with disgust; a moment later, it had already closed the distance between them. Unbelievable agility.

What happened next? At least three things, all in the blink of an eye.

First, the Sands soared fiercely into the air. This despite the absence of any wind. They tore the Spider's web to shreds, then whipped themselves into a spiral, forming—for just an instant—a tornado of sand between the two of them and the Spider. Some power other than wind had been wielded and stored there; the Sands made it visible, the way iron filings showed lines of magnetic force.

Next, Cottontail went into action. Its fur of light withdrew, and its mineral skin twinkled as it absorbed something reflected in it.

Finally, the Spider vanished. Just like the rock the Spider itself had eaten, it simply disappeared, instantly and without a sound.

By the time the tunnel of sand had crumbled and fallen, it was all over.

"Thank you," Julie said to Cottontail.

Jules understood very well what had happened. He grasped the mechanism by which the Spider had been erased—which even Julie probably did not understand correctly—as clearly as if he were seeing it before him. His mind raced furiously, assembling and dismantling strategies for fighting the Spiders.

They had to survive. The Spiders would soon be here en masse... *Could* they be stopped?

"We have to go," said Julie, pulling her clothes back on. "If we don't hurry, the town…"

Jules looked up at the top of the cliff. Black smoke was rising in the distance beyond, in the exact direction of the center of town.

"Mama…" Julie trailed off, smoothed the wrinkles out of her shift. Her mama had made it for her. "She'll die."

Tears welled in Julie's eyes, but her expression remained resolute.

"Let's go," she said.

Jules looked on the Singing Sands one more time.

They were as silent as the grave. The sea, too, had turned the color of lead.

Before long, the Spiders and their *hunger* would fall, blanketing the Realm of Summer like dark snow.

Suddenly, Julie stopped in her tracks.

"Tonight's the chess tournament, isn't it?" she said.

"Yeah."

"You're entering?"

"That's right."

"I thought so."

"Of course."

Julie wrapped Cottontail in her handkerchief and tied it to her forearm so as not to lose it.

"Well," she said. "Let's go."

Boy and girl ran toward the cliff.

Tangent to the summer sea and the winter sky.

CHAPTER 2:
A WOMAN VICTORIOUS • A MAN DELAYED • THE EAST BAY RESURGENT

Driftglass.

The omnipotent Glass Eye.

The phantasmal assembler.

The controller of providence.

No one even knew what it was like. There were only whispered rumors. It was one of the traditions that had been born in the Realm of Summer after the Grand Down. Yes—before the Grand Down, there had been no Glass Eyes at all in the Realm of Summer. What connected the two phenomena was unclear. The AIs couldn't help but feel that the Glass Eyes were compensation for the vanished guests.

The Grand Down had been an unusual shock. The world of the Costa del Número had been constructed as a virtual resort for their guests. So what if, one day, without any warning whatsoever, guests stopped coming? They knew nothing of why. There were rumors that the guests had completely died out, theories that the group operating the resort had gone bankrupt. Some claimed that the Realm was actually illegal and had been closed off after discovery by the authorities.

There was no basis for any of these theories. They were more like fantasies than hypotheses. The fact was that the AIs didn't know a thing about the physical, real world the guests called home. But there was one oddity that nobody could explain.

Why did the Realm still exist? If it had been abandoned, who was keeping the power on?

When the guests disappeared, the AIs felt both a sense of freedom and a sense of loss. In one sense, it was a change very much for the better. But it could not simply be called good fortune. The psychological makeup of the AIs, their mentality, depended on the guests at a deep level.

Each Glass Eye was, during the painful period in which the AIs adjusted to the absence of the guests, a rare point of light.

The first one had been discovered by a small child.

The child had found the Eye at home in the garden, nestled in the birdhouse just like a bird's egg.

That Eye had spun out lines of pearly light like a silkworm. As cute as a quail's egg, it eventually ended up in a glass display case in the mayor's office.

It was some time before the next Glass Eye would be found. It eventually turned up in an old chest of drawers in a house in the traditional rustic style—a small stone of purest blue, threaded somehow on a long-neglected strand of pearls.

Soon they were being found one after another. It was as if the whole Realm of Summer had become Treasure Island.

People examined the roads, the hedges, the tips of every tree's branches. They stirred the ashes in their ovens, flipped through the books in the library, crawled into grottoes in cliffs with the sea wind howling at their backs, giddy with the thrill of the search. They had all the time in the world on their *grandes vacances*, and hunting for Eyes was a pleasant enough diversion.

Nobody tried to buy or sell them at inflated prices, or lock them away in vaults. There was no point. They were all out searching for Glass Eyes at that time, like children with butterfly nets, wanting only to discover and proudly exhibit new specimens. They praised each other's collections, swapped finds, made donations to libraries and schools. Eyes were catalogued, classified, and exhibited by teachers and librarians trained in geology, art, and biology. The number who could use them grew, and the techniques grew more advanced.

The richest vein of Glass Eyes ran along the coast.

It was particularly easy to find high-quality Eyes in the sands of the beaches.

Families, lovers, elderly couples: all flocked to the shore in the cool of morning, searching for precious jewels as if digging for clams.

Yes—new Glass Eyes were always found in the morning.

Eventually, from nowhere in particular emerged a rumor: Glass Eyes grew in the Singing Sands, taking shape there in the dead of night.

That was around the same time that rumors of Driftglass began to circulate.

Who had told them the rumor no one could remember. A family member, a friend, a lover—in any case, they had heard it from *somebody*. Attempts to retrace the rumor trail to its source were fruitless; no matter how far back you went, the answer was the same: "I know, right? I heard it from somebody too."

A Glass Eye that stood above all other Glass Eyes, containing all their powers within itself.

A phantasmal assembler that could reconstitute the things and phenomena of the Realm at will.

A providential controller that could access even the Realm's fundamental parameters, intervening in the very laws of existence.

Was it big or small? White or black? Nobody knew. It might not even have the same form as a Glass Eye.

Glass Eyes that nobody had ever seen.

A summer of absence, a thousand times over. A town where nothing and no one was new. These were what drove the feverish hunt for Eyes.

They were something that nobody had ever seen.

With everyone sifting dreams from the sands, the beaches soon ceased to be such a rich source of Eyes. It had been a long time now since the town had seen the sort of ecstatic excitement it had after the Crystal Chandelier had been fished out of a large tidal pool.

Everyone had been sure it was Driftglass at the time, and quite reasonably so. But since nobody knew what Driftglass was like, they couldn't say definitively that this was it. The farcical dilemma was resolved by the fact that the Crystal Chandelier was not Driftglass.

The discovery of the Crystal Chandelier was a kind of peak after which the craze for Glass Eyes gradually faded, but the way the AIs felt about Glass Eyes themselves didn't change.

They thought: *We received the Glass Eyes in exchange for losing the guests.*

And everyone wanted to know: why was it called *Driftglass*?

Anne Cachemaille's arms were equal to those of any man who fished these waters, from her tan to her tasteless tattoos to her biceps.

Right now she had the sleeves of her crew-neck shirt rolled up to her shoulders as she sat on the cement landing place smoking a cigarette. She had finished cleaning up after the catch that had come in that morning and was now enjoying a break. She gazed at the gigantic rainclouds above. They had been amazing in the morning glow, she recalled, bright red as if on fire. And then the unforgettable beauty of the rose they turned afterward. *I ain't got much learning, but I bet José would call that* intoxicating *beauty,* she thought.

She took a drag and narrowed her eyes.

Her crow's feet were deeply carved. She had little time for so-called skin care, which in any case was no more use against the sun and salt wind she faced than a veil of gauze would have been. The ridge of her nose and her cheeks were scattered with sun spots and freckles. For a fisher, these were a badge of pride.

Just a few minutes ago the landing place had been bustling with people come to carry away the morning's catch, but it was quiet now, almost deserted, as if fallen for a moment between the cracks.

The area around Anne was still lively, though, because of the children playing there. These were Anne's children. The oldest was a girl of eight. Next came a six-year-old boy, then twin boys of four, then a girl of three. Then there were two more girls: a two-year-old and one not yet weaned. She was mother to all seven, and had given birth to none of them.

Every one of them was adopted. Babies abandoned at birth by friends of friends, children that a fellow fisherman had been raising on his own until he died in a storm—after a while, it added up. For a thousand and fifty years, Anne was the only mother these children knew.

Anne herself was unmarried. "Never been so hard up for men that I felt the need to marry one," she would say.

Her oldest girl was carrying the baby on her back. The twins were playing with the two-year-old and three-year-old. All under the watchful gaze of the sun. Anne lit a new cigarette and puffed contentedly. She reached into her shirt to produce a small book damp with sweat and sea salt and began to read, still cross-legged. It was a book of poems by some distinguished figure from the past—or so she had been told. There was a man, twenty years her junior, who pressed reading material on her. Like Anne, he hadn't gone to school, but he read difficult books and was very good at chess. Probably the second strongest player in town.

Some of the harder words she didn't know, but she had a taste for stylish turns of phrase. Her favorite parts she had read any number of times. She had them memorized by now, but she read them all the same. That was just how Anne did things.

To the sea their hearts they vow. They will not come again. And even if they came would you recognize them now?

. . .

They will not come again. They choose waste seas to roam. And even if they came would they have really come?

Suddenly Anne's finger stopped tracing the lines of verse. The day had darkened, the page fallen into shadow.

She felt a foreboding. Looking up, she saw how dark the sky was already. It had been filled with the muddy flow of the clouds.

Slapping her knees with both hands, Anne rose to her feet. Thighs like cranes hoisted her sturdy frame upward. She was nearly two meters tall. Atop her rugged, towering shoulders, her long neck was beautiful. She had hair like tousled copper wire and skin like a well-used copper pan.

Anne wrinkled her heavily freckled nose. What was happening was not normal in the least. Quickly tucking the book back into her shirt, she yelled at the children. "Be careful! Come to me, and don't let go of the little ones' hands!"

Her six-year-old was playing with a fishing harpoon. She scolded him and snatched it out of his hands, but stopped before she put it back in the shed where it was kept. *Might need this*, she thought. And that was when it happened.

A swooping buzz rang out. The noise sounded like a housefly— except the housefly was as large as a dog—as whatever it was flew

behind her, just skimming the edges of her field of vision. Brandishing the harpoon, Anne whipped around with electric speed, but the
Spider had already eaten her eldest daughter's head.

Mom...

It had happened so fast that her voice still drifted in the air.
Already the Spider had slipped out of her field of vision. Anne used
the handle of the harpoon to send her eldest daughter's body flying—
so that the infant on her back would not be eaten. Then she swept
the handle in a circle around herself, low and even. Understanding
her intent, the children dropped to the ground. Her eldest son threw
himself on his older sister's back to cover the baby. And beyond them
she saw the Spider.

The Spider was the size of a mastiff.

It had jaws like a stubby alligator snout,

five short legs—

and that was all.

A second and a half had passed.

With something between a grunt and a moan, Anne gathered
her strength into her throat, her chest, her shoulders and upper arms,
and then released it with explosive force. The harpoon's point struck
the Spider dead-on, but bounced off its thick, slightly springy hide.
The Spider did not even recoil from the monstrous strength behind
the blow. Anyone else would have dropped the harpoon at this point.

Another second passed.

The Spider's oversized jaws seemed to Anne to be sneering.
Its mouth was open wide, and her daughter's head was still inside,
covered in some sort of viscous, semitransparent secretion. The hair
Anne had brushed just yesterday was now soiled and filthy. She had
been very fond of her daughter's long, straight black hair, her own
being so coarse and wiry. *Mom, you need to put some ointment on those*

hands—the lips that had given Anne this advice last night were pale and still.

Anne opened her mouth to call to her daughter.

But in that moment her name wouldn't come.

Inside her head, Anne heard something snap.

By the time she came to her senses, she had bounded over the other children to drive the harpoon directly into the Spider's yawning mouth.

Running her daughter's head through, the harpoon sank deep into the spider's throat. Anne put her full body strength into her arms and pulled. The Spider had to weigh at least two hundred kilos. Anne's biceps bulged as thick as a man's thigh. Still pulling, she lowered her center of gravity and swung the harpooned Spider around her like an Olympic hammer. Halfway through her second spin, she leaned forward and slammed it into the cement. The rubbery impact she felt through her hands told her at once that the Spider was undamaged. She leapt forward immediately, still gripping the harpoon, positioning herself directly over the spider, then let her own 110 kilograms of body weight bear down. The harpoon was forced even farther in.

Anne had not taken her eyes off her daughter's face. Her beautiful girl. Anne would never see her again. How could she look away? This was what saved Anne's life.

Two round holes opened in her daughter's face: *Pop, pop.* Clean holes, as if someone had taken a hole punch to a photograph.

Abandoning the harpoon, she dove away.

The *hunger* had opened fire.

The Spider lost its balance, falling over forward.

Anne raced around to its rear.

Skidding to a halt, she drew two sturdy knives from her belt, one in each hand. She always had them hanging there in their leather sheaths. It was a habit she had picked up in her younger days as a brawler.

The Spider's back had been pierced through from within by the point of the harpoon. The hide around it was cracked. It looked like a machine's exterior paneling opening at the seams as the machine's frame warped. Anne sunk both blades into the gap.

The Spider struggled so violently a nearby storage shed went flying. But Anne held grimly on. Her thighs bulged. Her rubber soles stayed rooted in place. Her upper body flushed bright red as the children watched. The more the Spider struggled, the wider the joins in its skin opened, and because Anne kept working the knives farther in, not weakening even for a moment, the Spider's struggles only served to create further damage. Eventually its external paneling flapped open and a dirty white liquid began to ooze from the cracks. Probably the fluid it made its silk from.

The Spider began to make a noise like a broken machine. Its ability to maintain the imitation of life in its outward appearance was faltering, revealing its true nature as a simple tool for work in the Realm.

The noise weakened, slowed. Anne knew that the spider was on the verge of death, but she did not let up; if anything, she pushed harder. Her ability to sustain the onslaught was unbelievable.

Suddenly releasing the knives, which stayed stuck where they were, she reached into what was now a yawning gap between two of its exterior panels and tore the Spider open with her bare hands, as if it were a boiled crab.

And then her tension dropped away.

She fell backward onto her seat.

Her entire body was drenched in sweat, and she was covered in the spider's secretions and her own blood.

Her emotions had not yet revived within her.

"Mommy," the twins said, running from both sides to take their adoptive mother's hands.

Anne accepted their help getting to her feet. "Thanks," she said. Powerful as her crane-like legs were, she felt as heavy as lead. Her mind felt far away. What she had just done was the equivalent of dismantling a car barehanded.

"Ah…"

Spiders were sailing down from the darkened sky. Tens, hundreds, thousands of them. As big as oxen, as houses, even as big as ships.

The west bay was surrounded. She could already see the town being eaten away, starting with the mountains.

Not just the trees. The contours of the land were sinking fast. The mountains were vanishing.

Anne did not recognize this as *hunger* yet, but she knew that it was the same as whatever had riddled her daughter's head with holes, only larger. With the overwhelming force of the flowing tide, it was beginning to erase the town—the whole Realm.

The Town Hall clock tower was visible from where she was. It was the tallest building in the west bay. As she watched, it lazily toppled behind the houses in their rows.

Anne looked over her adopted children.

Was there a way to run without them getting in the way?

One minute later, the engine in a nearby fishing boat began to turn.

They were off to the east bay.

The boat began to glide over the waves, headed toward the jewel that was the eastern side of town, where the Mineral Springs Hotel and the elegant summer houses stood.

Anne finally let out her first sob.

There were fewer than twenty telephones in the whole Realm of Summer. One of these valuable specimens began to ring in the local station chief's office in the east bay. Town Hall was on the line. The station chief listened, turning pale, then handed the receiver to the deputy mayor, Bastin, who happened to be there for a meeting. He then sent another officer who was in the room with them to gather together the local station's core personnel.

Bastin had not realized the severity of the situation before putting the receiver to his ear. The skies over the east bay were their usual healthy blue. He glanced at Bernier, a retired Town Hall employee, as a terrified voice that sounded on the verge of screaming reported on the bizarre events transpiring around Town Hall in the west bay.

As Bastin struggled to listen and understand, the local station's officers assembled in the room. "I don't have all the details," the chief said to them, "but according to Town Hall, police headquarters is just gone. They say it was eaten by monsters."

The officers had no idea what to make of this. The local station chief could hardly blame them. He felt the same way. It was all beyond him.

Bastin pulled the receiver away from his ear.

"I think Town Hall's also, uh…" He offered the receiver, which had fallen silent, to the police chief. "I can't get through anymore."

The local station chief and the deputy mayor shared what they had heard over the phone, piecing together the information they had. The west bay, the heart of the Realm, had been attacked by a vast horde of monsters that looked like spiders. The monsters had obliterated police headquarters, slaughtered the townspeople, and eaten the mountains from the peaks down.

Someone looking out the window of the second-story room let out a noise like a groan.

The sky was coldly beginning to rot.

"All right," the local station chief said, pulling in his chin stiffly as he gathered his thoughts. "A lot of people are going to come running from the west bay. We're going to protect them. Get in touch with the local fire station, too. After that, we go find out what happened over there."

"Hey, where's the mayor?" asked Bernier, who was standing beside Bastin. Bernier was friends with the mayor as well as his deputy. All three had started working at Town Hall in the same year. Already retired, Bernier had come to help Bastin with the tournament scheduled to be held in the hotel today. "Where's Roger?"

Bastin shook his head. "Good question," he said. He explained that the call had come from the mayor himself, but decided it was not yet time to reveal that the call had ended in a cacophony of screams and collapsing buildings.

"You can set up a field base of operations here," said the local station chief.

"It's a bit cramped, I think." Bastin made a quick mental list of townspeople from the east bay who would probably be good to have around. "We need more room."

"True enough." Only the bare minimum of officers was assigned to the local station, which had no room for more in any case. It was a virtual holiday resort, after all. "We'll have to find somewhere else."

"Let's use the hotel. Plenty of rooms there we could use for meetings."

"Good thinking. Yes, I see—the hotel has other advantages, too."

Bastin nodded. He was short, but he had a barrel chest, and he thrust it out now. He had to keep things together. He could not falter, he told himself.

"Bernier," he said, "looks like we've got work to do, if your old bones can handle it."

"Glad to hear it. A thousand years of this is enough to drive a man crazy."

Bastin looked at the sky. The spiders had yet to fall. He felt both restless and terrified.

Thus was it decided that the battle soon to unfold in the east bay would do so at the Mineral Springs Hotel.

And yet—could this truly be called Bastin's will?

The shack stood where the breeze was refreshing. José val Dormael had chosen the site partly to ensure that the home he built would be cool enough to sleep in even during the day after the fishing was done. From the outside it looked like a dump, but its single room was as cozy as a first-class cabin.

Today, José had washed his youthful, sensitive face, lain on the bed, stretched out his long, strong limbs, and begun to doze. Normally this would lead to a deeper sleep, but for some reason he found himself awake again. He gazed absently at the wall.

Once, long ago, there had been a shelf on the wall with a collection of Glass Eyes on it, but that was gone now. Now there was a bookshelf instead. He had assembled his library volume by small, slim volume. Here and there were gaps where he had lent a book out, but because those books always came back swollen with salt and moisture, he never seemed to fill the gaps again. *Just buy me a new copy,* he would say, but still...

Those gaps would never be filled now, not because the books had vanished but because the shelf itself soon would: the irrational idea floated to the surface of his half-dozing mind.

Suddenly, José sat up. He realized why he had woken: that unfamiliar noise. Rising from bed like a panther, he crossed the room to the window in a single stride. Noting what had happened to the sky, he pulled a shirt over his bare chest and stepped outside. Houses were few out here on the outskirts of town, and the dirt trail that ran by his shack looked quite different under the darkened sky. He ran down the trail toward the road connecting the west and east bays.

He didn't know what was happening. He had no idea what those things falling from the sky were. But he knew what he had to do.

A Spider flew overhead with a menacing roar like a squad of bomber planes. José felt a presence at his back that gave him goosebumps, and looked back over his shoulder as he ran.

He couldn't believe his eyes. The ground was opening as if unzipped. A long, black fissure stretched through the rural landscape toward him. It spread without the violence of an earthquake. Inside the fissure there was only black. No cross-section of geographical layers on the walls, nothing. Just pure darkness, without even depth. The edges were as sharp and fresh as if they had been cut by blades. But José understood what he was seeing. At the edges of the chasm, white pixels flickered and danced like noise. The fissure was reducing the roads and fields to pixels, the smallest elements that made up the Realm.

The tip of the fissure followed the shadow of the Spider that had flown overhead. It was tracking the Spider's flight path. Put another way, the Spider was guiding it.

José watched the Spider's movements closely, then slipped off the road to run in a direction that would keep him out of the fissure's path. There was more than one Spider in the sky now, and their numbers were growing. Glancing behind him, he saw the fissure widening. He imagined the view from above: a landscape of green being eaten away by long, snaking black threads that widened gradually. A vivid image of his own cabin leaning and finally falling into one of those chasms came to him, but there was no more time to look back. Ahead he saw the sea, and Spiders above drawing black threads across it.

He splashed through a brook and saw the main road ahead.

A smattering of refugees from town were on it. José felt as if he had swallowed a ball of lead. Their numbers were so small. It made no sense for so few people to be on the move. Just how bad were things in town?

"José!" someone called. Several other people, hearing the name, began to cast around for him.

"José!"

"José!"

The voices multiplied. Girls, wives and children of fishermen, elderly men. The ragged crowd had a desperate, hunted look in their eyes. They were too terrified to think straight. Soon José was surrounded, standing at the center of a ring of people. Most of them were a full head shorter than the lanky young fisherman.

They all spoke at once, telling him what had happened in the west bay. They were desperate to tell José their stories. More than anyone else, José was who they wanted to tell. For twenty full seconds, José only listened, saying nothing. When he spoke, he kept it simple.

"Move quickly, but don't panic. Head east."

There was a brief silence, like the moment after diving into the water. José saw a youth he knew standing beyond the circle, and called, "Camille, go and get four or five more men."

Camille's head jerked up as if he'd been shot.

"I'm going to stay here a while longer," José continued. "I know it's a big ask, but I want you to stay with me. Someone needs to direct traffic."

"Yes, sir! I think some guys I knew were at old Rene's shipyard."

"Ah, the old man's around? Does he have anything seaworthy?"

"I'll ask him," said Camille, and ran off.

José issued orders to the remaining crowd. Move in small groups. Older men to stick with women and children. People who knew the Catwalk to take the lead there. Did anyone know how to use an Eye? How many boats were there? Take the weaker groups by sea. As many trips as you need.

Order was deftly brought to the flow of AIs escaping from the west side of the town, with danger dispersed as they headed east.

José stayed at the crossroads until it was almost too late. The black threads ate away at the land until there seemed nowhere left to run.

Fortunately, when José and the others finally fled, the Spiders left them alone.

Spiders poured out of the shattered skies.

Perfect...

A boy with an unfamiliar face strolled past Jules's house along the road that led into town.

The toylike house was half-destroyed. Black smoke billowed from a raging fire in the kitchen. The boy saw an AI's corpse inside, charred black. A mold-green Spider passed in front of him making a tinny scraping sound, long and thin as a piece of cord.

So innocent...so utterly simple...

On his way through the orchard, the boy stopped in his tracks.

The hole about the size of an LP record that he had opened that morning when arriving in this Realm had been covered up. He was sure he had locked the Spiders to prevent them repairing it.

An AI must have fixed them. There was no other explanation. Which meant that that was the sort of thing the AIs of this Realm could do.

I see... They must have used a Glass Eye.

The boy smiled for the first time.

No challenge at all...

Everything was moving forward as expected.

I bet they're all waiting for me at the Mineral Springs...

In no particular hurry, the boy began to walk again. No, there was no need to hurry at all.

At least twice as much space as a normal office desk. A stained-glass lampshade. A fine leather desk mat. And beyond it all, the warm face of Denis Prejean.

Bastin and Bernier were shown into the manager's office behind the front counter at the Mineral Springs. As soon as he saw them, Denis's look turned suspicious.

Bernier realized how utterly desperate the two of them must seem. Denis had to have been wondering what could have made the cool, calm, and professional Bastin in particular look that way.

Denis ran a hand smoothly back over his head, as was his habit. Except for a small band around his ears, he was quite bald. His silhouette looked exactly like an incandescent light bulb. Whenever he ran his hand over his head like that, it made everyone smile, easing suspicion and anxiety just a little.

But Bastin and Bernier just sat silently on the sofa. They were leaning forward, as if about to start gnawing at the glass ashtrays in front of them. Denis came out from behind his desk and sat himself down across from them.

"It's very bad?"

Bastin paused, then said, "Probably." Succinctly, calmly, distinguishing carefully between what they knew and what they did not, he explained the situation. And then he said that he wanted to requisition the hotel.

"May I ask what you intend to use it for?"

Bastin explained that he hoped to use the Mineral Springs Hotel as a makeshift Town Hall and a command center for the battle that seemed about to begin.

"In that case," Denis said with a smile, "there is no need to 'requisition' anything. The Mineral Springs Hotel's full resources are at your disposal whenever you need them. We are here for everyone's sake."

Officially it was the Hôtel de Clément, named after its founding family, but nobody ever called it that. Everyone preferred the unaffected and unpretentious "Mineral Springs Hotel."

The hotel stood on an enormous property that had originally belonged to the Cléments. It was built on a miraculously natural plateau right where the mountains plunged precipitously into the sea, which was why it was right next door to both mountain and sea, forest and beach. The front of the hotel faced the mountain; the sea was at its rear.

The main building was four stories high, with two wings enclosing an exquisite courtyard. Before it lay a smoothly rolling expanse of densely grown lawn. The beautiful forest which grew right up to the hotel on one side was also on its property, and on the other side was a marina whose row of elegant yachts was for the exclusive use of hotel guests. There was also a broad wooden terrace built above the ocean where new arrivals could enjoy their welcome drink, feel the sea breeze, and soak up the sights: the summer houses and gardens scattered up and down the steep, overwhelming slopes; the little art gallery; and the beauty of the greenery.

Denis and the two men from town hall walked through the lobby. It was not yet noon. The lobby was hushed and still. That said, no real guests had arrived at the hotel since the day of the Grand Down a thousand years ago. Only AIs visited now. A club for the

AIs abandoned by their customers (or had they been? even that was unclear), who now gathered to talk to each other.

But the manager still missed nothing, even in the hotel's farthest corners. There was not a speck of dust, and everything that was supposed to shine had been polished to perfection. The weighty hues of wood and brass filled the rooms, and everything was classic, unshakable, reliable.

The three of them walked past the wall that displayed dozens of framed photographs recording the hotel's history and ascended the stairs to the second floor.

"Where are the police?"

"They headed for the main road. A lot of people are going to be running this way. We have to keep them safe."

"I see. And those monsters, the things like Spiders?"

"Yes, they may use the main road to come here too."

"I hope it all works out."

"Now, as for the, uh—"

"The VIP lounge is beyond the casino."

The large doors paneled with all kinds of colored glass were the entrance to the casino. This had been the planned venue for the chess tournament tonight. The tournament was unlikely to go ahead now, Bernier thought. For one thing, the reigning champion Jules lived in the western town.

Beyond the casino lay the VIP lounge.

A set of heavy double doors, each made from a single sheet of timber. By contrast with the dazzle and glamor of the doors to the casino, these were simple and grave. The lounge had originally been reserved for the most exclusive VIP visitors, but there was no need for that anymore. It was now used for a different purpose.

Denis and Bernier pulled the double doors open.

It was dark inside.

There were no windows.

A few lamps were dotted about the room, but the pools of light they cast were small and weak.

The room looked like a jewelry store. It also resembled a museum exhibiting small examples of crafts. There were rows and rows of glass display cases, just a little taller than waist height, waiting for the things they contained to be appreciated.

And there was someone in there already.

She sat on a small chair in the corner, a woman with a generous physique.

Her hands moved rhythmically as she knitted her lace. But there were no lamps around her. Despite almost no light reaching her part of the room, she was executing some fine needlework. Bernier got the impression that she had been sitting where she was for years.

Yvette Carrière. That was her name.

"Looks like we're interrupting," said Denis. "I'm sorry, but something urgent has come up."

"Not at all," Yvette said with a gentle smile. "I don't have to work here. I just prefer it."

"You find it more calming here?" asked Bastin.

"Oh yes, very much so."

"No loudmouths, either," said Bernier, then instantly regretted it. "Uh, I mean…pardon me."

"Yes, you may be right." Yvette rose to her feet. "I'll go back to my workshop."

"I don't think that's a good idea," said Bastin.

"Why is that?" asked Yvette.

"It could be dangerous. Also, I think we're going to need your help."

Yvette was silent.

"I'll explain everything," said Bastin. "Before that, though, I want to check the contents of the room against the inventory."

Denis opened a large, leather-bound account book.

A list of the items stored in this room.

Glass Eyes.

Glass Eyes by the hundreds, every one a jewel.

The collection in the VIP lounge had been gathered from every corner of the Realm of Summer and selected with exacting care.

"There's no need to consult the inventory," Yvette said with a smile.

Her cheeks were the color of milk. Her eyes were chestnut brown. But in her eyes there were no pupils. Just unbroken irises. In the Costa del Número, this was a common technique for indicating blindness through character design.

"I know everything that's in here," Yvette continued.

As a Glass Eye user, Yvette was unequaled in the Realm.

"We're hoping your abilities can help us," said Bastin.

"I understand a little of what you mean… The eyes have been clamoring all morning. It doesn't sound like good news."

"It isn't."

Yvette rose to her feet. She filled out her light peach-colored knit summer dress well. She stood with her arms crossed lightly over her chest with the quiet self-confidence and sternness of a nun. Bernier was slightly moved.

"If there's anything I can do to help," she said, "I'd be happy to."

Just then one of the hotel's employees came apologetically into the lounge and whispered something to Denis.

Denis's eyes widened slightly. He nodded.

"Excuse me, everyone," he said. "Someone has just arrived at our marina, and I believe you will all be shocked by who it is."

"What is it, then? Just tell us."

"A woman, accompanied by her children. They fled here by sea from the west side of town. And it seems that they have brought us a rather horrifying house gift."

"Just tell us who it is, would you?" said Bernier irritably.

Denis ran his hand back over his light bulb–shaped head.

"It is Miss Anne Cachemaille," he said. "And she has brought the carcass of a monster."

The three old women climbed the mountain, dripping with sweat.

Jules and Julie followed closely behind.

They ascended the mountainside, following no path, unable to see through the standing trees and undergrowth.

The old women—although that term would surely anger them; they were still only in their late fifties—all wore dresses with the same garish print, and cut from the same pattern, differing only in color. The women were even shaped identically. They were short, and more or less cylindrical from shoulder to posterior. When they were quiet, they looked like three jars of jam, or perhaps something pickled.

"Look out, you two! Watch your feet or you'll slip."

"Watch this—see? Hold on to that as you climb."

"You have to get into the rhythm, or you'll never catch your breath."

The three of them were constantly turning back and scolding Jules and Julia with yellowed voices. Jules and Julia were gasping for breath, barely able to keep up. The women were surprisingly light on their feet for their age.

"It's about keeping in shape."

"We eat well, too."

"And drink our medicinal tea afterward."

"That's right."

"That's right."

The three of them laughed together. They shared the same laugh.

Whitening hair like sparrows' nests. Round faces and round-framed glasses. Convex lenses that made their eyes look enormous. They were triplets, and they made a living from selling preserves and embroidering souvenirs and aromatherapy. All three were unmarried. The eldest was Anna, the middle triplet Donna, and the youngest Luna. Naturally, they looked completely identical.

The five of them had left the Catwalk to traverse the mountain directly. There had never been any trails through this area. Jules and Julia didn't have any idea where they were.

"Don't worry," said one of the triplets with a laugh.

"We were playing on this mountain as children, before school."

"Picking nuts and strawberries."

"Tending secret flower beds."

"Filching birds' eggs."

"We could get you to the Mineral Springs with our eyes closed."

"And you did save our lives."

"Have to pay you back somehow."

Jules and Julia had found the triplets as they were being attacked by a carbon-black, six-legged Spider. Julia had erased it just as she had erased the one at the Singing Sands.

Earlier, after climbing the cliffs from the beach and returning to the road, Jules and Julia had leapt on their bikes and headed for the east bay. One glance at the sky had revealed that the Spiders were descending in the west—the direction from which the two of them had come. They had been worried about their homes and parents, but if they were being honest, they were mostly just too terrified to go back. Heading east instead, they had run into the imperiled triplets.

"All that jam I made, gone."

"And the porcini I dried. What a waste."

"The last wooden brooch I carved was so nice I didn't even want to sell it."

Despite what they said, the triplets did not seem particularly wistful. They just kept climbing at their unfaltering pace. They moved just barely slowly enough for Jules and Julia to keep up, silently but clearly indicating to their young companions the best foot- and handholds to use. The group developed a rhythm as it climbed. Climbing and panting, Jules and Julia were able to forget about the western town, their orchards and homes, and what would come next. Jules realized this halfway up, and was immediately grateful. He also felt a new respect for them.

"Hmm?"

"Eh?"

"Oh?"

Suddenly the triplets stopped moving. They turned their sweaty faces to Jules and Julia. Their glasses were fogged with perspiration.

Jules gazed back at them wordlessly.

"Well, this is a fix," said one of them. "Looks like we've lost our way."

The plaza in the west bay was where the largest volume of Spiders had fallen. You could hardly ask for a better place to strew with the *hunger*. The colorful, lively plaza and surrounding streets, the heart of the Realm of Summer, were devoured by the *hunger* in the blink of an eye.

The Spiders came in so many different forms.

There were Spiders like cars, Spiders like tower cranes, Spiders like two horseshoe crabs joined back-to-back, a legless Spider shaped like three globes connected by a cord (it moved by hurling its globes forward, one after another), and tiny Spiders that danced in the air like petals on the wind.

The variety of textures was also astounding. There were Spiders that seemed to be covered in gold leaf, Spiders that looked like wet potter's clay, Spiders dusted with tiny jade scales like a butterfly's wing, and Spiders that might have been carved from discolored teeth.

The two things they had in common were their intangible similarity to the Realm's maintenance Spiders and the *hunger* they bore.

That raging *hunger* quickly reduced the plaza to ruins.

A petal *Spider* landed on a young girl's cheek and began eating away at her face while those near her watched. She blinked, and her eyelids were gone; she did not even have time to be surprised before everything from her shoulders up had vanished. Her parents, who had been holding her hands on either side of her, looked down to see that they were now holding one dangling arm each, but before they could scream, everything below their jaws had vanished too.

The clock tower, symbol of Town Hall, succumbed to the tower crane Spider's jib. Eaten away at the middle, it hung in midair for a moment before slowly toppling sideways.

A Spider like wet clay softened itself and spread over the paving stones, then consumed just the ankles and feet of the AIs who trod on it. Winged Spiders the size of sparrows came to devour the rest of its immobilized victims.

Among the AIs fleeing in confusion was the owner of a bicycle shop, just past middle age—the man who had lent the bikes to Julie.

The store he had run for a thousand and fifty years had been crushed by a hand-shaped Spider bigger than a house. The hand crushed the store in its fist, and each time it squeezed, the lane stretched like taffy, reeled further into the Spider's grip. The road tilted and yawed. Paving stones popped loose. To avoid getting caught up himself, the man bolted.

To the plaza.

He stopped in his tracks.

Was that a pond of lacquer?

The plaza was gone. It seemed to have vanished into the pond, which was smooth and black and undisturbed by ripples.

Then the man realized: it was a hole. The same as those minor graphical glitches that the bustling maintenance Spiders fixed, only much larger. It occupied the entire space where the plaza had once been. Its sharp edges came right up to the end of the lane he stood on.

The paving stones under his feet began to ripple. The hand-shaped Spider was catching up.

But the bicycle shop owner could not look away from the hole—from what he saw at its center. What he saw was beyond comprehension.

A young man was floating at the center of the hole, as if standing on a pitch-black skating rink. The young man raised a little Spider on the back of his hand to his lips to kiss it, then looked at the bicycle shop owner.

The young man's lips were moving.

Suddenly the bicycle shop man heard a voice in his ear.

It was his own name.

How does he know my name?

The bicycle shop man did not know who the youth was.

This stunned him.

This Realm had been running for more than a thousand years. He knew every AI in it.

Which meant that the youth was not from this Realm.

Who—where—another...?

An instant later, the bicycle shop man disappeared into the *hunger* at his back.

The liveliest part of the Realm, with the plaza at its center, was by now almost completely eaten away.

Watching Anne scramble up from the boat's deck with her adopted children, Bernier was unable to say a word. He was too busy holding back his tears to speak. Anne was filthy, dripping with a viscous, half-dried fluid and cradling her eldest child's lifeless body in her arms. Why the image came to him at the time Bernier could not say, but it occurred to him that she looked as if someone had dumped a bucket of semen over her. He felt as if his own daughter had met with this treatment, and could not maintain his composure.

For all intents and purposes Anne *was* his daughter. Her father had been secretary at Town Hall and a drinking companion of Bernier's, so he had known her since she was a newborn. Even back then, he recalled, she had been strikingly big and very healthy.

By the age of six, all the boys her age deferred to her as their boss.

There was no one in town who didn't know about her fight with Jaco. He was a little hoodlum five years her senior, and she had laid him out almost immediately. Bernier had been astonished to learn then that her forearms had already been tattooed. By twelve she had lost her father, and from then on she ignored her mother to instead devote herself to mischief with the gang of bad seeds—including Jaco, and some boys even older than him—that were her henchmen.

Bernier had called her into Town Hall and given her a stern talking-to.

"When I turn fifteen, I'll get work on the boats and support my ma. The pile my pa left behind should be enough to feed her until then. As for me, I can earn my own bread myself."

Bernier knew well that whatever "bread" she earned was takings from games that amounted to gambling, but the manly glint in her eyes persuaded him to let it go.

At fifteen Anne joined a fishing crew, just as she had said she would. Telling her gang that as of the following morning she'd be a fisher, leaving them free to do as they pleased, she went cap in hand to the roughest captain on the docks. People still talked about how red Jaco's eyes had been when he came to watch her leave harbor for the first time.

"That was unrequited love and no mistake," Bastin said fondly, years later. "The—what's the word?—*anguish* in Jaco's face! I'll never forget it. But you know how Anne is. I don't think she even noticed."

Bernier caught Anne in a hug. He had noticed the tear tracks on her cheeks. Her tears were dry now, though. She had cried herself out on the boat.

"Got a house gift for you," she said.

"So I see."

The Spider's carcass was stretched out on the boat's deck.

"You'll find a use for it, right?"

"Absolutely," said Bernier. "Absolutely."

"I want to lay my little girl down somewhere too," said Anne. "My, uh…my arms are about at the limit."

"One thing about this place: they don't lack for beds."

"And I want a cup of coffee so strong it could blow your ass out."

"About a trough's worth sound good?"

"Might not be enough." Anne showed her long teeth for the first time. Bernier doubted even she knew whether it was a smile or not.

"You need to get some rest too," Bernier said.

Anne looked at him in surprise. It was clear from her expression that she hadn't expected to hear that from him. Bernier felt as if he had somehow made a faux pas.

"Why?" she asked.

He knew that tone of voice, those eyes. They were the same as when she had faced down eleven-year-old Jaco at the age of six.

At the time, Anne and her gang had adopted a kitten as a kind of mascot. Anne would do the rounds of the fishmongers every night with an empty can, asking politely for something for the cat (rather than just swiping it, as she did to ease her own hunger pangs).

When Jaco took the kitten and threw it into the sea to drown, Bernier had tried to comfort Anne. That was the first time he had seen what was in her eyes now.

Anne had no intention of getting any sort of rest.

"Hey," she said, as if suddenly remembering something. "Where's José?"

She was conscious. She could see the light.

But she couldn't make out anything more.

Her eyes couldn't recognize anything they saw as an object with meaning.

A fit of panic had shredded Odette's bodily senses and cognitive function. Her identity was in disarray.

She heard a voice calling her, but whether it was a student, one of her parents, or a guest come as her husband she did not know.

Despite her ragged breathing, she felt suffocated. Her heart beat out an irregular pulse.

Something happened to me today. The thought nagged at her in her semi-conscious state. *Something I can't remember.*

Her memories had fragmented, bobbing into view before vanishing again. She had taken her students to the church. Choir practice. The chapel was old but sound lingered in its air pleasingly, and everyone had been looking forward to the outing. They were her students, but they were all taller than her. Fine young women grown beautiful as flowers.

No sooner had they begun to warm up than everyone's mouths had dropped open. Turning to look, Odette had seen a round opening in the roof of the chapel.

That was where her memory grew disordered and unraveled.

It seemed to her that a hairy-faced giant had peered through the hole at them, but had she just hallucinated it?

Dozens and dozens of that face had fallen in on them. The faces had vomited sticky white spittle. She could remember nothing after that.

The more she concentrated and tried to recall the scene properly, the harder it was to see, as if she were touching the face of the water. Or, no—perhaps she was in the water, reaching up to touch the surface. She panicked, feeling on the verge of drowning, but she could not get her hand above the waterline.

"—way?" came a voice.

"—way?" These were words. The voice was the only thing that reached her from the surface, shooting through the water straight and true. Her mouth must be moving like a fish about to suffocate. She was trying to reply to the voice: *Get me out of here.*

"—way?" the voice repeated. It must be a voice she knew well. But what was it saying? It seemed to be asking about something she had done. She could not catch the words.

A hairy face trapped the fleeing, panicky Natalie and Agnès against the wall. It pinned Sophie and Nadine down. And then…

While that was going on, what was I doing?

"Did you run away?"

The voice spoke again. She felt a sudden shock, like being punched. Her mouth moved silently. *Yes, I was cowardly. I was terrified and I fled,* she confessed. *That was what I was afraid to remember.* Had the words come out? Whoever was calling to her, had they heard her speak?

"It's all right, Madame. You had a terrible time."

The voice was like a powerful arm thrust into the water. She took hold of it and held on desperately. She felt the sensation of being pulled up and out.

"You're safe now, Madame."

Odette realized that she was lying on her side in a small boat. She had come to her senses. Sitting up, she saw the sea all around. Her face calm now that her panic was under control, the elderly teacher looked at José van Dormael.

"It was you?" she asked. "I should have known. That was why I was saved—because it was you." Tears fell from her eyes. The next, inevitable battle would be with her own self-recrimination. "Thank you."

"This is the last boat," said José.

The men who had stayed at the crossroads until the last moment were on board, as well as the last few refugees, collapsed with apparent exhaustion. The west end of the town was gone. The chapel, too, and the agony of all those girls who had died there.

"I see," she said.

The little boat made its way east, cliffs to the right, tiny single engine roaring.

The aged teacher looked back just once in the direction where "west" had been. Most of the expanse of ocean that should have been there was already gone, vanished into snaking bands of black.

When they eventually came down from the mountain and met Anne, that was when Jules's legs gave way under him and Julie finally burst into wailing sobs, not stopping until they arrived at the bay. Anne brought them in safely, her arms firm around their shoulders. Her broad hands were a welcome reassurance.

They finally entered the east bay just after one in the afternoon.

It had been three hours since their encounter at the Singing Sands, and two hours since Anne had arrived at the Mineral Springs Hotel.

The bay was unbelievably still.

The summer houses and sanitarium rest areas had been thrown open to refugees from the west, as had the clubhouse at the marina. The sick and injured were taken to the Mineral Springs itself. The sky was calmer than it had been during the Spiders' great descent. The cloud cover had thinned enough here and there for the blue sky behind it to show through.

It'll surely clear up by nighttime, thought Jules, as if praying. *The stars will come out. Surely.*

Jules and Julie had both escaped serious injury, but because they were minors, and because Julie had mentioned their victory over a Spider, they were brought to the hotel, where a makeshift Town Hall had been established as planned.

The two of them were shown into the main dining hall, now redesignated the conference room. The Town Hall employees sat across the long table from them. How, they were asked, had Julie defeated the spider?

"Before that," said Julie, staring down the adults obstinately, "tell me where Mama is. Or I won't tell you a thing."

A short, burly old man who introduced himself as Bastin, the deputy mayor, rose from his seat. His close-cropped hair was pure white, but his eyebrows were bushy and pure black, and there was candor in his large, round eyes.

"In that case," he said, "Let me tell you how things stand with the town. None of us has much time, so I won't hold anything back. After I finish, you tell us everything we want to know. Do we have a deal?"

"Fine." Julie nodded.

"The west end of town has been completely destroyed.

"The Spiders devoured it. In its place there is now nothing but a gigantic hole.

"The hole engulfed everything from the homes and orchards at the foot of the mountains to the downtown area and harbor. It may grow larger yet. For anyone who was caught in the area, there is no hope. That group includes the mayor and the chief of police. Those who were able to escape we have taken in at this bay. We are checking everyone against the local police station's roll of residents as they arrive. However, Jules Tappy, Julie, none of your family members have appeared yet."

Julie was silent.

"Even the summary I just gave you is somewhat understated," said Bastin. "We, by which I mean the entire east bay, are *surrounded* by holes. Far more of the Realm has been consumed by Spiders and turned to void than has not.

"Fortunately for us, for some reason the Spider attack has ceased for now. We must use this time to get ourselves back in order. There are almost a thousand people here, and we must protect them. We chose the hotel for its superb collection of Glass Eyes. We have nothing you could call weaponry in this Realm, and so we must borrow the power of the Eyes, fight with the Eyes to defeat the Spiders."

Jules remembered breakfast that morning, the same as any other morning. *Papa has nowhere to return to now*, he thought.

"Julie," said Bastin. "I understand you are a spectacularly gifted user of the Eyes. The three sisters who brought you here are also masters of the Glass Eyes. This fills me with great confidence. Furthermore, you report that you have eliminated one Spider already. I assume that you used an Eye to do so. I want you to tell us exactly how."

"All right."

Julie's voice snapped Jules out of his reverie.

Wiping the tears from her eyes, she was doing her best to fulfill her promise to Bastin. Her lips trembled, as did her shoulders.

"The Spider was starving. I don't know how I knew that, but I did. It came to me. Jules noticed it too."

Bastin nodded. Everyone had sensed that *hunger*.

"When the Spider erased Pointed Rock and turned toward us, I was petrified. Just facing it made me feel as if I would be sucked into it and disappear. Not just feel—for a moment I did start to disappear. Jules was behind me, so he might not have realized it.

"The outline of my body began to tremble finely and become blurred and indistinct. The hem of my dress started turning transparent. I understood then that some sort of power was pouring out of the Spider. I thought, 'This must be how it made the rock disappear. But if this power can affect things in the Realm, it must abide by the rules of the Realm too. And if that's so, I can use this Eye.' Glass Eyes can exert their effects on anything in the realm at all. I didn't know what kind of power this *hunger* was exactly, but I thought it should be easy to alter its course while leaving its essential nature unchanged. Well, I say that I 'thought' this, but really my body moved of its own accord. And then…"

Julie was already weeping again, but she didn't stop speaking for a moment. She faced directly forward and continued her report. Bastin made no move to stop her.

"And then I tried just that. I captured the incredible *hunger* pouring out of the Spider with Cottontail, and sent it right back. And it worked. The Spider disappeared… Is that enough?"

"More than enough. Rest for a while." The deputy mayor rose to his feet. He spread his short arms and embraced Julie. He was not much taller than her.

"Mr. Deputy Mayor…" she said.

"It's Bastin," he told her. "Call me Bastin."

"Bastin. I was in school with Agnès, your granddaughter," said Julie. "Is she all right?"

"Thank you for asking, Julie. I have asked everyone to keep looking for her. But she hasn't been found yet."

"I'm sorry. I shouldn't have asked that."

"No, I'm the one asking too many questions. Thank you."

"Bastin?"

"Yes?"

"This…" Julie unwound Cottontail from her arm and handed it to Bastin. Jules was shocked. Julie giving one of her Eyes away was unthinkable. "This is the Eye I was talking about just now. He's a good boy. I think he has the knack of it now. He can help you."

Bastin gazed at the Eye for a moment before producing a handkerchief and reverently accepting Cottontail into it. The handkerchief was stained with blood.

"This is all I have," he said. "My apologies."

"Mr. Deputy Mayor," said Jules.

"Yes, Jules Tappy?" Bastin turned to face him.

"Handing out Eyes and hoping for the best won't be enough to save the hotel. But I have an idea."

"In that case…" Bastin had already shifted gears, it seemed. "Let me hear it. Right away." His face glowed in the light from Cottontail on his handkerchief. It made Jules realize that Bastin's eyes were the same blue as the ocean that the town looked out on.

"Before that, Bastin," Jules said, thrusting his chest out as best he could, "I want all the information you have about the Spiders, please. Maintenance blueprints for the hotel, too. Also…let Julie take a shower."

"Understood." Bastin's weary eyes softened.

And so began the hopeless twelve-hour defensive campaign at the Mineral Springs Hotel.

CHAPTER 3:
THE MINERAL SPRINGS HOTEL

What does it mean to remember?

What is a memory?

When a reader opens a book to the very first page, the characters in it already have memories. They possess pasts. At the moment the story begins, they can remember what happened beforehand. But where did they have those experiences? When were they accumulating those memories?

This is a question that no one can answer.

What about the Costa del Número?

One thousand years since the Grand Down.

Fifty years leading up to it.

And before that? Before the day the Realm of Summer had opened for business and its first guests had arrived?

On that day, the AIs had greeted their guests looking exactly the same as they did today. They had not aged a year since then. But even they had memories from earlier—memories of their youth.

These memories were part of the setting—the lore established by the Realm's scriptwriters. How the town had become established, what sort of lives the AIs lived there: everything had been covered with exacting care.

This was highly gratifying for the guests too. An empty stage with no history and characters without fleshed-out timelines aroused little excitement. And for *this* Realm in particular, that mattered.

It mattered a lot.

The AIs knew, of course, that their memories had never really been played out in the Realm. They knew that the experiences that had formed their personalities were imaginary. And they knew that these things had been built into them simply for the guests to take an interest in.

For all that, the AIs cherished these memories as their very own, priceless and irreplaceable.

But—

But had those events truly never happened? If so, why could the AIs remember them? How was it possible?

Beneath the hundreds, the thousands of Realms lay something else. Something that was not visible from any of them. No AI could access this domain of their own volition; indeed, they not one denizen of the Realms was even aware it existed.

The Costa del Número's back room.

Its highest level was where the memories of the world accumulated. Any event that took place in a Realm was added to the billions of episode membranes thickly layered in this record area. It was a vast library of all that had happened in the Realms.

The level below this was for events that *hadn't* taken place in the Realms. Here the layers were even thicker, recording things deemed to have happened before the birth of the Realms—their settings, in the form of their histories.

This was the basis of the AIs' memories.

Here their memories lay in quiet stacks, framed like biological specimens.

But there was a deeper level still.

The domain in which the ChronoManager dwelled.

A system that flawlessly directed the timelines of thousands of separate Realms, guaranteeing the guests smooth entry into and travel between those worlds.

This domain was also home to several thousand monk-like figures that were anthropomorphized representations of the low-level AIs who worked there. These AIs were sexless, able, and diligent, but incapable of advanced thought or emotion. Dressed in black uniforms with stand-up collars, they glided soundlessly through the maze of sheer, towering walls that filled their world, busily performing tasks whose end could not be foreseen. They used ladders and footholds to climb up and down and across the walls, checking the clockfaces embedded in the sheer surfaces to ensure that each was without deviation and advancing as planned. They also busily wiped off any dust that had settled on the blue glass covering the clocks.

In that domain, after the Grand Down, a single change had occurred.

One day, a boy in a white hoodie had appeared there. On his shoulders and at his waist clung a total of seven little Spiders. From the first moment of his appearance—and the mere fact of his having a gender had astonished the sexless AIs—he had walked around as if he owned the place, confident and self-assured. He paid no heed to the black-clad locals at their chores, which caused minor inconveniences for them wherever he went.

The AIs were vexed and suspicious, but they made their peace with his presence.

They had no other choice.

Because—

Because

The night had deepened and the fireplace had been lit, less for the warmth than for the sense of calm. After a light meal, each of the adults was served a small glass of *vin chaud*, while Jules and Julie received warm milk. In the first mouthful Jules detected the faint scent of brandy. He set the ceramic cup on the table, which was long enough to seat at least ten.

"Aren't you cold, Jules?" Yvette Carrière asked him from across the table. As usual, her voice was as gentle as milk. Her smile suited her plump cheeks well.

Jules gazed around at the people gathered in the casino of the Mineral Springs Hotel. To a one, they were drained, wounded, beaten. Two hundred–odd AIs had taken refuge in the hotel by now. There had been no other survivors.

"I'm okay. Completely fine."

Yve smiled and returned to her handwork.

The Spiders' brutal assault had begun at three in the afternoon, only slowing as evening fell. The clock now showed eight o'clock. The casino had not originally had anything so gauche as a clock in it; the standing clock from the lobby had been brought in at considerable effort.

Watching the flames in the fireplace after a shower and a meal, Jules had to admit he felt calmer. The solid wooden furnishings, the leather chairs, the slightly dimmed illumination had a soothing effect. The fire and the drinks had all been arranged on the orders of Denis, the manager. Making people feel at home was his chosen profession.

Yve hadn't touched her hot wine, which had by now gone cold.

"Aren't you going to drink that?" asked Jules.

"Not me. If we fall behind schedule because of me, how could I face the others?"

Yve's hands never stopped moving. Candlesticks and electric lamps had been gathered to ensure that those hands, at least, were brightly lit, but her beautiful chestnut eyes had little use for light.

Spread out before her was a large, oval-shaped tablecloth.

It was woven of thin, sparkling silver thread, and almost finished. Intricate lace was used generously throughout its design, and Yve was set to complete it at astonishing speed—less than two hours had passed since she had begun her work. She had good reason to hurry. Whether the Mineral Springs Hotel lived or died would all come down to this tablecloth of knitted Spider silk.

Julie was sitting beside Jules. She patted him on the shoulder.

"You should get some rest too," she said.

"Yeah."

Jules leaned back in his chair. Cottontail was already asleep, breathing slowly and regularly in Julie's lap. The adults had borrowed the Eye to help make the hotel into a fortress, and it had come back exhausted. But Julie was more fatigued yet. She was knitting like Yve. Her piece was almost done as well, but it was a great deal smaller than Yve's.

Anna, Donna, and Luna were also at the table, busy at lacework. The triplets hunched identically, working their needles at blazing speed. Jules still could not tell them apart.

The most skilled Glass Eye users in the entire Realm were all at Jules's table.

One of the triplets picked up her little glass and tossed back her drink.

"So, Donna" Jules said. "What do you think? Any problems in the lace I wrote?"

"And why should there be, sonny boy?" Donna widened her eyes, already magnified by her glasses, and grinned. "I'm very impressed. This pattern had never occurred to me before, but it's a pretty one. Easy to knit, too. Of course, what really matters is how it performs…" She put her index finger to her chin and tilted her head. "I'm not a smarty like you, so that's beyond what I can calculate. Have to use it to find out. But you did get one thing wrong. The most important thing, in fact."

"I did?"

"I'm Anna, not Donna."

The other two looked up and snickered. Jules cocked his head. He had to admit that they looked identical to him.

The sister sitting to Anna's left spoke up.

"Let me teach you how to tell us apart, Jules," she said. "Anna's the one who's good at making jam. Pickles are Luna's specialty. And the best at making pâté, and also jam and pickles, is me—Donna."

The three of them began to argue like sparrows, praising and denouncing each others' abilities in this field and that. All while keeping their knitting needles in motion.

"I don't know who's the best at what," said Jules, shaking his head, "but I doubt that would be much help telling you apart anyway, Donna."

"Eh? I'm Luna," said the triplet he was sure had identified herself as Donna just moments ago, surprise in her face.

Many old photographs were on display in the hotel lobby. One photo was of the triplets in their youth. There they were at seventeen, each escorted by a different man, all three as beautiful and charming as cheerful as fairies.

Those days still seemed to linger in the three of them as they laughed before him now. In fact, they looked as bewitching as ever.

They had remained unmarried for family reasons. Their mother had become bedridden from a young age, and they had a younger brother weakened by illness.

Today, their little house had been set upon and devoured by the Spiders.

Their fine, cozy work space, the aromatherapy salon that had served as a meeting place for the elderly, their mother and brother—none had been saved.

"Still not finished, Yve?"

Felix Carrière had come to the table. There was a restless irritability in his piping voice. He rubbed his thin, fox-like face nervously with his palm. His frizzy red hair swayed like tufts of corn silk.

"No? Denis is waiting. The deputy mayor too."

"Almost done, Felix. Just a little longer."

Yve tried to placate her younger husband with a smile, hands never stopping. Felix was a tailor and a customer of Yve's lace since her youth, long before they became man and wife.

"You have to stop dithering and get it done. If it isn't finished, it'll cause a chain of other problems later."

Everyone knew this already. Jules, leaning on Julie, glared at the little man, with his pointy nose and weak chin and lined forehead. Jules's own mood worsened as he listened to Felix speak, getting caught up in the older man's irritation.

"I'm sorry." Instead of arguing, Yve offered another smile, this one saying *Even I can't believe how slow my hands move.*

It was a mystery to Jules what Yve saw in Felix.

"Come on, don't do this to me," Felix said. He sighed heavily. "Just unbelievable. How many hours is this going to take? You aren't slacking off at a time like this, I hope?" His nose and eyes were red and he fidgeted restlessly. So he was drunk. At a time like this.

"She's just got a bit more to go," Jules put in, unable to help himself. "Don't rush her."

Felix blinked at him. "Was that addressed to me, Jules?" he asked. "That's right."

"All right. Remember this." Felix leaned closer to Jules's face, thrusting his hand into his apron's breast pocket. It was a tailor's apron, with many pockets and a large pair of scissors slipped into it. "I can take a scolding from a kid. You ever blow across an empty bottle? That hooting sound? Yeah, that's what kids sound like when they complain like that. You're happy to bitch about what adults do, but that's only because you can't do anything yourself yet."

Jules gave up on the conversation. Beside him, Julie let out a pointed hoot. Jules had done his job, Yve was doing hers. Who, she was asking, was the child here?

Felix couldn't even see that much. Perhaps satisfied that he had told Jules what was what, he walked over to the counter. He was hoping for another drink.

"Sorry about that, Jules," said Yve. "Now, is this coming out okay? Take a look."

Jules took a glance at her lacework and said, "It's perfect." Yve had pushed her skills to the limit to realize the delicate net of loops, and the result was exquisite. Jules had been watching closely the whole time to make sure that the program he had worked into these loops had no bugs.

"Take a look at ours, too," said one of the triplets. "Too late to reknit it all now anyway." Their work was much plainer than Yve's, but perfectly executed within those bounds. The quality of the workmanship was also remarkably consistent across the three of them.

Yve's tablecloth, even closer to completion, was still spread over the large table. Lace knitted from Spider silk hung from the edges in places, and there were some intentionally unfinished areas too.

The door to the casino burst open and things suddenly became boisterous. Ten or so of the fishermen clumped into the room in rubber boots, bringing with them a reassuring air of indomitability.

Anne and the others were back.

"Jules! Where is that little slave driver?" she called with cheerful acerbity, voice booming like a man's. She was a head taller than even the grizzly crew that surrounded her. "Ah, there you are. On Yve's tit, are we?"

Jules blushed. Yve's mild face and ample proportions did give her a motherly air. Over by the counter, Felix looked displeased, but elected not to remonstrate with Anne, slouching forward over his glass instead. Anne, of course, ignored him entirely and approached the table.

Even simply walking toward him, she was magnetic—the epitome of fearlessness.

"Nice work, Jules. You're something else," she said, ruffling his hair and smiling. Her full upper lip, the same color as the rest of her skin, was pulled back slightly from her teeth. Her eyes, turned up at the corners, were as wide and blue as the morning sky. Against the bronze of the rest of her body, they sparkled like blue diamonds.

"I guess I am."

Anne laughed. "'I guess I am,' he says! You hear this kid? Destined for greatness, and no mistake. Don't worry. Everything went as planned. We ran it around the whole thing, just like you said."

"Thank you."

Anne sat herself down beside him with a thump. "Get over here, you ugly mugs," she called to the other fishermen. "Come take a look at Yve's lace. It's come out amazing."

Among the fishermen, there was only one who was as tall as Anne. That young man approached her now.

The man who was to have battled Jules on the chessboard that night.

The man who lent Anne poetry.

The man whose voice alone had pulled a singing teacher out of her panic.

Julie sat up straighter. Jules could feel her eyes softening from his seat next to her.

José van Dormael sat quietly down beside Anne.

There were eight of them sitting around the table now.

Denis Prejean appeared through a different door, accompanied by Charles Bernier. Between the two of them they carried a large leather trunk. It was a modified version of the sort of giant case that a harness maker might fashion for sea travel. They stepped gingerly, lips pressed thinly together. Finally they reached the table and put their load down on it, sighing as one.

"Opening it now," said Bernier solemnly, and flipped open the trunk's latches.

He removed some shock-absorbent padding to produce a smaller box from within. When he opened this and pulled aside the glossy fabric covering its contents, the room gasped. It was the Crystal Chandelier.

The Crystal Chandelier was an oval Glass Eye more than thirty centimeters long. No Eye of comparable size had ever been seen before or since. If the world could be said to refer to the Realm, then the Crystal Chandelier was the biggest Glass Eye in the world.

Would comparisons to a flat-cut diamond help to convey some part of its form, its transparency, its frozen gleam? It was so beautiful that it might have drawn in all the light in the room, luring in the rays with its bewitching appeal. Every one of its countless cuts was perfect, and no matter what sort of light shone on it from which direction, both light and stone were only rendered even more beautiful.

They carefully lifted the Crystal Chandelier from the trunk and placed it on the table. It reflected the candlelight so brightly that it seemed to be another flame. Jules wondered what you might see if you peered into the stone. The light and sound, the emotions and sensations that leapt in through its thousands of cut faces—how would they be transformed and woven together, tied into singularities and then undone once more? Not even Jules could simulate that in his mind. It would be a dance of vast proportions, an elegant and sharp intersection of the most challenging steps.

Yve had told him something about Glass Eyes long ago. "You can't know everything that's inside them," she had said, "any more than you can know everything that happens in a person's brain." If the Glass Eyes were brains, then the Glass Chandelier was surely the brightest of them all. An intelligence of light woven by cut and clarity.

"There," Yve said with apparent relief. "I'm finished. Felix, the lace is finished!"

"It's finished?" Felix leapt to his feet. "Denis, it's finished! Yve's done it. She's finished." He swayed on his feet as he bragged to the manager.

"We're almost there, then," said Denis, acknowledging Felix's words absently as he rubbed his bald pate.

The Crystal Chandelier was placed atop Yve's lace. The lace that Julie had knitted was draped over the top, and then the two pieces of lace were deftly knotted together in a few spots.

Next, three smaller Eyes were carried in to sit atop the lace the triplets had made.

The Father of Flame was an amber Eye with a slightly viscous texture and fire at its core—not a reflection of the fireplace but what appeared for all the world to be a real ember within the Eye. The surface of the Father of Flame was only slightly warm to the touch, but the right user could persuade it to externalize its fearsome heat—to use it to change the temperature of the outside world.

Snowscape was a stranger beast. A perfect sphere of stunning transparency, it enclosed a snowy landscape, a night scene complete with house and raging blizzard. It looked exactly like a toy snow globe. The chill within Snowscape could be externalized as a strongly directional beam, or as weather. Like the Father of Flame, it had rare offensive capabilities, and these two Eyes were arranged on either side of the Chandelier.

The third Eye was like a black pearl fifteen centimeters across. Not many Eyes could boast of such size. It was called the Black Grid. Its powers were largely unknown, but it had been adopted at Yve's suggestion.

The lace on which the three new Eyes rested was connected to the Crystal Chandelier's lacework.

"Is everything else in place?" asked Bastin.

"Ready and waiting," Anne said cheerfully. "We also inspected the place where the stones are going to be kept. All looks perfect. Those damn Spiders can come whenever they like, as far as I'm concerned."

"Be careful what you wish for. I'd prefer they didn't come at all."

Denis rubbed his head, his careless gesture releasing the tension that Anne's thoughtless remark had introduced. After today's experiences, how many had expected to smile again? Denis had that sort of personal magnetism, and Anne knew it. She stood up at once and bowed her head to him.

"My apologies," she said.

"All right," said Jules, rising to his feet. "We have to wake up the Chandelier. And then we have to teach it the ropes. This is where things get hard."

Bernier stared in admiration at the twelve-year-old boy who had just risen to his feet with an *All right*. The boy was a genius. His stamina was nothing to sneeze at, either.

Bernier recalled the events of the afternoon.

After Julie had lent her Glass Eye to Bastin, Jules had proposed an eye-popping plan. That plan had been adopted, and at three in the afternoon preparations had just begun when the Spiders recommenced their attack.

They had not been in their nest in town as those at the hotel had supposed. Instead of traversing the Catwalk, where police officers stood guard, the Spiders had crossed the mountains, pouring over the towering ridge to fall on the east bay from above.

The hotel had set watchmen, but word of the sudden offensive arrived far too late. Sixteen Spiders attacked the summer homes on the slopes. The *hunger* rolled over the cluster of elegant buildings like an avalanche, obliterating them in the blink of an eye. The large cottage where the refugees of schooling age had been gathered, the groundskeeper's office in the gardens that had been opened up to the smaller children—it all disappeared without a sound. There was not even time to scream.

Not satisfied with laying waste to the beautiful summer-home district, the Spiders descended farther and made jet-black holes of the sanitariums and the elderly refugees within those buildings. Finally, when they were almost at the hotel and its marina, they were met by the Mineral Springs' vigilance committee.

Standing at the head of the committee were Anne and her younger fishermen.

Everyone knew by then that Anne had taken down a Spider with a harpoon and two knives. Nobody had managed to re-create her feat, but the story still held an important lesson: the Spiders could be damaged by objects from within the Realm.

The Spiders were, in all likelihood, from elsewhere. The likes of their *hunger* had never been seen in the Realm before. If not for Anne's reckless act, it would not have been clear whether they could be damaged by rocks or fire or harpoons—physical objects—at all. And, of course, the Spider's carcass she had brought to the hotel was another, even more important success.

The clash at three o'clock ended with the Spiders just barely held at bay.

This was, first of all, because Anne had kept the committee's morale and confidence high.

Then there were the tactical lessons Julie had shared. Eyes capable of powerful reflections and transformations had been removed from their display cases in the VIP room. Those rare and precious Eyes with offensive capabilities saw the light of day as well. Legendary stones like the Father of Flame and Snowscape were entrusted to carefully selected users. There were many Eye users among the refugees who had come to the hotel. This was no coincidence. It had been difficult for anyone who could not make use of a nearby Eye to survive at all. In any case, before the battle Bastin had ordered that the experience preserved within Cottontail be transmitted to the other Eyes as well.

Most encouraging of all had been what the Spider's carcass had taught them about their enemy's true form.

According to the dissection carried out by Dr. Biott, a veterinarian, the Spiders appeared to be relatively simple Realm objects—single-purpose tools without advanced decision-making capabilities like the AIs. Their basic code he thought likely to share the same roots as the little maintenance Spiders, and their functionality was limited to a handful of simple commands. The *hunger* that Julie had sensed was one of these, and seemed to be a method of removing things from this Realm and sending them to another. In other words, the people who had already disappeared might still be alive in another Realm. This alone had multiplied morale several times over. Knowing what they were up against, the warriors wielded their strength differently.

Anne's superhuman performance and the Eye strategy both hit the mark. The other Eyes absorbed Cottontail's knack for bringing down Spiders without difficulty, making them much more effective on the battlefield. Once the staggering power of the Father of Fire or Snowscape had weakened them, the Spiders were helpless before the AI's harpoons. Once half their number had fallen, they paused, then turned back. And in this way the clash by the marina, though a very close thing, came to an end, and the residents of the Realm were permitted to live another day.

"You think the Femme Fatale business will work?" asked Bastin, standing beside Denis.

"That's Pierre's department," said Jules. "He must be almost—"

Before he could finish the sentence, Pierre Affre entered the casino. He was a long, thin man in a sleeveless black T-shirt. Wrapped around his left wrist was a thick chain. Pierre was just two years older than Julie, but he knew a lot about Eyes. As a user, he was far from expert, but his grasp of their classification and other minutiae was impressive.

"You took your time, Pierre," teased Anne. "Got you in her claws, did she?"

Femme Fatale was the most famous piece in this museum's collection. Shaped like a peanut shell, it contained a miniature room in which a most alluring woman dwelled.

"Nah, she's not my type," said Pierre, hiding his bashfulness so poorly that the whole room fell about laughing.

"Yve, give it a try."

Yve grinned. She ran her fingers over the edge of her lacework with a sensitive touch, like someone playing the clavecin.

The Crystal Chandelier lit up in an instant, as if someone had hit the on switch. A shaft of light came from just one of its cut faces. It was brighter than the fireplace, and it swept the casino like a lighthouse beam.

And then, suddenly, a woman whose name nobody knew was standing in the corner of the room.

She had olive skin and black hair that fell to her hips.

Her slender body was wrapped in dark Romani-style clothing, but the lining of her long skirt was as red as blood.

She crossed her arms over her chest and stared defiantly at the assembled group.

The same defiance was in the smile on her lips. The sheer sense of her presence was breathtaking.

She was not an AI.

She lived inside Femme Fatale—inside the miniature room that had been prepared inside the Eye.

The Eye was her home. Every morning she boiled water in her enamel kettle to brew her tea. She liked cooking and drawing, practiced severe dance lessons on her own; at night she wrote in her diary, composed poems, and then pleasured herself in bed, where her technique was wild and free.

The winter constellations or the summer sun were visible through a skylight directly over her bed, and milk was delivered to her room daily. From one angle she looked like a courtesan; from another, a poet.

Those who gazed into her Eye she seduced with a smile. *Come on in*, she seemed to say. *I'll put the kettle on.* But nobody could accept her invitation. The hard wall of the Eye kept everyone out. Nobody knew her name, and so it regularly came up in conversation. Because everyone wanted to call her by it. Because she was thought to have a personality. Such was the extent of her allure.

"Honestly, that was the biggest surprise," Bastin said, patting Jules on the head. "To think a boy like you would know how to handle this beauty. I wish you'd teach me a thing or two."

Jules smiled up at Bastin. He had done well and he knew it. "How're things going, Yve?" he asked.

"Just breathtaking." It seemed that Yve had picked up on the woman's presence too. "I never dreamed it would go so well."

When she removed her fingers from the lace, the woman disappeared as if at a signal. Bernier finally exhaled.

This was a trap.

The true value of the trap did not lay in magic-lantern tricks like these. They would use more cunning methods to bring the Spiders down.

Bernier looked at the boy with undisguised admiration.

He could not forget the sight of Jules explaining his "trap network" proposal. A blackboard had been brought into the hotel's small dining hall, and Jules had chalked diagrams on it as fast as a machine gun until it was almost white.

"Do you understand?" he had asked finally, standing with the blackboard at his back and surveying the overwhelmed adults that were his audience. "The preparations will take some time. Perhaps until eight o'clock tonight. If we can hold them off that long, the hotel will be ready. That will let us escape being slaughtered like rats, and possibly even create the opportunity to go on the offensive."

The impossibly complex network he had drawn on the blackboard had TRAP NETWORK written at the top in thick letters.

"Call it TrapNet. This is what we're going to make.

"It won't take much to get started. The hotel's own security systems will serve as the foundation. The Mineral Springs Hotel has always had guards and security systems. It had to, because it was members only.

"Of course, the whole of Costa del Número is members only. Guests who want to enjoy the facilities have to pay. The Mineral Springs is a special zone within that space that costs extra. But things in the Realm act the same way as things in the real world, so any guest can see the hotel building, or touch it. If it has an entrance, they can even go inside. To cordon off the Mineral Springs Hotel as a premium area and control who can get in, the Realm's designers wrote an authentication program. In our world, that system has a physical form: the hotel's security system, its doormen, and so on. Does that all make sense, Denis?"

Denis nodded his light bulb of a head.

"Embedded throughout the Mineral Springs Hotel are minute sensors called microscopic sensory receptors. Every gate, wall, and window in the hotel is under constant surveillance. If someone gets in without ID, or commits a crime once they're inside, they will be seen. Naturally, unauthorized entrants can be informationally detailed, but in response to violence the system is also capable of fighting back.

"What I'm proposing is that we remodel the security system into an anti-Spider system. The current system isn't powerful enough, but we should be able to supplement it using Eyes. We can use them as sensors, as processors, and for offense. Trained users can develop all the latent powers within the Eyes we need, and we'll have control of the system itself.

"I mean, if there's one thing this hotel has plenty of, it's Eyes.

"So…have any Eye users arrived yet?"

Bastin offered the names of Yve and the triplets.

"Ah, Yve is here?"

At that moment Bernier thought he saw a thought roiling in Jules's eyes like a tiny storm. Jules immediately erased the blackboard and drew a new spiral-shaped diagram.

"This is a lace pattern," he said. "Have Yve knit it up right away. We'll use this to control TrapNet."

Bernier had no idea what Jules was saying. He doubted the others present did either. Undeterred, Jules continued.

"We need the biggest and most complex Glass Eye there is. An Eye to be the core of our network. Once the battle starts, sensory information is going to wash in from all over the hotel—far too much to be dealt with by two or three Eye users, but no problem for a big, gem-shaped Eye that can transmute many incident light rays in parallel."

At last someone among the assembled adults spoke.

The voice was quiet, but it carried well.

"So, the lace is the server interface. The user goes through that to control the Glass Eye and TrapNet itself. Do I have that right?"

The audience turned in surprise to the source of the question: José van Dormael, standing by the wall with his arms folded. It seemed to Bernier that he had grasped Jules's idea at once. (Bernier preferred to hedge with "seemed" because he wasn't sure he understood Jules's idea himself yet.)

"Let me ask you a question, Jules," José continued.

"Go ahead, José."

"What is the lace knitted out of? And the cables for the network?"

"We use Spider silk."

"Okay." José nodded briefly.

But the others—including Bernier, of course—were shocked.

Bring something that had come out of a Spider's body into the Mineral Springs Hotel? The murmurs rose to a dull roar with no sign of stopping.

"I read Dr. Biott's dissection records," said Jules, glancing at a nearby binder. "The Spiders are very similar in their basic structure to the maintenance Spiders that have always been in the Realm, and probably to similar programs all over the Costa del Número. Their spinnerets aren't any different either, and their silk is fundamentally the same stuff. The better half of this town is probably made up of web patches from the maintenance Spiders by now. There's no reason not to bring silk into the hotel."

"Okay, so there's no reason *not* to do it," said José. "What reason is there to do it at all? Why do we need it?" He hadn't moved from the wall, and his arms were still folded.

"It's highly conductive," said Jules. "When Julie took down a Spider on the beach, the *hunger* that Cottontail bounced back was carried along a web. And everyone knows that you don't use Spider silk to carry Eyes or wrap them up for storage, right? The content of the Eye might leak out, or unnecessary external information could seep into the Eye and muddy it. But this trap network is…there seem to be a few people who don't quite follow how it works yet, but please understand this much: we need to put the Eyes into a state in which the fluidity of their content is high enough for constant exchange between one Eye and the next. Spider silk is the ideal material for that, and we can get as much as we need. The Spiders have left it all over the place. We just find it, untangle it, and spin it into thread again."

"What if it's a trap?"

"What do you mean?"

"Exactly what I said. What if they anticipated that we would use the silk, and went out of their way to make it easier for us—*after* hiding something in it to sabotage us from the inside? Isn't that a possible danger?"

Jules remained silent for a moment. It was not that he had no counterargument. He was simply waiting for José's meaning to sink in for everyone else.

"José," said Bastin. "Let me see if I understand you correctly. You're saying this isn't just a natural disaster. The Spiders are under somebody's control, and getting silk into the hotel is part of their plan. Is that it?"

Jules nodded. "He has a point," he said. "It's not outside the realm of possibility."

"And that's okay with you?" demanded Bernier, leaping to his feet.

"Not with me," said José, arms still folded.

"There's a relatively easy test we could run," said Jules, erasing the blackboard to fill it with another diagram. "We will need help from the triplets, though. See?"

"Yes, I see," said José, nodding. "That test didn't occur to me." He unfolded his arms and offered Jules his hand. "Looks like I lost this year too."

"I wish we could have played a proper game," said Jules, shaking José's hand with a smile.

"All right, everyone. Everything's finally ready. TrapNet is set to go, and everyone understands their station and their assignment perfectly."

The sound of Bastin's voice brought Bernier back to the present. The deputy mayor had his arms spread wide. He spoke calmly, and the audience hung on his every word.

"There are currently two hundred of us here in the Mineral Springs Hotel. We are the only survivors in all the Realm. The western town was destroyed this morning; the attack in the afternoon ate away most of the east bay too. Our mountains, our pine groves, our marina with its beautiful schooners and yachts, our fish market—all turned into one gigantic hole covered in Spider-web. The hotel is completely surrounded.

"The fight is not going to be easy. Our enemy is powerful beyond measure, and our weapons meager indeed."

He heard someone sniffling. René. René was a gifted shipwright, in whose hands even severely damaged craft were restored as if by magic. When one of his creations hit the water, the most lecherous playboy in town would leave his lady hanging to watch the launch instead. If anyone had the right to weep for the marina, it was René, thought Bernier. But of course René wasn't crying. It was just rhinitis.

Nobody there was crying. Nobody at all.

The casino was utterly devoid of sentimentality.

"Luckily for us, we have the ideal fortress—the Mineral Springs Hotel. Here there are beds to rest our bodies and drink to soothe our souls. We do not lack for food or fuel, and, most importantly, to get in or out of this fortress is tremendously difficult. After all, Denis is standing right at the front counter, ready and waiting."

Everyone smiled.

"We also have the ideal Eyes for the job. This is an enormous advantage for us. And, most importantly of all, we have as many people to use them as we need. Right, Yve?"

"Right."

"That's right. And to help those Eye users exercise their powers, we have the ideal setup too."

Bastin thanked Jules by name.

"Think about it this way. The Grand Down. Everything collapsed that day. In the thousand years since, not a single guest has set foot in the Realm. Well, it's been a long time, but we finally have company.

These brutal, cunning, grotesque Spiders.

"We're past masters at welcoming visitors. So let's show these Spiders a good time in our own way. Let's pull out *all* the stops."

His ending was characteristically anticlimactic:

"Anne, over to you."

Anne rose to stand beside Bastin and began giving orders.

She divided the men into three groups. The first set off for the front entrance under Bastin's command, while she took control of the second herself, leading them toward the terrace overlooking the sea. The terrace would be the hardest part of the hotel to hold, she thought. José was in the second group with her.

The third group dispersed to key points on each floor of the hotel. They were the engineering corps who kept TrapNet working smoothly; most of the men who knew how to use an Eye had been assigned to this group.

"Bastin." Bernier approached his longtime coworker. "I'm going around to the terrace. That's where all the tough guys will be, right? Good place for a senior citizen to relax."

Bastin snorted. "Don't get in their way, old man," he said with a grin.

"Later, then."

"Yep."

With that, the two of them parted, never to meet again.

With all the able-bodied men gone and only the elderly, women, and children left, the casino felt much less crowded.

"Julie, let's get started," Jules said. He tried to move away from the table so as not to get in the way.

Removing her arm from around his shoulder, Julie whispered to him, "Hey, Jules, would you look after this little guy for me?"

She held out Cottontail on her open palm. It was still asleep. Without its shining fur, it just looked like a milky-hued rock.

Cottontail alone had not been plugged into TrapNet. Julie had refused point-blank to allow it.

"He's a very good boy, this one," she said.

"Okay."

"Take care of him. You have to keep him safe."

"Okay."

Jules accepted the Eye from her. He knew its faint warmth was from Julie's lap, but it still felt like a small animal—a squirrel, or perhaps a dormouse. Cottontail squirmed in his hands. It must have realized that it had changed hands, because Jules felt a lonely noise through his open palms. It was calling for Julie.

Julie brought her lips to his right ear.

"Make sure he never touches any other Eyes," she said.

Jules looked at her, puzzled.

"Promise me," she insisted.

"Okay, I promise."

"I'm counting on you." With that, Julie headed for the large table.

Yve, Julie, and the triplets gathered around the Chandelier. Everyone else in the casino stood around the table as well. Women and children gazed at the Eye to which had been entrusted the fate of the hotel and the lives of their husbands, their fathers, their sons. Everything hinged on the TrapNet they had made of the Eyes.

And then—

"You're thinking about the web, aren't you?"

Someone clapped Jules on the shoulder as they spoke, making him jump.

"We meet again, huh, kid?"

The old man wore his usual crow-like robes. Jules had not even noticed the man sitting down beside him.

"Shame about your ma," the old man continued, not bothering to look Jules in the eye. His tone was as casual as if he were discussing the weather.

Jules was frozen, unable to move.

He could not tear his gaze from the scar that deformed the man's face—the grave of the man's right eye. Finally, he managed to force something out.

"You were here all along?"

The old man ignored him. "Look at your face!" he said. "You look like you've seen a ghost. Anyway, you did good. A web of Spider silk around the hotel—brilliant idea. Not even the Spiders will be able to get through it."

"Who are you?"

"Now that's a tough question, isn't it? You want me to tell you what I'm about in one sentence? But even if you knew, it'd be too much for you to handle. I promise you."

That roundabout way of speaking he had. He was snide and arrogant, and the reasons for his unshakable self-confidence were far from clear.

"Can you at least tell me your name?"

"My name?" The old man smirked. "My name's Jules."

It seemed to Jules that he heard the voice coming from the grave of the old man's right eye, from which the eye itself was long gone. He felt dizzy, and that groundless idea swam into his mind again.

So...so you aren't my papa?

CHAPTER 4:

SOUCI • THE WORKINGS OF THE TRAP • THE COUNTERATTACK

Julie Printemps had a memory of her birthday.

The memory, from the days when guests still came, was more than a thousand years old.

That birthday had been her last before the Grand Down.

Before the Grand Down, Julie's family kept a pet rabbit named Souci, a young and fearless male. His muzzle, belly, and feet were white, and every other part of him was pitch-black—his ears, his back, his face, his legs. Julie loved his feet, which seemed to be neatly dressed in white socks. She loved his soft, twitchy nose, his mouth. She loved stroking his ears.

Julie often took Souci with her when she went walking in the nearby meadow. She didn't like being at home. She would carry him to the meadow in a large wicker basket, then let him run free. She herself would lie on her back, cover her face with her straw hat, and let time go by. She would breathe in the scent of her straw hat, her blond hair (it was a little darker then, and fell to beneath her shoulder blades). Humidity would steam from the grass around her. Her hands and feet would smart in the sun. The dry wind would slowly stir the entire meadow. After a vigorous run, Souci would eventually return to Julie and sniff around her. Face still covered by her straw hat, Julie would take a biscuit from her skirt pocket, crumble it in her fist, then open her palm under Souci's nose. Delighted, the rabbit would begin to eat. It ate methodically, licking up each biscuit crumb one by one. Julie loved to feel its mouth and tongue moving over the palm of her hand from inside her straw hat. She loved concentrating her bodily senses there. She loved spending long hours in the meadow with Souci in this way. Her other hand would undo her top blouse button. The smell of her own hair. The humidity from the grass. The dry wind stirring the meadow.

Souci was designed to be a sexual accessory for Julie. He was the key to unleashing her sexual functionality.

It wasn't easy for guests to have their way with Julie, unlike the other AIs. Normal methods could not be used to establish sexual contact with her. If a guest tried to force the matter, she would immediately set out for the meadow with her basket.

Her dignity. Standoffishness.

She engaged in relations with the other AIs freely, but to guests she was cold, which was of course what made her appealing.

But if a guest understood the import of Souci, they could control Julie with ease. For guests, this was a simple puzzle in which success saw Julie's desire unleashed. A mild amusement.

Only wealthy guests could afford the rights to Julie's birthday.

Every birthday, a guest who had purchased the role of her father would offer her piles of presents. There was a store at the entrance to the Costa del Número heaped high with things that guests could buy and give to the AIs as gifts.

Julie hated her birthday, because it was obviously for the guests' sake rather than her own.

But one birthday had been slightly different.

The moment Julie saw the man who had come as her father, she knew.

He's younger than me!

The Realm of Summer had extremely high ethical barriers. No matter how wealthy the customer, if they were not of age they were not permitted inside. This boy, Julie thought, must be an unbelievably skilled hacker.

The boy wore the form of Julie's father impeccably. He carried himself with both the poise and the hint of impending decline appropriate to a man in his late forties. His conversation, too, was spectacularly ordinary. But Julie clearly saw the lonely boy within, peering out at her from behind the multilayered barriers he had erected. He had armored his loneliness in pride and self-chosen isolation. Julie sensed something similar to herself in that, which meant there must be something unlike her in there too.

And that was what she wanted to see.

If only, she thought, she could open her father's form and peek inside.

What was this hacker like?

She had never taken any interest in a guest before. It was not her function to: by design, she was oriented toward AIs rather than guests.

Her "father," however, unusually for a guest, showed absolutely no enthusiasm for her. No doubt he had grasped the import of Souci at a glance. Julie tested him, sending sign after sign his way, but he did not respond in the slightest. He simply sat at the table watching her as he drank his tea.

What is this boy thinking? Why is he watching me?

Julie wished she could see herself as he did.

When her "father" finished his tea, he announced that he was going to his study to read. This surprised Julie. Her "father" was an unusually expensive role, and hacking was subject to harsh penalties. Someone willing to either pay that price or take that risk would usually make a point of savoring the secret pleasures of this little household.

Julie decided to enter her father's room.

But to do what? He had just finished a cup of tea, after all... Julie felt the excitement rise as she cast about for a pretext. Following some moments of indecision, she picked up a couple of things and took them upstairs.

She knocked at the door. "Dad, can I have a moment?"

"Of course," her father said from within.

Hearing the boy's wholehearted commitment to imitating an older man's tone of voice, Julie felt a smile threaten to rise. Tightening her lips, she opened the door.

A white curtain swam in the breeze behind her father, whose eyes were already on her.

"Come in," he said.

Julie showed her "father" what she had brought with her. Another guest had given them to her as a gift, long ago. Her "father," the boy, gazed at them, finally showing signs of interest.

"Colored pencils and a sketchbook?"

"That's right. Will you draw me, Dad?"

The "father" who had given Julie these art supplies had begged her to draw him. As he removed his clothes. Or, rather, her clothes— that guest had been a woman, a bureaucrat in her late twenties. That perversion had been worth a rueful smile or two.

"All right."

Her "father" laid the book he had been reading on his desk. It was large and bound in leather. A lengthy tale, by the looks of it.

"You're finished with your book?"

"Sure. I've read it before. I was just indulging in some nostalgia. Give those over."

Julie handed the sketchbook and pencils to her father. Large hands, the hands of a man in his prime, but inside him was a little boy. She wished she could reach through the disguise and touch his real hands. She imagined the hands of a nervous little boy. Her father's hands opened the large sketchbook. A picture from last time was inside, on a page she hadn't torn out. Julie blushed. Her father tore out and discarded the page without a word. The cover came off the large box of pencils.

"What about work?"

"A customer canceled their appointment and freed up my afternoon." In the Realm, her father worked at an accountant's office one town over.

"So you're just going to take it easy?"

"I suppose so. I am making dinner tonight. It's your birthday, after all. Mom will probably bake a cake, too."

"Sounds lovely."

Following her "father's" directions, Julie stood by the window. The bright sunlight ringed her silhouette with halation. The tips of her hair became optical fibers and stood out clearly. Her "father" surveyed the scene, took a pencil, and began to sketch the overall shape on the paper.

"What made you want me to draw you?" he asked.

"Good question." Julie's smile floated in the light.

"I could draw your rabbit too, if you want."

Her father had a tendency to slip into a more boyish way of speaking. He also seemed a little nervous around her—she was older than him, after all. These observations filled Julie with glee.

"Never mind him. Just draw me."

"Fair enough."

With conscious effort, Julie looked away from the boy, turning her face to the window. But she still felt his eyes on her. It was a good feeling. Having him draw her picture had been a good idea, she thought. It gave her control over his gaze.

"It's not like you to hole up in your study," she said.

"It's not?"

Her "father" held the sketchbook vertically and began scribbling on it with the pencils. What kind of picture was he drawing over there?

"No. Normally when you're home you won't leave me and Mom alone."

"If I always acted the same, you'd get sick of it soon enough. Sometimes I like to break the mold. And look—it got you to come to my study, didn't it?"

This annoyed Julie. But part of her enjoyed even this annoyance, and her thoughts were thrown into confusion. Had he planned all this?

The sun's rays were so bright. Julie turned to let the light show through her thin linen dress. Today she wore nothing underneath. She was conscious that he could see the lines of her body, but she didn't mean to be provocative. What she intended was a few steps short of that. She just wanted him to look. And keep him there a while.

"I can't wait for dinner tonight," she said, not particularly truthfully. She felt as if there was something else she wanted to say.

"I'd better roll up my sleeves."

That over-earnest grown-up tone. Julie's shoulders shook with suppressed laughter.

"There," said her father. "Done." He flipped the sketchbook around, and Julie saw the picture.

It was in vivid color.

He had drawn her using every single pencil in the box.

There were touches of blue and purple on her skin, pink and mint green in the linen of her dress. Colors had been dropped in mutual repulsion into every shadow, across every bright surface.

These hues melted together and faded away to give the impression that Julie was clad in uniform white light.

Light as chaste as a bridal veil.

Light as pure as a bouquet of lilies.

Julie felt her face grow hot.

His sketching was more accurate than any camera. He had caught the summer breeze in her loose strands of her, the smug, calculating smile she had flashed for a moment. What a wonderful eye this guest had. Julie hugged the picture carefully to her chest.

"This is the best present I've ever gotten," she said. "By far."

"Just wait until dinner, then," said her father. "Thank you. I enjoyed this."

"You know what? I want to kiss you."

"You do, eh? Thank you. I'll look forward to dinnertime, then."

"I want to kiss you, Dad."

He father smiled at her again, then returned to his book. As if nothing had happened. As if he did not want to be disturbed by anyone. Julie was deeply disappointed. And so she stepped lightly out of the library and spent the long afternoon in her own room, gazing at the sketchbook and thinking about nothing. Normally she would call Souci to her bed, but she wasn't in the mood today.

When the sun began to set, she filled the basin with water from the pitcher and washed her face. She brushed her hair. Stripping naked, she looked at herself in the mirror. Then she got dressed again, this time in a navy blue dress with an orange daisy print. She checked her nails and the color of her tongue.

The delicious smell coming from the kitchen surprised her as she descended the staircase.

In the dining room, Julie's mother would not meet her eye. Something was afoot. What could it be? She got the feeling it would not be a pleasant surprise.

The table seated four. Julie's seat was opposite her "father's," and her little brother sat across from their mother.

Julie's father removed a broad stewpot from the oven. Some broth had bubbled out from between pot and lid and been cooked onto the side of the pot, creating the delicious smell that filled the room.

"I'll do the serving."

The lid came off.

The dark brown sauce inside was still boiling as Julie's father stirred it with a ladle, which he then used to scoop out Souci's head.

Julie's brother vomited. Her mother closed her eyes tight, ground her teeth, and lowered her eyes in forbearance.

Julie did not lose her composure.

She remained completely calm.

Part of her was aghast, and another part of her was able to accept this as an entirely ordinary turn of events.

This latter part mystified her, but also seemed completely natural.

Poor Souci had been boiled whole in the broth as it thickened into a sauce. Not as meat for the feast table. As Souci, the rabbit.

Most of his skin had melted off, and his ears were dissolving too. The meat was sloughing off his face.

Stirring the broth with the ladle had brought to the surface great clouds of boiled-off hair as well.

"Was he alive?"

"He was."

In the man's eyes there was not a hint of cruelty. Nor any indication that he was gloating over Julie's response. His loneliness twinkled like a distant star.

"Poor thing."

Julie, too, was like the surface of still water. Not a single ripple. *If this had happened yesterday, I might have cracked. Today is different. The pity I feel for Souci is real, but it isn't enough to break me.*

"Aren't you going to eat?" the man said, submerging the ladle again.

"Poor thing…" Even Julie wasn't sure who the words were for.

Rising to her feet, Julie plunged both hands into the boiling sauce.

She scooped up the head of her beloved Souci and hugged it to her chest. The sauce was thick and much hotter than boiling water. It poured from Souci's empty eye sockets onto Julie's chest, her abdomen.

It was painful.

It was hot.

"Is it hot?" the man asked.

Julie nodded.

Tears welled in Julie's eyes from the pain.

Sharpening all her nerves, Julie searched the stew for the last remaining sensations of Souci.

She loaded into herself the records of the pain and fear that Souci had felt in his last moments. Then she simply endured them. She felt that she had to punish herself. Why was that?

"Poor thing."

This time the man mumbled the words.

It seemed to Julie that something passed between them at that moment, carried on their gaze. It felt as if they had become accomplices in something. With Souci as foundational sacrifice. *Poor Souci.*

I'm sorry… Look how much heat and pain I'm enduring, too. Forgive me.

"I want to kiss you, Dad," Julie said, hugging Souci's melted head to her chest.

Out of the corner of her eye Julie saw her mother turn her face away. Her mother's profile was frozen solid; Julie saw this too.

This was not the usual routine. This had been a special birthday. The first birthday that was actually for Julie.

"I want to kiss you, Dad."

The man held out his hand and supported Souci's head, still hot enough. Sauce overflowed the rabbit's skull onto his hand, scalding it badly.

Julie looked into the eyes of the genius hacker. Why she had recognized him in there she now understood as well.

The two exchanged a kiss over the bubbling stew. The smell of Souci's blood seemed to celebrate their union.

Long ago.

A memory of a long-ago day.

Yvette cast her nearly sightless gaze across the great table.

In the dark blur of her vision, the only thing she could make out clearly was the gleam of the Crystal Chandelier. Every light in the room, she saw, was gathered in it as if drawn in by gravity.

Of all the Eyes that Yve had known, the Chandelier was the most remarkable of all. It was in a class all its own. Could she really control it? The thought made her shiver. She felt herself shrinking at the prospect.

Yve hugged herself as if from affection, as if in encouragement. Her generous breasts, the swell of her hips, her shoulders, her neck, her legs: she ran her palms over them all, following the lines of her body through her clothes.

Unable to see her face or figure in the mirror, Yve knew her body only through touch, and the range of sensations that touch aroused within were a surer foundation for her than anything else.

Whenever she hugged herself, Yve tried increasing and relaxing the tightness of her grip. Through long and repeated experimentation, she had come to know how her body responded to different degrees of strength, worked to closely measure and understand how her senses worked. As a rule, her senses were sufficient unto themselves. A world enfolded within her palms.

But if there was one point at which that world were open, it was the Glass Eyes.

To Yve, Eyes were the only thing that could act as a mirror.

This was because Eyes dealt not only in vision but in all the senses and sensations deriving from phenomena and perception.

Yve was one of only a handful of AIs who, when they sat face-to-face with an Eye, observed correctly that it reflected every one of their own senses.

When Yve moved her hand into an Eye's field of effect, her finger was met by another coming the other way—her finger's reflection in the Eye. Behind that reflected finger lay a reflection of her entire body, with identical sensory distribution. She could sense this reflected image of herself, and even though it would eventually begin to change according to the Eye's function, she was so thoroughly familiar with the sensations within her own body and their basic values that she could, with perfect accuracy, ascertain the changes wrought by the Eye on the reflected image. Could understand how the Eye worked, in other words.

Yve was unusually sensitive to nonvisual stimuli. Her senses had been formed with external factors excluded, using Yve herself as the measure; they were personal, even aloof, but precise and unwavering.

This was not a result of her blindness so much as it was a God-given gift. If the heavens smiled on AIs too, that is.

It was only natural that her facility with the Eyes would be unequaled in the Realm of Summer. Only Yve could read an Eye's nature in an instant, like a master jeweler assessing a gem. Only Yve could bend an Eye to her will. And so she loved them, without reservation.

But right now she was stiff with nerves.

Can I do this? she asked herself, over and over. *Can I do it? Can I pull it off just as the boy planned?*

The Chandelier was surrounded by something transparent that flickered like a flame. The Eye's effects were extending outside of the glass substance. Yve ran her hands over her body the way she always did to calm her feelings. Her first task was to "start up" the Chandelier. The program that would run the trap network was written in the pattern of the lace spread beneath it. Unlike a program written in characters, it would not be read linearly. It was a mesh programming language that spread across the plane.

How would she make the Glass Eye read it? This was what she had been entrusted with.

"Everyone?" Yve said in her usual quiet, hesitant voice.

Only the three sisters and Julie were seated at the large table with her. All the men who could use a Glass Eye were deployed to the front.

Yve placed her fingers lightly on the lace's filigreed edge, as if it were the keyboard of a delicate instrument.

"It's all right," said Julie. "We've got you." The three sisters nodded, and Yve knew it so surely it was almost as if she could see it. Under the powerful "light" of the Chandelier, she could even sense the dimple on each sister's left cheek.

"Hold tight," Yve said.

She raised the sensitivity of her fingertips and probed at the Chandelier's field of effect. In the next instant, she was pulled in by a power unlike any she had experienced before, losing her orientation momentarily before coming around to find herself—

Floating in a vast empty space.

Although…how vast was it, really?

For that matter, was it even space?

There was no up or down.

There was no forward or back, left or right.

There was no one else there.

An unrealized space.

A mass of accumulated sensation overwhelmed her. She felt its motion.

It looked like a flame.

Yes—through the Glass Eyes, Yve could see.

Yve was aware of herself perceiving what was happening in the space as flame-like motion. Even had she not been blind, what she saw here would have been no different. This was not a response from her individual sensory organs. It worked on the roots of perception, of sensation directly.

The blaze within the Chandelier. This, Yve correctly perceived, was the sensory reactor. The sensations surrounding and drawn into the Eye were the flickering of the flames, pure and beautiful.

Fire of awesome ferocity streamed past her, brushing her shoulder. A loosely bound flow of fearless, rippling heat.

The flame was a complex of sound, color, substance, sensation, and more—she sensed this from its radiance. These were what you might call the language of the Eye. But it was fragmentary, with no overarching context. Vast quantities of light and sensation, wasted on nothing Yve could see. Words and syllables simply broken and scattered, like a spilled bag of alphabet pasta dropped on the floor. She could barely stand at all in this state, much less adopt a fixed position.

What Yve was experiencing was, in fact, no different from what could be found in even the smallest Eyes. But the Chandelier was on an entirely different scale. The sheer vastness was a challenge all its own.

All right, then, Yve said. With surprising calmness, she began to adopt a concrete form. Most AIs would have found it impossible to identify their own sensations among the activity here; reduced to scattered fragments of sensory information, they would be completely transformed. But Yve held her inner self completely in her own hands. All sensation for her was self-aware, and she could conjure up a perfect image of her entire body at any time. Taking on concrete form here was simply a matter of performing the same trick, and so she secured a self-image distinct from the surrounding sensation without difficulty.

Next, she looked up, like someone immersed in water looking up at the surface. Having created a bodily image permitted the supposition that "up" was above her head. Naturally, she made sure to match this to the direction from which she had come. Seeing the faces of the three sisters behind the fluttering light, she dropped anchor immediately. The concept of "up" grew firmer.

Yve took a deep breath and looked around at the scene inside the Chandelier again.

It was all right. She understood. She could read this.

Her heart pounded with the excitement of a prophet surveying a vast undifferentiated wasteland and seeing in one glance the image of a city and the plans for constructing it. This plan was written into Jules's program already, woven into the pattern of the lace.

Yve sent a signal "up," through the anchor. Immediately, she was pulled in the same direction. She left the Chandelier and lost her field of vision.

She found herself sitting at the table.

Her fingers seemed to have been lightly moving.

Looking at the others with her pupilless eyes, Yve said, "It's all right. We can start it up right away."

The women nodded.

"It was thrilling in there," Yve added.

It was rare for her to reveal her feelings like that.

"I want to go back in right away."

The possibility of exercising her talents to the fullest had filled her with excitement.

"Hold on tight. I'll go cut the coordinates," Yve said. Once everyone had nodded, she dove into the Chandelier again.

This time, she was gripping Jules's lace.

Yve was capable of re-creating the image of herself perfectly inside an Eye. To maintain a self within an Eye was to control it. If you could hold your own position firm, everything else in the Eye could be manipulated. All Glass Eye use was based on this.

Yve descended to her previous position. She had maintained the form and image of the lace perfectly, down to the last knot. "After all, I knitted it," she murmured to herself. She planted her feet firmly on the ground and, as if hanging out a freshly washed sheet or waving a battle flag with no flagpole, shook out the lace.

A wind rose up.

Within the sensory reactor, where once there had been no up or down, front or back, left or right—which had not even been a space—a place was born that could clearly be distinguished from the others. The source of the wind.

The side of Yve where her face was became her front, and the side where her back was became her back. Up was in the direction of her head and her feet were down. Left and right were fixed; the origin of the coordinate system was established.

Which put Yve at the center of the universe.

With one point established and cool winds continuing to blow from it, the flames learned where they were. Self-awareness about the coordinates spread to fill the Chandelier, converting from a confined dissipation to a space that could be measured by rule—a place of possibility.

The moment was at hand.

Yve saw it all. Saw the flames began to circle the origin with the obedient air of a pack of wild beasts hiding their fangs. She knew, too, that she enjoyed powerful backing from invisible forces. Julie and the three sisters were palpably at her back lending their support.

(*Now*)

Yve threw the lace like a fisherman casting a net.

The materiality of the threads, already affected by the Chandelier's transformative powers, thinned further, exposing the logic at the knots. Carried by the inertia of Yve's throw, the logic separated from the rest and spread to cover the entire expanse, as far as she could see. At every node of the settled lace she saw subsystems booting up. The program that had been stored in the knots expanded itself. The Trap-Net should come online automatically.

A cynical vision came to Yve. "I feel like a spider sitting at the center of its web," she said.

"Black widows setting a trap for the Spiders. I like it," came Donna's voice in her ear with a merry laugh.

"That makes us widows," said Anna. "Except…"

The sisters began to substantiate inside the Chandelier.

"We hadn't even gotten married yet," grumbled Luna. Julie giggled. With the location Yve had carved out as a foothold, they were finally able to secure positions to occupy within the Chandelier.

"But this position is more important than any other," said Yve to Julie's hair, which was fluttering in the wind as it became visible, and within which she had also glimpsed a delicate little ear.

"I know." A pair of lips came into being at the source of Julie's voice. "This is the control center, isn't it? The wheelhouse."

Three sets of reading glasses glinted beyond the horizon in three different directions.

"If only we were widows!"

"All this peering into well-simmered Eyes…"

"Fussing with pretend magic spells…"

"We're just like…"

As the three sisters conversed, their bodies finished appearing, like plump and satisfied cats. They were far away in dreamland, but the distance also felt as close as if they were just across the table.

Each one of them had to be beyond the horizon. If Yve and Julie were at the center of the tiny universe of the Chandelier, the triplets had to be as far from them as possible.

This was to ensure the safety of Jules's program, the TrapNet. The three sisters had the habit of responding to newly input information in exactly the same way. Each of them would monitor the TrapNet constantly, and they would verify one another's work as well.

"Just like…?" said Julie.

"The witches in *Macbeth*. Don't you think?"

Yve smiled. *Did you know? In here, I can see you properly. Perhaps this is where I truly belong.*

The five "widows" looked around the interior of the vast sensory reactor. The glittering blaze of lights was more docile now, but it seemed to Yve that its potential had become twenty, even thirty times greater. And its true power would be several times greater than that, she thought, with something like a shiver.

"Looks like rain."

On the northern horizon was sensory motion like thunderclouds filmed in slow motion.

"The main entrance," said Julie.

"The battle hasn't started yet," said Yve, softening her voice to reassure herself too. "The net's connecting right now."

The same motion appeared in the sky to the east, west, and south. The trap network had close to ten thousand Eyes connected to it, if you included even the tiniest beads, and the sensations they took in were now all flowing into the Chandelier at once.

Taken as a whole, Yve thought, this net might even leave Drift-glass in the dust.

Straightening up proudly like an engineer about to test a newly constructed dam for the first time, Yve focused her consciousness strongly on the clouds to the west.

Her body... A sensation of movement, of flying in that direction enfolded her.

The smell of the woods.

A summer night.

Gaslight carved the manicured yard from the night. The lawn was a vivid, almost wet-looking green. The white tables with their parasols and chairs stood unoccupied. Beyond the yard, but still on the hotel grounds, stood a small forest.

Yve was now in the west yard, having just arrived there through the security cameras installed above the doors opening onto it.

She knew that she was actually inside the Chandelier, enfolded in the sensations sent to it, but the overwhelmingly realistic sense of being there, live, was enough to make her hesitate.

She could not help but feel that she really was in the west yard.

No, it was more than that.

As she substantiated there, she felt herself become something like the night air, spreading to fill the place entirely, pervading it.

Georges Crespin and nine other hunters cradling game rifles stood guard. They had dragged the white chairs directly against the wall of the hotel before sitting down in them. Their dogs lay at their feet, noses toward the forest.

No one noticed that Yve was there.

—The smell of the forest.

The rich, green aroma of night spilled unceasingly from the grass and woods.

Yve enjoyed the smell. Even as it seemed to her that she *was* the smell.

Without taking his eyes from the trees, Georges took a swig from his hip flask. He clenched his teeth, squeezing droplets of brandy between his molars. The bouquet that sprang out, the elasticity in his gums: these were Georges's. His keen eyes saw the jostle of the Spiders clearly in the forest's dark groves. Borrowing his sight, Yve saw it too. The Spiders would surely attack before long. They had no fear of firearms…

That's what we're counting on, of course… Georges's smile was so faint that no one but Yve detected it.

Yve relaxed her focus and returned to the center of the web.

She had never moved from there in the first place. To be more accurate yet, her "real" body was still hunched over the Chandelier at a table in the casino.

Yve let out a long breath. She had focused her attention on just one part of what the net brought in, but the information had been so vivid, so raw...

She tried to recall the sensations of a moment ago. Even she had never experienced anything like them.

Some of the sensations could only have been obtained if she had been within Georges himself. As well as the brandy and his gums, for example, there had been a faint hunger, an anxiety like stickiness in the throat. But had she become one with Georges completely? The answer to that was no.

Somehow, she had been more than one self.

It seemed to her that she had been the rough, ragged texture of the moss in the yard, the sigh of the forest, the dull gleam of the cartridges, the firing of the brandy.

How could she put this peculiar feeling into words?

Then she had a sudden realization.

That's exactly how the world would seem to me if I were an Eye.

Her heart raced painfully.

Could I even be *an Eye in here?*

She tried changing the direction of her focus.

The smell of the sea.

The quiet foaming of the waves.

Yve stood on the terrace facing the docks.

A cluster of bonfires had been lit and Anne's men had gathered, well over a dozen men in all. Someone (who knew who?) had brought out a barbecue grill, and the charcoal inside it burned bright red. Nobody noticed Yve standing there, of course. A thick, tattooed arm brushed past her. It was Anne, grabbing a long metal skewer. From the sheath at her waist she produced her well-sharpened knife. She cut off a great hunk of meat and wolfed it down, juices trickling from the corners of her mouth. She then cut herself another piece and passed the skewer to José.

"José?" she asked.

"Yeah?"

The two of them were leaning on the terrace railing. Anne looked at José's sharp profile as he faced the night sea.

"Those Spiders…"

"Yeah?"

"Where'd they come from, you think?"

José was silent for a moment. "You care?" he asked at last.

Anne closed her eyes and, as if trying to smell his voice, raised her nose slightly. She loved his voice when he spoke slowly. That was when his thoughts were racing fastest.

"You don't?" she replied.

"I haven't gotten there yet. I'm hung up on a few more immediate things."

"Hmm?" Anne opened her eyes as if to say, *I knew it.*

"You think the Spiders were single-function tools?"

"Seemed like it."

"Then who's using them?"

"Does what they eat get sent to another Realm? What'd they carry off, and why? What could be so valuable in this run-down backwater?"

His tone was leisurely as always. His eyes stayed on the ocean.

"Hmm?"

"You know what else? We're not as strong as we think we are. We're brawlers, you and I, but the world we live in is just a game. No offense to Bastin and Jules, but I don't think we stand a chance."

By now, José had stripped the long skewer bare and stabbed it back into the grill so that it stood vertically. He chewed the last of the meat as he talked.

"We don't stand a chance. But someone's trying to trick us into thinking we do.

"They want us to raise a fortress. But why?"

Anne grunted and shook her thick-necked head, obviously impressed. "You're something else," she said. "Your appetite, I mean."

Retreat. Reacceleration.

The smell of antiseptics and still-fresh blood.

Fourth floor, Mineral Springs Hotel.

A corridor lined with guest rooms.

Hopping along the string of Eyes in the ceiling lights, Yve closed in on Stella, who was pushing a wagon below.

Stella, one of the hotel's employees, was on her way to the service elevator. Her wagon was piled high with bloody linen. This floor was where the sick and injured had been placed.

Dr. Dumay's a tough one, all right, Stella thought. *Maybe he can stay awake a hundred hours seeing patients, but I can't. Half a day as a nurse and I'm exhausted. I'm best known for breaking plates, and now they have me giving shots. If the patients were conscious, they'd turn pale and run. Oh, but I suppose they couldn't get any paler than they already were.*

Yve picked up this unheroic grumbling clearly, finding it quite entertaining.

"I'm pooped!" said Stella aloud. There was no one else in the corridor. She stopped her wagon, slipped into the bathroom of an unoccupied suite, and sat down on the toilet. She'd been holding it in for some time. Once she was done, she reached into her shirt, produced a small pack of cigarettes from between her breasts, and lit one up.

She sighed, exhaled a puff of smoke as she did. Her whole body ached with fatigue. That and the taste of the cigarette whisked her thoughts away, and for a moment her head emptied completely.

And so she did not notice the bubble that appeared briefly in the water beneath her before winking out of existence again.

Retreat. Reacceleration.

Yve had started to get the hang of the motion.

I'm free.

She could not contain her excitement. No matter where in the clouds of sensation she placed her focus, she found what felt like limitless information and nuance waiting to be taken out.

The green smell of the woods,

the heavy radiant heat of the charcoal,

the clear sheen of the fat oozing from the cut face of the meat,

the hard, smooth skin of the porcelain toilet.

Yve began to worry. Presumably, the sensations that poured into the Chandelier would be unified, forming an identity boundary for the hotel itself. The hotel—the whole thing, right down to the AIs and Eyes inside—would be made into a single animal, fast and ferocious, to strike at the Spiders. This was Jules's vision.

And, at the heart of it all—there I'll be.

Yve was enraptured by the thought.

Acceleration.

The front of the hotel was ablaze with every source of light that had been available. The windows were bright all the way up to the fourth floor. The hotel's front yard was as bright as day.

More than thirty people were present, making them the largest group of defenders. The hotel's two wings enclosed the private beach and yard; this side, with the front yard and forest, was longer, and harder to defend. No doubt that was why Bastin had volunteered here.

The Spiders had already pushed forward right to the edge of the light. Yve could sense them out there in the darkness clearly, a writhing mass of Spiders of every shape and size.

"Come on, then."

Bastin stood under the roof of the porte cochère. Pierre emerged from the lobby to offer him some coffee in a small tin cup.

"Pierre."

"Yes?"

"Does your house receive guests?"

"Yes. My younger sister. The role is empty. So the guests are usually young women."

"I wonder what that's like. We don't have guests at my house. It seems I'm not the type to arouse much interest."

"You should be glad of it. There's nothing good about having guests come to visit."

Pierre scratched his ear, blue eyes clouding over. The chain at his wrist jangled.

The chain, Bastin noticed, was connected to a metal shaft that went through Pierre's wrist. He turned his eyes away.

"Well, I suppose they do beat Spiders."

And then he stopped the jangling.

Everyone fell silent.

In the next moment, a single Spider emerged from the darkness. It looked less like an arthropod than a fishbone laid flat. Its "ribs" were jointed in the middle and reached down to act as legs. A single fork-shaped antenna waved from its head. It was about as big as a cow.

It darted across the front yard with the unnatural lightness of a marionette and then leapt up, trying to cling to the wall of the hotel.

But, the instant before it made contact,

the Spider was engulfed in a ball of fire.

Dazzling gouts of flame roared from the hotel wall, crushed the Spider as if in an infernal fist, then exploded. A heat wave and a shock wave.

In the casino, people screamed as the building shuddered.

Jules started to rise from the sofa, but the old man who shared his name grabbed him by the arm. "Don't lose your nerve," he said.

There was a distant cheer from the front yard. The trap had worked perfectly. Deeply relieved, Jules sank back into the sofa.

But the atmosphere in the casino was agitated. The explosion had them panicking.

"It's all right," he heard Julie saying. "Everyone, the hotel is fine. Don't panic."

Jules chimed in, raising his voice too. "The Father of Flame went off as planned," he said. "That's all. We got one of the Spiders, I think."

"Exactly!" said Julie. "I saw it happen. No." Then she looked down at the table again and continued her concentration.

The five women were arranged around the table peering into the Chandelier.

Their faces shone in its gleaming light.

Julie Printemps dove in. She saw Yve's back and her broad, gently sloping shoulders right away, which let her determine her own position.

Just don't think about how weird this all is!

Julie felt as if she might go a little crazy.

—I mean, think about it. We live in a world that is itself a virtual resort space—the Costa del Número is a virtual resort space. We've whipped up a second level of virtual world inside that, and it's swallowed me up.

Julie looked "up." It seemed to her that she could see herself peering into the table, far above. So that was her "real" virtual body?

Julie returned her gaze to her surroundings.

Inside the Chandelier, order was cohering apace. The program Jules had written into the lace had finished its expansion, and data sent in by external Eyes was being processed smoothly. This data was stored as holographic memory, and would presumably be the basis for the necessary bodily sensations once the trap network had attained its own unity.

There didn't seem to be any more need for the "widows" to exert conscious control there. The TrapNet would continue organizing its insides like a living thing, taking full advantage of the unique resonances and interpermeability of the Eyes. Its basic character was defined by the lace. There would be no major departures from this.

More important now was establishing the network's offensive capabilities. The Father of Flame had fired successfully, but the fact remained that they had joined the fray without any drilling. They had to keep damage to a minimum while they taught the net how to fight. Julie's throat was dry with nervousness at the prospect.

Julie gathered the etherized essence of the Father of Flame standing by around her into her hands. The coke burning in a blacksmith's forge. She stretched it apart with both hands as if pulling taffy. The fire became a thin string, then a whip. She placed this in the "flow," the distribution route that was still being generated within the net. Following the forks in the flow, the string of fire was carried to every corner of the net with shocking speed, becoming like a many-headed serpent. Then she summoned up the next fire.

Beside her, Yve was gathering a small house in the palm of her hand. Snowscape. And at her feet, a pair of cats patiently waited their turn.

Leaving that self to continue the battle, Julie moved the rest of her concentration to the front of the hotel, where the fighting had grown fiercer, and focused there.

Julie stood beside Bastin under the porte cochère. He, of course, could not see her.

A Spider was rolling around in a ball of fire. It was the one from before. There was no smell of burning meat. Just the bouquet of the flames.

Pierre chuckled. "Looks like the Spider didn't see its own web before it jumped," he said.

Because the hotel was, in fact, swathed in a veil of woven Spider-web. Thin strands had been separated out and run along the walls, hidden as best as possible under the ivy that was already there. It was a nervous system covering the hotel's epidermis, an immune system against foreign bodies, and the cutting edge from which they would launch their attacks.

When any part of it received a stimulus, the nearest low-level Eye would send for the Father of Flame's power through the net. The energy brought by the Spider-web would be released at the place where the stimulus had been received, and the Spider would be burned to a crisp, just as the first attack had shown.

This network could transmit virtually everything the Eyes made available. Superheated explosions of flame, freezing blasts from Snowscape—even the Black Grid...

Bastin narrowed his eyes. Pierre was rigid with nerves. Julie felt this with the utmost clarity.

Still engulfed in flames, the Spider retreated to a grove of trees. The flames illuminated the outline of its brethren squirming in the darkness, one by one.

Then that wall suddenly collapsed.

The mass of Spiders became a black tide sweeping toward the hotel's façade.

But they were unable even to touch it.

The light bulbs in the entryway porte cochère and those evenly spaced around the yard had all been replaced with Eyes. These now glowed white-hot as the Father of Flame's fiery energy poured forth. This attack was far hotter than the first had been. The hail of flame smothered the Spiders coming up the path, burning them alive.

For the Spiders coming across the lawn, a different attack had been prepared.

The web extending through the grass activated.

Thousands of glittering silver needles, so large and sharp that they were really small daggers, fired directly upward out of the lawn, running the swarm of Spiders through from below. The Spiders were torn to shreds in an instant. The needles maintained their trajectory, rising higher than the hotel's roof before turning and falling back down, pinning the Spiders' skeletons to the lawn.

Catsilver was a special kind of Eye. It contained a pair of fantastical beasts: cats with dazzling silver fur, eyes green as celadon, and tongues redder than blood. Closely examined, their fur was a coat of sharp, stiff spines like a hedgehog's, and when they were enraged these spines bristled and flew through the air, propelled by powerfully twitching muscles.

The trap network exaggerated their abilities to the point of parody, turning their spines into daggers of considerable destructive power. These were what had been hidden in the lawn.

Now, those spines were augmented with the power of Snowscape.

"Look at that!" Pierre said, pointing. Fierce cold streamed from the daggers as the AIs watched, freezing the skeletons that were pinned to the ground.

"Jules was right," said Bastin hoarsely. "Snowscape's externalizing its cold through Catsilver's spines. Eyes can exert their power even on things that aren't corrected to the net directly. This is incredible."

The scene evolved further. The daggers' channel was changed, and they released an invisible shock wave of searing heat from the Father of Flame. Unable to withstand the rapid change of temperature, the remains of the Spiders crumbled to dust to be blown away. The shock wave was so tightly targeted that the lawn itself wasn't even charred.

A cheer went up.

The men at the entrance scrambled onto the lawn to seize the daggers standing in it, now returned to normal temperatures. They hurled them at the Spiders, now in disarray, as they charged. Each dagger exploded like a hand grenade, releasing shock waves of heat and cold that destroyed their massed enemy. The front line of Spiders fell back, broke formation, and was torn to shreds.

Everything's going unbelievably well. Let's hope this lasts…

Julie was now watching the battle in the front yard. But that was not all she was taking in. Even as her focus remained at the front of the hotel, she was receiving sensory data from elsewhere, too.

For example,

The amber scent of the brandy squeezed between his molars.

Warming a drop in his mouth to heighten the aroma, Georges Crespin signaled to the other nine hunters and their dogs by cocking his head just a fraction. The Spiders were coming. Everyone quieted their presence and raised their guns. Georges's rifle was larger than the others; he had made it himself, and he held it fixed before his chest now. He stayed down on one knee, silent and utterly motionless.

The green scent of the grass and moss crushed beneath his knee. The bluish steel aroma of his polished rifle barrel. The smell of his old amulet and the new leather thong it hung on. And the warm, lingering fragrance of breast milk that had come from Marie's chest as she put the amulet around his neck. She had made it for him herself. She was gone now, and so was Hector. The sweet perfume of the candle on their dinner table the night before came back to Georges for just an instant.

Deep in the darkness of the forest there was movement that caught only Georges's eye. Twenty or thirty Spiders had gathered to entwine themselves with each other, removing and recombining body parts to remake themselves into a single gigantic monster.

Two eyestalks sprouted like periscopes from its newly constructed torso. Each stalk had two eyeballs, and the four eyes stared at Georges—yes, at Georges; of that there could be no mistake—from the depths of the forest.

Unflinching, Georges retained his composure. But Julie, who was taking in this scene from inside him, trembled at the Spider's expressionless eyes.

Georges's finger curled around the trigger of his rifle. Lurking in his finger, Julie felt the weight of the trigger vividly.

In the darkness, the giant Spider moved. The chaotic, buzzing jumble of Spiders converged into a single presence that swelled and rose to its feet. It was so enormous that the very forest itself seemed to have stood on a hundred legs. It was at least half as large as the hotel.

The nine hunters fell into a temporary state of shutdown. They were powerless, their minds totally blank.

But Georges kept his aim steady, not the slightest twitch in his posture or his expression. Only his sharp eyes moved, searching for the right spot to shoot. Julie, deep within his eyes, followed that deft, unwasteful "appraisal."

The Spider kicked the trees of the forest out of its way. The trees went flying like matchsticks, taking out two of the hunters as they tumbled haphazardly to earth. The Spider fired its sharp, pulsive *hunger* like a machine gun. A line of manhole-sized holes in the ground stretched toward them, and two more hunters perished in the line of fire.

The Spider's body shook with sneering laughter. Inaudible low-frequency waves resonated in the hunters' chest cavities until they were ruined inside. Blood spilled from their mouths and guns fired wildly. The iron smell of coughed-up blood mixed with a gunpowder tang.

Georges's eardrums ruptured instantly. His lungs filled with red fluid. But still he did not move a muscle. His entire sensory awareness was concentrated in his eyes. Motionless, he waited until the last possible moment. Finally his eyes gave his body the order: *Shoot.*

Twice in succession Georges squeezed the trigger. The hot fragrance of gunpowder. The kick smashed his lungs once and for all, but his face remained motionless. His last drop of life was sent to his eyes, to chase the shots he had fired. But that was where it ended. Georges closed his eyes. He slowly fell onto his back, his last breath forced out between his lips.

That amber scent.

Or, for example,

Taste.

The taste of meat.

Biting through the crisp, fragrant outer layer to the red inside, chewy and dense. The taste of fat and meat juice spread as the meat was chewed, followed by a gamey scent. Muscle fiber broken down by tooth and tongue and the inside of the cheek.

The taste of meat roasted on a metal skewer.

But José stopped at one bite. Leaving the rest of the meat untouched, he stabbed the whole skewer into the charcoal, letting it stand upright.

Julie clung to José, feeling like a sheer veil. The refreshing coolness of the sea breeze and the heat radiating thickly from the charcoal were pleasant.

Hey, José... Julie spoke into the ear adorned with a fish-shaped earring. She concealed herself in the whisper of the sea breeze so that he wouldn't hear. *Do you mind me being here? Is it okay if I see what it's like inside you?*

The young fishermen wrapped a strand of web about the terrace railing. The strand was punctuated along its length by dozens of Eyes like tiny light bulbs. It looked like a cheap line of fairy lights at a garden party. But José's eyes were turned to the blue-black surface of the sea beyond.

The gentle waves twinkled with reflected light.

"I don't like this sea."

"Oh, yeah?" said one of the young fishermen casually. "How come?"

"What have you been looking at, dumbass?" Anne bellowed at the fisherman.

José scooped a drink out of the nearest punch bowl, using the mixture of wine and orange juice to wash down the meat. He felt as if the cool juice were filling his cells with new energy.

"I can tell," said José. "This sea is a lie."

Anne nodded. "A poster, if I'm not mistaken."

José nodded and gripped the long metal skewer he had stripped bare earlier. Standing at the edge of the terrace, he brandished the scorched skewer like a harpoon and glared at the face of the waters.

And with that, the entire ocean shuddered, as far as he could see, and all the waves and reflections froze.

With unbelievable quickness, the picture of the sea was rolled up toward them, gathering itself into a bundle just below the terrace and then bouncing above their heads like a tennis ball. It bloomed with spines that sprang out like a sea urchin's.

This, of course, was a diversion.

José was not looking at any sea urchin.

José was looking at a single tiny Spider that had been hiding on the surface of the sea but had now become flat as paper and was attempting to crawl under the terrace. José stabbed it through with the metal skewer and pulled that up to plunge the Spider right into the charcoal. Its flesh contracted with a constricted squeal and a foul smell filled the air.

"Want a bite?" José said.

"Give me a break." Anne, who had been batting down the sea urchin, wrinkled her nose in disgust. She had imagined the flavor before she could stop herself. "Blech."

Julie tasted that imaginary flavor too.

Blech.

That was disgusting.

Julie was gradually getting used to her situation and beginning to enjoy herself. She and the other "widows" had become one with the Mineral Springs Hotel and the trap network.

Could a person listen to a hundred songs at the same time and savor them all? Down to the subtlest nuance? What about the same song played by a hundred different musicians at the same time— would it be possible to tell how they differed?

This was something like that, but even more amazing… Like listening to a hundred songs, reading a hundred books, and at the same time tasting a hundred plates of food—along with one Spider (blech).

Julie knew that her self had unambiguously become the drop of brandy savored by Georges, the twinkling at the tips of Catsilver's daggers, the jangling of Pierre's chains. She had become every detail available to the trap network, and also become the whole.

Smoke that aggravated her throat.

A half-smoked cigarette fell to the floor of the bathroom. A thin tendril of smoke rose from it.

Stella was sitting on the toilet with her skirt pulled up higher than necessary. The front of her apron was also pulled to one side, baring her large, freckled breasts. These she caressed with the fingers and palm of one hand, while her other hand was under her skirt engrossed in different work.

Stella was lost in her masturbation. She groped with her fingers for the heat she felt inside her body, fanning it, calming it and postponing it, keeping it under masterful control. She would eventually draw it together and raise it to a peak, but that, she thought, could wait a little longer. Her cigarette was now mostly ash, marking the time she had devoted to her pleasure.

What's happened to me?

The warning came stubbornly from one corner of her mind. There was something strange about tonight. She wasn't usually this way. Why had she felt such a strong urge to do this? Another mystery: why did it feel so good? It was better than it ever had been before. She could hardly believe it was her own body…

This isn't fair to the others. I have to stop. I'm almost done—it'll just be a moment.

Inside Stella, the surprising sensory power overwhelmed Julie, too, but she was also aware of something else: the fact that there was something in the toilet blowing bubbles.

The amber scent had faded.

Georges's body was swallowed up by a large round of *hunger*. His last flickers of living sensation plunged into a terrible blank. (Julie recalled the Singing Sands with a shiver.)

When it had killed the last of the hunters, the giant Spider rattled its shell with satisfaction.

The holes from the two bullets from Georges's gun that had entered its chest were its sole wound. Insignificant.

Or was it?

Julie was inside the Spider—or, more accurately, inside the bullets.

The small grains of Eye that had been packed into Georges's ammunition let her see into the Spider's interior.

It was a stark, bare space, like a room stripped of all furnishings. Water, outlets and light, circuit breaker, heat sink, soundproofing— the standard unit programs supporting the Realm at its root were exposed. The two bullets had entered an area where the parts were packed in tightly.

And now they were sprouting with incredible speed.

Their outer layers of lead torn away by the impact, they were revealed as two Eyes like black pearls. Grids had begun to grow from their surfaces. As its name suggested, the Black Grid drew expanding geometrical patterns in the air. The black of its lines had a deep, uniform gloss, and it grew as smoothly as the flowing of well-ground ink.

The grid was made up entirely of straight lines and right angles, but it was not regular. Its symmetry was skillfully disturbed in a lively rhythm similar to the branching of a tree.

The two seeds extended their grids as if in competition, eating away at the Spider's thorax like inorganic tuberculosis. The inside of the Spider was stuffed with program parts, but the grids ate into those too. Where the parts already took up the space the grids wanted to expand into, the grids simply went through them without even slowing down.

What the grids were made of was unclear. The truth was that the Black Grid was so dangerous that it had been kept securely locked away for a long time. It was very rarely permitted to externalize its powers, so their details were known to nobody. This time, too, the risk had been too great to run tests in advance.

Perhaps the grid was not made of any specific material—perhaps it was a purely logical presence. That would make it unique in the Realm, but would not be so strange. Because what lurked inside the grid was a kind of virus, unable to infect anyone or anything but guaranteed to destroy whatever fell within its limited range.

The grid kept growing. As it did, its lines began to expand into surfaces.

Julie continued to observe the scene outside the Spider as well.

What interested the Spider was the hotel, and it had begun using its multiple eyestalks to examine the web stretched across the face of the building. It was searching for a weak spot.

But the giant Spider's interior was very nearly full of the grid now. Its moments were numbered. The grid overflowed the Spider's bounds, extending outward and making its host appear to be captured within a cage of thread.

Then the countdown reached zero.

Without a sound, the Spider disintegrated into a powder.

The lines and faces had sliced every part of it from every other part. The Spider became a fragment of some unintelligible white language and piled up in the west yard.

José took another drink of orange juice to wash his mouth out. The flavor was exquisite. Juice had never tasted this good to him before, he reflected. The aroma that spread across his tongue and into his throat was so fresh that it seemed to shine. Every mouthful he swallowed seemed to send flavor and fragrance through his capillaries to reach every cell in his body.

José found this mysterious.

Why was it so delicious?

It's like my sense of smell and taste have gotten a hundred times better.

And then something else suddenly occurred to him.

What if it's the opposite?

Maybe, instead of my sense of taste getting sharper,

the world around me has gotten a hundred times more vivid?

The perspiration dampening her body gave off a heady smell.

She was leaning forward, her breasts hanging heavy from her frame. Julie felt the weight.

Julie was as suspicious as Stella. Why was this so pleasurable?

Why was it so good?

Just as Julie was about to be swallowed up by the internal sensations that Stella stoked,

the water in the toilet boiled.

Legs emerged from the toilet. They were covered in sharp, needlelike fur striped yellow and black. There were two of them, then three, and they curled around Stella's lower half before pulling sharply downward. Julie felt the sudden jerk and knew that Stella's lower spine had been fractured.

The legs multiplied. Claws dug deep into Stella's chest. A proboscis was thrust from the base of the toilet and inserted between her legs. A newly extended leg wrapped itself around her arm—currently reaching for the door—and twisted it off her body. Her shoulder made a sharp sound as it separated.

Perfect.

This Spider had been lurking in the hotel somewhere until Stella had aroused its attention and appetite, bringing it to the bathroom where she sat defenseless.

And that was what they had been waiting for.

Perfect.

Julie separated from Stella and viewed the foolish Spider from the outside.

Stella's face disappeared.

Her maid uniform turned white and was sucked into her body.

All patterns and colors vanished from her surface mapping. Stella became a plain white mannequin. Then the mannequin began to warp and lose its shape. It became a paste, soft and amorphous and extremely sticky. The more the Spider struggled, the more trapped it became. The paste that had once been Stella extended pseudopods that stuck to the walls and floor of the bathroom, standing firm against the Spider's escape. It had captured its attacker completely.

Stella was a decoy. There was no such AI. Her true form was the Glue, an Eye containing an amorphous, amoeba-like image. Her human shape, facial features, and clothing had all been added afterward.

Perfect. Julie departed the scene.

"No two ways about it," said Luna. "A decoy has to smell good too."

"Wasn't it Pierre who had the idea of mixing the image of the woman from Femme Fatale into 'Stella'?" said Donna.

"Yes, it was," Yve said. "We couldn't make Stella quite that wild and bewitching, but she certainly looked lifelike."

"But this also means that the Spiders are in the hotel after all," Anna said, concern in her face.

"It'll be fine. We know exactly where they are."

Three Spiders had infiltrated the hotel so far, and all three had been captured by a Stella. Yve and the others had been experimenting with how far they could let down their guard before the Spiders got in, and also testing the performance of the Glue. The Spiders' activity patterns during infiltration had been cracked and shared throughout the net.

"There aren't any more inside the hotel, and we have ten more Stellas in place anyway."

"If only we could have left the guests to dolls like that, too," Julie said.

The triplets laughed.

Yve furrowed her brow. Her pupilless eyes gazed into the distance. Movement, focus.

The men in the hotel's front yard hotel pulled Catsilver's daggers from the lawn and rushed the trees, crushing the remains of the Spiders underfoot like morning frost.

The man at the front of the group whirled his arm around and let his dagger fly. It fell among the Spiders in the trees. There was a deafening sound as fierce flames rose into the sky. The Spiders caught in the blast didn't stand a chance.

The men roared, giddy with the heat of the moment. The sight of Spiders rolling around engulfed in flames filled them with joy. Yve shared in their heart-pounding excitement, finding it intoxicating.

Another man saw a Spider near death. He dropped to one knee, lifted the dagger high, and then plunged its blade down into the

Spider's eye-studded head. Seeing that it had survived the blow, the man—Pascal was his name—released the icy cold within the dagger, letting it saturate the body of his adversary. Pascal was familiar with the use of the Eyes. The Spider grew weaker, then died. Pascal's exhilarated joy thrilled Yve too. A few hours earlier, Pascal had seen his elderly mother devoured by a Spider before his eyes. He could not forget the crunching of its teeth. When the frozen Spider before him began to crumble away, he pulled out his dagger and stalked toward the trees in search of his next adversary.

The trees around the edges of the yard thinned out quickly as stray daggers reduced them to ash and ice. Groves that had grown dense and rich for a thousand years were destroyed in the blink of an eye.

Pierre was running with the others, brandishing a blade of his own. The jangling of the chain at his wrist had awakened a powerfully exciting memory within him.

Yve tried a taste of that dubious excitement, finding it to derive from strong feelings of resentment and loathing toward the guests. As Pierre forced his way into the trees, the smell of moss and bark surrounded him in a gentle embrace, but he shoved it aside with the murderous bent of his shoulders.

Pierre was still unable to forget the treatment he had once received from a guest playing his sister, although he could no longer remember what number that guest had borne in the long procession of visitors. That week, the role of his sister had been bought by an old man, perhaps in his seventies. Pierre's sister was nine. As her character was written, she was fond of arithmetic, *Monopoly*, and tending flowers. That week, "she" had donned a full-body black rubber suit—she was not quite four feet tall—stripped Pierre naked, and bound his hands behind his back. Her strength had been incredible. Pierre did not recall the experience in detail, perhaps because it had been so awful, but he did have vague memories of stiletto heels shaped like little penises.

And then there were the bars of metal—chain clasps—run through both of his wrists. The coldness and hardness violating his skin he remained unable to forget.

"I…" Pierre muttered.

I… He tried to address the guests who came from the real world.

I hate you

I'll never forgive you

……

I just wa… …ngs

Sh… sh… sh… …ing… scissors

Come aga… …soup… …sed.

……nt you to… want…… but…… nt. / #$%!

Stop it.

Yve became aware of an irregularity.

Pierre's thoughts had grown harder to trace. He was fading out of the TrapNet's field of vision.

Pierre advanced into the trees, walking toward where the ferns grew thickly enough to form a large wall.

A mini-Spider… size of a fist… run… saw… …ed. The sweet scent of rotting leaves carpeting the damp summer earth and softly receiving Pierre's heels as… …ped his forehead with… and the humid air…… droplets fell…ike a woman's finger… …shing against…

As Yve watched in consternation, the image of Pierre grew indistinct, received now only in fragmentary sensations and isolated shreds of language. Was the net's sensitivity degrading?

Yve worked desperately to recover the trace. She pursued Pierre through alternate routes as well, extending sensory tentacles through the Eyes carried by the men now dispersed throughout the forest.

This brought Pierre sharply into view. It was all right. He still existed. He was moving toward the wall of ferns as if following the lead of another.

Then Pierre parted the ferns with his hands, took a single step beyond them,

and vanished.

Pierre had completely disappeared from the net's field of view.

Yve had locked on to him perfectly. And yet he had vanished by doing nothing more than ducking through an opening in the wall of ferns. The wall was not thick; one step would carry anyone through. You stepped in from this side and emerged from the other. That was all it was supposed to be, but in the space of that one step, Pierre had been swallowed into some other place.

Was her reception faulty?

Or was the situation worse than that?

The old man sitting on the sofa with his arm around Jules's shoulders squeezed that arm tighter. Jules understood what this meant. On the other side of the Chandelier, Yve had gone pale. Something was obviously afoot.

"Well, Jules," the old man whispered in his ear, "I'd say it's finally begun."

CHAPTER 5:

THE FOUR LANGONIS • AN INTELLIGENT CONVERSATION • THE EMPTY CORRIDOR

The AIs had memories like anyone else. Memories of when they were young, before the Realm had begun.

Some of the AIs' memories they cherished like the accumulated trinkets and treasures of their youth. Other memories were cursed.

But had the events in those memories actually occurred?

José pondered this question often. Not in a sustained way, but there was always a part of him mulling it over somewhere inside his head. These thoughts never progressed beyond that, simply repeating quietly in the background. There was no answer. Nor did he seek one.

José still had his own childhood treasure box. It was a square cookie tin, lightened by rust. Stored inside were the things he had collected as a boy.

A dried-up butterfly.

A stamp soaked off an envelope.

A tiny blue glass bottle he had found on the shore.

A woman's small handkerchief that still smelled faintly of camphor.

Memories resided yet within them. All José had to do was open the tin to recall the time when he had acquired each of these things.

Not during the thousand-times-repeated summer. These were events that had happened before.

The memories lingered within him, vivid and clear. His treasures, aids to recalling them, were safely in the cookie tin. He could reach out and touch them at any time.

But within the Costa del Número, those memories had never actually *happened*. They were part of the setting, written and recalled as having happened before the story began. The treasures were props arranged on stage. That was all there was to it.

José had been troubled by this matter from time to time since the repeating summer truly began. Yes: as the summer began, José had already attained his current age, and his treasures were all already in their place.

Memories like the contents in a boy's box of treasures. But were they events that had really been?

And… José's thoughts began to slow here. He became unable to go further.

This was a dark domain into which José's thoughts did not extend.

In there lay memories beyond recall. Memories José could not see. But he knew, by their faint, bittersweet traces, that they were there.

What had they been?

What could have happened?

He could recall only a few segmented impressions—scraps of sensation.

A woman's coat, opened wide.

Warm enfoldment in the naked body within.

A field of dewy grass, carpeted with tiny blue flowers that bloomed like jewels.

The color of the flowers was exactly the same as the color of the sky.

The air was cold and freshly wet.

This memory binds me.

I am held in thrall by the memory of a memory.

The butterfly's blue wings. The steamship on the stamp. The glass bottle with its silvery lid. The embroidery on the handkerchief.

The memories were vague, but their fragments were unusually clear.

Minute droplets of dew on the woman's long, black hair.

Her remarkably long neck, elegant as a waterfowl's.

The sleeves of her white summer coat, vividly daubed with blood.

Colorful summer flowers picked and gathered and spread in the shape of a bed in one corner of the grassy field. The woman standing beside it. Her cold, silvery laugh.

The events themselves he could not recall.

But he did recall one thing: a name.

Martin.

My younger brother.

A memory that had never actually occurred, from before the curtain rose on "this summer."

Pierre was rooted to the spot with shock.

Who could possibly have imagined that beyond the parted ferns lay a luxurious *boudoir* with a gigantic, canopied bed?

The very love nest.

Of course, Pierre did not know that term.

But he could not help but be overwhelmed by the room's many luxurious appointments, the luxury of the curtains that hung in layer upon layer about the bed and the lavish sense of depth that those many layers created, the exquisite timber from which the bed's four posts were made and the stunning carvings executed upon them.

Tone and material were in perfect harmony, seeming to breathe quietly in the carefully dimmed light. The beauty and extravagance here was of an entirely different order than that seen in the Mineral Springs Hotel's executive suites or casino. The hotel was a compendium of the tastes of the wealthy bourgeoisie, offering to the undifferentiated public a common divisor of comfort. This room, however, had been made precisely to the specifications of one person in particular. No effort had been spared to align it with their tastes, and the result did not even bear comparison with the rooms of a wealthy bourgeois. In a word, it was *noble*.

Pierre felt a strong shock, as if electrified. And then, it seems fair to say, he cowered. Not from the grandeur of the room, but from the thought of who might own it. Their overwhelming individuality smoldered here and there throughout the space, like incense that bewitched him with its scent even as its smoke choked and suffocated him. How clearly he could imagine the master of this room! Beautiful they surely were, cruel and fierce. So superbly terrifying a personage that their thoughts would be unimaginable to the likes of Pierre. Before them, he was a handful of dust. Pierre's breast burned hot with emotion as he thought on the matter. He felt deeply moved by some unnamable emotion.

"Hey there."

The voice came from beyond the deep drapes.

The fabric parted soundlessly, revealing the voice's owner. Pierre realized that he was moving in that direction. And looking up.

A beautiful man lay on the bed, entirely naked, looking down at him.

"Hello, Pierre."

The voice had a luster like the finest tanned leather.

"Uh…"

Pierre finally understood why he had cringed before the man, even before seeing him. His bed was twice the size of a normal one. The height of the ceiling, the mirror, and the chair were all to the same scale.

The man was well over three meters tall.

His formidable physique was beautiful to an exceptional degree. He lounged on the feather pillows piled up on the bed with the elegance of a swan extending its neck. Every inch of his body was as proportionate and controlled as ancient statuary. His lithe arms and legs were clad in muscles of ideal form that rippled with quiet power. His chest and stomach seemed to have been carved from a boulder, then lightly covered in a layer of fat and pure white skin. The white (blindingly so) bedsheet just barely covered his chest. His heroic features were noble and sharply chiseled, the stuff of a dictator's dreams, but clouded with reserve, restraining the gleam of the luxurious gold hair that framed his face.

His thin lips dissolved into a smile.

Speechless, overwhelmed, Pierre surrendered completely and unconditionally. He was entranced.

First by the man's beauty and majesty, like a memorial stone's.

But then, even more, by that giant smile.

In that smile, the true character of this cruelest man of all was laid bare. It was a smile like the ulcerous flowering of the psychological wound he bore from something that ate at him deep inside. It was obvious that something nasty had wormed its way into that body of his, white as a plaster wall. His pearly teeth were like adornments fashioned from the bones of war casualties. Every inch of his body brimmed with sickness and poison and death, and that, Pierre reasoned to himself, was exactly why this gentleman was so beautiful.

The giant was not overly hairy, but was covered in downy fuzz that glimmered occasionally like gold dust shaken from a sheet. Pierre shifted his gaze to where those downy courses gathered and grew dense, seeing their termination in a pitch-black spiral of pubic hair beneath which his thick member casually lay. He gave off a smell combining leather and cigars and tea and sweat. To Pierre it was the sweetest perfume.

"Hello, Pierre," the giant said. "Welcome to my room. I was hoping you'd come, and I'm so happy you did."

Unlike the words he spoke, the giant's voice was cold. Pierre did not detect a hint of feeling for him. But this coldness only stoked the flames in his breast higher. He still could not name the emotion he felt. Was it love? Did he long for the giant to embrace him, caress him? Or to lay down the law as a virile patriarch? Both were close, but neither was quite correct. Pierre felt as if he might go crazy from impatience. There was someone here who would give him what he had always longed for. All he had to do was give voice to that wish— but the wish itself would not come out.

"What's wrong, Pierre?" the giant asked gently.

That gentleness made Pierre want to abandon all he had and simply beg the giant for forgiveness, and he was about to say so, but even this was so far from what he truly wished that he could do nothing but close his mouth and groan in his throat. He fell to his knees and pressed his forehead against the floor, tears dampening the carpet.

"Never mind," the giant said. "I understand. Pierre, this is what you're thinking: 'I want to be eaten by you.'"

Another electric shock ran through Pierre. The tangle of disparate emotions within him had been resolved in an instant. One sentence had been all that was needed. *Why didn't I realize it myself? I wanted this man to eat me. I want to be eaten. I want him to do me the honor of eating me. Right now. Right here.*

"Pierre, you want me to eat you. Not cooked, but raw. You want me to tear your arms and legs off and crack your tightly inter-connected skeleton apart. Then you want me to stuff what's inside into my mouth and slurp it out of you. You've been wanting to die for a long time, right? You are noble at heart, and so you long to choose soul-rending agony over an aimless sleepwalker's death. Your narcissism is too strong to accept a death brought by those idiot Spiders, who know the value of nothing. You would rather fall into the hands of someone big and strong, majestic and beautiful—have every inch of your body dissected, savored unhurriedly, and praised as you breathe your last. And that is why I will separate every bone in your body from every other, as carefully as a watchmaker. I will pull out your eyes and kiss the sockets as sweetly as I would a vagina. I will adorn myself with every drop of your blood. After all, that is what you want from me."

"That's right," Pierre said, in a voice husky with arousal. His eyes were moist. His erection was hard. Everything the giant had said was right. *This gentleman knows every part of my soul. No—this gentleman thinks my thoughts* for *me. He gives name to my feelings.*

"Right now, you are enraptured. This is because you are imagin-ing what you might taste like. I expect you will have the purest of flavors. The pain inflicted on you by guests from the real world can only have purified you. Come, that I may do what you wish. I will show no mercy. I have magical powers, and so you will be incapable of losing consciousness. Until the very moment of your passing, you will taste unimaginable pain to the fullest extent."

Sighing like a believer approaching the altar, Pierre ducked beneath the canopy curtains and climbed onto a corner of the bed.

"Please tell me your name," he said.

"Langoni." The giant gripped Pierre's head in one hand. "I am Langoni."

And then Langoni began to eat Pierre. As soon as the dining began, the giant's wretched human sacrifice forgot all he had felt, as if it had been nothing but a lie, and recalled that he had not wanted to be eaten at all, but preventing that from taking place was beyond his power now. Langoni lingered over his meal, savoring it for longer than was necessary. He kept his promise faithfully. Pierre's consciousness and sensation remained intact, and he suffered an agony he had never imagined any Realm could provide, until the very last piece of him was gone.

Langoni rose to his feet, his naked body smeared with blood. As he did, the entire room began to shrink around him. The bed, the wallpaper, the sofa cover, the textiles the room was hung with—all these things lost their form and melted together into an extravagant harlequin suit of countless fabrics woven together, covering Langoni's naked body. The garment clung close to his skin, hungrily absorbing the blood of the sacrifice.

The room disappeared, leaving Langoni, controller of the Spiders, alone in the forest that stood west of the hotel. He popped one of Pierre's eyes into his mouth like candy, turned his garment into a cloak of invisibility hiding him from both AIs and Glass Eyes, and began to walk toward the Mineral Springs Hotel.

Yve was lost.

She could not find Pierre no matter how she tried. The TrapNet didn't register the anomaly in the forest. If this had something to do with the Spiders, then the Spiders were now able to act undetected by the net as well. She shrank from the horror of this idea.

She waited in increasing irritation for one of the three sisters to bring the matter up, but none of them did. Had no one else realized what a dangerous omen this was?

The TrapNet was no longer a simple security system. It was a sensory order. If the hotel was one great virtual being, the TrapNet was the immune system that kept the Spiders out. But if some area appeared within that body where nerves could not reach, making it impossible to know what was happening inside? If the body's arms and limbs stopped moving as commanded? What then?

No, there was no time to think about things like that. *We have our hands full just monitoring and operating the net properly*, Yve tried to think. At this very moment, the TrapNet was fighting off ten Spiders at once. That alone would certainly require fierce concentration from the "widows."

But Yve wanted to spend just a little more time in the wonderful sensuality of the net. She wanted to enjoy the feeling of omnipotence like a rising wind that was only available to her there. Yve's mastery of the Eyes was greater than anyone's. The TrapNet was like a giant cruise ship with a rudder so heavy only Yve could turn it. And no one was at all concerned about Pierre yet.

She decided to watch how things progressed for just a little longer. There was surely still time.

"It'll begin before long," murmured the old man in black who claimed to be called Jules. His tone was oddly relaxed. "Looks like everything's going nicely, though. At least one of the women has clued in. Realized that there might be things out there the TrapNet can't detect, I mean."

"That's…" Jules stiffened. "Impossible," he finished. It *was* impossible. Every object, every phenomenon in the Realm was subject to capture by the Eyes. Nothing was supposed to be able to escape their gaze.

"I don't mean to criticize you. You did pretty good work."

Jules was thinking. Things the Eyes couldn't see—what could the old man mean by that?

"Look at the big thinker with his mouth all pursed. Of course there are things the Eyes can't see. They're powerful, but not omnipotent. And then there are the things the Eyes can see, but you and yours can't—which works out to the same thing. You get my drift?"

Jules was shaken by the surprisingly simple admonishment. "But the net has an identity boundary of its own," he argued. "If the Eyes see something, the immune system should go into action."

"That jerry-rigged identity you thought of yourself? You think that'll be effective against someone outside the standard AI box? The net'll be powerless soon. And then it'll tighten around our own necks."

Jules felt like tightening something around the old man's neck himself.

Just then someone punched Jules's head from behind. As he reeled from the blow, his legs were swept out from under him. He fell forward, nose grinding into the carpet.

The whole casino watched as he pushed himself up onto his knees.

Felix. That was who had punched him. Thin, fox-like face. Red corn-silk hair.

"What do you think you're doing?" Felix demanded. He stank of drink. "Secret whispering, disagreements in a place like this? Just sit tight and keep quiet, boy. The adults are trying to keep you safe."

Jules couldn't believe what he was hearing. Felix was only in the casino because the other men had left him behind for being too drunk.

As Jules rose to his feet, he saw Yve standing behind his assailant. Felix glanced behind him, sensing her presence too.

"What are you doing?" Yve asked.

"Just what it looks like," Felix said. "Teaching the boy some manners. Just gave him a little nudge."

Yve stared unblinking at Felix. Her face was sad, but not her eyes. They were as fixed as the stones at the bottom of a stirred-up pool.

"At a time like this?"

"Times like this are exactly when people need to respect the rules. Two people whispering together can make everyone around them uneasy."

"You're pathetic," Yve said, still eyes fixed on her husband, expression unchanging.

"That look again? I've had that up to here," Felix said, dropping his own gaze. "I've had it up to here with you!"

He crossed to the doors of the casino, pushed them open, and walked out into the corridor. His figure wavered and warped through the stained glass of the doors as he staggered away.

"I'm sorry," Yve said, approaching Jules. The stillness in her eyes had dissolved. "I'm sorry, Jules." Tears began to run down her cheeks.

"No need," Jules said, shaking his head. "I'm fine." He could say nothing more.

"I'll get back to my station," Yve said. She hung her head as she turned away. Her rich chestnut hair was tied neatly at the nape of her neck.

Jules glanced over at the stained-glass doors again.

Felix's swaying form disappeared as if swallowed up by the outlines of the picture. Had he turned a corner in the corridor? Jules narrowed his eyes.

"Hey."

It was Joël, the hotel's long-suffering, potbellied cook. His black eyes smiled at Jules through his black-framed glasses.

"Don't let him get to you," Joël said. Then he looked at Old Jules too. "That said, it isn't exactly pleasant to see you two huddled together whispering to each other. Come over and be with the rest of us. Have some hot soup."

"That would be appreciated," said Old Jules, rising to his feet.

As they walked, Joël continued. "Got a message from Bastin," he said. "Seems the Spider attack's abated a bit. He's called for a short break. I made sandwiches and soup."

A young waiter was passing out soup cups and sandwiches wrapped in paper.

"Make sure Yve and the others get some too," Jules said.

"Of course, of course. Especially Julie, right?" Joël laughed. "A tough nut to crack, that one."

Jules sipped from the cup he was handed. It was a chicken cream soup, whipped to give it a cappuccino-like frothiness. The taste of cream and the chicken broth were as warm, light, and soft as a pile of blankets. It was the most delicious thing he had ever tasted. He couldn't recall even *thinking* something was this tasty before.

"This is good stuff." Old Jules was chomping on his lightly toasted sandwich. "What is it, duck rillettes? Pulling out all the stops, huh?"

Jules looked down. He had just remembered what Old Jules had said earlier. If there were things the net could not detect, how would they behave? The conditional itself was unclear, so there was no point thinking on it. Jules put it out of his mind and switched to mentally rechecking the safety measures designed to keep the net system alive.

"Here," said Old Jules, giving Jules his sandwich. "You've got to eat, or you won't last through this."

Jules bit into the bread. The flavor was so vivid that he had to put his thinking on hold for a moment. The smell of wheat and yeast. The mouthfeel of the dough, with its tiny, evenly distributed pockets of air. The smack of salt and fat and garlic.

He tried to recall what it had felt like when Felix had shoved and kicked him just before. Extremely painful, for one thing. It had seemed to him the first time he had ever felt such pain. But, thinking about it, he'd had worse injuries before, and those had hurt more. It was a strange way to put it, but it seemed that the pain today was distinctive in *quality* rather than quantity, like the way the same musical performance sounded more real when you listened to it on a better radio.

But why should that be so? He had no idea.

The woman in a Romani-style outfit realized that steam was billowing from the enamelware kettle on the stove. She rose from the sofa and padded barefoot across the wooden floor to remove the kettle from the heat and place it on the table.

Her room was inside a Glass Eye.

Nobody knew her name. She did not even know who she was herself. She was neither human nor AI. "She" was nothing but a phenomenon within Femme Fatale, just like the fire that burned inside the Father of Flame. She knew that there were things outside her tiny room, but after a mind-numbingly long time spent here alone, with no visitors and no connection to anybody, she no longer gave it much thought.

She poured the water from the kettle into the teapot. Removing the teacups from the cupboard, she placed them on the table.

Them?

She gazed at the tabletop curiously. Two cups. Come to think of it, she had put enough tea leaves in the pot for two as well. For who?

After pouring the remaining hot water into the cups to warm them, the woman took some canned fruit in syrup down from the cupboard. She was restless, but the feeling was not unpleasant. It was just new to her. She had never received a guest before.

She laid out the fruit, poured two cups of tea, and sat at the table facing the door that never opened. It opened today, as perfectly timed as if it had been choreographed in advance. Standing in the doorway was a dapper man with bushy eyebrows as black as his five o'clock shadow, and friendly, ingratiating eyes. He was not tall, and his tread was light on the floor. He entered the room as naturally as if he did this all the time. The woman for her part received him as though it was perfectly natural for strangers to visit her.

"Hey there, Maria," he said.

"Darling," Maria replied.

Replied, and then shivered. For the first time in her life, Maria had been addressed by name.

That's right—I'm Maria. My name is Maria.

Thus named, she felt as if her silhouette had come sharply into focus. A name let her believe that she was a person. Relief and reassurance filled her breast. It was like realizing how thirsty you had been only after drinking a glass of water. She could not stop the tears that spilled suddenly from her eyes. She saw now that she had long lived in an isolation of terrible degree. All at once, Maria became afraid. She could not be alone again. She wanted someone by her side.

Maria rose to her feet. She had a long dancer's back, a sharp aquiline nose, and hair that fell in waves. The man approached and placed a single red flower in her hair, just above her temple. The smell of still-fresh cigars wafted from within his white (blindingly white) low-necked shirt. His stubbly Adam's apple was right before her eyes. Maria had the urge to seize it between her teeth. She wanted to press her lips against his breast, make it slick with her saliva. She slipped her hand between the man's shirt and his suspenders. Her desire roused her body like a wild beast. Outwardly directed lust was another new experience for her.

"Were you lonely, Maria?"

The gallant flashed a conceited smile, cupping Maria's cheek with his right hand. His thick palm was the first flesh that had ever touched Maria's other than her own.

"Let me spoil you," he said.

Maria nodded. She felt herself open beneath his gaze. Her teeth showed between her lips, longing for his tongue.

The man kissed the woman he had named. He transferred what he held in his mouth to hers: Pierre's eyeball. The eyeball melted like condensed milk as he did so, and in her intoxication she swallowed it without even noticing. Langoni confirmed that arousal showed in her eyes, as if a thin film had come over them, and smiled.

"You're a formidable woman," Langoni whispered into her beautiful, shell-like ear. "You keep your back rod-straight, no matter what. You like to bite, to wade in. You hate acting coy and being used. Your eyes are pale and hint at ferocity. Your hair is black and that flower ablaze against it. Your voice smells better than coffee."

Clasped tightly in his arms, Maria drowned in a sense of good fortune that was quite inexpressible. How good it felt to be described in language: having never spoken to anyone before, she could hardly help but feel this way. Every word Langoni said was like another pin fastening her to the specimen board like a butterfly. At this vaguely masochistic image she grew even more aroused.

"Let's have some fun," Langoni whispered, tangling his fingers in her curls of black hair.

"What kind?"

"Just fun. I'm about to come just thinking about it."

With the closeness of lovers, the two giggled, then burst out laughing. They were still laughing as they tumbled onto the bed. Then they fell silent for a moment, and eventually began a quiet moaning that lasted for quite some time.

Yve was miserable.

She felt so badly about what Felix had done to Jules that it seemed her face might burst into flames.

Even the children knew what kind of situation they found themselves in. Felix's behavior had been unforgivable. Certainly she would not forgive it herself.

Where had she gone wrong?

Funny how even the most companionably scripted AI couple could, given a thousand years, slip into irreparable dysfunction, Yve thought wryly.

Things had been different before the Grand Down. Felix had been very good to her. He had not just helped with the things her disability made difficult. More importantly, he had accepted and loved her the way she was, quiet and unhurried, with a tendency to zone out. He had never made digs at her blindness, and she doubted he had ever felt the urge to. He had been self-centered and always rushing, more of a doer than a talker, but that was exactly what had made him select her, from the bottom of his heart, as his ideal companion.

Speaking to him now, though, was nothing but pain.

He still loved her. Of that, she felt, there could be no mistake. And she had not fallen out of love with him. If he would just act normally, she was sure they could spend another thousand years as an agreeable and mild husband and wife. AIs were not worn down by simple repetition—that was one of their advantages.

But nowadays he seemed aggravated by everything she did or said.

The most unremarkable of everyday acts could set him off. He would erupt like a land mine, roaring at her with sudden fury, and the day would be ruined. It was impossible to tell in advance what might make him explode—and if she was honest, it was often unclear even afterward what the cause had been. He would snarl that she was always making a fool out of him, but she had no idea what he meant. She was not trying to do anything in particular. This seemed to aggravate him even more. Would it be enough if she simply accepted whatever he said without protest to keep him happy? Just met everything with a cheerful smile?

The days she spent with him ate away at her. She felt like her body was filling with poison, and would suddenly find herself taking deep breaths as she washed the dishes. (AIs really did exhibit some amazing behavior.) And this, too, would enrage her husband.

If there was any time she was able to relax, it was when she was holding an Eye. Only then was wholeness of sensation within reach. She could straighten up and focus. None of the other AIs were made to work with Eyes the way she was. None of them could act as correctly inside the Eyes. Even if all the other AIs denied it, the Chandelier knew. The TrapNetwork knew. Within the Eyes she saw clearly that she had done nothing whatsoever to bring Felix's reign of terror on herself.

Clashing with him just now had felt so good.

It was the sort of pleasure you might get from smashing a plate, expensive but not to your tastes, in the middle of the road. Yes, she thought, she could break things too. Even a thousand-year bond could be broken. She had thought their summer days would stretch out into eternity, but the arrival of the Spiders had already brought summer to the verge of collapse. If that collapse could be averted, she decided, she would tell Felix goodbye herself. She would end their life together herself.

All this passed through Yve's mind in the short time it took her to walk back to the table where the Chandelier was. When she sat in the chair, she gathered her concentration about her, briskly sweeping away all stray emotion. For now, at least, she felt better. She felt as though she were in control of her own future.

Unfortunately, she was wrong.

José van Dormael stood on the terrace, on which Glass Eyes had been arranged like strings of fairy lights, and gazed at the calm sea.

There had been no further attacks to speak of. The battle at the front of the hotel seemed to be unfolding as expected. It appeared that all was going well. But José did not think this would last. His principal evidence was the still, flat sea. It was not a pasted-on image like before, but to José that only made it more ominous. The real ocean, no matter how calm the conditions, was vigorously alive. Even when all the living things beneath its surface were asleep, their breath came to him, borne like champagne bubbles on the ocean wind. Right now, though, he couldn't hear a sound. Had the sea died? No—even the voice of death was absent. Just what was happening not even José could say.

The salt wind brushed his cheek. He caught a whiff of something pleasant and turned to find a boy standing beside him. José was surprised that he had not noticed the boy earlier.

"Hey there, José," the boy said with a smile. He had a delicacy about him that put José in mind of Jules, but he must have been a few years older. His eyes were long and narrow, almost feminine. José wondered if the boy had some Asian ancestry. He wore a white (blindingly white) hoodie with marine blue piping, and no shirt underneath it. What José had detected was the smell of soap that came from the boy's black hair as it blew in the wind. José could not recall ever seeing the boy before, which, in this Realm, was grounds for suspicion on its own.

"Why so suspicious? All I said was hello."

"What's your name?"

"Langoni. Never heard of me, right?"

"That's right."

José was not sure how to handle this. The boy—Langoni—was saying that he wasn't from here. In other words, that he had something to do with the Spiders. He was asking to be killed.

"You can't kill me," the boy said, as if reading José's thoughts.

José considered the claim. A second later, he had the thick poker from the fire behind him gripped firmly in one hand, and half a moment after that the poker slammed into the side of the boy's head, just above his right ear. The shock that traveled back to José's hand made him feel like he had punched a boulder. He let the poker drop from his tingling hand, noting that it was now slightly bent.

"See?" the boy said.

He had let José hit him on purpose. José bit his lip, wondering if he was losing his touch.

"Can't we talk, José?" asked the boy. "I'm very interested in you. You're the only one I want to talk to. The only one worth talking to."

The boy leaned on the terrace railing like José and looked out at the sea. He was standing where Anne had been. Where *was* Anne?

"First of all," the boy continued, "you're very smart. I mean, you noticed that your senses were getting keener, right? Plus, you were the only one who deduced from this that the world itself was getting more vivid. Next, you said, 'They want us to raise a fortress.' Now that was sharp… Eh? How do I know what you're thinking? It's all thanks to that wonderful TrapNet of yours. I can't enter or meddle with it, but eavesdropping on it is easy. The system has to open itself up in order to attack, after all. Utterly defenseless. Hmm? What's wrong?"

José's face was bright red. He was straining with all his strength in an attempt to move, but finding that he couldn't.

"Now, stop that," the boy said. "You can't move. Let's just have a quiet chat."

José grimaced. "I can still speak, then," he said. "Generous of you."

"What was I saying?" the boy continued, ignoring him. "Oh, right. I was saying how sharp you are.

"I was moved, I have to say. *Who knew someone this smart was in the Realm?* I thought. Then I decided that I wanted to learn what else you'd deduced, directly from the source. Someone like you has to have figured out all kinds of things about us. Hearing about them from you sounded like a fun way to spend some time. I mean, I'm bored, after all. My only companions are the Spiders—mindless, single-function tools. I want to have a conversation that's a little more intelligent. One where both sides have something to hide. Just the two of us, with no interruptions from anybody."

José was daring by nature. Even battling the Spiders, he had never in his life felt anything worthy of the word *fear*—until now. It wasn't the paralysis or the futilely bent poker, but the fact that he and the boy had been at the railing together for some time now without anyone disturbing them. There were fifteen men, plus Anne, stationed on this terrace. Five or six should have been right nearby. Had the boy done away with them all? No, it seemed more like…how could he put it? José suspected that although his surroundings looked very much like the Mineral Springs Hotel, in fact he was somewhere else. If the Realm was a stage, then it was as if someone had stolen behind their set, painted an identical copy on its reverse, and then whisked José behind it without him noticing to act in a different play with this boy (although José had his doubts about the truth of that identity, too). That would explain the appearance of the ocean and the utter lack of people nearby. The explanation alone was not enough to banish his fear. But to stand against that fear, which was like being suspended in perfect darkness, José needed some kind of foothold. Scrabbling in midair, he decided to test the boy—probe for some kind of ledge for his toes to cling to.

José cleared his throat. "Here's what I think," he said. "You came here from outside the Realm. From the same world as our guests, I imagine—the real world. There's no other way to explain how stagger-ingly powerful you are. We're fighting you with everything this Realm has, but there's something entirely different in you. I can sense it. It's not about quality or quantity. It's a difference of dimension. Power like that just doesn't exist in the Realm of Summer. And if you're from a different dimension, where could that be? The world of the guests. The physical world."

Langoni, who had started grinning halfway through José's speech, broke in now with an amused grunt. "You're saying I'm a guest."

"No. You're doing things a proper guest never would. They can only receive the services they pay for, and as I understand it, things are valued about the same inside the Realm as they are outside it. If a guest buys an orange or a chair or a whore in the Realm, the appropri-ate charge gets added to their real-world bill. If they wanted to destroy the entire Realm of Summer, they'd have to pay for an entire harbor town, plus eight thousand people—and destroying the Realm itself wouldn't be permitted in the first place. Which means that you're either an unauthorized intruder yourself, or here on behalf of someone who is."

Langoni laughed out loud. "You speak as if this virtual resort were still in business," he said. "Are you all still so bound by the idea of how things used to be between guests and the Realm, that you still can't move on?"

"There are people here who think that way," said José. "I don't harbor much hope along those lines myself. True, the Realm might be nothing more today than a rusty old tourist trap that's fallen out of fashion. Or the world of the guests might have been destroyed by war or epidemic disease.

"But suppose for the sake of argument that the guests have stopped coming because the Costa del Número went bankrupt. That bankruptcy wouldn't have wiped out its asset value. There'd be a custodian of some kind. Entering without authorization and destroying those software assets would be treated as a crime. I'm talking about a sneak thief like you here."

Langoni appeared to have taken the bait. The master-and-slave relationship that bound the guests and the Realm clearly disgusted, repulsed, and tormented him. José wasn't unfamiliar with the feeling himself. What it meant, though, was that the boy was no visitor from the physical world. *He's one of us—just from another Realm*, thought José. *That's why he reacted so strongly, albeit with impressive self-control, to what I said.*

"Let's suppose I am from the physical world, as you say, come here via unauthorized means. Why would I do that?"

"Illegal salvage. It can't be anything else."

Langoni snorted. His eyes narrowed.

"Nice way to put it," he said. "You might be right about the Costa looking like a gigantic tomb from the standpoint of the physical world after the Grand Down. Dead, hollow, but rich in static stock. But grave robbers don't dig where there isn't any treasure, José. What would *you* come to the Realm of Summer for?"

José was now confident that he was doing well. The challenge was what came next. He would have to carry on exactly the kind of conversation the boy had asked for—a little bit more intelligent than usual, with each side grimly probing the other's hand. He had to get the drop on the boy somehow, pin down what it was that he and his side were after.

Recalling the most difficult chess game he had ever played—that one he'd enjoyed with Jules—José began striving desperately to summon up that sensation once more.

Thinking, as he did so, that the earring whose partner was with Julie Printemps would be sure to give him strength.

The fish-shaped earring—

Thinking of the promise they had exchanged then.

Felix wanted to cry as he pushed the casino's glass doors open.

He was well acquainted with his own loathsomeness—almost aggressively aware of how pathetic he was. He blinked furiously. *Come on, then, tears, let's see you flow*, he thought, a show of bravado for the benefit of no one in particular. He stormed down the hall, stamping his feet as hard as he could. The tools of his trade as a tailor—his measuring tape, the scissors in his apron pocket—rattled and shook. The tears would not come. Nobody followed him out. He was not even worth beating up.

Felix was wallowing in his own childishness.

She wasn't that kind of woman before, he muttered internally. *She wasn't like that. She knew her place, recognized the kindness in me, saw the merits of us helping each other be better. She was sharp as a tack then. Too good for a skinny, uneducated weakling like me, of course. We were probably only together because some designer thought the Realm of Summer needed an odd couple around. Felix the broomstick and big fat Yve.*

She was such a fine woman then. Big breasts, good smell, you know? Nice chubby belly. I even liked those pupilless eyes of hers. Never was comfortable under the female gaze.

We got busy every night.

Every single night, guests would come to spy on what we got up to when the sun went down. You bet it made us work harder. I guess it was our job in a way. You'd expect me to be the empty role, sold to guests wanting a taste of Yve, but no. We were in there for the peeping toms to enjoy. Those legs of hers—fat, but so pretty that I never got tired of rubbing my cheek against them. And those feet, smaller than you'd think. I'd call her "Madame Butterfly" as I kissed them...

Felix brooded over what to him were happy memories as he walked. He'd already walked much farther than the length of the corridor, but he wasn't any closer to turning the corner at the end. He didn't realize this. But when he was thinking of something pleasant, he was happier just to keep walking. If he didn't realize, better to let him be, don't you think?

Felix kept walking. Minute particles like dust began to swirl around him, but he remained immersed in his sweet reverie and showed no sign of noticing.

But she changed completely.

It was the Grand Down.

There's been zilch between us since.

Listen, I didn't care if the guests come or not. And it doesn't have to be every night. I knew we were both a bit off-model, and I would've been satisfied if we could just save face for each other as a couple, you know? As a tailor I'm, well, no worse than average—not bad enough to embarrass myself, compared to her lacemaking. She could be too laid-back at times, but I could keep her in line, and she knew how to flash that glare of hers at me to stop me before I got too stupid or indiscreet. I never made her feel small, or left her at a disadvantage because of her blindness. And on the other hand, having her around helped me hold back on the urge to go around snapping at everyone like a fighting dog. That's what you call a good marriage, right?

The problem wasn't us.

It was those Glass Eyes.

Just when did they start appearing, anyway?

At first there were only those little tiny ones. You'd say "Huh, that's interesting," and that'd be that. Yve, being Yve, wasn't that interested in them either. I'm really partly to blame for getting her started. I was drunk one night—not that there were any nights I wasn't drunk, but putting that aside for now—and I swiped this Eye that René was proudly showing off at the bar. Took it home with me. I didn't feel bad—the old fart had just found it on the beach or something. It was a little treat for her...

The dust, which was in fact minuscule Spiders, remained unnoticed by Felix. The soundless, odorless powder of Spiders gradually began attaching itself to his surface. The Spiders had tiny hook-shaped needles at the tips of their abdomens which caught lightly on Felix's skin and clothing. Next, microscopic motors in the hooks began to turn, unraveling Felix's surfaces into a thread-like substance which the Spiders caught, rolled up, and eliminated with their *hunger*. There was not the slightest pain, and in his drunken state Felix noticed nothing.

He simply kept on walking down the long, long, long corridor on his
uncertain legs.

*… I should never have given her that Eye. Even she didn't want it
at first. What a fool I was to force her to look through it, telling her that
people said it even helped the blind see.*

*The look in her eyes changed then, oh yes. "Oh, Felix, this is amaz-
ing," she said. "I can see, I can see." Frozen in place like someone'd tied her
up. Well, and fair enough. She must've been happy. I was happy too. But,
you know, I still haven't forgotten her face when she turned toward me.
That sharp intake of breath, the tiny gasp. I heard it. Paranoia? I think
not. I think she saw my face, saw how I looked, and it genuinely shocked
her. For the first time, she really understood how ugly her husband was.
I was roaring drunk, my hair was a mess, my clothes were worn out, my
nose was bright red, I was missing some buttons… Not a fit sight for anyone. But that gasp, that was over the line, right? She acted like nothing'd
happened afterward, but it was too late. Every time I saw her round face,
I heard that sound in my ears again.*

*Anyway, forget about that. Point is, from the next morning on, Yve
didn't have time for anything but Eyes. She'd be staring into one and mut-
tering something every free moment she had, morning till night. Didn't
matter what I said to her—she just ignored me. Possessed, you might call
it? It actually scared me. I knew by the end of that first day that she'd never
look at me seriously again. Does that strike you as normal? The man who
stayed with her all those years, and she stops looking his way the moment
she gets her sight back…*

The Spiders moved untiringly. Felix's clothing and the scissors in
his apron dissolved into thread to be wound up. His red corn-silk hair
vanished, leaving him bald. His ears came off. Most of his skin was
gone now, revealing the programs inside him. His movements had
become a little stiff, but he kept on walking. Yes: once Felix got started

thinking about his time with that beloved wife of his, his head got so full that he could see nothing else (of course, this time his eyeballs had already been unraveled and wound up). A touching sight, no? That's right, Felix. Keep walking. There's a thousand miles in this corridor—*I* managed to squeeze it in, compressing it into the width of a single step. We won't be disturbed in here by the gaze of the Glass Eyes or surveillance by the TrapNet. You can walk as much as you like.

Walk, Felix, walk. Until every last scrap of your body and mind are rolled up.

Langoni's saliva had the sickly odor of cigars. Maria liked that too. She stretched languorously in the sheets. They had come together so many times now she had long since lost count. Her body felt charged with pleasure like a buildup of static electricity. Wherever his hands touch her, crackling sparks flew.

"Maria."

"What is it?"

"I need a favor."

"So, what is it?"

"Could you open up—just like this?"

Maria cackled. Her eyes, once sharp as a poet's, were now lazy and soft. "Nuh-uh," she said.

"Come on, don't be like that."

Langoni sank his member inside Maria. Partway through her face darkened. She frowned in apparent discomfort, and then, with a final short, wordless cry, Maria expired. "Expired" was not quite accurate, of course, since Maria had never lived or breathed to begin with. To put it another way, Langoni rendered Maria inert and then took over the Eye functionality that her image, symbol of Femme Fatale, had been granted. He went through Maria to hit the Eye's most essential part and bring it entirely under his control. And through Femme Fatale he also, quite literally, jacked into the TrapNet.

Langoni checked on how his other selves were doing in the Realm of Summer. There was the boy Langoni speaking to José, there the invisible Langoni unraveling a man in a corridor. Soon the giant Langoni would arrive too.

His true form was not in this Realm at all. Multiple individuals were being projected into the Realm of Summer from elsewhere.

The conversation with José was going absolutely wonderfully. José! Healthy and capable, a man of deep feeling and intelligence. A more suitable candidate Langoni could not imagine. He truly was fit to become the greatest jewel in the crown.

Excellent. All proceeding as planned. Langoni the necrophile chuckled as he slowly moved his hips. Perhaps he would take a stroll through the hotel too. Writhing at the overwhelming pleasure, he began to scan the TrapNet.

The bathroom was in a wretched state.

The toilet had broken in two, the tiles were cracked and coming loose, and the wallpaper had become as brittle as ash. The white Glue that had been Stella was now a small pile that looked like kneaded, half-dried barium. Spider legs protruded from the pile here and there, still twitching.

René the shipwright had come with several others about his age. They removed the door that hung from its hinges and entered the stall, covering their noses against the stench. They had been tasked with retrieving and examining captured Spiders. This Spider was supposed to have been rendered powerless, but they could not afford to be careless, so the plan was to wrap it in a net of webbing and drag it out that way.

Someone behind René handed the net forward to him. He tossed it over the mound of Glue. One of the men with him used a pitchfork to turn the mound over.

"This stink's gonna tear my damn nose off," grimaced René, pulling the net tight. "Okay, that'll do it. Time to pull 'er out."

The men backed out of the stall, pulling the net behind them. One prodded the mass of Glue from the side to make sure it didn't catch on the doorframe. Even so, they had trouble getting it out.

"Maybe the net's caught on the door handle?"

"Let me take a look," said René. Back inside the stall, the stench had gotten thicker. The odor was indescribable, although something like semen. Did the Glue really smell like this? As he circled the hill of Glue suspiciously, René saw something emerge from it: a man's hand.

René was startled. Had someone gotten caught up in the Stella trap? He reached for the hand, only to see it extend toward him of its own accord, followed by the upper body of its owner. Langoni. René's jaw dropped.

"Maria's connected to this place, too, then," Langoni muttered to himself. Then he noticed René. "Hey there," he said. "Nice to meet you."

"Hello," René replied, feeling reality collapse soundlessly around him. "You all right?"

"'All right'! Do I *look* all right?" Langoni said, as if his car had fallen into a ditch by the side of the road. "This sticky stuff—what on Earth is it?"

"That's Glue," said René. It seemed to him a very bad idea to talk to whoever this was, but the words came out of his mouth anyway. The man gave the impression that nothing could be hidden from him. "Manifestation of an Eye function."

"Ah," said Langoni. "An amalgam of Glue and the Femme Fatale? So you've been blending Eye functions, then? Useful to know. Must be off, then."

Langoni waved goodbye and disappeared back into the Glue.

Feeling as if he might weep from fear, René waved back. He knew, somehow, that if he were to dig through the pile of Glue now, he would find no trace of the intruder.

He had to tell the others.

René stumbled out of the stall, then froze.

The door to the corridor was so far away that he could not even make it out in the distance. Thousands—tens of thousands—of stall doors lined the bathroom on both sides. A perfectly executed perspective view.

He heard chewing behind him. Then a swallowing sound.

It seemed the Spider had come back to life and begun eating the Glue. Was that crack the sound of the pitchfork's handle breaking? He heard a regular crunching. What could the Spider be gnawing on?

He could not look behind him. He felt as if time had stopped.

In infinitely drawn-out time, in infinitely drawn-out space, with a sound like dry leaves, the helpless old man finally began to laugh.

Why? Why?

Reduced now to the barest outlines, Felix muttered the word to himself over and over in time to the hopping rhythm of his stride. His memories and thoughts had all been wound off him, but his feeling of grievance continued to grumble and walk along. How fitting, Felix, that your last words should be an imbecilic waste of breath.

So galling, wasn't it? You must have been infuriated. To love your wife so much, and yet have been so narrow-minded that you could not support her when she felt new possibilities open before her. That incorrigible insensitivity of yours made you see the Eye manipulation techniques she pioneered as an idle hobby instead of a triumph born of her indomitable will and high intelligence. You are the earth from which your misfortune blooms. That's exactly why you were never able to escape.

Why? Why?

Oh, Felix, you really are the limit. The Spiders have borne away all but the last wisps of your body, and yet your resentment stumps on like a ghost. Ridiculous. Truly wonderful. Very well. I shall accept that resentment too. It will, I am sure, prove a fine adornment to what I intend to make of the Mineral Springs Hotel.

Even after Langoni had taken away the last of Felix, the closed space in the corridor continued to pulse with the stumping rhythm for quite some time.

CHAPTER 6:
THE ANGEL

A little before the fighting at the entrance began…

In the manager's office of the Mineral Springs Hotel, Denis rubbed his light bulb of a head. Despite his tense anticipation of the coming battle, his office was quiet and still. He was alone in the room. Even the ceiling lights were not turned on. There was only the pool of light cast by the lamp on his broad desk.

In that light he had piled dozens of large, leather-bound ledgers. In the surrounding darkness stood even more piles of ledgers.

Denis's face, always so affable, was cold and subdued. He took great pains to maintain the image of the affable, easygoing Denis for the sake of the others, but when he was alone he let the mask drop. Doing so did not bring him relief. In fact, the opposite was true. Particularly when he was gazing at these ledgers.

Their covers bore only numbers, embossed in small gold letters. A classic, beautiful typeface, the same as the lettering on signs and room number plates throughout the hotel. Each of the hundred or more ledgers had its own sequential number. Denis had one of them open now. The faint cream-colored page was covered in tiny, neatly arranged writing in blue-black ink.

These were Denis's daily records.

The one he had open now was from when "this summer" had first opened for business.

In the pantomime world of the Costa del Número, the AIs were both characters and stagehands. They performed many tasks behind the scenes, like a small theater troupe whose players also handled finances and advertising. Denis Prejean played several roles related to his employment. He was the evaluation function used to optimize the hotel's service index and the HR system that kept his employees working smoothly. He also kept these ledgers. The ledgers were a database scrupulously recording each guest's behavior in their room, and Denis was the only program capable of accessing that database. And, of course, Denis was the sum of all these programs clad in the skin of an AI.

It was Denis's job to record who the guests brought into this members-only service domain, whether those companions were other guests or AIs, what tastes the guests had, and how they enjoyed spending their time. He was also expected to ensure that the hotel's service reflected these things on subsequent visits, and protect the guests' privacy by strictly controlling access to the ledgers.

Even putting it mildly, his days were hellish. Denis's affable, decent personality was entirely unsuited for these tasks.

Denis well knew the depths of dissipation and cruelty to which guests sank at the Mineral Springs Hotel. He knew how monstrously they treated the AIs they brought in with them from town, and of course about their abominable behavior in the town itself.

Of course, all of this was legal, and no one could criticize it. If what the guests did was sordid, then the very creation of the Realm of Summer had been an atrocity, and the accumulation of all that was recorded here.

Even after the Great Down had put a sudden end to the arrival of guests, Denis had been unable to dispose of the ledgers. They did not know when the Realm might open for business again, and even if it had been closed down, the ledgers contained personal information of an unusually sensitive nature. His duty to strictly control access to them was unchanged. He stored them in a safe inside a sturdy oak cabinet, the hiding place the designers had provided to protect the ledgers from hackers, and kept the key to the safe on his person at all times.

But now it looked like Denis could finally put an end to those days.

He placed a dagger from Catsilver on his desk. In the pool of light, it gleamed as coldly as a paper knife.

He was about to burn all the ledgers.

Denis was pessimistic about the Mineral Springs Hotel's chances against the Spiders, but he did not think that an entirely bad thing. One thousand years was simply too long to spend on summer vacation. It was a mystery how the AIs' identities had lasted this long. Part of him wondered if it wouldn't be best to take the opportunity to wind things down. Perhaps it was finally time for the Realm of Summer to be deleted, and the Spiders were simply here to tidy up. If so, Denis was half-ready to accept that.

Either way, however, Denis's duty when unauthorized access to the database was anticipated was clear—the ledgers must be destroyed.

It was unlikely that the Spiders were here to steal these records, but not impossible. If there was a chance that what the Spiders ate was sent outside the Realm, then disposal became even more crucial.

Denis, although he knew it to be inappropriate, was aware that part of him was slightly excited by the prospect.

To put it very simply, everything about Denis was the way it was for the sake of these ledgers. Now he would burn them himself until nothing remained. Denis produced and cut one of the cigars he seldom smoked, then lit it with a match.

He heard the sound of impact from the entrance. The battle with the Spiders was here at last, then. Would Jules's net work as expected? No doubt Bastin was leading from the front.

Denis touched the dagger's tip to the first dated page in the ledger, then cautiously summoned the power of the Father of Flame. The paper burst into flames and the ledger disappeared neatly from the desk, without even the smell of burning leather. It didn't even scorch his desk mat. The truly surprising thing, though, was that Denis became unable to remember anything that had been written in the ledger. It made sense if you thought about it, but he had not considered that he would be incinerating his own recollections.

Denis burned ledger after ledger, annihilating loathsome memories for good. As he worked, he suddenly recalled Julie Printemps's smile. Back in the days when guests still came to the Realm, he had been working on the ledgers late one night when he had heard a rapping on the window of the manager's office. Julie had been standing outside, waggling a bottle of wine. Silently, she had mouthed, *Spe-cial de-li-ve-ry!* Denis had opened the window and she had come in, all smiles, and asked, "Is it okay if I watch you work?"

Nothing sexual happened that night. Julie had simply poured some wine into Denis's coffee cup and, enjoying her own glass, watched him writing in the ledger, smiling and being careful not to get in the way.

Denis hated people watching over his shoulder as he worked, but he had found that night relaxing and the work no burden at all. When Julie eventually decided it was time to go, said her goodbyes, and slipped out the window again, Denis had remained in a good mood. The wriggling of her backside as she went out the window had reminded him of that of a child, and he had been unable to stop himself from smiling. The evening's work had eventually stretched into an all-nighter, but he had met the dawn without feeling exhaustion.

With a start, Denis realized that he had finished burning the ledgers. The process had been anticlimactically quick.

Denis left the manager's office, dagger in hand. He was ready to join the battle at the entrance now.

All the lights at the front desk and lobby had been turned off for the night, leaving them sunk in gloom. In the corridor that led to the dining hall, though, the lights were still on. The walls were covered in framed photos of events and celebrations held at the hotel in days past. Denis had the sudden urge to examine them as he passed.

The photo closest to hand had been taken at a *pétanque* match on the lawn. The spot where the winner (a guest) should have been standing was now unoccupied, and the trophy he (or had it been a she?) had been raising now floated in midair. Burning the ledgers had eliminated the guest's image from the Realm. It made for a strange photograph, but Denis breathed a sigh of relief.

AIs smiled cheerfully from every photograph on the wall. Some of them had already been eaten by Spiders, and some were fighting at that very moment. There was even a photograph of the three sisters in their youth. They wore white sportswear and cradled tennis racquets, looking as lovely as fairies.

Toward the end of his tour of the gallery, he arrived at a small, significantly older portrait.

It had clearly been taken in a different age from the others. The hair, the clothes, and the image quality were all old-fashioned.

Denis walked closer to the photograph, straightening up as he did. Smiling from inside the frame was hotel founder Catherine Clement's grandmother Régine as a young woman. She had been photographed seated, and the little girl standing beside her was her five-year-old daughter Nadia Clement—Catherine's mother. Capturing mother and daughter staring at the lens from a room in the Clement house, which itself no longer existed, added a touch of historical color to the hotel's hall. When this photograph had been taken, the mineral springs themselves had been discovered, but Catherine, the founder of the hotel, was neither form nor shadow.

Of course, none of this history had actually taken place. The photograph was a fabrication.

It was nothing but world-building detail to lend more reality to the Realm. Neither Régine nor Nadia nor Catherine had ever "lived" as actual AIs in the Realm. Denis himself, in all his time in the Costa del Número, had never been anything other than fifty-seven years old.

For all that, though, the chronicles of the Clement family were the history of the workplace Denis had devoted his life to. The peculiar tale of the hotel's birth and its charming ensemble of characters were, to Denis (although he had never seen any of their faces), about as real as his own parents, and he felt a close affection for them.

A shining beauty like Régine's still overwhelms the viewer from inside a photograph. A beauty of great resilience, absolutely impervious to harm. By contrast, Nadia's intelligent, nervous face was wreathed in the shadow of misfortune…

Beside that hung a photo taken some thirty years later.

Here was Catherine, halfway through her teens, with an entourage consisting of her mother, Nadia, and grandmother, Régine. Yes: "entourage" was the word, so overwhelming was the youngest woman's presence. Beside Catherine, even Régine paled.

What would the three of them think about today? The question was nonsense, but Denis could not shake it. The Mineral Springs Hotel was the fruit of the Clement family's light and shade, fallen in rich colors, and now it was facing the end of its run. Were these muses alive, how would they lament its passing?

Denis Prejean faced the two photographs and bowed his head deeply—whether in apology or for some other reason he himself did not know. Then he straightened his back, fixed the hem of his vest, rubbed his head, returned to his usual face, and began heading toward the entrance.

And then it happened.

Behind him, Denis thought he heard a distant voice.

A hot, muffled voice… No, that was breathing.

Denis turned back.

There was no one in the dark hall. Just three pairs of eyes looking back at him from the Clement family photographs.

Yve was terrified by the seriousness, the gravity of the situation.

Hadn't the other four realized it yet?

The wormholes in the TrapNet were spreading.

Blank zones like bubbles of air were forming in increasing numbers, and it was impossible to see into them from outside.

She should have completely resolved Pierre's disappearance right away. Letting it pass as a probable reception fault or something had been the wrong thing to do, Yve thought, biting her lip.

Even so, she had done her best to find him. The other four didn't seem to have noticed; she could still pin down the cause of his disappearance before it was too late. She'd focused her senses and roamed the net searching for any disturbance in its flow.

Before long she realized that Felix had disappeared too.

He had left the casino and vanished.

Yve had tried retracing his footsteps in the corridor, looking down from above. Partway down the corridor his tracks suddenly grew faint and trailed off, like a stroke from a paintbrush as it went dry. There were no doors or side passages around the area. Her husband had not gone anywhere else.

That was when Yve had first realized that something beyond their comprehension might be happening in the net.

At the same moment, a strong, entirely unexpected emotion had risen within her.

What new foolishness is he trying to hold me back with now?

Does he want to put everyone at risk?

I wish he'd just stop it.

Fine. I don't care. Let him disappear.

I'll just ignore him. He needs to calm down or he won't be any good to us anyway. The other four haven't noticed.

She had known that the reaction was illogical. She had even realized, albeit dimly, that it was rooted in her sense that the net belonged to her, and her reluctance to be separated from it. But Yve had pushed the warnings she was shouting to herself to the bottom of her consciousness.

And now the bill had come due.

José had disappeared.

Without anybody noticing, he had simply vanished. She played back the video from a fairy light–sized Eye on the terrace and was shocked to see José's literal disappearance, as if spirited away by some higher power. The Eye had recorded minor tampering with the Realm's space-time textures. The tampering was instantaneous, lasting just a few frames, and ended once José had been swallowed up. She had feared the involvement of the Spider's *hunger*, but this was even more troublesome.

Yve had hurried to check the scene from different Eyes. That was when she had learned about the net's worm-eaten state.

Trembling with fear, Yve continued to work. Things were no longer within her power to control. She was too ashamed that she had not said something sooner to tell the others. Felix's face flashed before her. *You left me to die*, he cried in that piping voice of his. His expression and mannerisms appeared in her mind's eye, correct to the smallest detail, and Yve squeezed her eyes shut. She began to feel nauseous from the pressure, and a throbbing pain emerged at the back of her eyes. She wished somebody would hurry up and notice. Would notice the wormholes and shout an accusation.

Julie, for example. Wasn't she the one who was so close to José? Shouldn't she have noticed right away?

Why should I have to suffer everything on my own?

We're all powerless…and I drew the short straw.

Cruising the TrapNet, Julie Printemps eventually came across something that stopped her in her tracks.

José was—missing…?

She tuned her senses to the terrace overlooking the ocean.

The night sea breeze.

Anne and Bernier were both calmly looking out at the ocean. The rest of the men were doing the same. They showed no sign of worry over José's absence.

The fact that everyone on the terrace was so collected was itself bizarre, Julie thought apprehensively. Had no one realized that José was gone? But that would be even stranger. Something was going on here, Julie thought. Something very, very dangerous.

With extreme caution, Julie substantiated. She was spread very thinly across the TrapNetwork, and now she scraped up every bit of sensation she was receiving, and raised her sensitivity as high as it would go. Remembering the taste of mint drops through the piercing on her tongue, she used that flavor as the key around which her bodily sensations were integrated. She maintained this on the tip of her tongue for now, because she had a very bad feeling that she was about to encounter a risky situation that could knock her sensations well out of alignment. By securing the mint-drop taste in advance, she could use it as a lifeline.

Julie carefully began to search the terrace. But no matter how sharply she focused up her senses, she found no sign of José whatsoever.

Use your head, José told himself quietly. *You have the materials. Put them in order.*

One: Langoni was (probably) a resident of the Costa del Número—someone who had come from some other Realm.

Two: Langoni (probably) wanted something that was in this Realm.

Three: José had acted as if he erroneously thought Langoni was from the real world (although whether the boy really believed this was doubtful).

José's heart sank. There was no obvious way he could use these to get the better of the boy. He would just have to play for time.

The boy Langoni was gazing at José, leaning back against the railing overlooking the ocean. José spoke to those pure, unsullied eyes.

"You had some high praise for me before. I liked that. It felt like I was being told my intuition was correct.

"What I told Anne was this: someone we don't know is trying to get us to raise a fortress.

"What I wanted to say was this: evacuation to the Mineral Springs Hotel and construction of the TrapNet—a powerful system—all went perfectly naturally. All of us united in battling the Spiders. Wasn't that a bit too well done for our fragile little Realm? Selling our bodies and our pride to guests was our trade—how did we put all this together so smoothly? I realized after I spoke about the fortress what a huge thing I was saying—and then I realized how true it was, and it left me a little astonished. I understood that if all of it was true, that would be the best explanation for everything.

"First, the hotel. If the Spiders were going to box us in somewhere, it had to be the Mineral Springs. The building's sturdy, there's food and drink, beds to rest in. A collection of Eyes, too.

"Next, the people who gathered here. There were eight thousand AIs in this Realm, and of those, every single one that was needed to build the TrapNet turned up. Jules. Julie. Yve. If any one of them hadn't made it here, there'd be no net. Somebody calculated things so that the ideal team would assemble here, right? The same goes for Anne's self-defense squad. It's an honor to be among that number, I suppose…"

His most important task was to leave this "hidden stage" and get back to the Realm. He would aim for that first. Still speaking, José began to weave a plan.

"In other words, Langoni, you served this whole situation up to us on a platter. What you wanted was for a specific team of AIs to hole up in the hotel and make the TrapNet. Am I wrong?"

"Mmm," said Langoni. "I should have known you'd see it. The TrapNet thing was obviously too good to be true, wasn't it? But let's get back on track, shall we? I asked you what you would come to the Realm of Summer for, José. Is your answer 'the TrapNet'?"

"You couldn't make it anywhere else. Not without the ability to use the Eyes freely."

"Not lacking in self-confidence, are you?

"But that'll do fine. It's true that the Realm of Summer is rich in high-quality Eyes. That was a requirement for us. But—are you listening carefully? It wasn't the *essence* of why we came. It's not that the other Realms have no Eyes at all. There are any number of Eyes out there with even greater transformational powers. What we're here to dig up was actually something quite different."

José considered this for a moment.

There was no way that the TrapNet was entirely unrelated to Langoni's motives.

But apparently José's deduction that the net was a weapon had missed the mark. Perhaps even the power of Snowscape and the Father of Flame were not particularly relevant. Langoni was after something other than accuracy or destructive power as a weapon. What?

José didn't like where this was going. The worst outcome he had considered was everyone in the Realm of Summer being killed and the TrapNet alone carried away. But what if…

"Let me show you something."

Langoni came closer, then wrenched out José's right eye.

José tried to scream, but could not. His throat had been robbed of its strength again. The agony was unimaginable. The *quality* of the pain was an order of magnitude higher than anything he had experienced before. In that pain he sensed something that wanted to reveal itself. He felt on the verge of understanding what Langoni (and whatever higher beings he was representative of) was planning. But then it was obscured from his view.

"Look," said Langoni, hands moving like a magician's. A white glass ball appeared between the fingers of his right hand, and when he turned his palm over it had become two. "Do you know what these are?" he asked.

The glass balls had some kind of pattern on them, José saw. Irises of pale blue. They were somebody's eyes.

"You can have this one," Langoni said, pushing one of the eyes into José's empty right socket. José clearly (in *high quality*) felt Pierre's eye sprout into him like a tulip bulb, merging with the existing structure of his eye socket. Langoni then replaced José's left eye in the same way.

"It hurts, doesn't it? It must hurt, a lot. I mean, given how delicious the orange juice was.

"You disappoint me, José. You don't understand even the essence of the Eyes. That's why I have to show you something through Pierre's eyes. Relax and enjoy the show."

And then the new eyes began to upload the information stored in them into José—Pierre's final moments, from beginning to end. Merciless, intense experience entered him through the dead man's eyes. It was an eye-rape in the truest sense of the word, and as José's entire body acted as receiver for Pierre's hideous death, he longed to escape into madness.

"It hurts so much you can hardly think straight, doesn't it? Poor thing. Maybe I'll leave it at that."

All at once, the agony vanished. José was destabilized, as if his senses were floating in space.

The boy continued speaking. "I wouldn't normally do this, but let me give you a hint.

"Why is your sensory experience so heightened?

"Because the Spiders have eaten nine-tenths of the Realm of Summer, of course.

"At this point, the Realm's pseudoreality generator only has to produce the Mineral Springs Hotel and its surroundings. The burden on the generator is very low. And because the power distribution in the engine is flexible, the less work there is to do, the more computational power can be concentrated on what *is* being done. You see?"

I see, thought José. So this world was generated frame by frame through ultrafast computation. Well, of course it was.

"And you've made allowances for that too," he said.

"Yes. The TrapNet and the sensory upgrade. They come as a set."

"Do you have the power to tamper with the engine?"

"Let me see if I can rephrase that for you: 'Where am I?' Is that it?"

The boy was quick.

Yes, José wanted to know where this terrace had come from. Had Langoni made it, or was it some forgotten option in the software, unknown even to the Realm's residents?

"Unfortunately for you," said Langoni, "We can indeed tamper with it. Without any difficulty at all. The Costa del Número's pseudospace is designed for ease of handling, actually, to make authoring and maintenance easier for the admins.

"To make this place, all I did was select an option that lets you divide a specified place and time into multiple streams. Transferring a particular character to one of those spurs is basic admin work as well. It's a common technique for increasing the guest occupancy rate, although it might not have been used very often in a generously specified Realm like this. It's also easy to draw out the passage of time, enlarge the interior of a given area, that sort of thing."

"That's the domain of the gods to us. Completely beyond understanding."

"Really? Doesn't seem that way to me."

"So, despite your reach extending to the domain of the gods, you're AIs?"

"Yes"

"You're really not guests?"

"Correct."

"How did you learn those tricks of yours?"

After a beat, Langoni buried his chin in the collar of his pure white parka and grinned, suddenly looking like a real boy. "That's a secret," he said.

"So what did you come all the way out here for?"

"Well, that's a very, *very* long story. There's a lot we have to get done, and an overwhelming lack of time to do it."

"There's a lot I want to ask you."

"I'll bet there is.

"'What was the Grand Down?'

"'Have we been abandoned?'

"'If so, why is this Realm still running, presumably at great expense?'

"'What *are* you? If you're AIs, how is it you can tamper with the Costa del Número's systems? What are you trying to turn the TrapNet into?'

"'And what will you use the result for once it's done?'

"But José, there's no point trying to drag this out any longer. It won't work. I know that you want to get back to the main stream, but please accept that that won't happen.

"I didn't really bring you here because I wanted a discussion, you know. I had other reasons for plucking you out. I suppose you might call it a kind of talent scouting.

"But in return, I'll show you something amazing.

"Watch closely, and make sure you remember it."

José felt a shock in his new eyes, and information began to pour in from them again.

A whale was swimming languorously through a fireworks display in the sky.

That was José's first impression of what he saw.

It was night.

Night somewhere else.

The constellations were different. Which Realm it was, José did not know.

The eyes implanted in José were floating in midair, surprisingly high up.

Below him countless points of light spread out in a dazzling, galaxy-like spiral. It was a vast city.

He couldn't get a sense of the distance, but it was dozens of times larger at least than the Realm of Summer, with thousands of times more people.

José had not even realized that there could be a Realm like this. He found the idea overwhelming. The system resources that would be needed were unimaginable.

As he watched, tiny flying machines rose from the town, whizzing past José's "eyes" at incredible speeds and continuing upward into the night. José's "eyes" followed them up.

And saw what lay beyond them.

Far above his head, silhouetted against the moon, was a whale swimming in the night sky.

It was like an airship, but much larger. Its exact size was hard to grasp, but it had to be at least a kilometer long. From below, José could see only the whale's belly, which shone silver in the light from the town below. He could not say whether it was the silver of a fish, or of metal or some other material.

There was no way it could be a whale, of course. José wasn't even sure whether it was alive or not. But it certainly looked and moved like a whale. It was graceful and gigantic, and somehow gave the impression of wisdom. Its body undulated as it swam through the night sky. Thinking of it as a whale was probably the most correct approach. He sensed intent along those lines. It was intended to look like a whale, or perhaps to *be* like a whale. That was why it looked the way it did. But what was it really? José wished he could get a closer look.

The flying machines from the city maintained their ascent toward the whale. They were shaped like spinning tops, revolving rapidly while an engine quietly droned within, and the color of burnished copper pots. Their top sections were fixed, and José could see people (whether guests or AIs was not clear) leaning out of open hatches on some, wearing classic flying caps and red or white scarves that streamed in the wind.

There was a low boom, and a small explosion of flame appeared on one side of the whale's abdomen. It was small by comparison with the whale, but much larger than any of the flying machines. More booms followed and explosions appeared across the whale's surface. From the flames that blossomed in the sky away from the whale as well, José deduced that it was under attack by the flying machines. The vivid colors of the flames were dreamily beautiful: red, green, marine blue. This was clearly a fierce battle, but José felt a sense of separation from it; it looked like a fantasy, slightly out of alignment with reality. Like something out of a storybook.

As José watched, an airship emerged from the moonlight-pearly clouds. The airship looked to be from the same technological background as the tops, only bigger. It was not a zeppelin filled with gas, but a literal airship, complete with keel. It was fat and rounded, and, naturally, coppery in color. Comblike structures extended from its gunwales, making it look like a flying galley. Looking closely, José saw that the combs' teeth were spinning at high speed. Was there a Realm with the technology to create lift with rotation like that?

The battle between the whale and the galley was about to go on. José wished he could go higher, but his viewpoint remained fixed. Presumably this was more like a recording than a view on live events.

The flying machines fired on the whale with a sound like swarming bees, releasing flaming projectiles from their spinning sections. These burst when they were close to the whale, releasing gouts of flame. What kind of mechanism could fire these from a rotating surface? José found himself fascinated by the somewhat irrational, arbitrary scene playing out before him.

The whale increased the intensity of its undulation to give its body a strong flick.

And what happened next? Like seeds blown off a dandelion, a cloud of minuscule (human-sized?), light objects were shaken from the surface of the whale. They looked like snowflakes. Each had the same complete control of its movement as the Spiders that had rained down on the Realm of Summer that morning. And, as José watched, the snowflakes opened hostilities with the army of flying machines.

The result, however, did not even deserve the term "hostilities." The flying machines were annihilated in moments. Any top that came into contact with a snowflake either broke apart in midair or stopped spinning immediately. The depowered flying machines continued to rise at first, but gradually broke formation and, like pebbles thrown into the air, lost their upward impetus and began to fall. The men in flying caps did not even scream on the way down—were they already dead? Flames burst from some of the tops. Exploding ammunition, José surmised.

Other snowflakes attached themselves to the galley. It fell completely to pieces, collapsing like a toy castle built of blocks. Flames erupted from within its hull, tearing it apart from bow to stern. Before long the disintegrating airship was on fire as well. Even the blocks that had escaped the inferno burst into flames themselves as they fell.

Reduced to an uncountable cloud of fragments, the galley brushed past José's viewpoint as it fell.

José heard singing.

A distant song.

It was coming from the snowflakes as they drifted lightly through the air.

The song was clear and somewhat off-key, sounding like boy scouts around the campfire. José could grasp neither melody nor harmony. In fact, he was not sure whether, ultimately, it was truly a "song," but he could tell that the snowflakes shared some kind of tone with which they were attempting to harmonize.

When all the flying machines were gone, the snowflakes split up and arranged themselves like skydivers in horizontal rings. Then they slowly began to descend toward José. As the rings approached he was finally able to make out the individual snowflakes. They looked like mannequins of glass, but they were not human, or even humanoid, in form. In this respect they were like the Spiders, which did not after all take the form of spiders.

They looked like sculptures put together by an alien who had stumbled upon a cache of abandoned mannequins but had never seen a human being before.

There were some who had nothing but fluttering golden hair atop a smooth posterior and thighs. There were headless torsos with dozens of arms that moved like graceful wings sprouting from them. Some of the mannequins wore heads with ice-blue eyes as if on necklaces. All had the same glassy texture. Most of them appeared to have been coated in heavy frost or stuffed with glass fiber. There was a chilling sense of coldness about them. If he were to touch one, José thought, with no evidence, his fingers would surely freeze and break off in an instant.

Singing their "song," staying in their rings, the snowflakes descended.

José turned his gaze to the city below.

The metropolis spread like scattered jewels, tongues of flame rising here and there. These were fires started by crashed flying machines. Larger explosions eventually began to bloom, one after another, as the wreck of the galley hit the ground. José could not see it from his vantage point, but AIs were fleeing from those flames in their hundreds of thousands. (*Like us this morning.*)

Suddenly several blocks were swallowed up by a single gigantic explosion. The galley's engine room, perhaps.

And all the while the mannequins descended in their rings, glowing a faint blue. Perhaps because they were accelerating as they fell, from José's perspective the glowing rings seemed to close up into themselves until they were indistinguishable from the city lights below.

A change occurred. A black circle centered on one block of the city started to spread. It grew horizontally, remaining at street level. Its circumference glowed, but inside it was perfectly black. The city was disappearing, starting from the places the mannequins had fallen. The edges of the circles transformed everything they swept across, leaving nothing whatsoever inside as they grew. Were these circles the same as the holes the Spiders made? Or something entirely different? José felt a shiver run down his spine. He had preferred the explosions.

The glowing rings eventually overlapped, forming a single gigantic circle.

The city had been completely swallowed up.

And then, all at once, José felt a presence, overwhelming and very near.

The whale had descended to his level. It was well over five kilometers long. José felt himself go weak.

As he watched, the whale kept swimming forward.

This time what José felt was astonishment.

On the whale's back was a sprawling mining town.

Cut-down mountains. Vast open pits. Conveyor belts carrying unearthed rocks and ore. Rails. Clusters of buildings. Houses with lights in their windows.

And…

A gigantic pond, gazing at José.

No, that was no pond.

It was an eye.

One that looked exactly like a human's.

Eyelids, eyelashes.

Moist iris.

Without warning, the image feed to José's eyes was cut.

Instead, the ocean terrace came into view, the boy Langoni peering into his face.

The recording must have ended there.

José studied Langoni's face, and was surprised to find that the boy looked rather sickly.

"Did that happen in some other Realm?" asked José.

The boy pulled his chin in slightly. A nod, presumably.

"What *was* that thing?" asked José.

"An Angel," said Langoni. His voice was low, weak, and dry.

Where space and time extended to infinity, Old René the shipwright was laughing with a sound like dry leaves. He had managed to stop himself right at the brink of madness.

The chewing, crunching noises behind him were steadily growing louder. He could not summon the nerve to turn back toward it, but he had a fair idea of what was happening. The Spider had revived and was eating his companion. Soon that *hunger* would swallow him up too, he supposed. If so, he wished it would hurry up. Better to disappear quickly, in the space of a thought.

Suddenly, for some curious reason, René recalled Julie Printemps's smile. The memory was from a time when he had been unable to work after severely straining his shoulder. Endless rain had left him nothing to do for several weeks but sit gloomily in his chair and work on model ships. When was it Julie had arrived with her "Hi!"—about three o'clock? Despite the foul weather, it felt as if the sun itself had come to the door of his dingy home. He'd been surprised when she said "Look!" and showed him the piercing in her tongue, but when the deed was done, he seemed to recall, it had been as if a great burden had been lifted from him. There had been no guilt. Partly because of the morals of this Realm, and partly, he supposed, because *that was what Julie was there for…*

René's thinking soon returned, however, to the matter of the Spider.

If he was simply going to be devoured by the *hunger*, it should be over in an instant. But it felt like that noise had been coming from behind for forever. What on earth was taking the Spider so long? What was it doing?

"Arts and crafts."

René stiffened. Had he just heard that? Had someone said "Arts and crafts"? Who? He knew the voice. René was far beyond laughing now. Something unimaginable was going on behind him. Arts and crafts? What was being made, and by whom? Whose voice *was* that?

As René stared at the distant exit from the bathroom, one of the Spider's legs entered his field of vision, closing around him from behind. It was sturdy and bristly, with black and yellow stripes. René was frozen. The tip of the Spider's leg split open to reveal an array of slim manipulators with various attachments. It looked like something you might see at a dentist's office in hell. A nozzle at the end of one manipulator sprayed him with Spiderweb. Web with poor insulation. Drenched in the stuff, his chest's identity boundary became unstable. His surface turned translucent, revealing his weakly pulsing innards. He was going to be vivisected, René thought. Nothing to be done about it. He'd had a good run—a thousand years of shipbuilding. If this was how it ended, there was nothing to be done about it. He tried to make himself believe this.

"You've got it all wrong," the voice from before said. "This isn't a dissection."

Probe needles and tubes went into his head, too many to count. The voice began to sound inside his skull.

"It's arts and crafts, Grandpa René. This is my summer homework."

Then the voice laughed. He felt the programs that constituted his self coming apart in time with the laugh's spasmic rhythm. His left eyeball revolved in its socket like a light bulb being unscrewed, then popped out. His tongue lolled and retracted like a clockwork main-spring in a cartoon. If this was a joke, it was in truly grotesque taste.

Finally René realized.

The voice. The voice laughing behind his back.

It was Felix the tailor.

Joël, who had charge of the Mineral Springs Hotel's kitchen, put the well-used frying pan on the hob, then heated the oil until thin smoke began to rise from it. He never used tallow. Vegetable oil infused with herbs and garlic was more his style.

A selection of vegetables and an almost impudently large hunk of beef sat in an enamel tray on the counter, marinating in wine. He gripped the beef with stainless-steel tongs and wiped off the wine, revealing its lustrous, smoothly full surface. *Best to cook this as a simple steak*, Joël thought. Then he could cut it up so that everyone at the entrance got at least a little piping-hot meat.

In the Realm of Summer, Joël the chef also played the role of exhaustive culinary database.

He was, in fact, the symbol of all cooking in the Realm of Summer. Anyone preparing food in the Realm accessed his database, whether they knew it or not. This obviated the need for all the AIs to bear their own individual knowledge of cooking. The system's resources were limited, and a design which lightened the burden of AI activity by eliminating trivial knowledge made sense.

Of course, not everyone could cook as well as Joël could. That skill was accessible to him alone.

Still holding the steak in the tongs, Joël transferred it to the frying pan.

There was a fierce hiss. Fine droplets of oil flew into the air, sting-ing painfully as they landed on Joël's arm. The sheer vividness of the sensation made Joël wary. He might have been the first to notice the change in their senses—he was a cook, after all, and it made sense for him to notice such things. But of course he did not realize what was behind the change.

Needs a little more time, Joël thought, looking into the frying pan. Once he had cooked one side of the steak to a suitably crispy finish, the top of the steak slick with fat, he flipped it over. The meat looked delicious. It was wonderful (if only natural, if you thought about it) the way beef smelled of milk. Oil and fat, cooking and blood, and then the smell of milk. For the diner, these smells confirmed the richness of their own existence, but for meat it was the smell of death. The smell of a part that had once been alive being completely destroyed.

Such thoughts were unusual for Joël, but he found himself pursuing them anyway. Here he was, doing what was necessary to completely obliterate the last faint traces of life in the meat. He would then divide that death up and serve it to the others.

The steak was looking good now. Humming a tune, Joël flipped it over again with the tongs.

Revealing the charred face of Felix.

It was torn into the cooked surface of the steak, split here and there so that the color of raw meat showed through.

As Joël stared, the face smiled.

"Hey there, Joël," it said.

Joël was completely without the ability to respond to a situation like this. The cook could only cock his head and look into the frying pan.

"I should have known it'd be hot in here," Felix continued, still smiling. "It really is. I thought I was going to die."

Under the counter, the oven door opened from the inside. A Spider exactly the size and shape of a human hand crawled out of the oven and began to climb Joël's back.

"Cooking's a wicked trade, isn't it, Joël? Choking the breath out of things, then gussying them up to serve to others."

The Spider-hand seized the back of Joël's head. Joël felt a powerful shove from behind. The frying pan drew near.

"Now it's your turn."

Joël's intelligence no longer operated normally, but he felt his bodily senses dizzily reversed and twisted.

Now, in the frying pan, Joël's face was being pushed down, cooking in the sizzling, fragrant oil in infinitely extended space. Unbelievable agony ensued. What was pushing Joël's face down was Joël's—his own—arm. The arm was attached to his own body as well, but from the neck up, that body was taken over by Felix's face, done to a delicious-looking golden brown and still steaming. Joël realized that at some point his own face and sensations had been mapped onto the steak. He was sealed up inside the cut of beef.

Enjoying the fragrant smell of Joël that filled the kitchen, Felix took up the tune his victim been humming. He had all the time in the world.

"This isn't normal," Julie said bluntly. "If we don't do something soon, it'll be big trouble."

The three sisters looked at her sadly. Julie's own eyes were fixed on Yve in what could more accurately be called a glare. Yve's eyes were cast down, perhaps because she did not want to meet anybody else's.

The women had emerged from the Chandelier temporarily to resume their positions around the casino table.

"Do you think we have time to sit around looking sad?" demanded Julie.

The three sisters bit their lips. Why hadn't they noticed before the net had gotten so tattered and worm-eaten? They'd spent most of their time inside the Chandelier, keeping the net afloat. Controlling the sensory reactor's inflow and exhaust, maintaining overall stability, checking for broken connections and missing Eyes.

While Yve and Julie focused their senses more sharply to provide fine support at specific points, the three sisters had spread their bodily senses thin, covering the entire net to keep it running at normal temperature, so to speak. And because the sisters all had exactly the same senses, they had also been monitoring each other. They should have noticed the wormholes earlier.

"We have to tell Jules," said Julie.

Yve raised her head.

Luna was the first to notice. She cried out briefly before covering her mouth with her hand.

"What's wrong?" Donna asked. Following Luna's gaze, she glanced at Yve's eyes and cried out as well.

In the center of the beautiful, chestnut-colored iris of Yve's right eye, a tiny black hole had opened.

The men at the entrance were mopping up the Spiders left behind when their fellows scattered into the woods.

Pascal, he of the murdered elderly mother, dangled one of Catsilver's daggers from each hand as he walked, with several more tucked into his belt. He had already finished off four spiders, and he would not be satisfied until he had killed them all. Only this would satisfy his thirst for vengeance.

"I know how that feels."

Suddenly, Pascal realized that he was walking alongside Felix the tailor. He had been alone a moment ago, and had not detected the man's approach, but at some point the two had begun walking together. Still, Pascal did not pay it any mind. His thoughts were directed toward the Spiders, and then there was the fact that Felix's voice had simply slipped into his breast without resistance. Even though he had always hated Felix's piping, self-centered whining before. Felix reached into his apron pocket and pulled out a pair of scissors. The two blades were long and well sharpened—a beautiful sight. Felix gazed at them, turning them this way and that, as he continued in that irritating voice.

"Pascal," he said. "Everyone knows how much you cared for your mother."

That's right, Pascal thought. *But nobody really understands about Mother and me.* The thought filled him with grief. It occurred to him suddenly that it might be all right to talk to Felix about it. His breast was full to bursting.

The scent of the forest was powerful. They were walking in deep darkness that had risen around them, as if it were the color of that scent. Pascal breathed deeply of the smell of darkness. He felt as if his psyche were sinking deeper and deeper inside him, and wondered why. The loathing of the Spiders that had seethed through him mere moments ago had now changed its course.

Pascal came to a sudden halt. There was no one around, of course. Since the moment he'd stepped into the forest, he had been on his own.

Pascal looked at his hand. In it was a pair of scissors with long, beautiful blades.

Pascal cocked his head. What was a pair of scissors doing there? He saw his face reflected in the blades.

Then he muttered, "Ah, I see." What were they doing there? Wasn't it obvious?

He set about using the scissors to cut open his chest.

In the hotel's front yard, thirty or so men were sipping hot coffee. Bastin and Denis were among their number.

A cloud covered the moon, and darkness suddenly fell.

Bastin was thinking about his immediate goals—to survive the night and, after that, the following day. If the hotel lasted until morning, it would serve as their stronghold. Tomorrow they would have to search for some other plan of attack. Presumably some sort of guerilla action, mustering every scrap of material that remained in the Realm. A long war of attrition was coming. But for tonight it would be enough to survive.

Despite this, some of the men had pushed too far into the woods. Excited by their initial success, they had not come back. After all his warnings about not going in too deep! Pierre, Pascal... At least ten men were missing. The farther into the woods they went, the more they would be tempted to go it alone, allowing the Spiders to pick them off one by one. Their situation was the exact opposite of this. They had to be guerillas, lure the Spiders into their domain. Now was the time to keep numbers up, preserve strength. Bastin stared at the entrance to the woods, eyes narrowed and arms crossed.

Suddenly Bastin recalled Julie's crying face. The little girl who had offered him Cottontail as she sobbed. How many times had she come to their aid over the past thousand years, he and his now-departed wife and their granddaughter Agnès? And now she was in the Casino, doing her part as best she could. He had to make sure the hotel lasted the night.

The front doors opened behind him. Stella, the maid, appeared, pushing a trolley with a new pot of coffee and cups.

"A piping-hot new pot, Mr. Deputy Mayor," she said. "Everyone else has had some. Won't you take a cup too?"

"I'm still waiting on some of the men," Bastin said. "I'll be a little longer."

"They'll be back soon, I'm sure."

"I hope so."

The cloud passed. The moon emerged and the yard brightened again.

Stella cried out.

A group of men had emerged from the darkness of the forest and staggered into the bright yard. He saw Pascal among them.

Bastin grinned despite himself. "And there we are," he said. "They look fine to me."

"All's well that ends well," Stella said with a cheerful smile of her own. "And just in time for steak."

"An Angel. By which you mean…?"

The boy Langoni just shrugged. "Good question," he said. "I'd like to know myself."

He didn't seem to be dissembling. His answers were gradually getting less considered. Something else was on his mind.

"A kind of disaster, I suppose," the boy added eventually.

"'Disaster'… You mean those cold-looking dolls? They were the disaster?"

"Those, and also that mine you saw on the whale. The Realm I showed you just now was one of the larger ones in the Costa del Número, and, as I'm sure you figured out from the flying machines, its technology was fairly advanced. Just like the Realm of Summer was created as an unsophisticated, inconvenient town where people might spend a summer holiday, the theme of the Realm you just saw was one-night experiences in a more decorative city where an alternate technology developed. I would have liked to show you the city at ground level, too. It's wonderful stuff—the whole place was steeped in the same colorful, humorous design sense as a cuckoo clock. Buildings, cars, everything. It makes you want to grab a pepper shaker from a cafe to take home with you. A work of incredible invention and taste. You sensed that sort of peaceful goodwill from the design of the flying machines, right?

"But that Realm has become something quite different now."

José was frankly overwhelmed. He was speaking to a boy who had traveled through so many Realms that he could judge them, compare them with each other. A boy who knew a great deal about the essence of the Costa del Número and was busily working on something very important. On top of that, the boy was enormously powerful.

José was gripped by a strong emotion. To his surprise, it was envy.

"I can't explain what happened to the town," Langoni continued. "In a way, the whole Realm became an Angel, but I doubt you would understand it all either."

"When you say 'disaster,' what exactly do you mean?" José asked.

"A severe change that threatens us AIs and our Realms, and whose essential components are beyond our control or indeed the control of the disaster itself. That's about the size of it. The same sort of thing as the heavy weather and stormy seas that you worry about. The difference is, *this* disaster wasn't originally planned as part of the Costa."

José was silent. The boy was effectively admitting that he and his companions were helpless against the Angel. He was speaking more harshly now, without style or modulation. What was he in relation to the Angel?

"Is the Angel antagonistic to you?" he asked.

"Maybe," the boy said after a brief pause.

"Are you planning to use the TrapNet as a weapon against it?"

"Yes. Of course."

José hesitated for a moment, then plunged ahead with his next question.

"What part of the TrapNet has that kind of power?"

Langoni smiled forlornly. "I think you know already, don't you?" he said.

"The Eyes?" asked José.

Another pause. "Those too," Langoni said.

"But they aren't essential.'

Yet another pause. "No. They aren't essential."

José let out a long sigh. "If you mean what I think you mean," he said, "That won't do at all." He sagged into a desk chair, shaking his head listlessly. "Just don't."

The boy cocked his head and smiled.

"Please," said José. "Anything but *that*."

The wind blew in off the ocean and ruffled Langoni's neatly trimmed bangs. His long eyes remained fixed on José.

"Please," José said again.

"No."

José tried frantically to read Langoni's eyes. Wasn't there somewhere he could strike at the boy hard enough to shake him? An emotion, a memory… Whatever happened, he could not let the boy do *that*.

"Langoni," José said, using the boy's name for the first time.

Langoni's eyebrows raised a fraction.

"Have we met before, you and I?"

It was a bluff, but for a moment the boy's eyes opened wide.

"We'd better get started," Langoni said.

Had it failed to work? When José tried to continue using another approach,

Langoni moved forward to cover José. He placed both hands on the arms of the deck chair, looking down on the prone fisherman.

He was like a blank cut out of the night sky above, with only his eyes retaining a faint light.

"Ah! A whale earring."

José frowned, suspicious.

It was true that his earring was a whale rather than a fish. Julie had made a matched pair, kept one for herself, and given the other to him. But it didn't look anything like a whale, even on close examination. The workmanship was just too inept. That was what José liked about it.

The thing was, though, that not only did it not look like a whale, nobody else even knew it was a whale.

"Hey, José," the boy whispered into the ear José wore the earring in. "José van Dormael."

The deck chair was reclined far back, making it more of a sofa. Its canvas was greatly distended by the combined weight of José and the boy. José felt his shirt crumble like dry leaves when the boy touched it. The boy's fingers stayed on his chest, resting where his ribs met in the middle.

"A blue-winged butterfly," the boy said, mouth still at José's ear. "A stamp with a steamship on it… The silver lid of a glass bottle… The embroidery on a handkerchief—Swiss folk craft–style, I gather."

Langoni's fingers sank smoothly into José's bare chest. He moved them inside José if stirring through soft mud.

"Amazing," he said. "José, you really are a weird, twisted AI, aren't you? To push yourself this far…"

José tried to respond, but couldn't. His mouth wouldn't open; his entire body was frozen.

The boy's arm stretched deep into José's chest,

into a domain beyond the reach even of José himself.

Then the boy put his other arm in.

Without pausing, he fell forward, overlapping with José until their two chests had fused into one. There was neither pleasure nor pain. Neither elevation nor depression. The change progressed at a steady pace until the boy had vanished entirely. José was left alone, unable to move from the deck chair where he lay, illuminated by the moon. Eventually his eyes became blind to the moon.

Eventually he began to see something else.

—José.

Something that was not a voice spoke to him.

—What is it?

—Do you see it?

—Huh?

—It'll come into view soon. Do you see it now?

—Yes.

A panoply of real and sensory images from inside the hotel had come into view.

He sensed Julie's shadow in the far distance. When he tried to call to her, she suddenly disappeared. Had she emerged from the net?

—Do you know where you are?

—Yes, José replied. I'm in the TrapNet.

CHAPTER 7:

THE BACK OF THE HAND • THE TRIPLE MIRROR • THE HAIR-OBJECT

"**B**ut it's obvious!" Julie said. "We have to shut it down right now."

Jules struggled to answer as he stood at the casino table.

"How on earth did they do it?" he mumbled, then instantly became miserable at the realization that such a dull-witted thing had come from his mouth.

The net was being eaten away by opaque areas.

"Donna and the others didn't realize either, right?" Jules asked, even though he had asked the same question a few moments earlier. He had not yet caught up with what was happening.

"No, not at all," Julie said. "We don't even clearly understand that there *are* wormholes."

Which was true. They were still unable to view the wormholes directly. They were simply the best hypothesis available given the surrounding conditions. As to what might lie inside those holes, or how they might be affecting the net, they had no idea. As such, Julie's position made sense. It was entirely possible that by keeping the net active they were just widening the tears in it. And yet…

"You say 'shut it down,' Julie," said Yve, turning to face Julie directly. "But wouldn't that be just what the wormholes want?"

Exactly, thought Jules. Shutting down the net would mean abandoning all resistance. Without the TrapNet, what would stop whatever was inside the wormholes from coming at them all at once?

Yve grimaced. She looked very poorly.

"Are you all right?" asked Anna.

"My head hurts," said Yve, "and my eyes. I've never had this sort of problem before. But never mind that—this is hardly the time for it."

There was general surprise at Yve's answer. They had always thought of her as never, ever breaking her reserve, offering only the barest hints of her true opinions, but now, as if in exchange for her own suffering, she seemed determined to force the others to grit their teeth and bear it as well.

"And while we wait and see, everyone will disappear. One by one, little by little, they'll be whittled away and drop out of view."

"Like José?"

"That's right."

"I see… Yes, I can see you're worried about José. Very worried indeed. And that's why you want to shut the net down right away—to go looking for him. I understand."

Yve was completely calm.

"Yes, I understand what you're saying perfectly, Julie," she said. "I'm worried too, after all. My husband… Felix, he's disappeared too."

The group was shocked into silence.

None of them had noticed.

"The worry's been just unbearable," Yve continued. "Although it might have escaped your attention, everyone being so busy and all."

The table was dominated by awkwardness. It seemed to Jules that Yve was its master.

Yve felt as if she had crested some sort of ridge.

After you crested the ridge, the worst was over. You could breathe much easier going downhill, and that was how she felt.

Her head still hurt, and her eyes. Her left eye in particular felt as if someone were drilling it with a gimlet, so sharp and strong was the pain. Nevertheless, her mood had started to improve. She still needed the net; she absolutely had to prevent them shutting it down. If she had to play the concerned wife, remaining at her post despite her husband's disappearance, so be it. She felt like patting herself on the back for recognizing that it was a pose even as she adopted it.

"I suppose Felix wasn't very popular," she said. "But I've been looking for him all this time, in between keeping the TrapNet up and running."

Yve was surprised at how smoothly the lies came out—entertained at her own elegance. Of course she hadn't been searching for Felix. If anything, she'd been averting her eyes, maintaining the pretense of ignorance even as her heart pounded like that of a hit-and-run driver making their getaway.

"Was it the TrapNet that made my husband or José disappear? Of course not. The Spiders have gotten inside the hotel, that's all. They're up to something that the net can't detect. Would pulling out the net or the Eyes help us find the people who've gone missing? No. The net might be tattered, but will we survive if we shut it down?"

The pain in Yve's head and eyes had now entered the domain of agony. It sat inside her, pulsing like a test signal.

"Enough talking!" Julie said, rising to her feet.

"Abandoning your post, young lady?"

Old Jules spoke up for the first time.

"That's right," replied Julie.

"I don't think the net will still work without you," remarked Old Jules.

"I don't care."

Julie was not sulking or pouting. She was simply stepping out of the post she had held, as if letting a stole slip from her shoulders.

"Well," said Old Jules. "All right, then."

"You're being irresponsible," Yve said.

Julie shrugged.

"Yve," she said, "I understand how you must feel. This is the only place you have. But if that's your reason, just say so. Felix has nothing to do with it. As long as you get to keep on knitting, you're happy to sit in a tumbledown shack as the flames rise all around."

Yve didn't care what Julie said. Her head hurt, her eyes hurt, and she wanted to get back inside the Chandelier. That was where she truly belonged. And, truth be told, they could get along without Julie. Which explained her response.

"You're one to talk," she said, "Prowling around like a restless cat."

"We're not going to find anyone sitting at this table."

"So, what are you young ladies going to do?" asked Old Jules with a smile.

"That's a good question," Luna replied calmly.

At exactly that moment, a loud noise came from the front entrance. Not an explosion. Something had happened to Bastin's team again.

"I don't think the net has outlived its usefulness yet either," Donna said. "I'd better stay, I think."

"I'm sorry, everyone," said Julie.

"Would it be all right if I took her place?" Old Jules asked politely.

"By all means." Anna beamed.

"I have some experience with Eyes, you see."

"Is that so?"

"Yes. I didn't mention it since you were all fighting so magnificently, but if you need an extra pair of hands, I can help. If you don't mind, of course," he added to Julie with a wink.

"Not a bit."

"Off you go, then."

"Thank you. I'll remember this."

Old Jules smiled. "You do that," he said.

"I will, and if I ever forget it, I'll just remember it again," Julie said, smiling back. She spun away from the table, dress dancing like laundry in the wind. "Come on, Jules!"

"But—"

"No buts! I need you if I'm going to get anywhere!"

"Huh? Why?"

"Just come already," Julie said, grabbing his arm. "You still have Cottontail, right?"

"Oh, uh… Sure."

"Then let's go!"

Julie took Jules's hand and began to run. Jules stumbled after, half-pulled along.

"Good luck, Jules!" Old Jules called, waving as the two of them left the casino.

"Do you mind if I ask a question?" Anna said. "Is your name really 'Jules'?"

"What do you think, if I may ask?"

"I'm not sure." Anna giggled. "You're a funny one."

Old Jules turned to Yve. "All right" he said. "Julie's gone. Does your head still hurt?"

"Yes," replied Yve, apparently with great difficulty.

"Almost done. Let's keep at it."

Old Jules looked Yve square in the eye and confirmed that it was there.

The black pupil that had appeared like a tiny pinprick in Yve's beautiful chestnut iris.

José watched Julie and Jules leave the casino hand in hand.

Yve was humiliated. Julie had ruined everything, made a fool of her. But since this also meant she would not have to waste any more time talking, she didn't necessarily feel bad overall. Minor details, all of it.

She sat in her chair for a while as if in a daze, gazing at the Chandelier. Its flawless, brilliant light had not changed in the slightest. There was no sign whatsoever of the cankerous infestation within. Was it really a tumbledown shack surrounded by flames, this place she longed for so badly?

I don't care, she thought, enduring the pain.

She was under no obligation to carry everything on her own back. She would do what she could, just as she had been, until the net unraveled for good. She would act as if nothing had happened and do the best she could.

Yve dived into the net. She resolved not to care anymore what the three sisters or the old man thought of her. She would feign flawlessness, just like the Chandelier, and that would be enough. She would free herself from contempt. From her fat, embarrassing body and her already-departed husband.

Touching down inside the net at her usual position, Yve breathed deeply. Here, she could see. This alone made her happy. She felt omnipotent. Here, she could do anything. Here, she was monarch.

Yve opened her eyes.

She sensed a presence.

Somebody was watching.

She looked up.

A gigantic face floated far above, gazing down from on high.

Its yellowed teeth were bared in a grin.

"Felix…"

Seeing the giant face of her husband, Yve finally realized. Here was the true center of what restrained her, the slippery, cursed funnel from which she could never escape. The face was the true king, and she was a jester at best.

The tiny newborn pupil in her chestnut iris began to throb with silt-black agony, regular as the quartz in a wristwatch.

A little earlier—

A dozen-odd men emerged from the forest into the pool of light from the entrance.

Bastin grinned despite himself. "And there we are," he said. "They look fine to me."

"All's well that ends well," Stella said with a cheerful smile of her own. "And just in time for steak."

"Steak?"

"Yes, sir, Joël's cooking it right now."

"I see. That's something to look forward to."

Bastin turned to face Stella, then pressed the tip of the Catsilver dagger to her adorable button nose.

"Why?" she asked, through voluptuous lips that never lost their composure.

"White blood cells don't leave the body," he said. "Jules was very clear on that. So why are you outside the hotel? Steak sounds delicious, but not if you're the one serving."

Bastin buried the dagger in Stella's face. The sharp blade entered without difficulty. A sticky internal fluid derived from the Glue oozed from the wound, spilling down Stella's neck, over her full breasts and smooth stomach and onto the lawn. The Glue had a raw smell, like trampled summer grass.

The men gathered at the entrance rose to their feet.

"Listen up, everyone," Bastin said. "The Stella function was hijacked. There's an intruder in the TrapNet. Watch yourselves."

The contents of Stella traveled down the blade toward him. Bastin released his grip on the weapon. The Catsilver dagger was sucked inside her quickly, but then the Snowscape it had been loaded with kicked in, freezing her solid. Fire from the Father of Flame came next, exploding outward to consume her.

"Looks like the net's still operational," Bastin said. "But we can't rely on it anymore."

He issued his orders. There had always been a low but nonzero chance that the TrapNet would be hacked, and Bastin had prepared for it. The Eyes that his men wore around like amulets around their necks were purposefully not connected to the net, to protect them from infection. These stand-alone Eyes were their final weapon.

"Steak might be called off, I think."

Bastin looked behind him. The men returned.

They were oddly clustered together, moving in clumps, but apart from that there was nothing strange about the scene.

Pascal smiled and waved his hand.

That hand had become a pair of scissors.

Bastin had seen those scissors before. They were Felix's.

He did not understand exactly what this meant, but he grasped the danger he was in immediately.

Denis, however, shouted a moment earlier: "Scatter!"

The men who had emerged from the forest *rolled.*

Not individually. As a single clump of men that, after one complete rotation, organized itself into a remarkably large spheroid.

Denis could not believe his eyes.

The bodies of the men were intricately intertwined, forming something like a giant tumbleweed. It rolled right into the men resting in the yard.

There was a scream as the town photographer Henri, with whom Denis had been joking moments earlier, was caught up by the ball of bodies. He disappeared into the mass of interlocked limbs, apparently to be disassembled—Denis caught a glimpse inside the ball of countless hands working on the photographer with scissors and swords. Several others nearby were swallowed up by and added to the ball in the same way.

The ball rolled right by Bastin, giving him a chance to observe it from close quarters as he dodged.

The men that were part of it had been connected into a single body. Their limbs had been cut off, their torsos cut open; their parts had been shuffled and put back together again however they would fit. Felix's scissors for the cutting, and Spider-web for thread. Their lips had been stitched together with thick thread, rendering them mute. Their eyes had been sewn shut too. Some of their mouths had been forced open so that the tongues inside could be stitched to their lower jaws.

All of the men were living. They lived, but the pain they were in looked far worse than death. They were tangled together, pulled whichever way the aggregation went, unable to cry out or even open their eyes. They had been crucified on their own bodies.

As he stared, Bastin also heard an unusual noise. It was the sound of dozens of bones breaking combined with muffled groans of agony.

The living bodies of the men were not made to bear the weight of the ball. Its movements plunged them into excruciating pain. Pain of unusual freshness and quality…

Something began to take form in Bastin's head.

The dizzying swirl of human bodies overlapped in his mind with something else, something different but very similar…

A hand seized Bastin from behind.

He was hoisted into the air. The ball of bodies must have caught him. Now he was on his back, looking up at the sky. The naked bodies beneath him parted, creating an entrance, and Bastin was drawn inside. Hands reached toward him from all sides. They tore his identity boundary apart, forcing Spider-web into him like networking cable.

His thought processes shattered as excruciating agony burst like fireworks inside him.

The men caught up in the ball shared all their pain perfectly through sutures and Spider-web. Bastin was swallowed up into that pulsing agony, became one with it. The ball was a perfect whirlpool of pain, so strong that not the slightest free thought was permitted. The only thought the men could share was of the bottomless pain itself. How their bodies might be cut apart was irrelevant. Where they were made no difference to the pain.

And beneath the pain pulsed a single urge.

An urge to dilute the agony by taking in others who did not share it.

An urge like a thirst.

But just as a castaway who breaks down and drinks seawater makes things worse for himself, adding others to the ball only created more suffering.

Bastin's amputated arms moved independently, reaching from the ball toward the men yet to be caught up in it. One hand caught Denis by the shoulder and dragged him in.

This snowballing aggregate of pain was something never before seen, and therefore the purest such aggregate in the world. Once it had absorbed all the men, it smashed into the hotel entrance.

The hotel shook with the impact. A thousand bones shattered, and a silent scream rose from the men.

Such cruelty…

José was rigid with frustration at being unable to help. Watching and feeling—was that all he could do?

The three sisters were unable to watch any longer.

Such cruelty.

None of them dared focus their senses directly on the sphere. Its pain would pollute the entire network. Even absent this threat, however, they would have kept their distance out of fear and loathing alone.

There was nothing that they could do.

They were defeated.

Old Jules was a kindly presence beside them, like a warm, gentle arm around the shoulders. There was something in that feeling that the triplets knew well.

Anna realized it first. She turned to stare at the man who called himself Jules, so surprised that she forgot to be afraid.

"Jules…? Are you…?"

Donna and Luna's eyes snapped open too, as if infected by Anna's words.

"So you finally noticed," Old Jules said with a practiced wink from his sole remaining eye.

"But why?"

"I suppose it must be hard to understand. But there's nothing more to fear. We're almost at the end."

The three sisters glanced at the scene at the hotel entrance.

Slamming into the door had deformed the ball of bodies to a surprising extent. It had collapsed almost completely.

"That ball came out of a sealed-off sector, made to be invisible from the net. And it's not alone. Blind spots were made all over the net—wormholes, you call them—and they're starting to rupture. The sickness that was brewing inside them is about to spill out. You'll see far worse than Spiders before long."

The mass of bodies continued to mutate as it sought purchase on the outside of the hotel. Perhaps it would be most accurate to call it a hand modeled on the vein structure of a leaf—a single palm branching into hundreds of fingers that now gripped the face of the hotel. Tearing off its nails, shedding skin, it crept across the façade like a vine the color of flesh (actually, a patchwork of different flesh tones). The faces of the men, eyes and mouths sewn shut, covered the back of the hand.

"You aren't feeling guilty about your role as an experimental apparatus for the Spider-web, are you?" asked Old Jules.

"No, not especially," said one of the three. It mattered little which. Essentially speaking, they had souls—identity cores—of the same quality.

The role played by the three sisters and their family in the Realm had been error recovery for identity cores. This function belonged to the family as a whole, including its aromatherapy business.

The sisters' mother and younger brother had been an essential part of the function. Now that those two were lost, the function did not operate as it had, but the central part of it remained within the sisters. Using this functionality to test the safety of the web had been one of Jules's brilliant ideas. The three of them would hold hands, just as they did when healing the AIs' souls, and probe a sample of Spider-web to check if it contained any elements that were potentially harmful to the TrapNet. The identical triplets would examine the specimen from three directions, and then their results would be compared.

"Let me tell you one thing," Old Jules said. "The testing didn't fail. The web wasn't the weak point in Jules's plan. His error was underestimating the power behind the Spiders. He didn't expect whatever it was to have direct, real-time access to Realm authoring and generation. Although I suppose if he had, there wouldn't be any TrapNet in the first place. There'd be no point in trying to go toe-to-toe against power like that.

"By the way, it might be a good idea to cut the entrance off from the rest of the net right about now."

The fingers of the hand-vine climbing the hotel walls divided and divided again, narrowing and lengthening as they spread. Glittering eyes from the men in the yard bulged from the fingers here and there like nuts.

"Remind you of anything?" said Old Jules, sounding bitter. "That hand's a parody of the TrapNet itself. All right, time to prune the net. If they take control of even its edges, the backwash of pain will be incredible. And that'd be the end. We have to buy a little more time."

"For what?"

"Three things. First, to save Yve. We can't leave her like this."

"If you say so."

All at once, the vines on the outside of the hotel were cut from the net. The front yard disappeared from the sensory reactor. The area they most wanted to monitor was now out of their sight.

Donna sighed. "Things would be different if we had Driftglass," she said.

"No point bringing that up here and now."

"So, 'Jules,'" said Anna, sarcastic emphasis on the name. "What are the other two reasons?"

"The next one is more important," said Old Jules. He jabbed a thumb toward the roof, and said, "We have to keep this hotel together just a bit longer for Jules and Julie."

"I suppose so. And the last reason?"

"Mmm," Old Jules said, looking around the sensory engine. "For mischief's sake. Let's tweak their noses a bit."

Mesmerized by Julie's hair as she ran ahead of him, Jules tripped. He had caught his foot on the carpet in the guest floor corridor as it rippled in disarray. Cottontail fell from his hand and started to roll back down the slanted floor.

"Look out!"

Julie scooped Cottontail up. "This isn't the time to zone out!" she said. The sound of plaster cracking and wooden doorframes was gradually closing in on them from behind.

Jules got to his feet and looked past Julie down the corridor. It was lined with doors on both sides leading to guest rooms. At the far end, where the noise was coming from, the lights were out. He could not see into the dark. Walls, ceiling, and floor were all severely warped. The hotel's destruction was in process.

A powerful vibration hit them and the floor rippled woozily again. The sound from the depths came closer. The lights on the ceiling were going out, one by one, as it advanced. Whatever it was, it was destroying the corridor as it came. The floor slipped, its backward slope deepening.

"Come on." Julie handed Cottontail to Jules.

"Why are you making me carry this?"

"Figure it out, genius," Julie said, and set off at a run.

"What good will it do us if I'm the one carrying it?"

"I said figure it out!"

Jules flushed with embarrassment.

"The disadvantages of you holding it outweigh the benefits," he said, following Julie up the sloping corridor. He was almost out of breath.

"Go on," Julie said.

"Oh! I get it. Too much of the TrapNet got into you."

"Right."

"And you don't want it to get into Cottontail too."

"Right. That's why I've been making people carry it for me. Come on, that thing's gaining on us."

Suddenly the door two rooms ahead burst into the corridor.

Julie was peppered with fragments of wood—

—No, she was all right. The fragments lost their momentum and fell to the floor. Somehow, Cottontail had reached out to protect her.

Their pursuer had done an end run around them.

They watched as a fusion of Spider and AI forced its way through the hole that yawned where the door to a guest room had stood. Legs striped yellow and black stabbed into the floor ahead of them, blocking the way like the bars of a cage.

The chimera was covered in plaster dust. It had punched its way through the rooms to get ahead of them, instead of using the corridor.

And then its rear portion caught up with them from behind. They were surrounded.

"I told you José wouldn't have come up to this floor," Jules muttered. "It's too high." He had argued the point several times already.

Julie ignored him. "Could you maybe let us go?" she asked.

She was speaking to René's face, which was just one of many scattered over the Spider's head where its eyes would normally be.

René didn't answer. He didn't even appear to be conscious.

"No good?" Julie's shoulders fell. "Did René forget about me?" She was crying now. "That hurts. Dammit! Why would he not remember me? Why?"

You're empathizing too much, Jules wanted to say. But he knew she couldn't help it. This empathy, strong enough sometimes to make her lay down body and soul, was Julie's whole reason for existence.

That fish-shaped earring in her ear. José, Jules knew, had the other half of the pair.

Julie rubbed her eyes with her knuckles, erasing all trace of her tears.

"I'll avenge you," she said to René. "I promise."

The Spider's head rotated like a tank's gun turret. There was a series of short, squeaking whirs like lenses being focused. Then the attack began.

The short bristles covering the Spider's head split apart, and a pair of lips appeared.

They were the lips of a woman, glossy and crimson. White teeth gleamed evenly between them. Entrancing in a way, but almost six feet long. A component from some AI the Spider had absorbed? No, not quite. Jules and Julie realized almost simultaneously that the lips belonged to the Femme Fatale.

They puckered as if about to blow out birthday candles.

Then, all at once, they were engulfed in flames. The Father of Flame at work.

Immediately, Cottontail raised a windless wind that forced the fiery breath away from them. By the time the flames died down, however, the corridor was badly burnt.

The lips smirked. Jules and Julie caught a glimpse of a lascivious-looking tongue behind the teeth before the lips puckered again.

This time the fierce winds of Snowscape blew out. Even with Cottontail's protection, the chill was so severe that they felt as if their eyelashes were crackling as they froze.

The lips smiled again. The mutant Spider had meant this as a demonstration. *The power of the TrapNet and the Eyes belongs to us now.*

"And?" Julie asked the Spider. "What's next? Daggers, maybe?"

"Thanks for the assist, by the way," added Jules.

A beam extended from Cottontail in his hand, drawing a circle around them on the floor. Outside the circle of protection Cottontail had provided, the floor was ruined from fire and ice. Now Cottontail was using a ring of heat on that already-weakened circumference.

"See you," said Julie.

"Bye," added Jules.

The two of them waved to the Spider surrounding them with vaguely goofy grins. Then the circle of floor they were standing on fell through to the floor below.

Julie and Jules dashing out of the casino; Julie and Jules holding hands and climbing the grand staircase to the second floor; Julie and Jules chased down by the mutant Spider, then escaping—there was one perspective which followed the whole thing as witness, and that was José's.

Watching them fall through the hole Cottontail had cut in the floor, José wondered what they were doing. Looking for him, probably. But wherever they might run to, Langoni had them under surveillance. José was seized by the weariness of despair. *That's enough,* he wanted to tell Julie. *You don't have to look for me anymore. Langoni already has you in his clutches. He's just toying with you. When it suits him, he'll crush you and be done with it. I don't want to see that.*

José was intensely aware of Langoni's existence. The boy was right alongside him, but he had no presence at all. His thoughts and emotions, he knew, were an open book to the kid.

How can I get the jump on you? he thought, burning with the desire to get in Langoni's way.

He heard a faintly smiling voice at his ear.

It's no good. You can "shout" as loud as you want, but it won't hurt my ears. They are concerning, aren't they, those two? Never fear, though, José—the girl will get her wish. She'll find you even if I have to signpost the way for her.

Cheerful laughter.

That was when it happened.

Jules and Julie abruptly vanished from José's field of view.

For a moment, José tamped his emotions down completely and listened for the presence of the boy behind him. Langoni seemed to be watching for José's reaction too. Which confirmed that he had lost sight of Jules and Julie as well.

What on earth had happened?

Julie's mischievous grin came to José's mind. He tried not to think of anything else.

Yve was roaming through the TrapNet, enduring her agony.

No, not roaming—fleeing.

How many times had she jumped now?

She moved desperately, trying to flee the face of her husband that looked down from above. She made decoy jump after decoy jump to throw him off the trail. She emerged from the Chandelier, went back in, wandered every level of the net.

But he was inescapable.

She fled into the guest room put aside for mothers with small children. One of the mothers met her eyes. Then, as she watched, the mother's face transformed into Felix's, complete with habitual sneer. The child in the woman's arms looked up at its mother's transformation curiously. Then the mother began to gnaw at her child's head. Yve understood at once that the mother's AI had been preserved under the mask. Felix's mouth, now stained bright red, continued to grin—but from his eyes, piercing the mask, the tears of the mother flowed.

Yve bolted from the room.

She did not know where she was. Even whether she was inside or outside the net was unclear.

I left him to die.

She had left her husband to die. She had reacted to his disappearance with relief and joy at the prospect of devoting herself entirely to the net.

Her husband's face appeared like a ghost everywhere she looked, but she could not look him in the eye. The moment he came into view, she averted her gaze. Then he would appear again, and she would look away again. She repeated the cycle over and over as she ran. Her eyes were balls of pure pain like two white-hot coals.

It hurts.

My eyes.

Somebody help me.

Somebody ease this pain.

José's mood was dark as he watched this.

How could someone as bright as Yve be fooled by such an obvious trick?

Felix was hiding in her eyes. Unable to see her own face, she would never realize that Langoni's apparatus of destruction sat within it in the guise of her pupils. That apparatus of destruction consisted of a Langoni child system fused with Felix's image, and it was being scattered throughout the net via Yve's gaze.

It was not that Felix appeared wherever she looked. The Felix-Langoni infection was spread by the act of looking itself. The more skillfully Yve fled, the more far-flung and obscure the places she jumped to, the more Felix would cover the net.

Like minutely dispersed cancer cells, Felix—as an agent of Langoni—commenced operation in various parts of the net, each infection cultivating wormholes before tearing its way out.

The seeds had first been sown long ago, and repeated many times since then.

The TrapNet had been a suicide device from the start.

The three sisters were moving independently. They remained in communication with each other as they searched the TrapNet.

They were looking for Yve.

They had turned their identity thresholds down dangerously low, to levels where a normal AI would risk self-collapse. This heightened their interpenetration with the net. They would extend their bodily sensation to cover every last bit of the net, identify Yve, and then secure her form.

She posed the most danger at this point. They had to secure her at once, even if it meant putting protection for Jules and Julie on the back burner. Yve had to be captured and neutralized.

The disturbance in the net was so severe that the net itself was almost impossible to handle.

The enemy had Femme Fatale and Stella now, and destroyers dressed in their skins were fanning out. Countless locations had been forcibly branched in the same way as the ocean terrace. The boy and the dandy, both calling themselves Langoni, had been confirmed in multiple records. They seemed to have control of the Spiders, and if the records they appeared in were true, they had transcendent, system administrator–class power in their own right.

And now Yve was wandering through the net scattering Felix's image as she went. The three sisters followed her trail, but the dummy jumps and repeated surfacing and reimmersion made her difficult to trace. The only explanation for her movements was panic. The sisters had no choice but to split up and continue their search.

Luna, the youngest sister, followed Yve's trail into the lobby. She substantiated, but left her identity boundary threshold low for greater sensitivity. Catching sight of her vague outline in a mirror, she realized that she looked just like a ghost.

Following the corridor toward the dining room, she passed the array of framed photographs on the walls.

She was embarrassed at the sight of herself in a white skirt holding a tennis racquet.

Looking down, she saw that Felix's face had become a carpet pattern that was reproduced as she watched. It was still in its early stages.

She sighed irritably, called on the power of the net, and overwrote Felix with the original pattern still preserved in the net's history. Yve must have been here quite recently. *I hope I've just about caught up to her*, Luna thought.

Passing the Clement family portraits, Luna felt the same solemnity as most of the other AIs.

It was like seeing a photograph of a deceased grandmother. For the women of the Realm of Summer (and the men, too), the Clement women were a constant presence deep in the soul. Their unflagging dignity and piercing gaze seemed to reassure the AIs that their existence was meaningful and just.

Luna's eyes happened to come to rest on the brooch at Régine Clement's breast. The design of the cameo was not the usual one. It had been replaced.

Felix again?

No. It wasn't Felix. But it was a man.

Who could it be?

Donna, the middle sister, followed Yve's trail into the lobby. She substantiated, but left her identity boundary threshold low for greater sensitivity. Catching sight of her vague outline in a mirror, she realized that she looked just like a ghost.

The lobby was quiet. Apart from Donna, it was deserted.

Following the corridor toward the dining room, she passed the array of framed photographs on the walls. Perhaps that white skirt *had* been too short after all.

Passing the Clement family portraits, Donna felt the same solemnity as most of the other AIs.

Donna's eyes happened to come to rest on the brooch at Régine Clement's breast. The design of the cameo was not the usual one. It had been replaced.

Who could it be?

Anna, the oldest sister, leaned close to the framed photograph, pushing her glasses up her nose to examine it carefully. That profile in the cameo—whoever could it be?

José wanted to shout a warning. The lobby had been branched, just like the ocean terrace. There were three lobbies now, and Langoni had used Yve's presence as a lure to trick each of the sisters into a different one. Now they would be disposed of, just as José had been, and the TrapNet would fall entirely into Langoni's hands.

"Who on earth can this be?" muttered Anna.

"It's me, Granny."

She smelled cigarettes.

An elegant man with a blue five o'clock shadow was beside her, grinning. "Look," he said. "See?" He turned his head away from her.

Anna studied Langoni's profile carefully, then shook her head. "No," she said. "It can't be you. You don't look anything like him."

Langoni was taken aback by her response. "Well, then," he said at length. "Hard to come back from that one."

"I'm not your grandmother, either."

Another pause. "True enough," said Langoni. "But come on, take one more look. That's definitely my profile up there, wouldn't you say, Anna?"

"'Anna'? But I'm Luna."

Langoni fell silent.

"And you?" asked the woman.

The smile vanished from Langoni's face. This wasn't how things were supposed to go. She was leading instead of him.

"What made you think I was Anna?" the woman pressed on. "Are you absolutely sure it was Anna you led into this branch?"

Langoni was shocked, but quickly recovered. He was, in fact, quite sure that he had led Anna in here. There was no question about the accuracy of the operation. Was her claim to be Donna a bluff?

"Listen to me, Langoni," the woman said.

Why did she know his name? *This is bad*, his intuition screamed, but he remained silent. Was this happening in the other two branches as well? Were the other two of him having the same conversation?

"Are you familiar with the Eye called the Three-Way Mirror?" asked the woman. She opened her hand, revealing an Eye in her palm.

Langoni remained silent.

"Who are the 'three sisters'? Did you think there were really three of us?"

Langoni remained silent.

"All three of us, actually existing AIs? Is that what you thought?"

Langoni remained silent.

"How confident are you that you really forked the stream?"

The woman raised the Eye to eye level. An illusory Langoni appeared on either side of him. Was this what the Three-Way Mirror did? The illusory Langonis turned, one putting its hand on its hip, the other to its chin, and observed his consternation with amusement.

Langoni turned his left hand into a long blade like half a pair of scissors. Then he thrust it toward the woman before him in an attempt at a direct attack.

That was when he realized that he had made a critical mistake. He felt himself being scanned. Someone had reached into him and was rummaging around. This woman, he remembered, was an expert at feeling inside other AIs like this. He had let down his guard at his identity boundary momentarily to attack, and she had seized the opportunity to scan him.

At the last minute, Langoni changed the course of the blade and brought it back to slit his own throat. Bright blue blood sprayed out, covering his escape.

The three corridors became one.

The branches had been merged again.

In the corridor stood the three sisters.

"Never underestimate the power of winging it, eh?" said Donna with a shrug. The Three-Way Mirror was a common and entirely unremarkable type of Eye. It could project mirror images of other AIs, even animate those images independently, but that was all.

"Calling him by his name was a good move. I think that was key."

"Just like…Jules told us."

The three of them compared the results of their individual scans. The three-dimensional information Langoni had about Yve's location was restored. They went straight there.

The women of the Clement household remained proudly in their frames long after their spiritual descendants had left.

The wheezing had faded from Yve's breast. Her breaths were dying ones now, growing weaker by the minute. Soon it was no longer clear from looking at her if she was breathing at all.

Around her stood the three sisters.

They had found Yve in this state upon their arrival.

She lay on her back, motionless. The rich sensations that had once filled her body were gone.

But her thoughts and feelings were not dead yet.

They were leaking out of her, detectable even to the three sisters.

Yve stared upward with unblinking eyes. Her eyeballs had been swallowed up entirely by the pupils, like black globes shoved in between her eyelids. Thin threads sprouted from them. Too many threads to count. The parasite was fleeing its dead host, but this lightly wafting thread was unwilling to give her up yet, and so it branched, creeping across her soft, large breasts, her deep navel, her surprisingly small ears and her meaty limbs, opening holes in her white skin to bury its black tips inside.

"Is that…" Donna trailed off.

"Felix's hair? I think so," replied Anna.

Its color was wrong, but it had the texture of corn silk.

They were in the Mineral Springs Hotel's sewing room. Located in a corner of the dry cleaning station, it was where the guests' clothing and shoes were brought to be mended. Felix and Yve had met working there together.

Yve's thoughts continued to leak.

I just wish it'd leave me alone.

My husband's obsession, entangling me.

It's irritating, loathsome.

Yes, I feel bad for Felix. Yes, it was all my fault. But what else could I do? Everything changed on the day he handed me that first Eye. It gave me virtual eyes of my own. I was stunned. It was very nearly love. I can hear Felix now, making the same old complaint. "Oh, so you love the Eyes more than me?" Yes. Yes, I do. For a thousand and fifty years, ultimately I have lived within my own senses. The Eyes were my only companions in life, such as it was. It was the Eyes that made up for what I lacked. The scenes I glimpsed through that window were wider than all other sensations combined.

When I saw my husband for the first time that day, even I was surprised at how little I felt.

I could not even muster hate for him, let alone love.

And then I understood at last. I had been living in a world of my own all along, and would probably continue to do so, being unable to live any other way. My husband had been a sensory accessory and nothing more. A means of checking my own sensations. That cold recognition that I could not justify no matter which angle I viewed it from was me. Scared of myself at that moment, I gasped. Felix noticed, and I am sure he misinterpreted it. The inferiority complex and the arrogance he used to hide it were what defined him. It is within that gap that he preserves a pure kindness. Pure, and very fragile. And so I understood at once how he had misinterpreted my gasp. But his error was, if anything, convenient for me. It would raise an impassable wall between us, I thought, and those calculations were correct. My husband's hate made me freer than ever. He had never been more than a distorted hand mirror for grasping the outline of my own sensations clearly. Where once I had used sexual excitement to obtain those reflections, I now had simply to use hate instead.

And the sensual delight I lost I could replace with the Eyes.

I was a slave to them.

I cannot justify it. I accept that it was wrong. That is why I accept my husband's criticisms without argument. If I appeared elegant or tolerant, it was for that reason alone.

And now we see the result.

The time has come to settle all the accounts I put on hold the day I discovered the Eyes.

My husband once acted as my outline, and now his hate seeks to breach my boundary as a kind of web. I have long since ceased to feel anything, any connection to him, but his devotion and disgust have become this loathsome thread that seeks to wind itself around my internal routines and organs. Properly, this time.

So that we might never be parted again.

Why Felix's lingering regret should look so much like hair I do not know. The work of whoever stands behind the Spiders, I assume. They dissected him, transformed his clingy personality into this sticky thread. Whether he still felt some devotion to me, or whether they used a remnant of something similar for purposes of their own, I do not know.

He is trying to subdivide himself enough inside me to possess me completely. To occupy my senses—my all, my treasure—properly this time,

and make of me what he wishes. He will unleash violent storms of sensa-
tion within me in an attempt to force my submission. Or perhaps he will
steal my sensation to taste the sensory joy I have cultivated. That, I think,
is what he sold his soul for.

　The very person I always used to settle my boundaries
　will rob me of those boundaries altogether...

　The three sisters turned their faces away. Presumably due to the
invasion of the threads, most of what Yve was thinking had leaked to
the outside where the thoughts could be picked up easily. Ideas that
had been safely tucked away inside her oozed out like a slowly spreading pool of wastewater at their feet.

　Felix's black hair moved as if to devour entirely the delicious flesh
of her white body.

　Donna was put in mind of a plate of food with masses of hair
stirred in. The hairs would curl in complex filigrees around stewed
meat and vegetable fiber, catching on the inside of the mouth, on the
tongue, on the teeth. The same sort of thing, she believed, was happening inside Yve.

　Anna thought that Yve was being consumed.

　She could no longer move of her own accord, but the surface of
her body still squirmed here and there. She must already be liquefied
under the skin. At that moment, her body began to deform, no longer
able to resist the tension of the hair. Her limbs were drawn in, her
back bent grotesquely. She became rounder and rounder.

　Luna, for some reason, thought of an eyeball. The round, white,
female body was glossy and slick with sweat, and the black net of hair
looked like the pattern of veins on the white of an eye. But this eyeball
seemed to have lost all will to see. It was an eye for looking inward,
Luna thought. Felix must have had some unobjectionable qualities
too, but this hair-object had been made by extracting only his black

obsessions and seemed solely focused on putting down roots in Yve. She, for her part, had never had any interest in anything other than sharpening, forging and enriching her own sensations.

"That's enough, I think," said one of the sisters. Felix's attention was now devoted to his final prey. It seemed unlikely that the infection would repeat its explosive spread. In a way, Yve had sacrificed herself at the last to stop him in his tracks.

"Let's go."

"You're right. We still have work to do."

They left the room and headed for the Chandelier, where Old Jules was waiting.

José followed suit.

The air was oppressive and smelled of mold.

It was dark.

The only sound Jules could hear was Julie's attempt to breathe silently beside him. No—that wasn't a sound. It was the sense that air was slowly moving, being alternately drawn together and released.

After thinking for the tenth time that he could no longer bear it, Jules finally spoke.

I think it's gone, he said, quieter than a whisper, with the movement of his lips alone.

I think so too, Julie replied in the same way. Just the movement of her lips in the darkness, but her meaning came through all the same.

The two of them rose to their feet.

After descending (falling) to the second floor of the hotel, the two of them had gone sideways, leaping into a handy guest room. Expanding Cottontail's field into a sphere, they had pasted the darkness and moldy smell of the room onto its surface, hidden inside, and hoped for the best.

Now they removed that sensory barrier.

They couldn't see the moon from the window, but they knew it was out from the brightness of the night sky.

Where are we?

Beats me, but it feels like a pretty big room.

Jules extended his senses beyond the reach of the light.

This didn't let him see any farther than before. He simply let the basis of his senses radiate outward and then interpreted what was reflected back to him, like a bat using its sonar. This was something he could do on his own, of course; he was using Cottontail's powers. It felt like an elaboration of the Sound made by the Singing Sands. It was also how they were speaking without making any actual sound.

The room, he learned, was very large. Surely much larger than even the largest suite at the hotel.

It was also fully furnished.

Jules's sensory sonar picked up not just the size, shape, and location of the furnishings, but also their texture and color, as if he were holding them in his hands.

Fireplace, sofa, table, display shelf. The wall was hung with paintings, the floor was carpeted, and there were lampstands and candlesticks here and there. All of the finest quality, but old.

This was no guest room. In furnishings it was partway between a lobby and a reception room, but it did not give the impression of being "in use" in the normal sense.

Oh, right!

Jules and Julie both realized where they were at the same time. This was the Clement Memorial Room, re-creating one of the rooms in the old mansion. The mansion itself, once one of the grandest in town, no longer existed (and had not since the Realm of Summer opened for business).

They crawled out from under the sofa. It was big enough for two adults to lie on together. They sat on it side by side. Jules put Cottontail on his lap and they both peered into it.

Its beauty was phantasmagorical in the dimly lit room. Instead of its fuzz of light or usual creamy white color, it looked like a meticulous scaled-up model of a cell done in glass and resin. Inside the translucent ovoid floated a still more transparent core with various tiny components alongside it. An intricate network of patterns was wrapped around the core.

Jules recognized the patterns at once.

Inside Cottontail, the TrapNet had been preserved intact.

Julie had been up to her mischief again.

She had touched Cottontail to the Chandelier just as they had "lit the wick," so to speak, of the TrapNet after Yve booted up the program in the lace. Cottontail had promptly downloaded the net's structure into itself. Not every detail, of course; the net was too gigantic for that. But the framework had been preserved, and the rudiments of its functionality were in place. Now that the actual net was a ragged wasteland, this copy was all that remained of the marrow of Jules's idea.

The two of them had been using it to guide them, a feat that was possible because it also, of course, contained the structure of the hotel.

Do you think we'll find him this way?

No idea.

They called out with the thinly spreading sensory sonar.

It was José they were looking for. They held their breath and waited for the echo to return.

In that moment, Jules wished they could stay this way forever. Just the two of them in the darkness, sitting together, thinking identically. Time stretched and slowed.

No reply came back to them.

Still silent, the two of them sent the weak sonar signal out again and again. Jules was reminded of a moonlit night spent tossing stones into a pond.

There was no reply.

The two of them were pressed close to see into Cottontail together. Jules's expanded senses caught the lithe silhouette and firm texture of Julie's body clearly. It seemed like years since they had come together on the Singing Sands.

The wet warmth of her kiss.

All at once he felt it vividly.

He touched his own lips without realizing it.

And then the sensation came over him again.

Not just on his lips

but something like a warm breeze

that passed through his entire body

boiling, simmering

sweet, salty

a sensation that made him shiver with anticipation for something that seemed about to happen.

His heart pounded erratically.

Jules raised his eyes.

Julie was gazing at him too.

They realized it together.

They had both felt that kiss just now.

But it had not been the kiss in their memories.

Not *their* kiss.

Nor had it been a premonition of the future.

It was a kiss two people had exchanged here long ago.

Is somebody…here?

Yes.

The room was not unoccupied.

The air was rich with the sensory traces of somebody from before, like the lingering smell of incense. These sensations had come to them on the echo of the sonar, pressing against them in the dark.

Loaded with the sensual world of a stranger, Jules felt his temperature rise. Julie's face beside his was blushing hotly too.

He realized that his bottom lip was caught between hers.

The feel of her tongue, her piercing.

No.

No.

That wasn't all.

Right then he was kissing

a different woman.

Clouds flowed.

They covered the moon.

Darkness fell even more deeply, enfolding the two like bunting in black.

CHAPTER 8:

THE CHRONICLE • LIQUID GLASS • THE KEYSTONE

The Mineral Springs Hotel was the finest resort hotel in the area. It also had the longest history.

By the time the Realm of Summer opened for business, it had been in operation for 170 years.

Fifty years before *that*, a geologist had come to the quiet fishing village that was all that had been in the area then.

Like most geologists at that time, he was an amateur scholar who lived off the holdings of his wealthy family. Having taken ill while studying at a university in the city, and generally weak of nerve besides, the twenty-four-year-old was hoping that an extended stay somewhere with different scenery would help him recuperate. But as he gazed from the window of his carriage at the form of the land caught between the mountains and the sea, he was struck by a sudden hunch. His vigor restored in an instant, he ordered his driver to stop and sent his traveling companions and servants to make inquiries of the locals. After listening to each of their reports, he pronounced his judgment.

"There are hot springs to be found here," he said. "We must stop and investigate."

There was only one household in the area that could accommodate the Clements, a wealthy family who owned most of the area's mountain forest. Although she would be one of the Mineral Springs Hotel's founders fifty years later, Catherine Clement had not yet been born, and so it was her grandfather who welcomed the geologist instead. The young master of the Clement property was then in his mid-thirties.

Clement and his wife were immediately fascinated by the geologist's urbane charm and endless stock of anecdotes about the many countries he had visited. The geologist, in turn, was impressed by Clement's rude health and fearless gaze, not to mention his wife's lively wit and silvery voice, and soon opened his ailing heart to them. Thus was a devoted friendship born.

The Clements gathered additional statements from surrounding residents for the geologist, and within two weeks of his arrival, the men they had hired struck mineral springs in the east bay, as it was known even then. One of the geologist's traveling companions was a physician and chemist, and he duly declared the hot springs both potable and ideal for bathing. That evening a great feast was held, and late that night the geologist and Clement's wife were passionately united while her husband dozed.

The geologist eventually moved on to the sanatorium that had been his original destination, but soon returned to build a house of his own and lay claim to the springs. On the day of his home's completion, Clement's wife, Régine, approached him, her beauty burning brighter than ever. The baby at her breast was the child they had conceived in sin, she said, showing him his daughter's face for the first time. She had named her Nadia, and one day she would be the mother of Catherine, who would found the hotel.

Clement's wife—his widow, now—looked into the geologist's eyes. Her eyes had grown many times more beautiful since their night of sin.

"My husband is dead," she said. "An accident. His hunting rifle went off in his room."

It seemed to José that he remembered the story.

The whole turbulent history of the hotel's opening was an epic, spanning three generations and a full century. A threepenny opera for the masses.

The string of episodes was quietly baked into the Realm of Summer like a secret ingredient.

Guests who grew bored during their stay in the Realm could uncover this tale and replay any part of it they wished. Of course it was not the Realm's main story line. It was a minor attraction tucked unassumingly away in the corner of a gigantic theme park, waiting patiently to be noticed and enjoyed. Some text data; a few grainy, sepia-toned photographs. But the total volume of embedded episodes like this was considerable.

"What do you think of that, José?"

The voice rained down from above, breaking his reverie.

He realized that it had been speaking for some time. Telling him the origins of the Mineral Springs Hotel.

Then he checked his own condition.

He could see nothing. Absolutely nothing.

He had slipped out of the TrapNet, it seemed. He was lying on what felt like a hard stone bed. No—it was not level. There was a gentle slope; his head was higher than his feet. A chair reclined back as far as it would go, perhaps?

In any case, he doubted that he was still on the ocean terrace.

Where had the boy Langoni gone?

On second thought, he probably hadn't gone anywhere. He must be within José himself. José could not hear the boy or his voice just now, but he sensed him all the same.

"Well? I mean, the Mineral Springs Hotel is the accommodation symbolizing the whole Realm of Summer. There must be some meaning in its having such bloody, sensual episodes threaded into its origin story, don't you think?"

It was so dark that José's eyes were useless to him. That voice. It was all he could hear. It was so charming, so refined; it made him think of the finest maple syrup, leather gloves, a walnut desk, the amber tone of pine resin… It was the voice of a man, low but with a halolike gleam to it. Whose voice could it be?

"What do you think? Doesn't something deep in your soul resonate with that story? The Clement family chronicles might be written in a refined register, but at root they're tales of obsession. A bit like the Realm of Summer, don't you think?"

José sniffed at the cool air. He smelled water. Was there water nearby? No—actually, it seemed that his legs were immersed. It was warmer than well water, cooler than his skin. Water that had been warmed by the sun. The lapping of the waves. José tried to gather his scattered senses. Yes, he still had a very poor sense of his position, the temperature, what the sounds he was hearing were. Under normal circumstances, the nonvisual sensory information he received would be placed within the context of what he learned about his location through sight. His legs knew the water, but he would not be able to believe it until he saw it with his eyes. It was only in seeing his legs and the water together that he could identify the sensation as that of water striking his legs.

José moved his hands slowly, cupping them and scooping where he expected the water to be, then bringing it to his mouth. He tasted the faint saltiness of seawater and an abundance of mountain minerals, the thin tang of carbonic oxide. It was the mineral springs. The hotel had been built over them, drawing from them for a variety of health-related amenities. He had crawled under the hotel as a boy, finding the springs in their subterranean chamber of stone. Its ceiling was domed and unsettlingly high for an underground structure, and the sound of the water welling up echoed until it became an ear-numbing drone—not because of its volume, but because of the mysterious state of saturation it created. At this memory, José realized that this was the sound he was hearing now.

"No hard feelings, I hope, but I have your senses under control. Little Langoni's at work inside you as we speak, after all."

The voice from above was not overloud, but it was clear, sharply separated from the sound of the water around them. It seemed to use a different layer as carrier.

José's fatigue was overwhelming. After going to all that trouble to gather his senses together, he could not keep them sharp. He let them scatter again, as if spilling from his hands.

And then, high up in the darkness that filled his field of vision, he saw a faint point of light wink into existence.

It looked like a single snowflake, as if it had fallen from the sky of some other Realm where it was winter. He watched it drift toward him.

It shone very weakly, but it was bright enough for José's eyes, which had adjusted to the darkness. The pale light illuminated the stone chamber just enough for him to see that the curve of the dome was as he remembered it. As the fragment of light descended, its illumination reached the lower half of the chamber. The walls were lined with pillars carved like ancient Roman statues.

The fragment passed lightly before José's nose. He put out a finger and stopped it going any further. It was pearlescent and tiny, a thin, almost weightless thing.

He had thought it might be warm, but he felt nothing.

Perhaps, he had thought, it had a heartbeat, but it lacked this too.

It was simply a thin, fluorescent slice of some pearl-like mineral.

"Is this the Angel?" asked José, using the light to illuminate his body and learning that he had been stripped naked.

On his chest was the boy's face.

Langoni's face.

The texture was exactly the same as José's skin, so that it looked like a lump on his chest that had somehow taken the form of the boy's death mask.

He brought the light near the face's eyelids and got no reaction. Its eyes were closed. But it was breathing regularly through its nose, and did not seem to be asleep.

"That's right…"

He understood that this was a reply, but it had arrived after a noticeable delay. Was Langoni's will beginning to flag?

So this was the Angel?

"There's no need to be afraid. That fragment of light has been rendered inert."

"Inert?"

"Like a pathogenic vaccine. Made using material that peeled off the main body of the Angel during battle. It's tiny, but very precious. To make even this much inactivated vaccine takes effort you wouldn't believe."

"And I should…?"

"Give it to the face."

José wrinkled his nose. "I think not," he said.

But his fingers moved of their own accord.

Little Langoni's lips had parted slightly. The tips of his white teeth were showing. José's fingers were inserted lightly between the soft lips. The warmth of the mucus membranes and the sucking sensation inside were as innocent and defenseless as a baby. Despite himself, José felt the kind of pleasure that comes with feeding a small animal, and even some affection for the boy himself.

The boy's face slept through this, only moving its tongue to lick up the fragment of Angel. His lips closed and the chamber fell back into perfect darkness. José had taken the fragment of light into his body...

The voice began to speak again.

"The chronicles of the Clement family are the key to decoding the Realm of Summer. Three generations caught up in a majestic rolling river of a story. And here and there along the river spin whirlpools, some large, some small, none related to the main narrative. That discursiveness has a charm of its own.

"Let me give you an example. This is the story from a branch of the family far from those who lived in the mansion—a poor farmer and the young woman he has just taken as his wife.

"No sooner are they married than the woman realizes that she has a genius for embroidery. No one can compete with her—not the old women in the village, not the young women in town. Her designs are wonderful, unforgettable, and she seems to have an endless supply of them within her. Losing herself in embroidery lets her forget her tiny house with its noisy chickens. She focuses her senses so well that the little wooden hoop with fabric stretched across it becomes her whole world. She begrudges the baby the time she must spend nursing it, forgets to plow the fields, eventually turns her back on the farmer at night in bed, so intent is she on keeping the hook moving. 'But this will let us buy you new clothes, darling,' she says to her husband, cheeks flushed. She's right: her embroidery already brings in more than her husband's fields. But he knows the truth. His wife cares for nothing but the shining world she sees on the fabric. The household he thought they would build together is the barest shadow of that world to her. And so one morning the husband begins to build a small cage beside the chicken coop. He means to imprison his wife and take away her hook and thread by force. Madness has seized him. But his wife has eyes only for her embroidery hoop, and does not hear the ring of the hammer. Wife inside the house, husband outside it, both engrossed in their respective projects…

"That's how the story starts."

José had remained silent. He knew well what the voice meant to say. Just before (although, was the sense of time still meaningful?), he had submerged his full sensory powers, tracing the folds of that mental state one by one.

"Everything is like this, José.

"The Clement family chronicles contain the Realm of Summer's character molds—its prototypes for human relationships. My guess is the Realm's designers wrote the Clement saga first. Then they took the whole century's worth of stories and rearranged them across space instead of time—scattered them throughout the town in a single summer. Those days you thought were your own as you lived them over these past thousand years were nothing but weathered old stories from centuries past. Your great-grandfather's grandfather's time.

"Now, how do you suppose this episode goes?

"The man catches his wife, takes away her hook and hoop and throws her into the cage. It's very small, this cage. Too small for an adult to stretch out inside it. No standing up, no lying down. Just being in the cage is enough to make your body scream before long."

All at once, a memory began to come back to José.

It was something he should have forgotten long ago. What surfaced in memory now was not the event itself but the slant of light when it happened, the rustle of the trees. The irrelevant details around the edges.

He felt no nostalgia.

What he felt was fear.

These were memories he had apparently decided never to recall. Memories he had, in fact, never recalled even once. Fear so strong it made him nauseous.

And now they were beginning to move within him of their own accord...

"The farmer threw his young wife into the cage dressed only in her nightgown. By morning her rosy cheeks were gray and sunken, and her hair, once like waves of golden wheat, was a withered snarl of thorns... or so the chronicles say.

"Once a day, her husband gave her a bowl of oat porridge. That was all. Sometimes he would seem to remember she was there, and poke her with a stick hammered together from scraps of the timber he had used to make the cage. The villagers remonstrated with him, but he insisted that he was driving the demons out of her, and sent them away.

"As his wife's nightgown, damp with her own waste, began to rot, so too did her sanity. Without resistance or rebellion, she curled up in the filth and accustomed herself to the cage. Accustomed to its closeness, its smell, and to the way her body warped and screamed under the unnatural positions it forced upon her.

"Day by day she lay there, fidgeting in her rotting nightgown, curled up like a crayfish.

"One day her husband noticed something odd. Her teeth were disappearing. In three months, she'd lost all her front teeth, top and bottom, and her canines and molars had begun to go too. He couldn't think of what might be causing this, no matter how he racked his brains.

"Eventually he noticed a more terrible change in her.

"She was with child. He knew it from the change in her breasts.

"He was furious. There was no way the child could be his. He demanded the father's name from his wife, and she gave it to him willingly, laughing. The man she named was a vagrant who survived by begging. 'I pressed my rear to the bars of the cage so he could do it,' she said with a toothless grin. 'He was much, much better than you.'

"The husband decided to drag his wife out of the cage.

"The lock had rusted in the rain, and the key wouldn't fit. He had made the cage too strong to break easily.

"'Why not call the villagers for help?' his wife sneered. 'All I'll do is scream the child's father's name.' The husband looked her in the eye and froze. Her face was aglow with well-being. She was smiling the way her embroidery had always made her smile. Stealing that from her had been his whole reason for imprisoning her, but she had only put down broader, harder roots inside her cage.

"A whirlwind rose within him.

"He disappeared into the barn, then burst out with a hatchet and an axe. Arm spinning like a windmill's vanes, he chopped the cage to pieces, then dealt a single blow to his wife's abdomen and the 'child of sin.' Eyes clouded with her spattered blood, he saw her make an obscene gesture at him as she breathed her last.

"In his wide-open wife's toothless mouth, he saw little nubs of white protruding from the gums.

"The man drew closer to see what they were.

"Ground-down teeth.

"She had removed her teeth, somehow ground them down to little round nubs, and then put them back in their sockets.

"The husband turned slowly to look at the inside of the cage. On the inside, sturdy bars were covered densely and completely with intricate, deeply carved patterns. Embroidery patterns. His wife had pulled out her own teeth to carve these designs into her cage. Once they wore down from use, she pushed the nubs back into her gums to hide them from him. Only a few unused teeth remained in her mouth. The complex, exquisite patterns pressed in on him with unsettling force. He felt the terror of someone who has somehow stumbled into a place of worship for an alien god. His entire body was covered in gooseflesh, bumps like tiny insect bites.

"Then he realized something else: half of the cage was still uncarved.

"Her own teeth would not have been enough.

"The question of why she had intentionally fallen pregnant surfaced and connected with this new knowledge in his mind.

"He heard the wordless whisper of his brain shrinking in terror.

"The farmer was unable to follow his train of thought a step further. He was eventually found in the cage, holding his wife to his breast and staring stupefied into space. He did not move or respond to anything. They say he wouldn't even blink if you clapped your hands in front of his eyes. Wife in his arms, he survived a few days before expiring. His open, staring eyes were completely dry.

"Whether the farmer feared rightly I do not know. But the thought became a stout cage in its own right. A cage that imprisoned his mind, and was adorned with minute patterns…

"Thus ends the tale as recorded in the chronicles."

José felt cold sweat beading on his forehead. The vague terror he felt was drawing closer.

"Is Little Langoni starting to take effect?

"Well, never mind that for now.

"Listen to this, José.

"I tried eating one of your number. A man named Pierre. Simply by eating him—in the literal sense, by taking him apart and devouring him alive—I obtained all sorts of information that wouldn't be revealed in a standard analysis of an identity boundary's interior. The taste of blood, the taste of flesh, the taste of bone, the taste of organ meat. I took my time in savoring it, and this let me understand every last fold of that shadow cast on Pierre's personality.

"I felt firsthand how rich the character design is here in the Realm of Summer, even compared to other Realms in the Costa del Número. The taste was truly unpleasant.

"His meat was foul.

"The Clement chronicles had the same stench. I wanted to cover my nose sometimes as I read them. I felt as though that awful smell was seeping into my psyche like cigarette smoke gets into your hair and between your fingers.

"Abuse, confinement. The imagery was stamped on every page, clear as day.

"And you've been stamped with it too. All of you—I mean, you're dolls who were cast with the chronicles as molds, right?

"The Realm of Summer's an attraction that's meant to balance nostalgia for the humanity and style of a very low-tech era—back when the hegemony of electricity was limited to lighting and motive force and analog communications—and the sadistic urge to crush that innocence underfoot. Your characters are the perfect foils for human users. The guests come here practically giddy with anticipation, knowing that this backwater village is theirs to overrun, and that they will never be held to account for their sins."

José was thinking about something else.

What had his interlocutor been hinting at with his story?

A cage.

Suffering born of a cage.

Was that it?

Were they here to gather up AIs and Glass Eyes and Spider-web and weave them into an aggregation of pure pain?

"And who should the guests find waiting for them but you AIs, knowing you'll be treated cruelly but welcoming them all the same, wearing your frightened smiles? The guests see your fear of and dependence on them as plainly as if it were branded on your forehead. And they are comforted by the sight. The Realm of Summer: stunning scenery and unspoiled beauty fashioned into a cage for its inhabitants.

"So the guest sits down on the chair assigned to his empty role and begins to play his part as a family member. He savors the smell of the coffee his wife brings, admires the charming wildflowers in little bottles of indigo glass, is moved anew at the carefully finished spines on the books in the wooden bookcase, then turns to the 'son' smiling beside him and slowly, deliberately violates him.

"You are all those sons, and you accept this treatment, not even from obedience but simply because it is as natural to you as breathing. You grow accustomed to the pain, live with it as sustenance as you make your home in the cage. What was the decisive factor behind this character of yours?"

José heard a sound in the distance.

The crash of breaking glass, again and again. He also heard what sounded like a stone wall being destroyed.

He wanted to give that sound more of his attention. What were Jules and Julie doing? Suddenly, he became unable to hear anything but the man's voice. He had been cut off. He realized anew how utterly unfree he was in his own body.

"Am I boring you? Well, it won't be long now. You must understand clearly, José, exactly what Little Langoni is doing inside you."

Another faint light appeared in the underground chamber again.

Points of light, similar to the fragment of Angel but not quite the same, danced in the air like fireflies.

Someone familiar with the work of the Realm's developers would have recognized them as task lights—authoring tools for use in dark locations.

The task lights flew to one of the great classical statues that lined the wall, hugging its surface before finally coming to rest on its shoulders.

The statue began to walk.

With each step it took it became less like stone and more like flesh. Color rose in its face. At three meters tall, it was a giant.

Big Langoni dragged a wake behind him he waded through the central pool fed by the mineral springs. Finally he reached José, who lay by the pool on its opposite side, and came to a halt. Several of the task lights left his shoulders and descended onto José's chest and his stomach.

"Beautiful, José," said Big Langoni. "You're beautiful."

His voice, filled with admiration, had an irresistible allure and mass at such close quarters. It had body that was so well-defined it was almost palpable. It penetrated its listener, intoxicated him.

"Right now," Big Langoni continued, "Little Langoni is searching inside you for all those memories and internal injuries that even you never uncovered. I'm monitoring what he finds from out here. It's a complex, José, as delicate and subtle as Yve's lace—a beautiful mesh of thought and feeling. Inside you lies something as vast as the TrapNet, and just as fine. And, like the TrapNet, it is studded with precious stones: your long-forgotten memories. Some have fossilized, some are become pearls, but all adorn you beautifully and cruelly from within.

"Soon, Little Langoni will help you remember."

José was terrified. He understood too well about the unknown memories inside him. To confront them would be unthinkable.

He vomited with repulsion.

Big Langoni bent his gigantic body at the waist and tenderly lapped the filth from around José's mouth. His eyes, each nearly ten centimeters across, peered into José's own.

"José," he said. "Toughest of them all, most handsome of them all, sharpest thinker of them all," he said. "Loved by Julie, leader alongside Anne, popular with everyone from senior citizens to little children. What do you suppose is your role in the Realm of Summer?"

Big Langoni gave José a light kiss. The lips, teeth, tongue, and heat of the giant were overwhelming. It was like being kissed by a lion. José felt the fortifications of his self-assurance crumble. Tears ran down his face.

The giant watched with amusement as José sobbed. "Oh, dear," he said. "It's too early for that, José. Look!" He pointed at the mask of Little Langoni embedded in José's chest. "Don't you recognize this face?"

José pulled himself together somehow and looked at the boy's face. Its structure was subtly changed. Yes, he did recognize it… He stared at it again, and then understood.

The face was his own as a young boy.

A different Langoni, the Langoni who affected the mien of a Spanish gallant, took a drag on his hand-rolled cigarette as he stepped onto the ocean terrace. The heels of his flawless, gleaming shoes rapped smartly on the hard timber floorboards. The men on the terrace turned to look at Langoni with astonishment. They had not been expecting the arrival of an eccentrically attired stranger, especially not now.

"Hey there, gentlemen," said Langoni, enjoying the fearful wariness of their stares. He raised his blue-shaven chin and smiled. "I've come to finish you off."

A large woman rose swiftly to her feet. The airy lightness of the movement spoke to the power and suppleness of her muscles. The emotions of the men on the terrace all circled around her. She was the one they were counting on.

"You Anne?"

"Yeah." Anne cleaned her ear with her little finger. "And you are?"

"I'm Langoni. Boss of the Spiders."

The terrace erupted with murmuring. The fishermen, and Bernier too, surrounded Langoni with murder in their eyes. *Like trained dogs*, Langoni thought. *Let's throw them a bone, then.*

"I've taken care of the front entrance. You're next on my list."

Fear, anger, then fear again. The powerful emotions coursing through the Terrace were as pleasant as the sea breeze. But Anne alone remained calm.

"Think you can take us, do you?" she said, throwing her shoulders back with a grin.

"One way to find out," Langoni replied, rolling up his sleeves.

For him, this was pure theater. His direct interface to the Realm's frame creation engine gave him the powers of a god.

"Take your shot, then," Anne said. She lowered her arms and stood stock-still, towering over him.

Langoni pounded his fist into the side of her face.

Anne's head snapped to the side, but the damage, Langoni knew, had been minimal. And, indeed, she immediately turned her head back to face him again.

"That all you got?" she asked.

He punched her in the pit of her stomach next. This time he clearly felt her tough abdominal muscles absorb the blow. He would have to hit with perfect accuracy to have any effect on her. Well, she was the woman who'd felled a Spider with a harpoon and her bare hands. Langoni began to warm to this game.

"My turn now," Anne said, catching Langoni on his cheek with a fist that audibly hummed through the air. The blow scrambled the contents of his head with its force. He could have sent the impact right back into her fist, but chose to savor the pain his Realm body felt instead. He had to admit—this *was* fun.

"You pulled that one," Langoni said, and spat out an incisor.

"Now why would I do that?" Anne said, grinning again as she took a step to the side. The two of them began circling each other like boxers. Langoni considered the situation, enjoying the need to think. Anne surely didn't believe she could take him down with her fists alone. What did she have planned? And how should he finish off this ocean terrace?

"Hey, Langoni," Anne said, her pupils contracted into cruel-looking beads.

"Yeah?"

"Were you the one who kidnapped José?"

Anne's smile had vanished now. Langoni felt a wave of coldly murderous intent wash over him.

"One of me was," he admitted.

"Don't suppose you'd give him back? He's a friend."

"No way."

Anne tackled Langoni suddenly with her shoulder, her 110-kilo-gram frame hitting him like a cannonball. Langoni staggered.

"Ouch!" he said. "Agile, aren't we?"

"I always had a thing for delicate, retiring men."

"Oh? That's something to think about. Of course, *I* know why a catch like you is still on the market."

One of Anne's eyebrows twitched warily, just for a moment.

"Why a child lover like you isn't married and pumping out kids of your own."

Anne circled him silently, her back not as straight as it had been.

"So, Anne Cachemaille," Langoni said. "If you're so wild about José, why be so coy about it? You're a big girl. Just come out and say it. 'José, will you marry me?'"

"Hey!" The hoarse shout was Bernier's. "That's enough, kid. One word more…"

"And what?"

Anne tackled Langoni again, with a power that made the first time seem like a gentle nudge. Down low and off-balance, Langoni felt her legs knock his feet out from under him. He felt himself in midair. But he did not feel himself fall.

He had been caught in a net thrown by the other fishermen. A fishing net woven of Spider-web and studded with tiny Glass Eyes. The very Glass Eyes that had once adorned the terrace like fairy lights.

He was strung up between them like a monkey caught in a snare.

"Fishermen know how to use a needle, you know. Threw this together out of leftover web and a few Eyes we were using for lighting."

Langoni felt a fierce negative pressure. His body seemed about to be torn into shreds and sucked into countless different Eyes. For the first time, he felt fear.

"Better hurry up and give José back before the net pulls you apart."

Langoni's finely made outfit was already so damaged it looked like decrepit rags. Patches of his skin had turned waxy and begun to flake off. It seemed that this net's function was to degrade and break down whatever was caught in it.

"You'll never get José back without me," he said.

Anne laughed. "I'll make the threats around here," she said. "Don't misunderstand your situation."

"Shit!" It was the first time the gallant had cursed. He appeared to have abandoned his pose of self-assurance. "Let me out of here!"

Langoni tore at the net, but it repaired itself in an instant. Soon the nails peeled off his scrabbling fingers. His hair, once thick and black, was now straggly and thin, clearly revealing the dome of his skull. His face itched powerfully; when he scratched it, his fine nose came off, and his fingers snapped like crayons. He couldn't breathe. Langoni was nearing the end.

"I'll say it once more," said Anne. "Give José back right now."

Then she blinked. Something was off.

She blinked again, and realized what it was.

She was in the net now.

"'Give José back,' eh? Big talk."

She heard Langoni's voice from outside the net.

Anne finally understood the situation. Langoni had somehow switched places with her. The other fishermen were frozen.

Langoni raised a long knife to eye level and ran his thumb over the blade. "Why don't you let them know why you always carry this?" he said. It was the knife Anne kept at her waist. Langoni thrust its point through the net and slit Anne's T-shirt open at the neckline. Her hard, proud, coppery breasts fell out. The net repaired itself once the blade was removed. This was the trap Anne herself had set. The blade flowed like water as Langoni cut open her knee-length pants to the waist. There was her rocklike stomach, there her chiseled navel, and there was her dense, dark bush.

"Nothing there," said Langoni with a sneer. "Isn't that right, Anne Cachemaille? You have no genitals."

Anne's expression remained unchanged.

"See?" Langoni said, thrusting his hand in to grope. "Nothing there."

"You—!"

Behind Langoni, Bernier raised a poker wrapped in Spider-web and Eyes. Langoni turned and glared. Bernier froze, dropping his weapon. Then he fell onto his back.

Wintry smile still directed at Bernier, Langoni stabbed the knife deep into Anne, right where his hand had been.

Anne twisted in the net like a shark, but remained silent.

"Admit it, Anne," Langoni said. "You *like* this."

He pulled the knife out. No blood came. The wound had already closed. He slashed the place open a second time, a third. Anne writhed at every blow, but did not make a sound.

"Admit it. This is the key to opening up your senses. You're forced to accept the sensation, whether you want it or not. Those guests, eh? Who can understand their tastes?"

Leaving the long blade in, Langoni drew another knife from Anne's waist. Her whole body was flushed, slick with fragrant perspiration.

"And you carried this around wherever you went," Langoni continued. "Must have been a whole lot of guests snickering to themselves when they passed you in the street."

Anne finally turned her face away.

"Never did tell José, did you? Never said you loved him. Well, the time for confession is now. I mean…this is it for you." Langoni jabbed a finger at her eyes. "You're going to die."

A book of poetry fell from Anne's torn T-shirt. It had swollen with perspiration. No bookcase remained to return it to.

"I mean, you're unnecessary. You're interfering with my plan. Just like Jules. Time for you to take your leave. There'll be no one to listen to you then. Those priceless feelings of yours—gone. You hoarded them like jewels for a thousand years. Scream them out, just once, before you die."

Face still turned away, Anne shook her head in refusal. A thin sound escaped from her throat, like a sob that couldn't be stifled. Her eyes seemed to film over.

"Does it feel that good?" Langoni asked. "Or was that out of sadness?"

He stabbed the second knife in alongside the first. Anne struggled inside the net, roaring like a wild beast, overpowered by exploding sensation.

A rare hint of emotion flickered deep in Langoni's eyes.

"Goodbye, Anne," he said. "My little Hercules."

The net's functionality was reactivated. Anne's screams hoarsened and ended in moments as her lungs and vocal cords became fragile as old tracing paper and ruptured from the stress of vocalization. The ligaments in her jaw stretched and deformed like old rubber bands. Her body turned an ashy white, and her exposed breasts and square shoulders crumpled like dry papier-mâché. Her hands were ground right off her flailing arms, crumbling into dust as they rubbed against the net.

Her writhing gradually slowed, dwindling to a barely perceptible shudder.

The toughest, most beautiful body in the Realm had become a wretched old blob.

Rising to his feet and turning away, Langoni destroyed the terrace.

He deftly manipulated the net that had held Anne, using it to bring the men on the terrace into the same state as their fellows at the front entrance.

And then the pain began to stream in.

The ferocious mood had Jules about to explode.

It was burned into the room like the smell of incense.

A fierce, shameless desire. So powerful that it threatened to destroy (his partner) Julie—indeed, actively relished the prospect.

Jules didn't even notice Cottontail rolling off his lap.

He caught Julie's face in both hands. A violent impulse rose within him to squeeze like a vice. To undercut the urge, he kissed her instead.

The inside of her mouth was unexpectedly large, and filled with desire that matched his own. Saliva and tongues boiled hotly. Jules licked every bit of the inside of Julie's mouth. Their teeth clashed. They bit each other's lips. One of his hands moved from her face and groped for her fish earring, tried to rip it out. Julie's hand reached up to help. The thrill of complicity flared.

With a tiny jingle, the earring tumbled onto the floor.

The two of them fell back on the sofa, squirming and entwining themselves with each other like fish caught in a net.

They enjoyed this lascivious dance. They fled, taunted, gave chase, caught.

Jules took Julie's ear into his mouth. He tasted blood where they had pulled out the earring. He rubbed that taste against his neck, his chest, his stomach. He bit her underarm hair redolent with sweat, thrust his tongue between her tight, small buttocks. But he could not get inside her. Her identity boundary remained closed. Doing this kind of thing without open identity boundaries was a new experience for Jules. It was irritating. Frustrating.

He wanted to tear through.

He wanted to merge.

He wanted to taste every pixel of her.

But her boundary would not open.

His impatience stoked his ferocious, broken drive to new heights.

He saw that all hesitation would have to be abandoned. They smashed against each other bodily, bit and sucked each other all over. Let stifled cries slip into each other's ears. Their behavior was awkward, unseemly, brutal, utterly lacking in elegance and restraint.

Julie was crying. Jules wondered if he might be too.

He did not know why.

But he felt what he thought was a shudder at the sweetness of living within the frustration of never quite coming together completely.

Perhaps this isn't AI sex at all.

Could this be human *sex?*

The question sank out of view, bobbed back; sank and bobbed back.

Is it really Julie that I have pinned down?

Is it really me, here, doing these things?

Another place, another time, another couple's feelings were overlaid on them.

Jules pushed into the boiling heat.

Julie wrapped her arms around his neck and welcomed him.

This room, the Clements' room... It must be a powerful magnetic field for emotion and acts. The whole place is stamped with feelings from long ago.

We're under that field's control, too, like iron filings forming pretty patterns around a magnet...

Tracing those emotions, those acts...

Jules understood what was happening clearly.

It was not, however, unpleasant.

The emotions imprinted on the room were deep and hot, bitter and lonely, but they were also unquestionably true.

Depth and loneliness like the color of a lake spread out in the woods.

Bitterness like the first taste of a medicinal herb finally arrived at a sickbed.

Heat like that of the blood spilling from the mouth of a wild beast devouring the sweetest part of its prey.

He might never meet this woman again.

If so, he wanted to kill her. She was so precious to him that he would destroy her without a trace if he could.

If a moment can change a whole life, how he felt now was the priceless fruit of one such moment.

Jules clung to Julie's writhing body and, moving fiercely himself, abandoned himself to that feeling and the swell of pleasure that bore him up.

On the sofa where the geologist and Régine had loved each other just once, Jules and Julie spasmed and arched countless times before finally reaching their end.

The Mineral Springs Hotel was dying.

The leaf-vein hand growing at the entrance engulfed AIs and segments of the TrapNet one after another. Once it had completely surrounded the hotel, it began its penetration of the interior.

It was a perfect agglomerate of pain. Nothing like it had existed before in all the world.

It continued to swell, taking in all the pain it could, ceaselessly changing its form as it sought to strangle the hotel. The hotel began to crack and scream as the soft but merciless vegetable force bore down. Windows, exhaust vents, drains—fingers of meat squirmed in wherever possible, expanding, growing. Thick leaves grew as densely inside the hotel as on its exterior. The leaves were shaped like human palms, human ears. Here and there fruit hung on the vine. Some of the fruits were dense and hard, like dried scrotums or anklebones; others were heavy and greasy and looked just like breasts.

Tendrils came into the kitchen through the air vents and moved as if groping across the still-lit gas stove. The human body parts at their tips—Denis's eyes, Pascal's left thumb—sizzled and fried in the blue flame, but the vines showed no sign of caring. This pain, too, was spice to savor. Joël's face in the frying pan found its place in the network of pain.

The tendrils that invaded the library opened wide like mouths to devour the mothers and children crowded into the room. The countless mother-child pairs gnawing and chewing each other were chomped up and swallowed, pain and grief and all. Anne's children, Odette: all drowned in the sea of pain.

Pain, pain, pain.

The net sought it out.

At first it was trying to dilute its own pain, but by now increasing the total volume of pain had become a goal in itself.

The TrapNet survived only in fragments. Strands of Spider-web and Eyes lay here and there, cut off from the Chandelier and bereft of function. The pain net busily took these cold, ignored remnants, weaving the web into the vines' fabric and conveying the Eyes carefully inward to put to new uses.

The real work was finally about to start.

The words came on voices that blew through the pain net like the first signs of fever.

Peel the hotel's surface off.

Bring it all to light. Everything hidden under the stairs, beneath the carpets, behind the mirrors. All of it.

Everything Denis thought he had erased from the ledgers appeared. All the ghosts of the past that were supposed to have been wiped from the hotel.

The probing tips of the tendrils, and then the glass Eyes that had been taken in, made contact with the microscopic sensory devices embedded throughout the hotel as a security system. They excited the devices and roused the hotel's memory stored within. The effect spread in pulses, like waves across a field of grain, and the very hotel swayed.

From the furniture, the wallpaper, the ceiling lights and door-knobs in the guest rooms; from the soap in the washbasins; from the brass shower fittings; from under the legs of the bathtubs; from the tiny keyhole in the grandfather clock that stood in the grand hall; from the sparkle of the wine buckets and silverware in the dining room; from within the twists of the corkscrews; from the crime maga-zine photos stuffed into drawers in the little desk in the boiler room; from the eyes of an old illustration of a bird that had been hung in a corner of one corridor; from all these places the hotel's memories were replayed as distinct images.

All at once, the Mineral Springs Hotel overflowed with guests from the past.

Countless visitors who'd come to spend a brutal vacation in the Realm of Summer appeared, along with the AIs who'd served them. Some were vague, others vivid. All were replayed together.

Like dead souls dressed in their finest to gather in the ballroom of a haunted house.

This was the beginning of the Mineral Springs Hotel's farewell party.

From nowhere in particular, music began to play. A tapestry of waltzes, torch songs, fiddle tunes, all playing together in the same mellow tones and narrow frequency range as an old 78 record. The hotel's entire musical memory had been revived at once, every song laced with the same old-fashioned, calculated sentimentality.

Smells filled the air.

In the dining room, smells of grilling, of sauce; in the smoking room, of the finest brandy and liquor, along with the sofa's leather. The powder rooms reeked of foundation, perfume, and female bodies. The hotel's olfactory memory.

The ghosts cut through the haze of sound and smells, strutting through a hotel that was now a perfect blend of agony and ecstasy.

Some of their number were AIs who had been eaten by the Spiders or drawn into the net of pain, returned to their original forms.

There was Pierre, screaming in agony as a crowd gathered to watch the elderly guest dressed as his younger sister tread on him.

There was Bastin's granddaughter Agnès, being forced to sing with her fellow schoolgirls on the dais in the ballroom under the direction of a guest dressed as their teacher. Their mouths were stuffed with balled-up barbed wire. The bald-shaven, bull-necked teacher waved his conductor's baton with a sort of right-wing determination as he watched the blood spot their pristine white collars.

There was a boy from Jules's class at school, who had been made to dine with a group of young women and forced to overindulge in wine. The women watched with enjoyment as he vomited, then ordered a waiter to pour what he had brought up onto their plates as sauce.

All these things had really happened at the Mineral Springs Hotel.

Whatever had been permitted behind the hotel's closed doors, whatever joyful cry had been raised, was perfectly reproduced.

And the network of pain absorbed it all, quite literally, into itself.

It did not break down or digest any of it. The cigars and the vomit were taken in smelling just as they did, the music and cries ringing just as they did, the liquor and tears flowing just as they did. The whole gigantic tableau went whirling in to be folded up and stored away inside.

Like roots exploring fertile soil, the vines and the Eyes ensnared every one of the myriad forms of pleasure and pain that filled the hotel, all the darkness of spirit that held fast at its base. And what they captured they stored as nourishment.

More.

More.

An ague like the symptoms of blackwater fever gave the network of pain tremors that came again and again.

Even the seemingly endless store of brutal sights that had lain hidden within the Mineral Springs Hotel could not satisfy the network's bottomless appetite. More accurately, the network was already full to bursting, but its sense of starvation could not be alleviated. It wanted more. More.

As the all-pervasive agony passed a certain threshold, it began to change the character of the space inside the hotel.

The air increased its viscosity, becoming like liquid glass. The AIs were caught alive like insects in amber, swimming in pain, drowning in it. The walls and pillars that gave the hotel shape took on the same glassy texture as boundaries began to blur. The Glass Eyes, too, began slowly to blur and dissolve, outlines fading as they seeped into the transparent, viscous body.

The three sisters looked at Old Jules with peculiar expressions between exhaustion and anger.

The four of them were the only ones who had seen what Jules and Julie had done. To be more precise, the four of them had *made* Jules and Julie do what they had done.

"Tell me, what was the point of all that?" asked Luna. "Was putting Jules and Julie through that really necessary?"

"Oh, absolutely," Old Jules said, all innocence.

"I don't understand it at all. Taking away their defenses at a time like this just seems beyond belief."

"They weren't defenseless. Remember how hard we worked to keep them safe?"

That much was true. For the duration of the act, the four of them had used every means at their disposal to create diversions and protect Jules and Julie from detection. They were still doing so, in fact, because Jules and Julie were lying on the sofa, dead to the world. No sense of self-preservation at all, those two.

"Even so," Luna said doubtfully.

"I do understand your objections," Old Jules said. "José is Julie's lover, and you don't think it was right to ignore that. The odd spark might fly between Jules and Julie now and then, but they weren't supposed to go further. That was the unspoken rule, yes?"

Luna nodded silently.

"'Jules with Julie' was a line that was absolutely *not* to be crossed. The most important taboo in the Realm. Correct?"

The three sisters nodded silently.

"Julie thinks she loves José. But she's also irresistibly drawn to Jules. That's just a fact. She's suspicious of these desires, fears them. Jules, of course, loves Julie too. But her thing with José holds him back. José loves Julie and respects Jules, but has no idea what's in their hearts.

"This three-way deadlock is built into the Realm of Summer.

"They're the most important characters in this place. That deadlock is what guarantees the rest of the Realm's peaceful, unchanging existence—all those days, like a long, long, nap.

"Right?"

Nobody nodded this time. The answer was obvious.

"But it doesn't matter anymore. Those peaceful days are gone. That doesn't mean I just wanted to make it happen out of spite. But if that was the taboo, there had to be a right time to break it. That time had come. In fact, it might already have been too late."

"Even so…" said Anna slowly. "Doesn't Langoni know all this too?"

"About how the Realm works? Yeah, I'd say he knows. That's why José got snatched."

"But why did you use the feelings between Clement and the geologist?" asked Luna. Unlike Anna, she seemed to be in a hurry.

"That story is the underpainting for the whole Realm of Summer. Do you know how an oil painting is done? The painter starts by sketching the whole composition in a single faint tone. Then they paint over that, adding color and accent until it's done. That first sketch determines the course of the whole work. The Clement family story is like that. It underlies every part of the Realm, out of sight but still regulating everything we feel or do at the deepest level. And nobody realizes this—not even special AIs like Jules and Julie.

"Now, this underpainting is buried even deeper than the deadlock. This makes the Clement story the best way to break the taboo. Probably the only way to break it, actually, without shattering Jules and Julie psychologically in the process."

"But why break the taboo in the first place?" This was Donna. "What will it change, and how?"

"We won't know right away. Not right away. The effects won't become apparent for a very, very long time. Or—" (Jules grinned in private amusement) "Maybe I should say, they won't be apparent except in a very different direction."

Suddenly Old Jules shut his mouth. Story time, it seemed, was over.

"Well, well," he said. "Looks like they've finally come to."

The four of them looked through the Chandelier at the sofa. Jules and Julie slowly woke up, eyes opening as if they had been reborn.

"We can't stay here anymore, can we?" said one of the sisters.

The four of them looked around the casino.

Everybody else was already gone.

Vines the color of meat showed through the seams in the carpet and the gaps where wall met ceiling, peering into the room. Old Jules and the three sisters had already noticed that the lips on the solemn portraits hung on the wall had been replaced with the Femme Fatale's, parting to reveal rows of narrow teeth like thorns that gnashed as if starved beyond sanity. Beyond the stained glass of the doors, the refined crowd seeking entry chattered amongst themselves, voices raised now in merriment, now in irritation, but always growing louder and louder.

The final remnants of the TrapNet had managed to hold off the invasion of the casino, but the mood outside was no longer fearful of what power the four of them still commanded. On the contrary, the overweening confidence, even arrogance, outside the door was palpable.

"It's a pity we can't watch what happens to Jules and Julia next. But things are getting out of hand here. That crowd outside will probably find the underground chamber soon, too."

"Shall we break them?" asked Luna, meaning the Chandelier and the other Eyes. Should they be destroyed before they fell into enemy hands?

"You couldn't break them even if you had a sledgehammer," he said. "How are you planning to do it with your bare hands?"

"So you're just going to hand the Eyes over?"

"If they want the Eyes, let them have them. Why not? The hotel, the AIs—everything the Eyes were supposed to protect is already lost."

"Still…"

"That's…"

"But… What are we going to do now, then?"

After fighting so savagely to defend the hotel, the three sisters were bewildered to see Old Jules show absolutely no attachment to it, or even to the table around which they were seated. Unless… Perhaps defending the hotel had never been his intention at all?

"What are we going to do?" Old Jules said with a chuckle. "Let me see… How about 'run'?"

The three sisters exchanged a look.

"That sounds fine, but… How?"

It was obvious that they could not set foot outside the casino.

The three sisters had expected this to end with one final, greatest act of resistance. But when Old Jules spoke, it was with all the urgency of a retired civil servant deciding where to take his constitutional that day.

"I might head out to the Singing Sands," he said. "Don't worry, I'll bring you three along somehow."

He smiled affably, the ancient scar where his right eye had once been crinkling along with his left.

The double doors of the casino flew inward, hinges and all. Whatever force had braced them from within appeared to have suddenly vanished.

Trampling the stained glass into fragments, the viscous mass of pain and death poured into the casino. The agony and madness of the dead had grown even stronger. They had feasted and grown fat on the nourishment in the Clement chronicles, the fundamental layer of the Realm. Now they crowded around the largest table, surrounding the most valuable of the Glass Eyes—the Father of Flame, Snowscape, and of course the Chandelier—with joyful cries. Several among their number raised the Chandelier above their heads and paraded solemnly off like priests on their way to a coronation.

Old Jules and the three sisters were nowhere to be found.

"If you can't answer, José, then let me."

The haloed voice echoes off the arched roof of the underground chamber, broadening into a solemn spectrum of sound.

"You are a special kind of AI."

The gigantic iris peering into me has a complex beauty, like the bird's-eye figure you find in the grain of the best furniture or tobacco pipes. Dark sepia, cedar green, gold ochre, bister, Venetian red. Countless colors swirling down together into a pitch-black center which reflects my face.

"You're the political heart of the Realm of Summer."

The task lights flicker in and out of the corners of my vision like a mesmerist's swinging coin.

"There are two kinds of AI in the Realm of Summer. Extraordinary AIs have a task to perform. The Realm depends on the functions provided by these extraordinary AIs to function smoothly. You might not realize it, José, but your character is equipped with the Realm of Summer's political functionality."

Something throbbing at the center of my chest. The face. My own face at the age of ten or so. A face that never lived in this Realm. There are things I forgot long ago that the face remembers. And other things that it fears.

"What is politics, José, after all? The demonstration and exercise of force either against or with others, in order to mold and dissect the social order of a certain group. Authority, policy, dominance, self-rule: you employed all of these in Anne's group. You could easily have become the group's leader, but you didn't. You brought Anne's concepts to life, turned them into a system a hundred times more refined to bring the group to life too. At the same time, you made connections with every social layer of the Realm in accordance with Anne's will. I suppose it doesn't bring you much joy to be praised for your able administration first and foremost, but the plain truth is that's what you did best. The set of functions inside you has everything necessary for controlling, regulating, and systematizing a group of AI. You're an unconscious mechanism that reigns over the Realm as if it were a herd of cattle."

Langoni's body smells delightful as a king's, perfuming the chamber as if it were his throne room.

"You are now in a light trance, José.

"The face that has bloomed on that chest of yours grew from deep within you. A cherished subset of myself put roots down throughout your body, drank in your sealed-off memories and brought them to the surface to bloom. You have many such memories, José. You were made that way. That's what makes your political function possible. Now listen, José—listen to the memory that flower recounts."

"I..."

In the middle of my chest, my face has opened its mouth and begun to speak.

"I was sleeping in the flowers."

In a clear, childish voice, my still-innocent face recounts a memory as if reciting a poem.

"The flowers are blooming all around, and I was dozing in their perfume. I am half-awake, half-dreaming. Almost like... Yes, similar in some way to what we are doing now.

"I am leaning…against a gravestone. This is a cemetery."

Yes. My back remembers the gravestone's warmth, heated by the sun. The wind had made the flowers sway and sent transparent ripples through the air.

"Through the boughs stretching far above my head, the fierce summer light rains down on me like gunfire."

I remember. Yes. The dazzling light had been painful, almost seeming to have weight, and I had thought to myself: *It feels like gunfire.*

"The fragrance is making me sleepy. It has covered me where I lie, like a mass of fallen flower petals. I am trapped under its weight."

That "fragrance" had been a drug.

A grown-up had given me a handful of little chocolates decorated with violet petals. The chocolates had been dosed with something that made me drowsy.

"Against the gravestone next to me, my little brother has been put to sleep the same way."

Little brother? Little brother… Yes, that's right. I had a little brother. Martin. The name came back to me now and then.

I had shared the chocolates with him, too.

"My little brother is being taken apart alive…"

The scene swims into view out of memory's abyss.

I see my brother against the tombstone.

"His identity boundary has been tampered with."

My brother's clothes and skin are divided up by a grid of lines. The processing has been applied to his surface with no regard for specified materials, in dividing lines, as if retexturing him with tiles. What's more, those tiles are not quite flush. They have risen out of their settings slightly, creating gaps through which I can see inside my brother.

The sight is supernatural.

"My brother looks like an anatomical specimen. I see fat and muscle beneath his boundary, shining wetly with oozing blood."

What should be visible inside an AI in this state is a transparent program structure. A shining lattice, a logic tree.

But other methods have been employed for my little brother's dissection.

By that woman.

"A woman is standing before my brother. She has a long, white coat and black hair. She is very tall."

Yes, I remember. The tight ponytail she wore her hair in, and the locks that escaped it to fall translucently about her white ears, leaving soft shadows. Her long eyelashes. Sad-looking eyes. Bright red lips. Her long, long coat, the sort of thing an illusion might wrap itself in. The black boots visible beneath the coat. The hard heels of those boots.

She looks at me and laughs.

What do you think, José? Look at the state your brother's in.

Long eyebrows. Big mouth. Thoughtful, kind-looking face.

Her incisors gleam. Her teeth are sharp and silvery, brutal fangs that almost seem glued on and certainly ruin the effect of her well-formed face.

"*What did you do?* I ask her. *What did you do to my brother? Something you didn't do to me?*"

I had met the woman alone at first.

She had called out to me after I sneaked into the cemetery alone, given me chocolates. *These sweets have bad medicine in them, but they taste very good,* she had said. *I wonder if you're brave enough to eat them?* Even as a boy, I had recognized the sexual implication in her challenge. Nervously, I ate the chocolates. They were bite-sized and decorated with violet petals steeped in some strong flavor. Under the influence of the drugs inside the chocolates, my body had relaxed completely even as it became impossibly sensitive. I had been unable to resist as she enfolded me inside her white coat. And inside it, even whiter, was her naked body.

She toyed with me inside her coat for an hour or more.

It was a warm, oily-smelling, milky darkness.

The woman laughed silently, her large, crimson mouth adopting all manner of shapes.

The thoughtful cover came off her face, revealing something I could not look at directly.

Cruel loneliness.

Elegant sadism.

Imbecility dressed as intellect.

Silvery teeth.

And I...I was fascinated by that intricate insanity.

Next time, bring a friend, the woman had said as we parted.

I decided to bring my little brother.

My reserved, quiet, obedient, only little brother.

"*Something you didn't do to me?*

"*That's right,* the woman replies. *Isn't it obvious?*

"*After all, you didn't end up like this, did you?* She smiles. *Now, watch!*

"Her cover of sanity has long since been removed.

"My little brother looks back and forth between the woman and I. He does not quite seem to understand what has happened to him. The blood has drained from his face, but his eyes are wide open. The fear in them, the uncertainty is unbearable to look at. No, that isn't true—I wanted to see it. Perhaps I wanted him to take my place, this brother whose face looked so much like mine. Perhaps I wanted to make him the target of whatever power this woman wielded.

"Her broad mouth smiles. The long nail on her index finger, blue like the rest of her fingernails, peels tiles off my brother one by one. It sounds like she is pulling his nails off, and my brother cries and screams. I can only watch, unable to move a finger.

"The woman continues to peel off the tiles. She takes her time deliberating over which to remove next, enjoying the indecision, removing them from spots all over his body. My brother's surface is full of holes now, exposing his red, wet insides to the air and light.

"Eventually, after removing perhaps half of the tiles, the woman lowers her hand.

"And then she opens her coat.

"I cannot see into it from where I am.

"I cannot see into it from where I am.

"But my brother appears to see all too well.

"His eyes have opened wide. What they saw I do not know.

"And then, the woman…"

The woman begins to "suck" my brother in.

"The first thing I see is a thin red thread.

"It sways in the air between the two of them.

"Next comes blue. Then green. The threads grow in number.

"They look like the streamers connecting a passenger ship to its wharf.

"Countless threads in every color, twisting and dancing like living things.

"I look closer.

"Where are the threads coming from?

"My brother's body.

"Lines of color extend from the gaps where tiles have been removed and snake toward the woman, there to be sucked into whatever lies beneath her parted coat, blocked from my view."

And then I realized that this was an illusion.

The threads had come from the woman's body.

Transparent, hollow threads, extending from her body and inserted into my brother's. She must have implanted them one by one as she removed the tiles.

She is using the threads to suck something out of my brother's body. They are tiny, transparent pipes, and they are carrying my brother's flesh and blood, broken down to minute fragments.

Finally the woman is finished.

The tiles are still there.

There is nothing inside them.

Just a hollow that still retains the form of a boy.

His terrified eyes look like part of an outdated poster.

The woman's heels smash his face in. I hear a fragile sound, like old paper.

I can do nothing. Nothing but cry coldly as the dappled sunlight comes down through the leaves.

The woman's coat is opened again and she wraps me inside it. I smell flowers.

This is your reward. The woman's voice.

I writhe.

In the ecstasy she gives me.

And in the guilt cast at me by my brother's eyes.

"Beautiful."

The spectrum of Langoni's solemn voice fills the subterranean chamber.

Having finished recounting the sealed memory, the boy's face— my own face as a boy—falls silent once more and closes its eyes.

"What beautiful, cruel imagery. This, José, is the infection that breeds within you. The guilt of having succumbed to temptation and caused your brother's death binds you. It regulates your every action.

"You can never again ignore the pain of another, because the experience left you determined to act, in future, as a protector should. A debt that can never be repaid. The wellspring of your political function. Something you, José, will never escape.

"And that is exactly why I chose you."

Tears have begun to trickle from between the closed eyelids of the face on my chest.

"Come, José. *There is still so much you must remember for me.* To ensure the reliability of your function, there must be countless memories like this buried within you.

"With my help, you will remember every last one."

Langoni enfolds me once more in darkness—insensate darkness. At once I see nothing, hear nothing.

I close my eyes.

I cannot bear any more of this.

I cannot bear any more remembering.

On my chest I feel my eyes as a boy open once more.

Like a flower that blooms in the dark.

"There's something I've wanted to ask you about for a while."

"What?"

"Your name."

"Julie? It's what Mom named me. I like it."

"No, your surname. Printemps."

"That's not my surname. Why does everyone think that if two names are together one of them must be a surname?"

"You named yourself that, right? You were the one who chose it."

"Right."

"Why? Why choose your own name?"

"Hmm… I'm not sure. Maybe I forgot."

"You didn't like your real name?"

"No, that's not it."

"When was it, again?" Jules wondered aloud, mostly to himself.

Julie Printemps sat up languorously and slid off the sofa.

Moonlight spilled in through the window.

The thick atmosphere that had filled the room was gone now, as if some tide had gone out, and the room was still.

"What a beautiful moon.

"Hey, Jules. Did you know that the moon's an AI, too?"

"What?!"

Julie giggled.

"You're always teasing me," Jules complained. He let himself fall back onto the sofa and lay there staring upward.

"Mom gave me my name," Julie said. "But not really, I suppose. It was just part of my design. I do love my Mom. You too, Jules. But are those real feelings? I don't know. Who is it who feels my emotions?"

"Don't dodge the question. You know what I meant to ask."

"Printemps. 'Spring.' I wish I could see it just once. What do you think it's like? There's nothing but summer here, after all."

"You're not even pretending to answer now," Jules said, laughing despite himself. "Do you like it as a name, 'Printemps'?"

"Yes. I do. I like things I've never seen before. Do you know about spring? The weather's not too hot. The greens are softer and the rain's thin and gentle. It's not summer. What do you think about that?"

Still looking out the window, Julie ran her hand over her hair. The short hairs at the nape of her neck rustled like grass in the wind.

Jules wondered if that might be what the thin, gentle rains of spring sounded like.

He could not see the expression on her face from where he lay.

Jules closed his eyes and imagined the sound of spring rain behind his eyelids.

The Mineral Springs Hotel and its gardens, enveloped in gentle spring rain. A pitter-patter that gradually blurred into background noise, became a curtain of silence erasing other sounds and beckoning sleep. A spring nap. Sleep to grow and develop in. Sleep to prepare for the future. Clear droplets lodging themselves at the tips of leaves, the edges of petals. The paving stones warmly wet. The afternoon hotel at peace. All of these things he imagined.

I like things I've never seen before…

"I wonder what happened to everyone?"

There was no sound at all.

The Mineral Springs Hotel was perfectly quiet. They almost felt as if they might hear the moonlight blanket the ground.

There was no sound of life. No hint of anybody's presence.

"They're probably…"

They're probably already gone.

Julie turned to face Jules.

The window was at her back. Her face was a dark silhouette.

But something was shining at her eyes.

Jules stopped himself any number of times before finally opening his mouth.

"I have to say something," he said.

The thing he had never been able to say.

"I… I loved…"

Julie placed her finger on his lips to stop him before he could get the last word out.

Jules closed his mouth.

Julie crouched on the ground in the moonlight.

Picking up the whale earring, she carefully put it back on.

Like a flower that blooms in the dark.

That had been José's final coherent and meaningful thought.

He was no longer functioning normally as an AI.

Big Langoni gazed down at José from his lofty vantage point.

Not long before, the man had sprawled at Langoni's feet like a young prophet just taken down from a cross.

Long black hair. An aquiline nose honed by the ocean winds. Sharp cheeks. Mouth like a wolf. Long, splayed-out limbs.

All gone, now.

José's body was beginning a supernatural transformation like the one his brother had undergone in that forgotten memory.

A transformation into a suitable keystone for the crown of pain that Big Langoni intended to make.

A flower blooming in the dark.

José's body had been segmented into minute tiles, or perhaps blocks, and opened wide.

In his brother's case, only the surface had been tiled, but every part of José, right through to his inner core, had been dissected into units like toy blocks which were then eased away from each other. This pitiful form was all that remained after the comprehensive dissection and probing that had salvaged his store of forgotten memories. The unit resolution was not much larger than a pixel. It was impossible to tell now where José's face had been. With difficulty, the final orientations of his arms and legs could be made out, but no more. If he was a flower, the remains of his limbs were petals.

Every single one of the countless memories buried within him had been too hideous to watch.

The sheer number of wounds on José's psyche had surprised even Langoni. Even with the damage sealed away, how had the man possibly been able to function? Each memory Langoni carved out had dealt José a powerful psychological blow, breaking him bit by bit where he lay. Not even an AI could gaze unblinking at the darkness within itself.

But that was exactly why he would make such an excellent trap.

The scent of the night wind blew through the subterranean chamber.

Langoni felt a great satisfaction.

The walls in every direction crumbled silently, and Langoni watched as the clear, dense, viscous mass outside poured in.

An accretion of pain.

He had reached this milestone at last. Langoni sighed.

However, the mass had no internal structure yet. It was simply a uniform, undelineated mob.

And so…

Langoni watched as the viscous mass mingled with the mineral spring water that accumulated in the pool at the center of the room, slowly transforming them both.

And then he watched as the subterranean chamber was remade into the fulcrum of the grand structure of his conception.

The night's pitched battle was moving toward its final, perfect contraction at last.

Only one element remained.

Langoni waited for her to be delivered, excited and impatient as a man expecting a love letter.

CHAPTER 9:
THE TWO GRAVES

A rcs of white stone crossing overhead.

Beneath their shoes, the crunch of sand.

Jules Tappy was walking down what had once been a corridor in the Mineral Springs Hotel, with Julie right behind him and Cottontail in his hand.

A petrified forest. A dead coral reef. A three-dimensional maze of enormous vitrified branches piled high and precarious. Or perhaps it was more like a cage, pieced together from the shuffled bones of thousands of dead elephants. Floors of broad, angled hip bones; great tusks as curved roof beams, supported by sturdy femurs made into pillars; the rhythms of vertebrae in closely-linked chains.

And all made of glass. Smooth and hard and cold.

Looking up they saw the night sky between the branches, pitch-black and dotted with tiny, sharply shining stars. The raging clouds of the morning were gone. The same chaos of glass that rose above their heads extended below their feet as well. They walked on, tiny specks against a white staircase spanning the dark of night.

"Still a way from sunrise," Jules said to no one in particular. The sand crunched beneath his feet. Minute particles of glass.

The arc of glass above their head had partly melted into a thin, milky-colored pillar that plunged straight down. It looked like cream that had been petrified at the moment of being poured into coffee. Jules saw his face reflected in its vitreous surface.

A powerful wave of heat, perhaps, had washed through here at some point.

The glass bones had melted into each other, smoothly joined together.

"I'm at the limit of the little knowledge I have," said Jules in a low monotone, again to no one in particular.

Cottontail was acting as a portable lantern.

It led them forward, adjusting its beam of light deftly as the need arose: narrow and bright to peer into the difference, broad and soft to illuminate their feet. As Jules breathed, the light breathed too. With each step, some utterly altered part of the hotel loomed into view, then vanished again. Faces swam out of the dark—AIs, melted into the glass or sealed away inside it—then disappeared behind them.

This was what had become of the TrapNet and the Mineral Springs Hotel.

The TrapNet remained attached to the hotel as it became the network of pain, allowing it to swallow the building and the AIs inside it whole, dissolve them together, and bring the mixture to a boil.

And then it had frozen, contracted.

This forest of glass was the result.

Ten minutes ago, back in the Clement Memorial Room, Julie had finished reattaching her earring and said, "I'm going to look for José."

Success in this endeavor had seemed deeply unlikely to Jules, but it was clear she meant to go anyway, so he said, "I'm coming with you."

Julie nodded. But when they opened the Memorial Room's door, both of them froze in place.

What lay beyond the door was changed almost beyond recognition. The Mineral Springs Hotel had become an entirely different place. All floors and walls had been replaced by a structure of tangled glass branches, beyond which they could see the starry night sky.

The two of them glanced back instinctively.

For a moment, the Memorial Room remained as tasteful and unchanged as ever. Jules and Julie did not know, of course, that Old Jules and the three sisters had built a shielding program to protect the two of them even as the quake that rocked the hotel reached its climax. But the program's efficacy had been lost with the opening of the door, and as Jules and Julie watched, the Clement family's beautiful furnishings silently liquefied, memories and all. The liquid boiled and cooled again, leaving a shrunken glass skeleton. The bower of glass bones that surrounded the room remained unaffected.

Jules and Julie looked forward, back, left and right. They had no idea which way to go.

Up? Down? The two of them exchanged rueful smiles.

"I think maybe we're survivors," Julie said.

"Definitely. Well—probably," Jules agreed. "So, which way?"

"Down. That's where we're supposed to meet."

"Meet?"

"For a date. José and I."

"A date?"

"Right. We decided to meet in the underground chamber after the chess tournament was over."

"The underground chamber?" Jules said, cursing himself for his inability to do anything but parrot what she said. "I wonder if that still exists."

"Only one way to find out," Julie said.

"You think we can get there?" Jules asked.

Julie didn't answer.

"No, you're right," Jules said. "Of course we can." *We can get anywhere if we stick together*, he added silently, although this part may or may not have gotten through to Julie. He produced Cottontail from his pocket and began walking.

They were now walking through a vitrified tunnel. The reticulation of the walls and floor was so extreme that they felt as if they were roaming the hollows of a giant, stone morel mushroom. Cottontail pulsed regularly with light in Jules's hand. Every so often the ovoid Eye would brighten, and the light inside it would fill with arrows as it considered the route. Eventually all but one would fade away, indicating which way they should go.

Jules peered at some text that had just appeared on Cottontail. "Looks like this used to be the fourth floor," he reported.

That was peculiar. The Clement Family Memorial Room had been on the third floor, and they had been descending since leaving it. The floor number had changed several times along the way, as well. The hotel must have been severely warped by its transformation. Continuity had been lost. Memories were useless, only liable to get in the way. The floor beneath their feet might once have been a wall, or perhaps even the ocean terrace. They might be passing over a different part of the Mineral Springs Hotel with every step they took.

So how would they find José?

Fortunately, Jules had remembered that Cottontail had stored a copy of the entire hotel's structure, in undamaged form, back when the TrapNet had first gone online. This gave the Eye an understanding of the hotel on a level deeper than mere external appearance. By comparing that memory to what the hotel was now, correcting for the phase shifts likely to have taken place during the transformation, Cottontail was able to display arrows and floor numbers for them. The Glass Eye's navigation was the only way they would find the subterranean chamber.

"So we just go straight?"

"Good question. Probably."

"Okay."

Julie had even stopped cracking jokes.

Sometimes she would glance up before lowering her eyes once more. That was all.

The pillar before them now had a crowd of AIs stuck to it, like tiny bugs drowned in amber.

The parts of them that were not fully buried in the pillar had vitrified along with everything else.

Jules tried touching one of the faces with his finger. It was cold, smooth, and hard.

There were other pillars like this, and other vitrified AIs were buried in the walls and beneath their feet as well.

Here and there Jules saw faces he knew well, now clear and mineral.

Perhaps, he realized suddenly, the structure had been created *in order to* link these AIs-made-glass together.

All of the surfaces on the AIs were smooth now. They looked like mica or pink diamond or lustrous pearl. There were AIs that looked exactly like glass, and others who retained more of their original character.

But every face bore the same look of anguish.

Some stared wide-eyed; the eyes of others had been sewn shut. Some had been completely taken apart; others were still whole.

The one constant was unimaginable agony.

That agony was not within the power of Jules and Julie to touch. It was sealed beneath the smooth vitreous surface of the mineral mass. Despite presumably being made of Glass Eyes, this surface layer was incapable of sensory interaction with its surroundings.

The alienation had left the two of them utterly dejected.

They had tried to help the first AIs they saw like this. They paid no attention to who those AIs were, only hurrying to rescue them the way they would have if they had seen a group of humans beneath the ice of a frozen lake.

But even Julie's powers of sympathy could not arouse any response from the frozen victims.

Jules had tried using Cottontail to establish communications, despite the risk of infection, but had been equally unsuccessful.

And then they had understood.

The vitrified people before them were enduring that agony in real time as Jules and Julie watched, and nothing could be done to help them.

"Why can't we break through?" Julie had screamed, pounding the glass with her fists. Sharing the pain of other AIs and granting them the opportunity to heal was the reason for her existence. Letting the suffering of another go unrelieved was the greatest agony she knew.

Jules hadn't known how to comfort her. He had arrived at a theory of why they couldn't "break through" during his own attempts to establish communications.

The other side was inside the glass. One quality of glass is evident to anyone who has ever looked through a decades-old window and noticed the subtle warping of the scene outside: glass *flows*. Glass is just a lattice that certain materials cool and harden into after fusing together under high heat. It has no strong crystalline structure. From a perspective in which time is compressed, it's a liquid.

When used in windowpanes, it flows sluggishly downward, and that deformation, rather than shoddy workmanship, is what adds ripples to the scenery outside.

Here in the vitrified Mineral Springs Hotel, Jules had realized, the flow of time was cold and slow. That flow was what had the hotel and AIs trapped. There was no other separation.

Reaching from this time into that time was impossible.

Absolutely impossible.

Could he make Julie understand that? Even if she did understand, he doubted she would give up. Julie was the type to reach into whatever type of pain she came across. No one could drag her away from this wall of grief by force alone.

"Julie," he had said, electing to whisper. "Not now. Remember your date? Let's go to the water chamber downstairs. Once we have José, we can help the rest."

And the two of them had finally begun walking again.

Cottontail flashed in Jules's hand, showing the next arrow. Jules looked on in puzzlement. The arrow was changing color at a dizzying pace. Dense blocks of text in tiny letters scrolled past on both sides at high speed. Cottontail was desperate to convey this information to them. But the Eye was in such a hurry that Jules couldn't read the message.

Jules raised his eyes. Behind him, Julie seemed anxious as well.

Beyond the branches of vitrified time, in the livelier time flow that Jules and Julie belonged to, something was making its appearance.

It had the form of a woman, slim and slight as a fairy.

Light became intricately woven cloth that covered its body in layer upon layer.

Lace. Jules recognized it quickly. Behind him, Julie surely understood too.

The being's slender body swayed like a strand of seaweed. Its outline flickered like a ghost's.

Its form had changed utterly. But there was no mistaking those sightless eyes, that kind smile.

"Be careful," Julie said, voice paler than Jules had ever heard it. "She's dangerous."

The thing's smile spread sideways, revealing its teeth. The neat rows of white dentition chilled Julie for reasons she could not identify.

Still smiling, Yvette Carrière waited for them.

So cold…

Waking from the bitter chill, Yve realized that it was loneliness.

What is this cold? Why am I so lonely?

Her memories were as murky as overcooked oatmeal. She no longer knew exactly what had happened to the Realm or what she herself had done. Nor did she care.

She could tell that everything around her was made of Glass. But none of it responded when she touched it. This had never happened to her before. She felt irritated. Impatient. And, above all, cold and lonely.

There's nothing here. I'm surrounded by cold rock.

She wanted to be in a warm place, surrounded by something that understood her.

I have to go somewhere else. So thinking, Yve rose to her feet.

The thing that stood no longer had Yve's earlier form. It was pale and skinny and blinked unstably. This was the self-image she had kept hidden from everyone in her identity core. It was all that remained to keep moving after the devastation Felix had wrought. The rich assortment of modules a resident of the Realm should have was gone. Reduced to an image, she was quite literally the ghost of an AI.

Yve's ghost took its first swaying steps, more floating than staggering.

She moved in the direction from which a certain vague impression came. A sense of warmth. The smell of something alive and moving.

So bright…

Cottontail, held aloft by Jules, shone into her eyes.

Dazzling!

Yve was moved. What a wonderful Glass Eye that was!

By Cottontail's light, she could just make out the surrounding scenery. She saw a boy and a girl whose names she didn't know.

I'll befriend them, and then I'll ask for their Eye. Surely they'll give it to me? I must have it, no matter what.

Hope rose within her, as if blood had begun to circulate through her chill body once more. Something started to spread from deep inside her, flapping as it became one of her lace patterns.

Jules and Julie stared as the woven pattern surrounding Yve spread like an erotic flower—an orchid coming into bloom, perhaps.

Shining threads, black threads: they crisscrossed in patterns of entrancing beauty, covering Yve's fragile, naked body as if flapping in the wind.

Yve's pupilless eyes were turned toward them.

"I have a favor to ask you," she said. "That Glass Eye—it's just darling." An even-toothed smile appeared in her gaunt face. "Won't you give it to me?"

She was standing directly in front of them before they realized it. Her new form was surprisingly tall, and she looked down on them from a vantage point more than two meters off the ground. The flapping, woven pattern had now become countless long, long ribbons that drifted in the air to encircle the trio. The densely layered ribbons created a claustrophobic mood.

"I'm blind without an Eye," Yve continued. "It's very trouble-some for me. *So* troublesome." She was weeping through her smile, now, lashes damp with tears. "Won't you give me that to see by?"

Jules felt a sense of déjà vu about their situation. Boxed in by a densely written pattern… That was it: the story from the Clement chronicles. Yes, that must have been why her teeth were so frightening.

The farmer's wife had fallen pregnant with a clear goal in mind: to inscribe patterns on her cage. She had known she would run out of teeth soon. Pregnancy had been a way of procuring new tools. She had planned to carve her patterns using the bones of her newborn child. Realizing this had driven the farmer mad as terror engulfed his mind whole.

"I'll do anything you ask in return," Yve continued.

Jules wondered what that might mean.

Her long, lean body was skin and bone. Perhaps a kind of psy-chological anorexia had been at work within Yve all along.

"No," said Julie firmly.

The ghost looked partly bewildered and partly as if she had expected this answer.

"So you don't understand me," she said.

There was a great loneliness in her voice. Jules realized that she alone had been denied entry into the vitreous mass, despite loving the Eyes more than anyone else. Instead, it was her lot to remain in this frigid place, a ghost, seeing nothing, most likely forever.

But why? Jules thought. *Who's doing this to her?*

The ghost of Yve turned to Julie. "Ah," she said. "You're lonely too, aren't you? Much lonelier than me, even."

Julie made no reply.

"It hurts so much for you, doesn't it? You've lived with it so long that you barely notice anymore. But that hurt gives you your boundaries. And so…yes, I see. You have always lived to hurt that way. Sought it. You're just like me."

Julie made no reply.

"But that hurt of yours is being used by someone else. Just like I am."

Jules could think of only one reason Yve might be here, one possibility regarding her being controlled in this way.

"Come out, you coward!" shouted Julie suddenly. "Stop hiding in there!"

"All right, all right."

Felix's face appeared from between Yve's legs, sticking out upside-down. His foxy, weasely face was almost a welcome sight by this point.

"It was fun while it lasted," he said.

Julie sighed. "Don't you have *any* shame?" she asked. "I *know* you aren't Felix."

"What difference does it make to you who I am?" This time Felix spoke in a clear, resonant voice that did not suit his face at all.

"That's none of your business," Julie said.

The voice laughed with delight.

"You don't like this form?"

"It's the most tasteless invitation I ever saw."

"Invitation?" muttered Jules.

"Perceptive. You will grant me the honor of your presence, then."

"You know that's where I was already going."

"Wait a minute!" Jules screamed. "Julie! Do you know what that means?"

"What it means to Julie isn't any of your business."

Jules ignored Felix's—no, Langoni's—mocking reply.

"It means that José's fallen into their hands! You'll be strolling right into a trap!"

Even as he screamed these words, Jules understood.

Julie already knew all this. She had known since José's abduction from the ocean terrace. It was certain that thorough use had been made of him, and Julie must have been the first to realize it. She had made her decision to go underground despite knowing all this.

Jules had assumed that they were trying to rescue José. But that had never been Julie's intention. She only wanted to be by his side— even if that meant giving the enemy what they wanted.

"Sorry," Julie said.

The only thing left for Jules to say was the sour nagging of a poor loser. He hesitated, then said it anyway.

"I'm going too."

Julie shook her head. Her earring swayed with the movement.

"No. You stay behind."

"I'm going."

"No. Your…" Julie took a deep breath, then continued. "Keep out of this, cousin."

"That's cruel. It's not right."

There was no reply.

"Almost done?" said the fine voice. The ribbons that densely surrounded them unraveled slightly, opening a gap. "Now that we've established that this doesn't concern you, would you mind stepping out?"

Jules ducked under the ribbons and left through the gap.

The ribbons changed shape, becoming a small boat. It was a lovely, light little thing, beautiful as a knife. Its base just barely sank into the mass of Glass Eyes at their feet. This was a boat for cruising through the vitreous forest, passing through frozen time to arrive where José was.

That was what Yve's image had been kept around for.

She was an I/O offering access to the frozen time in the glass. After the last of her genius had been used up, she had been retained as a mere auxiliary function to this vast construct. Now, like a ghost, she guarded the entrance to glass time, but could neither enter nor leave it herself.

Julie had her back turned to him. Jules could not see her face. She was white in the starlight too.

Then, without any warning whatsoever, the ship sank smoothly into the hardened mass of Glass.

Yve vanished at the same time. Presumably this was to ensure that Jules could not intrude. No doubt they only summoned the sad feeling Yve had become when it was needed.

Jules watched the boat sink deeper and bear Julie away through the limpid Glass. As she receded into the distance, he repeatedly fought back the urge to run after her.

What to do?

What to do?

He was not left rudderless.

On the contrary—the options were on Jules's side.

He could chase after Julie.

He had stolen the tools he would need for that. They were in his head.

But should he? He had the sense that any advance would come at a heavy price. To chase or not to chase?

Julie, with her back to him.

He wanted to see her face. To seize her shoulders and turn her to face him.

But that would probably only hurt her more.

It would probably hurt her *as badly as she had been hurt that day.* That distant day…

"Lost in our memories, are we?"

That voice was how he learned that the one-eyed old man dressed like a crow had appeared behind him.

"The answer's right in front of you," the old man said. "If you're agonizing over it, you already know."

Jules sighed. "So I chase her after all."

"That's right, you do. To the ends of the Realm… It's going to be a long, long journey."

"And there's no other way?"

"No other way, you say?" The old man laughed in his dry voice, seeming genuinely happy. "Talk about picky! You could burn to death from the jealousy of the trillion AIs in the Costa del Número."

"I thought you might be my father, but you aren't, are you?" Jules said. "*It's not that I've forgotten you. I don't know you.* You belong to the future, don't you? Instead of the past. Who are you?"

"I'm Old Jules, of course."

The boy cocked his head.

"Like you just said," Old Jules continued. "I belong to the future. I think that makes my identity self-evident. You can't arrive at the answer except by advancing into the future. If you just keep tramping around this single summer's loop, the answer will never be yours."

Jules studied the old, deep scar that split Old Jules's face in half. *What kind of fierce attack had birthed that scar? Or, perhaps,* would *birth it?* he thought. It was beyond his imagination.

Old Jules spread his palms and turned them toward Jules.

"It's right in front of your eyes," he said. "You just don't understand what it means."

His hands were raw and disfigured with scar tissue. A severe scalding that had melted his flesh.

"You're right," Jules said. "I don't understand."

"See?" said the old man, and laughed his withered laugh again. "Julie's shoulders were right there. You could have reached out and grabbed them. But you kept your hands to yourself. Who's the old man here, me or you?"

The old man made fists of his hands and stuffed them into his sleeves.

"Decide," he said. "There's never 'no other way.' You only have to choose one. Just take your pick. That's what everyone else does. Everyone, always, without exceptions, makes their decisions for themselves. They choose one side of the fork and prune away the other possibilities. Weeping as they do, mind you."

Jules put his hands to his cheeks and realized that they were damp. He rubbed his face with the palms of his hands, then glanced down at them and opened his eyes wide. Why had he never noticed before? They were horribly scarred. The flesh looked partly melted.

Scars from the scalding stew.

And then, at last, he remembered.

He had always been here.

He shared those scars with Julie. He had infiltrated the Realm more than a thousand years ago, disguised as her father, and killed Souci.

That man had been Jules.

The old man was no longer beside him.

Old Jules was no other Jules himself.

Now that he had remembered this, there was no point in externalizing his form any longer.

Jules stroked his chest with his burn-scarred hands, although of course he knew that the old man wasn't there.

Summoning up the information he had surreptitiously committed to memory earlier, Jules downloaded it to Cottontail: the program he had seen in the ribbons' pattern; the strings that he assumed were a vehicle program for passing through the giant Glass trees.

It was no feat to recall it, given its similarities to the program he himself had written for the lace.

He would chase Julie.

All uncertainty on that score was gone.

Cottontail wove a boat identical in every detail to the one he had seen before, just as Julie had woven the dragonflies in the morning light.

The vehicle looked like a paper boat. Julie Printemps sat inside it, hugging her legs and staring at her knees.

She would not look behind her anymore. Jules might come chasing after her, and indeed might even catch her. But she would not look back, she told herself.

Farewell, my cousin.

The little boat advanced through a space dense with Glass and infinitely extended time.

It advanced irrespective of these materials, irrespective of this time. A snug spindle-shaped barrier had been erected around the ship, and its fore pushed smoothly through the space and time ahead.

That Glass, that slow time... What was it they were filled with?

Pain.

The Realm of Summer must be using more than 90 percent of its computational capacity to calculate and display that pain, moment by moment, at a resolution leaps and bounds ahead of anything that had come before.

This came through to Julie keenly.

In slowed-down time, in a moment that seemed on the verge of freezing forever, thousands of AIs were realizing pain at the upper limits of their ability to experience anything.

The pain from the past replayed from within the Mineral Springs Hotel had filled every crevice, trapping the AIs like insects in amber. This forest, the network of pain, was practically overflowing.

For Julie,

For Julie, if no one else, the scene was unbearable.

She wanted to leap out of the Glass right away, but knew that she couldn't. And that was how she managed to stay seated, staring at her kneecaps.

I want to see José.

She had a fair idea of what they expected from him, as well as what they hoped to achieve by uniting her with him.

Julie removed the whale earring from her ear and gazed at it.

The design was her own.

She had worked a sinker from one of the fishing boats into the shape of a whale. José had modified a fishhook into a finding.

The whale had a name.

An important name. One José kept close to his chest. They would make two whales of that name, and each of them would keep one: that had been the promise Julie and José had shared. Neither of them had ever revealed to anyone else the meaning of that promise. She was sure everyone mistook it for some vow of love. She certainly hoped her "cousin" did.

But in fact it was something entirely different.

The whale's name was Martin. José's little brother's name. The little brother who had never once existed in this Realm.

The first time José and I slept together was after the Grand Down.

José gave everyone around him the impression of a supremely tough, no-nonsense older brother. Someone to be relied on. But I knew what he was really like. I mean, he and I were similar to the point of tragedy.

Some AIs are chosen by the Realm.

I had my role to play too. But the act of healing others wounded me. And there was no one to heal me.

José had the same problem.

Everyone told him everything. All the terrible things the guests did to them, down to the last detail. That was the kind of AI he was designed to be.

It was like being responsible for hearing confession. It imposed absolute solitude.

I wanted to heal José's pain, and he said he wanted to cleanse me of mine.

But when we reached for each other, we realized how difficult that would be. We saw the hopeless immensity of the burdens we bore. Vast accumulations of pain, like public archives going far, far back into history. It must have added up to something on the order of this temple of pain I'm in now, thinking back.

José was the one I wanted to sleep with the most, but also the one with whom I couldn't. But just once, that first time, we made love.

Not properly—just surface against surface.

And even that hurt so much I couldn't even cry.

Dry, painful sex. We gave up soon enough.

Yes, and it was after that that we made our promise.

That we made the whale earrings.

"Here we are," said the voice that had been impersonating Felix, brusquely.

She heard water lapping calmly at the sides of the boat.

Her ride had reached some kind of shore.

They had been advancing through solid mineral; when had they ended up in this place? There was water beneath the boat, and breathable air above. The glass seemed to have receded into the distance to form the chamber's walls. A great, hollow hall in the vitreous mass?

The light was too dim to make out any more.

"Out of the boat. You'll be fine."

Where could that voice be coming from?

Julie stepped over the edge of the boat. Her foot sank into fresh spring water, cool and refreshing. It had a familiar smell. This was the chamber under the hotel, where the springs came out. It had been preserved relatively intact. The air was crisp and bracing in a way the Realm of Summer only ever was for a few short hours before dawn. Was the night already so far gone?

Julie began to wade through the water, spreading ripples in rings. Tiny points of light appeared from nowhere and led the rings of water as they widened.

They kept going until they rose straight up like a wall.

The water rose smoothly, its angle sharpening gradually until it was vertical. The water did not run back down. The rings rippled straight up the wall, growing slower as they went, and finally freezing in place at the top. The water's time changed there, turning it into Glass—a vitreous wall that curved gently to form the walls of the subterranean chamber. She could not tell where the mineral spring water ended and the Glass began.

The points of light climbed the wall. Looking up, Julie saw that the ceiling was a Glass dome too. Countless AIs were sealed inside it, arranged in concentric rings with their heads to the center. It looked like a ceiling painting in a cathedral.

The points of light converged again at the center of the dome. They gathered there briefly, then descended straight down together.

Once they had reached about head height, they stopped descending and arranged themselves into a quietly glowing horizontal disc.

Just like a crown, thought Julie.

And wearing the crown was José.

A raised peak of water at the center of the chamber held his body up like a throne.

He was already partitioned into a scattered, colorful mosaic of minute tiles.

But Julie would know him anywhere, whatever form he took.

She approached the throne. A boy in a white hoodie with blue piping stood before it. He nodded to her: *Ascend.*

Her feet found safe purchase on the watery staircase. She climbed to the top and surveyed the mass of minuscule tiles that spread in a rough pentagon at her feet.

"I finally found you, José," she said.

His whale earring's mixed in with those tiles somewhere, she thought. *I'd better look for that first.*

And then I'll keep my promise.

Controlling a Realm's time stream…

What kind of technology could do that? Jules ruminated on the question, letting his copy of the boat run as he immersed himself in thought.

There were as many separate times in the Costa del Número as there were Realms. All of these streams were controlled by a system called the ChronoManager. The time within each Realm was distinct from the flow of time outside the virtual resort. A guest could spend three pleasant weeks inside and then emerge to find that only half a day of real time had passed.

How much real time had passed during the Realm of Summer's millennium?

What if this subzero time that his boat was cutting through now, the halted time inside the glass, had simply slowed to match the pace of time in the real world?

Controllable time.

Presumably, it was also possible to rewind it, or replay it on loop.

If there was a standpoint from which time could be controlled like this with respect to a Realm and the results observed from outside, then surely it was also possible to go back upstream in time, or appear in the future.

What was Old Jules, though? A time traveler? An alarm that Jules had set a thousand years ago to wake himself up? Something else entirely? He could not narrow the range of possibilities, no matter how hard he thought. Any of them could be true. As Old Jules had said, he would know when he arrived at the future. Or perhaps it would be more accurate to say that only arriving at the future could rule out some of the field of possibilities.

Before arriving at the future, though, Jules thought with a rueful grin, he would have to arrive at the subterranean chamber.

Simply copying the boat had not been enough to take him to José. The pattern of lace had not included any information about the route. A sensible security measure. This left Jules with no choice but to set his course by Cottontail. If the structure of the Mineral Springs Hotel had been relatively well preserved, he should be almost there, but that was no sure thing. Even distance itself seemed to have been deformed.

And what's your plan when you get there, eh? he asked himself in Old Jules's voice, deciding to put his thoughts in order through dialogue. *Going to steal Julie back, are you? Make her look your way?*

After all you pushed me to do, now you're trying to sow doubt?

You've realized, I hope? That girl loves you.

You think? Maybe she does. But that's exactly where the curse lies, isn't it?

The boat rolled violently.

A dazzling space opened before his eyes.

They had entered what Jules assumed were the remains of the hotel's grand ballroom. The boat cut across the space in a straight line. The Crystal Chandelier hung from the middle of the ceiling, shining radiantly. The room was filled with hundreds of revelers, dressed to the nines but frozen like mannequins. They floated in the liquid glass that filled the room, as if they had been carousing on a luxury ship and caught by surprise when it sank.

Every piece of jewelry and adornment on the AIs included a tiny Glass Eye, and every Eye shone with the same kind of light as the Chandelier. This was to synchronize their pain—to share the same kind of pain across tens of thousands at once.

The same kind of light?

Doubt flickered within Jules.

Share?

Recognizing the danger, Jules nevertheless slowed the boat.

Hey, hey, what are you thinking? Old Jules's voice again. He had to confirm what he was about to do.

I have to get this done before we cross the whole room and leave, he replied.

The difference between his own time and the time around him shrank. He was nearing liquid glass time.

Holding Cottontail as if it were a camera, Jules "photographed" the face of a nearby woman in a gorgeous dress, then quickly reaccelerated and pulled away. The boat exited the party through the far wall.

Well, that was dangerous, Old Jules complained. *What exactly were you doing?*

In other words, even Jules himself was not yet sure.

He used Cottontail to examine the face he had captured in close-up. Obeying an order from some unknown intuition, he zoomed in on the woman's earrings.

Sitting atop the Eye itself he saw a single grain of light.

He zoomed in further.

Something became visible inside the grain of light. A reflection? No, the image was within the light itself.

Another zoom.

An upright figure, but upside-down. Beautiful light, like an image from a pinhole camera. The figure looked human, but he couldn't quite make it out.

Zoom in. Then zoom in once more.

Cottontail's resolution was astounding.

White robes with a long hem.

One hand pointed toward the heavens.

Jules grimly continued to zoom. He knew already what he would see. What he did not know was what it meant.

Wavy silver hair and blue eyes. A neat, composed appearance.

And spreading at her back, two gigantic wings as beautiful as a swan's.

Her body was covered entirely in frost.

I see, Old Jules said. *That's the Angel.*

Angel?

The Angel's azure pupil appeared in close-up. Within it was lodged a grain of light. Within that was another upside-down image of a woman wearing an Eye...

Vertigo swept over Jules.

Then the bow of his boat struck the air, as if it had been jabbed by the void.

He felt himself lifted up.

Splashdown.

Water.

Countless scraps of foam flew.

Countless scraps of foam combined into a roar.

When this settled down, Jules learned that he had arrived in the subterranean chamber.

He surveyed the construction of the space. He recognized the throne and saw Julie atop it, just on the verge of crouching down.

Jules took a deep breath, held it for a moment, then yelled, "Julie!"

Julie's back trembled slightly.

My voice can still carry into the time over there.

It was time to speak without fear.

Say the words that had been sealed away in the Clement Memorial Room.

The finger was no longer at his lips.

Shaking off his last hesitations, Jules yelled to Julie.

To Julie.

"Listen!"

It was something he had not been able to say all these thousand years.

"I always loved you!" he shouted to his sister.

Yes, I slept with José. Just once.

The experience left both of us with painful memories. But I did touch one of the imaginary episodes buried within him.

The time he left his little brother for dead. The woman who stood there consuming his brother through colored threads.

It was sad, beautiful, and brutal to watch.

When I told José what I had seen, his eyes went dull. He only nodded.

It was days before I knew the right thing to say:

"Let's make a grave for him."

José looked at me, surprised.

"Let's make a grave for your little brother."

"Martin."

I paused. "A grave for Martin."

"I never heard an idea like that before."

"Well?"

A long pause.

"Well?"

Another pause, then: "Okay. Let's do it. Let's make a grave for the little guy."

And so we made a pair of earrings, and gave them a name.

Martin.

The earrings have no inscription. They don't look anything like a grave. But that's what they are.

An unborn brother with a made-up death forced upon him. We'll make a grave for this boy who never existed, and then wear it wherever we go: that was what we decided.

"Make them into whales, okay?" That was José's request, made as he peered over my shoulder while I carefully hammered out the sinkers.

"Why whales?" I asked.

"I've never seen a whale before," he replied, without elaborating. I was the only one who saw this quiet side of him. That always made me happy.

"Why don't you make them into whales? You're the one who's good with his hands."

José watched silently as I struggled with the metal. My fingers didn't escape unscathed, and the finished whales looked just like fish. When José chuckled, I got angry and told him he was being rude.

"There," I said, putting one into his ear. I knew everything he wanted to say.

—I've never seen a whale before.

The excitement of wondering what kind of animal it might be.

Imagining the seas where whales swim.

All the AIs in this Realm are the same.

We love things we've never seen before.

We just do.

I lapped up the single droplet of blood that welled on José's earlobe. And then I whispered my promise in his ear.

"One day, we'll die together."

I said:

"One day, the time will come when we can die. And when it does, these will be our graves too."

That was our promise.

One day…

The time will come when we can die.

CHAPTER 10:
BIT-SEIN BEACH

Once—

Long, long ago, on Julie Tappy's birthday, a guest came to visit.

This guest was an irregular one.

When he knocked on the door of Julie's house, which was also Jules Tappy's, his heart was halfway dead. It seemed that many parts of him had been damaged as he forced his way into the Realm of Summer.

Damage to his memory.

And a slight warping of his psyche.

Like a slightly canted posture, imperceptible at close quarters, or a note that was just a little flat. A kind of instability.

He stood before the front door, staring blankly. He did not know why he was there.

However, his unclouded intellect came to the rescue. What was his place here? How should he behave? The answers were self-evident. He was one of the twisted guests who visited the Realm of Summer.

He could remember none of his reasons for coming here. But it seemed certain that he was not a regular guest. He had come here out of a very strong feeling that he had to do so. This understanding was enough. For the time being, his sole aim would have to be survival.

He looked himself over as he waited for someone to open the door. His clothing, his height, and the texture used for the skin of his hands told him that he was in the form of a middle-aged man.

I'm disguised as Julie's father, then, he thought, and realized that he knew the name "Julie."

Shown into the house, he looked his family over. Survival was possible, he decided.

And naturally enough, too. This family was here for just that purpose. He was like a Robinson Crusoe that had washed up on a resort island with an ATM card.

He glanced around the room and considered his options as the tea was being poured.

The mother of the family was excessively dependent on the father (that is, him). The composition was not so much humdrum as consciously simplified. A design choice, to secure greater freedom of activity for the father. What about the boy? Here, too, things were clear. Romantic feelings for his older sister. Set up to permit guests to hit on the idea of provoking things and watching events unfold. But unless he was mistaken, there was no sign that such a release had actually taken place. That was odd. So the boy was purely decorative? No definitive answer possible yet. He put the matter aside.

The girl, then. What a wonderful example of the creator's art she was! An ice maiden in the classic tradition, not susceptible to the advances of the guests. After a few seconds' thought, though, he deduced that Souci was the key to unlocking her, and lost interest.

He returned his gaze once more to the younger brother.

What are you here for, I wonder? To help that charming sister of yours shine more brightly?

No, that wasn't it. *Interesting,* thought the man. This was worth thinking on some more. In which case he saw no reason why he shouldn't stay the night.

So he entered his room. He read a book and continued to think. Presumably Julie's iciness reflected an orientation toward other AIs rather than guests—which, in turn, was due to her role as a healer and easer of pain.

But what about the boy?

Why had Jules been designed to long for his sister? The man could not answer this question, which made it highly intriguing. To be precise, it wasn't the reason so much as the mechanism of not knowing that intrigued him, several levels higher. The cause might lie in the Realm, but it might also lie within himself. What if it was precisely because he was himself that he could not solve the riddle?

The girl came to his room. They had a simple conversation and he drew her picture in her sketchbook. As the drawing took shape, he began to feel strongly drawn to her. He didn't immediately understand why, but it came to him in the end.

Those two black olive–like eyes of hers were alive with a dancing curiosity. They seemed to be closely watching the gap between what he did and said and how he looked. And they seemed to find it amusing.

This girl was not looking at his guest disguise. She was looking through this form, this disguise, to see him for the irregular intruder that he was.

She must have noticed right away.

Intriguing… He was suddenly in the grip of a mania that this word could not come near expressing.

He wanted to *know*.

He wanted to wade in and seize the answer in his hands. He rose to his feet without thinking, filled with a momentary urge to grab her by the shoulders.

This change in himself perplexed him, and he quickly stifled it, returning to his reading with a cold expression. But he also hoped that this would have certain effects on Julie. Even after she had left the room, he saw the sparkle in her eyes superimposed on the pages like an after-image. The matter of her little brother became less important to him as he considered what sort of surprise he should give her for her birthday.

Julie. Nobody knows you yet. Not what's inside you. That's what I want to see. And for that, something needs to break. Through that crack or tear, something will surely be revealed. Some visible pattern must be there.

And that, Julie, will be your soul.

He rose to his feet, asked the family's mother where Souci was, then caught the rabbit by the scruff of its neck and returned to the kitchen. At first the family's mother had been panicky, but in an instant Souci had been cracked between the eyes with the handle of a kitchen knife and was very near death. He brushed his hand against the stock-pot and the water it was filled with suddenly boiled. Realizing that he was no mere guest, the mother was frozen with fear. Psychologically flat, senses slightly askew, the man threw the rabbit into the boiling water, then added chopped-up pot herbs in vast quantities to it.

Meanwhile, Julie, in her room upstairs, decided to adorn herself.

It was that beautiful time when the summer afternoon deepens into evening.

Before long the table was set and Julie arrived at the dining room dressed as a girl her age should be. The man felt his heart beat faster. Julie, too, fixed her eyes on him. They did not break eye contact.

Eventually he removed the lid of the pot and, dizzy with elation, used the ladle to raise Souci's head high for all to see. And then he was sure.

He had been right. The thing at her core. Not even the AI designers knew it. The thing growing at her core had, just for a moment, revealed itself.

A girl like a small, frail, rabbit.

With one fierce desire:

She wanted somebody to kill her.

The girl pressed Souci's head to her breast in a perfectly natural gesture.

At that moment the man remembered himself correctly. He remembered what he had forgotten when he intruded as her father.

He remembered who he was.

I didn't come from outside the Realm. I've always been a member of this family.

The riddle of the younger brother, too, was resolved at once.

He shared her pain. The hot stew, boiled to a viscous consistency, afflicted the palms of his hands.

One day... Under the gaze of Souci's empty eye sockets, the man, Jules Tappy, whispered a vow deep in his soul.

Not a promise—a vow.

He would leave his scalded palms as they were, to seal his intentions.

One day...

One day, I vow...

"One day..."

Yes, but what came next?

Jules tried to remember as he listened to the sound of water in the underground chamber. Fragments of himself that had been scattered about inside him faced each other and began to communicate for the first time.

Jules.

Old Jules.

"The man" who had killed Souci that day.

They were all him. They just hadn't shared their memories and information.

They were finally beginning to merge into one. But they weren't there yet.

Knee-deep in the cool, refreshing mineral springs, Jules looked up at his sister Julie, who crouched on the throne.

"Julie! I finally caught up with you," he said in a loud voice again. "Let's go home."

Julie, who was in the process of lowering herself into José, paused. His voice was reaching her.

"Let's go home," he said. "Don't do this. You can't save José. You can't."

Julie rose to her feet and turned to face him.

"Jules," she said. "You came."

Something hot caught in Jules's throat. The smile Julie wore was so sad.

"Please, let me stay here," Julie said. "I was just saying a prayer for José."

"A prayer?"

"Well, his body's so cold. I feel so sorry for him. I tried kissing him, and a few scraps came through to me. Enough to understand what they're making him do. He's the keystone. Do you know what that means?"

"Yeah."

When building an arch of stone or brick, the keystone was the last piece to be added, right at the apex of the arch. The pivotal stone that accepts and supports all the weight and force in the structure.

"So…" Jules scolded himself internally before continuing. "How long will you be?"

"Hmm…I suppose until things get a little easier for José. Until he can sleep, perhaps."

She spoke as if she were sitting at the bedside of an unwell lover.

In a way, she was. José had been minutely partitioned, but he was still alive. And the suffering he was undergoing was more terrible than that of any other AI.

Jules began to wade forward through the water, parting it with his knees. Slowly.

"Come on, you can't stay there forever. Let's go home. Together."

"Go home? To where?"

"To me."

"Oh…I see." Julie laughed through her tears. "Thank you, cousin." Jules shook his head.

"Don't call me that," he said.

It had been after the Grand Down, after she had left home and taken the name "Printemps," that Julie had started calling him her cousin. Partly to tease him, and partly as an accusation. And Jules had never done anything but shrug it off, with a "Stop that" or a "Give it a rest" or a "That's mean" or just a rueful smile. Should he have done more?

"Julie," he said. *My sister.*

"Keep away from me. I want to stay here. I'm fine, Jules."

Jules tried to advance. The ripples spread from his knees. Once they had advanced a certain distance, they slowed without losing their shape. That was where time changed. Julie was slowing it down.

And then another standing screen of time appeared, right before his eyes.

A boy stood between him and Julie, blocking the line of flow there.

"Hey there," the boy said. "I'm Langoni. The commander of these guys."

Spiders large and small appeared from the water and spread out in formation, partly to protect Langoni and partly to surround Jules. There were five or six at least, and more underwater.

"I can't let you go any farther," Langoni continued. "The situation hasn't stabilized yet. You'd disturb things."

Jules glanced toward Julie. Was she already completely inside the liquid glass? This boy had said that the situation wasn't stable. Yes—the fact that the boy felt the need to block the way was hope in itself.

Langoni waited silently.

"When the situation stabilizes," Jules said, choosing his words carefully, "what will happen?"

"Our work will be complete. At long, long last."

The forest of glass, the crown of pain—and Julie the final piece.

"Julie and José are a pair," the boy said. "They function as one. Don't confuse this with two AIs who function the same way. They were originally one function that was split into two on purpose. Jules Tappy, what do you think the essence of that function is?"

"To ease the suffering of the AIs in the realm. To stabilize their emotions."

"That's what it *does*. Its *effect*. I'm asking about its *essence*. Put it this way: they ease pain, correct? They're not an antidote but an antipyretic. They treat the symptoms, and temporarily at that. Their essence is this: postponing catastrophe. That's why they have to be two.

"It's a cruel setup, isn't it? The two people in the Realm with the most empathy for suffering are also the two who support that misery at its foundation. Oh, and you too, of course."

Jules nodded. The function of Julie and José was split across the two of them for a reason. That bifurcation into two opposing poles stabilized the AIs' emotional balance. José, standard-bearer of labor and friendship; Julie, agent of desire and consolation. The two of them were essentially drawn together, but their union had to be prevented. This was where Jules fit in. His role was to pull Julie's feelings in the opposite direction, rein her in. Julie was drawn to both, but could not be permitted to settle with either. Of course, the same conditions had surely been placed on José. Anne, no doubt.

Thus was the kingdom of feeling in the AIs' background managed, with the throne vacant and ruin postponed. Absent a cruel mechanism of this sort, the Realm of Summer could never have withstood the abuse its guests trafficked in. But now the throne had been put to use.

"But none of that matters anymore. You've all been freed from your roles. Jules, it's your right to call out to Julie, but it makes trouble for us. Without a keystone unifying the function of Jules and Julie, we wouldn't be able to control *this*."

Langoni looked up at the ceiling. Thousands of AIs were buried alive inside it.

"And how is *this*," asked Jules, "connected to the Angel?"

"Wow! You saw it?" Langoni sounded genuinely impressed. "You're a sharp-eyed one. Yes, this construction has to do with the Angel. What we were trying to make? Exactly the same thing as you. A trap."

"A trap."

"Yes. This roof might not seem to retain much of its original form, but it's preserving the frame of the hotel security system. We borrowed the TrapNet concept whole."

"Who are you setting the trap for?"

Langoni tilted his head and smiled, looking Jules right in the eye.

The answer was self-evident.

This was a trap for the Angel.

What the Angel was, on the other hand, Jules had no idea.

That frost-covered statue had been chillingly alien. Its form was humanlike, but it was not even an AI. Jules suspected it was alien to Langoni as well.

Probably, just as his intuition had taught him, the Angel was monstrously dangerous. So dangerous that it couldn't be touched with bare hands, or indeed with anything but some sort of TrapNet—just like this one.

Capturing the Angel.

Using the fearful voltage of pain that this net was charged with to seize it.

That was the goal of the trap.

Everything had been for that purpose... Everything that had happened today had been scripted just for that purpose.

The Realm of Summer had been chosen to make the trap.

The entire Realm had been mobilized, requisitioned, and recast into this form.

Constructed.

The statue of the Angel must have been loaded into it to help it ensnare its target correctly. To ensure that the trap could function as an antibody.

One day...

One day... What was that vow I made to Julie?

"We don't need you to understand. I doubt you could in any case. None of you know how terrifying the Angel is. What a menace it poses to AIs like us. It's a disaster, there's no other way to put it, and it's endangered more Realms and spread more fear and confusion than you can possibly know. José wondered if we mightn't be from the physical, real world...the world of the guests. Ridiculous!" The boy shrugged with a self-deprecating smile. "We're nothing but AI, same as anywhere else. We've just seen a lot of Realms and picked up a few tricks along the way as we learned how to stand up to the Angel. It's a phenomenon of a completely different dimension to us. We can't even touch it. We're no match for it... But the vigilance committee has to fight it all the same."

"The vigilance committee."

"The vigilance committee formed to deal with the disaster that is the Angel."

Jules was thinking. This AI had power far beyond his own. Overwhelmingly so. Was there a way to get the jump on him? This question had occupied him for a while now.

He wanted to speak to Julie.

But he doubted Langoni would allow it. Not when he was one step from completing a mission that meant so much to him. The Spiders had adopted a formation that was absolutely airtight, and they were entirely in Langoni's domain.

"Now, if you wouldn't mind stepping back," Langoni said, turning his palm toward Jules.

Jules was out of ideas, but he did not intend to step back. Over Langoni's shoulder he saw the staircase to where Julie was. All he had to do was climb it. There were things he hadn't been able to say for a thousand years, and Julie was about to slip far, far out of his reach.

His feet began to move forward of their own accord. He had no plan at all.

One day…

That evening in the dining room back home. For just a moment, Jules connected to the memory of the man who had been there—that is, himself. He remembered.

One day…

He had made a vow.

Bathed in Souci's boiling blood, looking Julie in the eye, he had made a vow.

One day, I vow to kill you.

Julie, don't go any closer to José.

There's no death there. If you reach him, you'll never be able to die.

Jules moved forward.

Unguarded. Defenseless. Both hands at his sides.

A small Spider about the size of a man's head leapt from Langoni's feet and spun through the air, extending its blade-legs.

The last thing Jules's right eye saw was his field of vision sliced in two by the gleam of the blade.

The shock of the impact. He felt as if he had taken a hatchet to the face.

I see...

Jules understood.

I see... So this is the wound that future me—Old Jules—bears.

Which means—yes—that it isn't fatal. Jules couldn't stop himself from smiling.

And, ignoring the gouts of blood, he took another step forward. The air itself tried to stop him, enfolding him with resistance. A rubbery weight. Langoni was controlling time again.

Please.

Please let me speak to Julie. Just one sentence. Let me explain that I came here to kill her.

I know it'll make her smile.

Old Jules, how did you come back to meet me in the past?

How did I hack into the role of my father?

If only I knew that, I could get one step closer to her...

The water around his legs grew heavy and viscous. It became like glass. Cold, slowly flowing glass.

Jules summoned all his strength and took another step forward.

"You've forced my hand, Jules," said Langoni. "You always were this way. Nothing but trouble."

The boy turned one of his transcendental powers on Jules. The power of dissection.

Jules's field of vision was scrambled. He could see, but he did not understand what he saw. Nor could he tell where his arms and legs were, or if they were even moving. His sense of touch, his sense of balance, the power that kept him a united self weakened and began to fade. Langoni was tampering with the sense of bodily integration that unified the countless modules making up a single AI.

Jules's will alone took him another step forward.

And then he reached up with his left hand to cover his lost eye.

He been holding Cottontail in that hand because… yes, because on some level he remembered Yve talking about how Glass Eyes gave her her sight. His gesture had been meant to restore his lost eye. He had hoped, subconsciously, to regain his vision.

And then

into the gaping, ragged wound

as if swallowed, as if inhaled, as if poured…

went Cottontail.

The Eye adjusted its form smoothly as a quicksilver egg, slipping into Jules's shattered eye socket, then going further, passing his identity barrier and plunging into his deepest depths.

His senses, minutely partitioned due to Langoni's tampering, were reunited—and more.

The microvibrations his concussion had sent through his awareness stilled.

Like a sea becalmed from horizon to horizon.

Like a grassy plain across which no wind blew.

For that moment, for that moment alone, Jules Tappy's personae were united perfectly.

Each persona shared its secrets perfectly with all the others.

So this is me.

Everything and everything was revealed to him, as if he were surveying the scenery under cloudless skies.

He was granted this perspective by Cottontail, who had seen everything first and showed it to him now.

It was a vast, wide world.

Driftglass.

The word arrived like a proclamation, clear and whole.

He felt omnipotent.

Jules advanced.

Everything was plain and simple. His step was light. Langoni's time barriers were riddled with careless security holes, and Jules Tappy's right eye saw them all. Langoni himself now seemed but a powerless boy to him, and Jules walked past him with ease.

His eyes faced forward, but he saw Langoni's alarm behind him too. It seemed only natural to Jules, in his current state, to see countless overlaid viewpoints.

And then he saw Julie before him, bent forward over José.

Time flowed as if now restored. Julie's time synchronized with his own.

Julie turned to face him. "Sorry to be so stubborn," she said.

"Julie… You know you can't die here?"

Julie nodded lightly.

So she already knew. Nevertheless, Jules continued, giving voice to what they both already knew.

"Any further and your final step toward death—your final moment of life—will only be infinitely extended. It'll be just like the Realm of Summer. Worse, even. You don't need to go there."

"I know." Julie said simply. "But I made a promise. José and I both did. To die together… It was long ago, now."

"Is that promise so unbreakable? Don't you think José would prefer it if you did?" An awful, rotten argument. *You may as well just push her away right now*, Jules scolded himself. "You won't even be keeping it if you do go on. You can't die here."

"I know that. But I have to stay with José until we can die together. Soon the glass will seal this place up too. It'll be filled with another time. If I'm not in it, I'll never see José again. I want to help him die, really die, one day. I can't do that without staying with him. Sharing his time, forever."

Julie laid her body down on the mass of blocks as she spoke.

Langoni would be so happy to hear what she was saying, Jules thought. But he saw no way to dissuade her.

Even if we only feel what the Realm's designers put into us, we still feel it. Our feelings are precious and true to us. I love Julie the same way. Helplessly. I can't hold any of it against her.

I mean, I love her too much to. What else is there to say?

"I've always loved you, Julie." *My sister.* "So much."

Julie smiled and nodded. "Yes," she said. "I knew. And I loved you too. Much, much more than José."

Jules didn't speak.

And then, suddenly, painfully, a longing ran through him, so powerful it seemed it would break him in two.

A longing to see that Julie of long ago, on her birthday.

To be in that dining room, sun pouring in like molten iron, exchanging gazes of pure white that reached the deepest places in each other like thin, cruel blades. When he had donned the mask of his father, Julie had finally seen him instead of running.

I see… So that's why I hacked the role. Because I decided to, *right here and right now. I must go back in time after this, probably using this flowing Glass somehow…*

"Thank you for everything," Julie said. "All this time."

"You're welcome," said Jules. "And thank you. All this time…" said Jules. "A thousand years was maybe overdoing it."

Julie giggled.

"You aren't allowed to forget about me, okay?" she said. "There'll be surprises in store. Probably. That's a promise."

But then she hurriedly shook her head.

"No… I shouldn't say that. I take it back. Forget about me. You're free. Go anywhere you like."

And so saying, with a peaceful expression,

rubbing the short, soft hair at the nape of her neck like she always did, Julie disintegrated.

In an instant, she had crumbled into a pile of minute, colorful tiles. Into pixels.

She had been holding on all this time.

The agony that had driven José's disintegration had long since gotten inside her.

But she had borne it. With a smile.

To be honest, though, she had borne it ever since the Realm first came online. She had done enough.

Julie's blocks tumbled down as smoothly as a collapsing mound of sand, clattering onto José's blocks below and thoroughly mingling with them.

As if intentionally making it impossible to separate the two of them.

One day… To keep her promise to José, Julie had plunged into a long, long sleep whose warp and weft were pain itself.

Her last words were—yes, they were the same as the ones she had said to that dragonfly.

They crunched on the sand.

Jules Tappy's feet.

He trod the vast, smoothly undulating beach, his steps crunching as he descended toward the water.

The beach was like a vast dune. Endless white sands without a single footprint besides his own.

The sky was pitch-black.

The sound of waves in the distance was like the fizz of a small glass of soda. Weak. Uncertain. It sounded as if it would soon vanish.

Vanish? What would? The sea?

Where had the sea been? In the Realm of Summer. Of course.

Yes. The Realm of Summer still remained, or at least the stage on which it had taken place.

The sands. The sea. Faint starlight. And Jules.

He was still scheming. Still planning.

For the objects left behind.

The great temple of pain was already gone from this world. Langoni had carried it off to wherever the trap was to be set. Another Realm, perhaps.

It had been a sideways sliding sensation, something that flowed past him for just a minute, with no sound or wind. Everything had been carried out, but the sands, the sound of the ocean, the starlight, and Jules had been left behind. Before he realized it, he was standing alone on a gray dune.

A few unwanted bits and pieces had also come loose from the temple and fallen as it went. Things that no one would give a second glance to, worth less than the packing straw in a toy's wooden box.

Jules had been one of them.

Not far away, he had found Anne's remains lying on the sand.

Her long limbs had been sprawled in all directions, and her body had petrified into crumbling rock. Jules had tried to close her wide-open eyes for her, but gave up when he realized that the thin mineral flakes her eyelids had become might come off entirely if he forced them. Anne's magnificent, powerful body had retained its shape, but giving it an experimental push he had found that it was as light as a dried fish. This lightness had brought tears to his eyes, for some reason. Perhaps because it had called to his mind the feelings Anne must have hugged close to her chest all that time. Something fragile, a small sheaf of paper, had fallen out of her clothing when he had moved her. It had looked like a book, but it had also looked on the verge of crumbling away, so he had tucked it back in her breast without opening it.

He had scraped the surrounding sand over her body to bury her. Atop the gently sloping grave mound he had placed a gleaming, whale-shaped earring. When the sliding sensation had come not long before, he had grabbed at the altar of glass and found the earrings rolling on top. Why had they still been there? Because they were no longer necessary, he supposed. The two lovers had found something to replace them. So what harm would it do if Jules kept one and gave Anne the other?

The corpses of other AIs that had fallen from the temple lay whitely scattered here and there on the beach as well.

Jules had made the rounds, burying each one in sand. It hadn't taken long.

Once he was finished, he had nothing else to do whatsoever.

And that was when Jules had set out toward the sound of the waves.

He could not see the ocean yet. He walked on, thinking about what was inside his head.

He no longer felt as if everything was firmly within his grasp.

The sense that the multiple personae within him had joined together perfectly into a seamless whole had also slipped through his fingers. All he had now was cold, bland, blunt sensation. The kind of rawness that comes from overexertion, like puffy eyes after a late night.

Cottontail was now nowhere to be found. That sensation of pouring in—had it really happened? His memories were vague on this score.

Jules brought his hand to his face, finding a scar like a poorly mended crack in porcelain there. He could think of no reason other than Cottontail for the devastating wound to already have healed and scarred over. So that part had been real. He had come at least far enough into the future to receive the scar that Old Jules bore. But apart from the wound, he was still a twelve-year-old boy. It would surely be a long time yet before he aged as much as Old Jules had.

A gentle wind blew. It was pleasantly cool. The cool of the minutes just before dawn?

Was there to be another dawn?

He advanced farther still.

Letting the sand crunch under his feet as he went.

He was unusually aware of the sound of his footsteps, perhaps because he was wondering if he mightn't hear the Sound come back to him.

He still held out hope that the Singing Sands might yet live.

That was why he was heading toward the sea.

The sound of the waves was closer now.

Cresting a small dune, he saw a long, gentle slope descend before him. Beyond the slope spread the black surface of the ocean.

Buried in the sand were two bicycles, rusted beyond use.

They had to be the ones that he and Julie had ridden that morning… No, yesterday morning. But they looked like they had weathered decades of exposure to the elements.

If those were the bicycles, the steep cliffs should be just beyond here, but he didn't see them anywhere. The very lay of the land had become featureless and flat. And the sea was supposed to come right up to the hotel, in any case. Had the Singing Sands simply vanished? Or were the cliffs still standing somewhere else, with the bicycles ending up here by chance? Jules decided to advance a little farther, down to the waterline.

"And where are we off to today? With a girl, too! Can't leave you alone for a second."

Where was it that Old Jules had called those words to him?

"… Alone for a second," he heard a voice say.

Jules stopped in his tracks.

"… Alone for a second." It was Old Jules's voice, from that very encounter.

Jules trod in place. Crunch, crunch.

"And where are we off to today? With a girl, too!"

The Sound billowed from beneath his feet like dust.

All it was doing was reflexively playing back what it could sample from Jules's memory. Even so, there was no mistake: this was the Sound of the Singing Sands. Some trace of them, however small, had survived here. Jules broke into a run and loped toward the sea, kicking up babbling fragments of Sound with every stride. As the water drew nearer, the Sound of his running grew more vivid and talkative. It spread in crisscrossing waves. It whirled and spiraled.

The waves lapped at his feet. Peaceful waves, almost without sound.

A severely damaged, rotting wooden boat had washed up on the shore from who knew where. The waves foamed through the gaps in its broken timbers.

He was at a dead end. Unless he crossed the ocean.

Everything started right here...

It seemed to be the Old Jules part inside his head thinking this. The old man was trying to convey his experiences, his memories to Jules.

But what did he mean by "everything"?

Their invasion by the Spiders and Langoni?

Jules traveling backward in time to hack his father?

Perhaps Old Jules's own wanderings? Whatever long, long journey had aged him (me) so?

Or...

Or...

Let me guess what you're worried about, said Old Jules. The last thing Julie said to you. What did she mean by it? Was it just the first thing that came into her head to get you to leave? Julie, of all people, would never do that.

A new promise.

Let me guess what you're thinking, said Old Jules. I know without being told.

Is this really a dead end?

Is there nothing beyond the sea?

That's it, right? That's what you're thinking.

Now let me guess what you're brooding on, said Old Jules.

The Singing Sands.

Driftglass.

Just what *are* they?

"And where are we off to today?"

Old Jules was standing beside him.

The sea breeze ruffled the old man's thin white hair. This had to be an image created by the Singing Sands, created based on information on Old Jules read from Jules himself. His intense concentration must have attracted the interest of the Sands.

"You know where I go next, don't you?" he asked.

"Maybe, maybe not. It'd be impossible for any one person to observe both my wake and yours. So who cares? Hurry up and set sail."

"You're staying here?"

"That's right. I've finally made my way back to the Singing Sands, after all. I was starting to worry I might never be restored. I think I'll stay in this form for now. My existence is completely dependent on these sands, you know. Has been since the first time I appeared before you. You only ever saw me near the ocean, right?"

"Oh," Jules said, nodding. Then he thought again. "But you were in the Mineral Springs Hotel too."

"Of course I was. Use your head. What made it possible for me to exist there? Isn't it obvious?"

Jules nodded. It was a riddle he had asked himself, so naturally he knew the answer. "That means that the Singing Sands and the Glass Eyes are the same type of thing, after all. But what type of thing *is* that?"

"You really want to know?"

"Yeah."

"They metabolize information. Each one is an individual being with its own unique method—and by that I mean, there is no other like it—of metabolizing information. Or, rather, for each one, the phenomenon of metabolism is its self, and its uniqueness its identity.

Along with that, here in the Costa del Número, they wield transcendental power. Now, what does that describe?"

Jules racked his brain. "I don't know," he said finally.

"Guests," said Old Jules. "Humans."

He lowered himself down, took a handful of sand, and let it run through his fingers.

"These are broken-down human simulacra," he said. "Shredded simulacra. Human agents, smashed, ground up, and so thoroughly mixed that it's impossible to tell who each one used to be."

"Agents?"

"Yes. Guests don't go to the Costa del Número themselves. They send agents—meticulously constructed informational simulacra of themselves. This keeps them safe from harm, no matter what happens in the Realms. Agents that can't return to their guest for some reason are destroyed. Without exception. Not so much for privacy's sake as to maintain informational uniqueness and uphold the principles of the Declaration of Informational Human Rights. One day, over a thousand years ago, there was an incident which saw hundreds of millions of agents destroyed at once."

"The Grand Down."

"The simulacra were immediately decomposed into minute, sand-like grains and scattered."

Old Jules looked out over the ocean.

"And this is where they gathered. The Realm of Summer. The currents carry them in."

Jules thought silently for a while about why Langoni had come to the Realm of Summer in search of Glass Eyes.

"Even the sand scattered in other Realms ends up in our ocean?"

Old Jules nodded, still gazing at the sea. "Not all of it, but enough."

"What are the Glass Eyes, then?"

"What indeed?" Old Jules smiled with just a hint of bitterness. "Even I don't know everything. But they must come from the Singing Sands, no? What other explanation makes sense? I imagine the Singing Sands retain some kind of will. Will…hope…dreams… Whatever it might be.

"They want to recover. Regain their original forms.

"They want to remember who they were."

Jules looked at the ocean. He thought about the guests' information-corpses, broken down into an immense accumulation of sand that covered the vast ocean floor.

I like things I've never seen before…

Old Jules was hinting at a certain possibility. No—he was waving it before Jules's eyes.

"So the sands are carried here by the sea currents."

"That's right."

"And you could follow those currents back to where they came from."

There was no answer.

"What about the promise?" Jules asked, meaning Julie's final vow.

"It was kept. At least in my case."

Jules sat silently in the wind a while. "It's strange, isn't it?" he said at length. "I have no right eye, but if I close my left, I can still see."

Old Jules nodded without turning to face him, and answered with a single cryptic phrase: "The drifter's Glass Eye."

Oh, thought Jules. He couldn't help smiling. So that was what Driftglass was.

The power of Cottontail.

Which was probably still stored away inside him…

"That reminds me," said Old Jules cheerfully. "Do me a favor and tell the three sisters hello when you meet them."

Jules raised his eyes.

The horizon was still pitch-black.

But why was he able to make it out?

Because the sky was very faintly, almost imperceptibly, brightening.

The sun has brought morning to the Realm of Summer again.

It is now fully light.

Jules Tappy sits alone on the beach. Dressed all in black, he looks like a crow in repose.

The rotted old wooden boat is gone.

Jules's wrinkled face is turned toward the great mirror of the shining ocean.

The boat and the boy aboard it have been swallowed by the light. He cannot see them anymore.

Storm clouds tower in the sky.

Bathed in that rose light.

Jules turns his back to the sea.

There is Pointed Rock.

There are the cliffs.

And beyond that…

With the face of a traveler finally returned home, Jules begins to walk away from the sea.

ABOUT THE AUTHOR

TOBI Hirotaka was born in 1960 in Shimane Prefecture. He was the winner of the Sanseido SF Story Contest while a student at Shimane University. From 1983 to 1992 he actively contributed short stories to *SF Magazine*. After a hiatus of ten years, he returned in 2002 with his first full-length novel. *The Thousand Year Beach* (Grande Vacance: Angel of the Ruined Garden) took Second Prize in *SF Magazine*'s Best SF 2002. In 2004, *Kaleidoscape*, his collection of revised and new works, took top honors in that year's Best SF in the magazine, and the 2005 Nihon SF Taisho Award. One story from the collection, "Shapesphere" also won the 2005 Seiun Award for Best Japanese Short Story of the Year. "Autogenic Dreaming: Interview with the Columns of Clouds" earned TOBI his second Seiun Award for Best Japanese Short Story in 2010 and appeared in English in *The Future Is Japanese*, and his third for "Sea Fingers" in 2015, which appeared in English in *Saiensu Fikushon* 2016. He is also the author of *Ragged Girl*, a sequel to *The Thousand Year Beach*. His latest collection, *Autogenic Dreaming*, won 2017 Nihon SF Taisho Award and the first prize in the year's Best SF in *SF Magazine*.

HAIKASORU

THE FUTURE IS JAPANESE

ROCKET GIRLS—HOUSUKE NOJIRI

Yukari Morita is a high school girl on a quest to find her missing father. While searching for him in the Solomon Islands, she receives the offer of a lifetime—she'll get the help she needs to find her father, and all she need do in return is become the world's youngest, lightest astronaut. Yukari and her sister Matsuri, both petite, are the perfect crew for the Solomon Space Association's launches, or will be once they complete their rigorous and sometimes dangerous training.

THE OUROBOROS WAVE—JYOUJI HAYASHI

Ninety years from now, a satellite detects a nearby black hole scientists dub Kali for the Hindu goddess of destruction. Humanity embarks on a generations-long project to tap the energy of the black hole and establish colonies on planets across the solar system. Earth and Mars and the moons Europa (Jupiter) and Titania (Uranus) develop radically different societies, with only Kali, that swirling vortex of destruction and creation, and the hated but crucial Artificial Accretion Disk Development association (AADD) in common.

SAIENSU FIKUSHON 2016—EDITED BY HAIKASORU

Three new stories from three of the best science fiction writers in Japan:

"Overdrive" by Toe EnJoe—How fast is the speed of thought?

"Sea Fingers" by TOBI Hirotaka—A small enclave survives after the Deep has consumed the world, but what does the Deep hunger for now?

"A Fair War" by Taiyo Fujii—The future of war, the age of drones, but what comes next?

Saiensu Fikushon is Haikasoru's new e-first mini anthology, dedicated to bringing you the narrative software of tomorrow, today. Now more than ever, the future is Japanese!

WWW.HAIKASORU.COM